T0120413

Praise for *Savage Ridge*

'A richly drawn, haunting and unforgettable mystery'
  Chris Whitaker, *Sunday Times* and *New York Times* best-selling author

'An unusually intelligent, exceptionally involving thriller. Part morality tale, part classic procedural, part domestic suspense – think *Mystic River* by way of Harlan Coben – that's kaleido-scopic in structure but very direct in impact. And you haven't met an investigator quite like Sloane Yo – she's a genuinely original creation, tough and true and vulnerable'
  A. J. Finn, #1 *New York Times* bestselling author

'A superb crime novel set in the Pacific Northwest for fans of Jane Harper and Nickolas Butler. Loved the claustrophobic small town setting. Wonderfully atmospheric and engrossing'
  Will Dean, *Sunday Times* bestselling author

'Gloriously bringing to life small town revenge and simmering resentments, *Savage Ridge* is a one-sitting read, one that will make even the most moral of readers question exactly what they would do. I loved it'
  Lisa Hall, author of *Between You and Me*

'Full of tension and suspense, I couldn't put this down. The twists and turns kept me on the edge of my seat. Brilliant!'
  Simon McCleave, author of *The Snowdonia Killings*

'A stunning whydunit that inverts readerly expectations, *Savage Ridge* is both a gripping mystery and a wrenching story about the corrosive nature of guilt, of the price we pay for what we do and what we leave undone. Morgan Greene is a suspense author to watch'

Jeff Abbott, *New York Times* bestselling author

'Dark, gut punching and satisfying all at once. Expert handling of characters and pace, and a glorious evisceration of moral duty! Simply brilliant'

Rachel Lynch, author of *Dark Game*

Savage Ridge

Morgan Greene is the pen name of British author Daniel Morgan. He studied Creative Writing and English Literature at Swansea University with a focus on narrative structure and theory. Author of the bestselling Detective Jamie Johansson series, Daniel currently lives in South Wales with his partner and snow-loving collie.

MORGAN GREENE

SAVAGE RIDGE

CANELO
US

San Diego, California

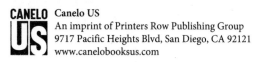

Canelo US

An imprint of Printers Row Publishing Group
9717 Pacific Heights Blvd, San Diego, CA 92121
www.canelobooksus.com

Copyright © 2024 Daniel Morgan

The moral right of Daniel Morgan writing as Morgan Greene to be
identified as the creator of this work has been asserted in accordance with
the Copyright, Designs and Patents Act, 1988.

All rights reserved. No part of this publication may be reproduced,
distributed, or transmitted in any form or by any means, including
photocopying, recording, or other electronic or mechanical methods,
without the prior written permission of the publisher, except in the case
of brief quotations embodied in critical reviews and certain other
noncommercial uses permitted by copyright law.

Printers Row Publishing Group is a division of Readerlink Distribution
Services, LLC. Canelo US is a registered trademark of Readerlink
Distribution Services, LLC.

This edition originally published in the United Kingdom in 2024 by Canelo.

Published in partnership with Canelo.

Correspondence regarding the content of this book should be sent to Canelo
US, Editorial Department, at the above address. Author inquiries should be
sent to Canelo, Unit 9, 5th Floor, Cargo Works, 1–2 Hatfields, London SE1
9PG, United Kingdom, www.canelo.co.

Publisher: Peter Norton • Associate Publisher: Ana Parker
Art Director: Charles McStravick
Editorial Director: April Graham
Editor: Traci Douglas
Production Team: Beno Chan, Rusty von Dyl

Cover Design: Lisa Brewster
Cover Images © Depositphotos and Shutterstock

Library of Congress Control Number: 2024931022

ISBN: 978-1-6672-0731-5

Printed in India

28 27 26 25 24 1 2 3 4 5

To Sophie,

For your unending support, both on and off the page. It means more than you'll ever know.

THEN

Chapter 1

Nicholas Pips

As the last remnants of light drained from the sky, Savage Ridge held its breath.

The town had been in shadow since mid-afternoon, the steep valley sides shielding it from long days. They loomed above the tops of the houses, pine-laden and jagged, sentinels at watch.

There was always a stillness that hung in the air, sharp in the winter, thick in the summer. And it was summer now. Which was why it wasn't unusual, or suspicious, for the three of us to be in the Main Street Diner, sipping on milkshakes like on any other warm Sunday evening. Except this wasn't like any other warm Sunday evening – because we'd just finished burying Sammy Saint John.

Right after we killed him.

Emmy Nailer was sitting opposite me, in the window of our booth, the shiny red vinyl upholstery behind her clashing dangerously with the colour of the skin around her eyes, raw from the tears. She stared into the gathering dusk, vacant and damaged.

Peter Sachs was next to her, hunched over, not touching his strawberry float, incessantly picking dirt from under his nails, a wild look on his face. The clicking sound was deafening to me despite the chatter surrounding us.

A few other bodies filled the empty seats: a squat guy in a weathered plaid shirt and tight Wrangler jeans spilling over the sides of his bar stool; a family at the far end next to the door, their booth frantic and loud, the two kids all hopped up on sugar.

The bell above the door dinged and I turned, looking over my shoulder, seeing the last person in the world I wanted to.

Sheriff Barry Poplar.

His eyes found mine. He nodded his head. I nodded back, heart hammering.

Pete made a sharp *psst* sound and I twisted around, hands flat on the table in front of me, trying to control my breathing. *Fuck. Fuck! Why was he here? Why now?*

Emmy had gone white as a sheet. Pete was leaning forward, the straw of his shake between his lips, but he wasn't drinking, wasn't moving a muscle. His eyes were fixed on Pop over my shoulder.

I heard the sheriff's voice from behind me. 'Hey, Darlene,' he said to the waitress behind the counter.

'Working late, Pop?' she asked in her rasping voice.

Sheriff Poplar chuckled a little. 'Yep, just thought I'd stop in for a little pick-me-up.' His keys jangled in his hand as he leaned forward onto the counter.

'Large black to go?'

'You know me too well.'

'Coming right up.' She busied herself with the pot.

In front of me, Pete's eyes leapt to the table in front of his glass and I knew that Pop was looking our way.

Everything was still for a second, and then the sharp crackle of Pop's radio cut the air.

I jolted in my seat at the sound, turning my head just enough to see out of the corner of my eye.

'Sheriff? Come in,' came the tinny voice, barely audible.

Pop stood straight and turned it up on his shoulder, resting his chin next to it. 'I'm here, what's up?'

'I just got a call from Thomas Saint John, said he's trying to reach you, there's no answer.'

4

Pop sighed before toggling the talk button. 'Just getting a coffee, my phone's in the truck. What's going on?'

'He said he needs to see you at the house, right away.'

Darlene placed his cup on the counter and Pop smiled at her, picking it up and taking a steaming slurp. He winced at the heat, put it back down, then spoke again. 'Something wrong?'

'It's about Sammy,' the voice said. 'He's missing.'

Pop hesitated, brow creasing. 'Missing? Since when?'

'I don't know,' the voice replied. 'But he sounded pretty annoyed. You better get up there.'

Pop let out another long sigh, picking his coffee off the counter and heading for the door.

As the bell dinged, I risked turning around again to watch him go.

He stood there at the threshold, looking back at me, coffee in one hand, open door in the other.

My heart as good as stopped. All I could think was that he knew. He knew what I'd done. What *we'd* done. That we'd killed Sammy.

But then he was gone, getting into his truck. The headlights flared and he pulled out onto the street. The flashing blue lights on the roof of his car lit up the empty road and he accelerated hard towards the hills at the edge of town, streaking through the red light at the intersection and off Main.

I slowly turned back in my seat. Emmy and Pete were staring at me. I wondered if they were asking themselves the same question.

Was killing Sammy worth it?

I didn't know if I'd ever have the answer.

But it was already done.

And now there was no going back.

Chapter 2

Barry Poplar

The road climbed out of town, the streetlights ending and plunging Sheriff Barry Poplar into shadow. The sun had already disappeared behind the western ridge and Savage was winding down into night.

The hulking engine of the Chevy Tahoe waned and then flared, changing down two gears to keep pace up the hill. He'd driven this road a thousand times, but never like this.

There were no other cars and he hugged the middle yellow line, splitting the cracked blacktop down the middle, snaking up and up into the hills.

A few miles on, he pulled left down a road that only led to one house. The biggest in Savage Ridge. The house everyone knew, owned by the family everyone knew. The family that owned everyone.

The stone pillars loomed.

The engine was hot, gulping air. It quietened to a chugging idle as Pop slowed towards the intercom, leaning out of the driver's window, the massive golden 'SJ' emblazoned on the black iron gates ahead filling his windscreen.

He pushed the buzzer, massaging his mouth nervously, moustache bristling along his knuckles. He sighed and checked his watch. It was 9:37 p.m.

His thumb drummed the steering wheel.

'Saint John residence.' The voice echoed from the intercom, formal and polite, but strained all the same. When Thomas Saint John was unhappy, everyone felt it.

6

'Sheriff Poplar,' Pop replied, keeping his eyes ahead. The night was warm, sweat beading on his temples, his tan shirt darkening under the armpits. He wasn't overweight, but his uniform felt tight, constricting, all of a sudden.

The gates began to open and he crept through the widening gap, one hand on the wheel, the other still squeezing at his cheeks.

Gravel crunched and spat from under the tyres as he pushed the accelerator, heading for the front door, hemmed by a pair of stone lions keeping guard on either side.

Before he could even kill the engine and climb out, one of the house staff was standing at the open door, a massive oak thing, waiting for him to come inside. Despite the urgency of Thomas Saint John's call, Pop still had to come to him.

Luckily, he knew the way, walking straight up the steps and into the foyer. His heels squeaked on the polished marble tile floor as he hung a right and headed towards Thomas Saint John's study. He would approach, knock, and wait for an invitation to go in. Like always.

So, he knew something was wrong when he saw Thomas Saint John striding towards him down the corridor.

The man was big, with a sagging body, and hands that never quit. He'd always be turning a pen, or clicking the dial of his watch around, cracking his knuckles. Today, he was rotating his reading glasses. Over and over. Over and over.

'Poplar,' he said, stopping abruptly in front of him. 'It's about fucking time.'

Pop dragged his eyes from Saint John's fighting hands and took in the look on his face. It wasn't worry, but it was close. The wrinkles around his eyes seemed more numerous, the craters under his cheekbones, the skin dripping down to his loose jaw, seemed deeper than normal, his shade paler.

'I came as soon as I could,' Pop said. 'What's wrong?'

'What's wrong,' Thomas Saint John replied bitingly, glasses pausing for a moment, 'is that Sammy is missing, and you're not doing a damn thing about it.'

'Missing?' Pop hooked his thumbs into the front of his belt, and drove his bottom lip up to meet his moustache. 'What do you mean missing?'

'Missing. How else do you want me to goddamn say it? He's not here. I don't know where he is. No one has seen or heard from him. And he's not picking up his phone. He *always* picks up when I call him. Always. He knows to.' Saint John brandished his glasses at Pop.

He drew a breath. 'How long for?'

'Since this afternoon.'

'This afternoon?' He knew if he lifted his watch to illustrate, or even suggested that it'd been a mere matter of hours, he'd only anger him further. 'Okay,' he added, 'let me give Beaumont a call, and we'll ask around, see if anyone's—'

'No one has. No one knows where he is. And the staff didn't even see him leave. He could be anywhere, with anyone. And you know it's not safe out there. Not for him.' The glasses turned faster than before, Thomas Saint John's eyes fierce and cold.

'Alright,' Pop said, taking his hands from his belt. 'Someone must know where he is. He could be out with friends—'

'Friends?' Thomas Saint John spat. 'You know damn well he doesn't have any friends.'

'Alright,' Pop said calmly, trying to defuse the situation. 'All we gotta do is ask around, and—'

'I know where he is.' The voice echoed from over Pop's left shoulder and he turned to see Ellison Saint John, Thomas Saint John's eldest son, standing on the mid-landing of the staircase. The boy was twenty, Pop thought. Tall, handsome, blonde. He'd been away for a few years, studying at a private college – Whitman, Pop thought. He hadn't realised he was back.

'Ellison,' Pop said, taking in the boy. Bigger than Pop remembered. Almost a man. 'I didn't know you were back.'

'I got back last week,' he replied, hand on the bannister. He came down a step, eyes locked on his father, movement tentative, cautious almost.

'How's college?' Pop called up. 'Fancier down there than here in Savage Ridge, I imagine?'

Ellison smiled awkwardly, abashed. 'Yeah, it's, uh—'

'For God's sake,' Thomas cut in. 'Your brother. You know something? Why didn't you say so before? Spit it out. Now.'

Ellison's mouth hung open, then he lowered his eyes, nodded a few times, staring at his feet. 'Yeah, of course, sorry.' He cleared his throat. 'Sammy, um, earlier, I mean, he said—'

'Words, boy,' Thomas Saint John urged. 'And look at a man when you speak to him.'

Ellison snapped to attention but didn't look at his father.

Pop watched in silence, waiting for what came next.

'He said he was meeting someone. A girl.' Ellison looked at Pop now, his blue eyes bright in the soft, pale glow of the chandelier above him.

Thomas Saint John's breathing was heavy and fast at Pop's shoulder. 'Who, dammit? The name.'

'Emmy Nailer.'

'Nailer?' Thomas Saint John repeated, shocked.

When Pop turned to look at him, Thomas Saint John was grave, hands clamped around the glasses tight enough that Pop was surprised they hadn't snapped in two.

'Nicholas Pips. Peter Sachs. Emmy Nailer,' he growled. 'I want them arrested. Immediately.'

Pop just stared at the man, slowly hooking his thumbs back into his belt. He nodded slowly, swallowing.

He knew there was no arguing with a Saint John. Ultimately, he didn't have a choice in the matter.

Chapter 3

Nicholas Pips

I didn't sleep at all.

I kept waiting for a knock at the door, for the phone to ring, for blue light to filter through my blinds and strobe across my ceiling. And they came, of course, but morning broke first and the birds were singing by the time the deep rumble of Pop's truck filtered through the glass of my window. The knock followed shortly after.

Mom and Dad had been up for an hour, maybe a little more. I couldn't get up, couldn't face them.

The sound at the door told me everything I needed to know. The kind of hammering that you did with the heel of your fist when it wasn't a polite request to be answered.

Dad got there quickly, muttering to himself. I could hear it through the floor. I held my breath as he did, unlocking the latch, sliding the chain off, and then pulling the door wide.

My heart beat quickly, the soles of my feet sweating under the covers.

'Sheriff,' my dad said, confusion in his voice. 'Everything alright?' He had no idea.

Pop's voice was muffled, but I could still hear that he sounded tired. 'Gene,' he replied, 'sorry to call so early.'

'No, no,' my dad said, 'not a problem. You want some coffee? Come in, there's a pot, and—'

'Not a social call, I'm afraid,' Pop said. 'Nicky here?'

I pulled the covers higher, fists balled into the fabric.

'Nicky?' My dad sounded surprised. I heard his footsteps, the squeak of the door as he stepped through it and pulled it closed behind him. They were on the porch, right below my window now, the voices coming up from underneath, through the floorboards. 'What do you want with Nicky?'

Pop drew a laboured breath. 'It's complicated,' he said, seemingly with some difficulty. No doubt my dad was giving him a hard look, the one that always made it tough for me to speak, too. 'I'm in a bind here, Gene,' Pop replied. 'I just need Nicky to come down to the station with me, answer some questions, and—'

'He's not going anywhere until you tell me what's going on.'

There was silence for a few seconds. Then Pop spoke. 'It's Thomas Saint John. He—'

'Fuck Thomas Saint John. That bullshit with the pool? We cleared that up. It's done. You said so yourself.' I couldn't see it, but I knew my dad was cutting the air with his hand and then folding his arms.

'My hands are tied,' Pop insisted. 'Sammy Saint John is missing.'

'Missing?' This time, there wasn't much surprise in my dad's voice. 'And you think Nicky is involved somehow?' He paused for a moment. 'Let me rephrase: *Thomas Saint John* thinks Nicky is involved.' It wasn't even a question this time.

'The longer this goes on, the worse it'll be.'

'You're not taking my son. If you want to talk to him, you can do so right here, with me in the room.'

'If I don't take him in, it's not me that's going to come knocking next time.'

'You can tell Thomas Saint John, and his lapdog, to go fuck themselves, alright, Pop? I knew your father, he kept order in this town for a long time. And he kept his integrity, too, despite that big house on the hill. We'll always need at least one honest cop in Savage.' That blow must have hurt.

Pop deliberated for a few seconds. 'Alright,' he said then, sighing audibly. 'Tell you what, you bring Nicky to the station this morning yourself. We'll talk, amicably, and get all this straightened out. You know where Nicky was last night?'

'He was at the movies with Pete and Emmy.'

'Well, there you go, nothing to worry about. Just come down, have Nicky say that, and we can put this behind us. And then Thomas Saint John'll be off both our backs.'

'Goodbye, Pop,' my dad said, the door creaking again as he pulled it to close shut.

There was a slap, hand on wood, the door stopping abruptly. I jolted a little.

Pop's voice came through, low and a little firm. 'Don't make me come back, Gene. It'll be worse if I have to.'

The door latched and I heard my mother's voice. 'What was that about?'

I slipped from bed as they spoke.

'Nothing,' my dad replied. 'Just Pop. Seems like Sammy Saint John's gone for another joyride, and Saint-Prick Senior's ready to burn the town to ashes to find him.'

'Well, if the boy ends up in a ditch somewhere, it's no great loss,' my mom spat.

My father hushed her. 'Quiet, Nicky's still in bed. And witch hunt or not, Pop said he needs to go down to the station, make a statement. Just a formality,' he reassured her.

Mom scoffed. No doubt she had plenty to say, but she'd said it all already. The Saint Johns weren't a popular family in our house. And this wasn't likely to change that fact.

'I'll take him,' my father said, decisive. 'We'll go after breakfast, be back in an hour. You want to put some eggs on? Nicky's not going to like this. Least he can do is have a full stomach before he's dragged through this shit again.'

It was just last week I was there, at the station, giving a statement about what happened at the pool party. I wasn't keen to relive it, especially not before I checked in with Emmy and Pete. We needed to make sure we had our story straight. If they heard I had got hauled in already... shit, not worth thinking about.

'Sure,' my mom replied. 'I'll get some going. You want to give him a call?'

Footsteps on the stairs.

My dad's laboured breathing as he came up, hip sore, hand sliding up the smooth rail, shushing along the wood. 'Nicky?' he called.

No answer.

He came along the landing, paused at my door, knocked. 'Nicky?'

The knob turned, door swinging inwards into the empty room.

My dad stared in, his expression even. Not much surprised or rattled him.

I watched him stand there for another second through the guest room window, crouching on the slanted roof above our side porch, and then I turned away, scuttling down to the edge and sliding off over the drainpipe, landing softly on the loamy flower bed below.

By the time the last grains of earth had settled, I was already through the back gate and running.

Chapter 4

Lillian Dempsey

Light splintered down through the browned needles of the black alder, sun-baked and dusty with the summer. It was morning, the heat not yet strong, and Duke, the boxer dog, was snuffling through the undergrowth, looking for squirrels. They chirped and skittered up into the canopy as he bounded after them.

Lillian and Simon Dempsey's house backed onto the outskirts of the Okanogan-Wenatchee National Forest, so it was out the back door and straight into the woods. When Lillian was home, this is where she spent her mornings, her evenings, and every minute she could. With Simon, with Duke, or alone.

Her phone buzzed just as they were halfway up the trail to the bluff that overlooked Kachess Lake. Lillian stopped, catching her breath, and fished it from her fanny pack.

Simon paused on the trail behind her, resting his hand on a boulder. He squinted up at her from under the brim of his fisherman's hat. Lill always hated it. He'd worn it in college when they'd met, and he was still wearing it now. It was dorky then, and it always would be. But it was as much a part of him as his slightly too long fingers, overly hairy shins, and the biggest, kindest heart she'd ever known.

He looked at her with that look he always did when she answered her work phone on 'us' time.

She looked away guiltily, putting it to her ear. 'Dempsey,' she answered, knowing that saying she wasn't back in to work for another week was a little redundant. She turned slowly to look down at Simon, listening to the voice on the other end. 'Where the hell is Savage Ridge? What? That's a little below my pay grade, don't you— He's not even been missing twenty-four hours? Then what the hell are you calling— Tonight? You're serious? No, I don't know who that is. Should I?' She shrugged at Simon apologetically. He sighed and headed up the trail, walking past her.

He whistled softly, clicked his fingers at Duke who looked down at his mom for a few seconds, then scampered up the trail after Simon.

Lillian lowered herself onto a rock on the side of the path, listening as the information came through. Not that there was much of it.

'Right, right,' she said. 'Yeah, I'll, uh…' She checked her watch. 'I'll head back, get packed, and then head out. I'll call you when I get there.'

She hung up, stowed her phone, and looked around. No sign of Simon or Duke.

Great.

She sucked in a breath and levered herself up onto the next step, long, pale legs straining as she quickened her pace. She was tall, her red hair glowing in the early morning sun. Her skin was alabaster, covered in bruises. She didn't know where they came from, they just appeared after the slightest knock: the dog running past, banging them on a chair leg, it didn't take much.

Lill reached the head of the trail, breathing hard, and found Simon perched on their boulder, watching the sun play off the surface of the lake below, a million diamonds turning.

'Hey,' she said, approaching slowly.

'Hey,' he replied.

'I, uh…'

'Gotta go to work.' He nodded as Duke sidled up to him. Simon's hand rose, ruffling the dog's head, his fur greying around the jowls despite his puppyish nature.

'Yeah, some nowhere town up near the border, Savage Ridge,' she laughed, throwing away the name. 'Some local kid never came home last night. No big deal, but the father's some small-town big fish or something, I dunno.'

'And they want their best guy on it,' Simon said, not looking at her. He knew the script.

Thing was, Lillian Dempsey *was* the best guy that the Washington State Patrol Criminal Investigation Division had. She was a senior investigator with fifteen years of experience under her belt. The next step up was either being chained to a desk or heading for Quantico. But she had no intention of subjecting herself to office work, and the Quantico ship had sailed for her at least five years ago. She had a house, a husband, and the best-worst dog in the world. She was happy at home, and respected at work. But apparently not enough that her first vacation in two years couldn't be interrupted.

'I've got to head off right away,' Lill said, throwing a thumb over her shoulder. She watched the side of Simon's face, clean-shaven and rounded beneath the brim of his battered hat.

'Of course you do.'

'You want to come down with me?'

'Think we'll hang here for a while.' He turned to look at her, eyes hard, without love in that moment. 'It was a long climb, you know? Be a shame to waste the view.' He gestured out at it, the valley sweeping away before them, sides rounded and scooping up to sharp peaks that cut the sky in two.

'It would.' Lill shifted from foot to foot, knowing she needed to go, hating that she had to. 'I'll be back in a few days, three, tops.'

'I'll be here.'

She nodded. 'Right here, or back at the house?' She laughed at her own joke.

Simon smiled a little, offered an arm to her.

She bent down, hugged him.

He kissed her on the cheek, then on the mouth, pulling her against him.

She let him for a moment, then released.

He took the signal and did the same and she stood straight. 'See you soon?'

Simon nodded, reaching out and lacing a finger under Duke's collar so he didn't follow her down.

'Look after Dad, okay?' She pointed to the dog.

He panted happily. Blissfully unaware.

Lill gave them a wave, then turned her back on the lake and her vacation, and started down the trail, heading for home, her badge and service weapon, and whatever mundanity the town called Savage Ridge had in store for her.

Chapter 5

Nicholas Pips

Pete lived on my street, about five houses down on the opposite side. His mom and dad were already up and moving around, I could see them through the front window. His mom liked the natural sun coming into the living room, so she always drew up the blind first thing. The houses on the street were all built in the Fifties. Boarded exteriors with gentle sloping shingle roofs, classic porches, front yards letting down to tree-lined sidewalks with big leaf maples and ashes lining the roads, their roots forcing the paving slabs into uneven bulges.

I walked quickly between the trunks, shaded by the canopies. They were still, the air hanging thick and quiet like it always seemed to on those summer mornings. The heat would come later, beating down into the Savage bowl, the surrounding ridges keeping the wind at bay.

You could see all the way through Pete's house, to his mom and dad at the kitchen table beyond the red suede couches. His father was a taller guy with thick hair, greying at the temples, a streak of light, stark against his dark skin. He peered down over his oblong reading spectacles, reading his paper. He received the *New York Times*, an educated carpenter. He was smart enough to do anything except leave Savage Ridge.

Pete's mom busied herself at the stove, long black ponytail swaying along her spine as she stirred something. But there was no sign of Pete.

I thought about stopping, about knocking. But it's the first place my dad would check for me, and I needed to get ahead of him.

Emmy was two streets over. Cutting through the alleyways between the back gardens, I was there in a minute or two, sweat beading on my forehead, hands slick with it, too.

I clenched them a few times, wiped them off on the thighs of my jeans, and approached her house.

It was a little older than ours, a little narrower, a little taller. There was a bigger porch at the front, a basement beneath elevating the first floor. I couldn't get a look in through the front window, but there was an old dryer sitting next to the house that'd been destined for the scrapyard for as long as I'd known Emmy. It was rusted and overgrown with weeds and grass, but you could stand on it, get your eyes to the sill of the side window on tiptoe.

Pete and I would often peek in there to see if Emmy was home, or if her mom wasn't. She was a great lady, warm, welcoming, always cooking something. But shit, you couldn't get away. It was always a conversation, a long one. *Where you going? How you been? How're your folks? Did you hear about this, what about that?* She was best avoided if possible.

I skulked across the road, the hour still early enough that most cars were in their driveways, people not yet at work.

I made for the dryer, heading across the overgrown front lawn, and stepped up onto it, running my hands up the peeling wood panelled exterior of the house until my fingers reached the sill, hooked over, and bore weight, the old wood creaking and bending a little as I raised my eyes to the glass.

Emmy.

She was there, on the couch – green velveteen with buttons and tassels – curled up, knees to her chest, arms wrapped around them, staring at the floor in front of the TV. She wasn't moving, wasn't doing anything, but her eyes were full and shining, ready to burst with tears. Her brown hair hung in dull waves to her shoulders. She'd always looked so bright, so full of life. But now, now she looked… hollow. A shadow of her former self. And I couldn't help but feel like I'd done it to her.

My breath caught in my throat, an ache developing there. I scanned the room quickly, looking for her mom. The window was open above me, the bug screen keeping the mosquitos out, but letting sound carry. I listened carefully for her mom's humming, any banging in the kitchen. There was nothing. She must be upstairs still, or in the basement doing laundry.

This was my chance.

I lifted my hand, ready to knock on the glass, but before I could, a shape emerged from the kitchen.

I fell still, knowing I was obscured by the bug screen. If I didn't move, he wouldn't see me.

Pete walked from the kitchen carrying a steaming mug of something. Tea. Earl grey with honey. It was her favourite.

He approached the couch, nervous. He *looked* nervous, biting at his bottom lip. The bags under his eyes told me he'd slept about as well as I had.

'Em?' he asked quietly, offering her the tea.

She didn't look up.

'I, um…' he started, then trailed off. He moved in front of her, put the tea on the floor, and then knelt there, reaching out to take her wrist. He stared at it, like she might shatter when he touched her. She was looking right through him.

His hand rested on her forearm, his thumb moving slowly over the peach fuzz on her tanned skin. 'Em?'

She looked at him now.

My heart seized a little in my chest.

Pete swallowed. Em kept her eyes on him, a tear rolling down her cheek. She lifted her arm from her knee, turning it through the air so she could take hold of his hand, tugging him softly from his knees and onto the couch.

He went with her, eyes wide, fixed on Emmy, her full, pink lips quivering.

Pete sat and she twisted around, pulling her bare legs, long and smooth below the hem of her jean shorts, onto the cushion under her.

She curled into him, into his shoulder at first, and then slid down until her head was in his lap, hands clasped in front of her face like a child.

Pete's arms were raised, like someone had just spilled something on him. But slowly, he seemed to soften, to relax, lowering one hand until it was on her ribs, the other he let move towards her head. His fingers shook as he pulled a strand of hair from her face and tucked it behind her ear.

Emmy curled tighter, tears filling her eyes, rolling over her cheek and wetting Pete's cargo pants. He stared down at her like she was some sort of wild thing, some sort of exotic creature.

He'd always looked at her like that, like she was everything.

My nails dug into the half rotten wood of the sill, splintering it. Why Pete? Why did she call him? Why was he here and not me? Emmy and I were closer than they were.

It was obvious though, wasn't it? The second she saw me bury that shovel in Sammy Saint John's skull, that was it. Anything, everything she'd ever felt for me – could have felt – was gone. In an instant.

As Sammy Saint John fell still, we fell apart, away from each other, into darkness. The edge of that shovel did as much harm to each of us as it did to Sammy.

My jaw shook. My cheeks burned.

Rage.

Jealousy.

Guilt.

Loathing.

But not remorse. Not regret.

If this was the price, then this was the price. We knew nothing would ever be the same. We accepted that. We traded it.

If I had lost Emmy, then I had lost her. But to turn to Pete? He was in this with me. He helped me dig that goddamn hole.

He had blood on his hands, too, whether he swung that shovel or not. Fuck. *Fuck!* That moment, it was seared into my mind. Playing over, and over, and over as Pete made curls in Emmy's hair, watching her, cradling her.

We were so sure the fall would kill him. So sure, that by the time Sammy came to rest at the bottom of that hill, he'd be dead. We stood there, Pete and I, fists locked, shoulders pumping, Emmy hanging across the centre console of that old, rusted out Impala, breath held, waiting for us to say something, the engine idling lumpy like it always did. And we just watched. Watched him tumble, roll, like a rag doll, legs and arms flailing, crying, screaming, bones crunching as he hit trees, pine needles cascading down after him.

And then, stillness.

Emmy asked from the car, voice tiny, 'Is he... did we... do it?'

And then he started moving. Groaning.

The hole was already dug there at the bottom, the shovels back up here with us, leaning against a tree, ready to be thrown in the trunk and taken somewhere very fucking far away.

Pete looked at me in the fading light, the pines swaying and creaking around us, the air cold for an August afternoon. And I saw it in his eyes. That he wasn't going to have it in him. That a few more seconds of silence would have him saying something stupid like: *We shouldn't do this. We can't go through with this.*

So, before he could say it, I turned away, reached for the shovel that was only supposed to dig the hole, and started down the slope.

Gripping it tight in both hands.

There was a click to my left and gooseflesh erupted across my skin, my mind flashing back to the present moment. I don't know that I'd ever heard the hammer of a revolver being pulled back before, and yet, somehow, before I looked over, I knew what was waiting for me.

Richard Beaumont was a big guy. Six feet tall, broad. He was overweight, but his frame carried it, his shoulders wide and pointed like he had a coat hanger under his shirt. His neck was thick, his jowls wide and low, his features close-set. His lined forehead was shining, the hair around the sides of his head short and bristly, his pate practically bald.

'Don't move, kid,' he ordered, his gun trained right on me, glinting silver in the morning sun.

His patrol car was parked behind him at the curb. I didn't hear it coming, couldn't over what was replaying in my head.

'Hands, now,' Beaumont said, not advancing, just standing there on Emmy's lawn, pointing a gun at an eighteen-year-old.

'I...' I began, about to explain what I was doing here. For a second, I thought a neighbour had called me in, but then sense prevailed. Beaumont knew me, my mom and dad. He was here for me, looking for me.

Everyone knew that he was Thomas Saint John's gopher. Pop had been sent to collect me, and had failed, so Beaumont was picking up the pieces.

'Come down off there, slow,' Beaumont ordered. 'Walk towards the car. And don't try nothing.'

My heart thundered, my hands raised next to my head. I couldn't speak, my mouth dry.

There was a creak of floorboards and I risked a glance into Emmy's living room, saw that Pete and Emmy were standing a foot from the window, staring down at me wide-eyed. There was so much I wanted to say, so much I needed to do before this happened. Before we got taken.

But Beaumont was on a short leash, and what I really didn't know was whether if I spoke, if I did something, he would pull that trigger.

And I really didn't want to find out.

The three of us crammed into the back of the cruiser, an early-2000s Ford Crown Victoria that stank like burgers and body odour. He'd probably had the shirt on less than an hour and he already had pit stains down to his fucking muffin top.

I glared at the back of his rolled neck as he drove through town. We'd all turned eighteen. Technically, we didn't need our parents with us if we were being brought in. And he knew that.

He didn't say a word as we wound down Main towards the station. There were just a handful of cops in Savage Ridge. Sheriff Barry Poplar, Deputy Richard 'Dickie' Beaumont, a couple of other officers, and a clerk. Not much ever happened here, so there was no need for a big force. Fewer than 5,000 people lived in Savage Ridge, and that was counting the houses dotting the highways for ten miles either side, too.

Beaumont pulled in at the curb, the street quiet. There wasn't much this end of Main, just an old mechanic's garage, a warehouse that stocked plumbing supplies, an office with four units, three of which remained empty, and a little further down, a lumber yard.

He let the engine idle, watching the sky, lazy blue over the treetops.

It was as though he were waiting for us to speak.

Beaumont drew a laboured breath. 'You wanna start, or should I?' he asked, trying to catch our eyes in the rear-view mirror.

None of us spoke.

'Sammy Saint John,' he said then. 'What do you know?'

We all kept our eyes down.

'It's no secret you kids got a bone to pick with the Saint Johns. Hell, Pips, just last week they had to pull you off Sammy, beating on him, threatenin' to kill the kid.'

'That's a lie,' I snapped, looking up, meeting his eye.

He kept my gaze. That's what he was looking for. 'Is it? So, you wouldn't be glad to see Sammy Saint John out of Savage?' He raised an eyebrow, the hairs long and curling up his forehead.

'I think everyone in Savage would be glad to see him gone if they knew what he was really like.'

Beaumont ran his tongue over his bottom teeth. 'So, what happened? You scare him? Make him leave town? He's not handcuffed to a radiator in your basement, is he?'

'I don't know anything about Sammy Saint John,' I said, looking at my knees again. Emmy was in the middle, Pete on the far side. They were holding hands, knuckles white. 'I haven't seen him since the pool party, and honestly, I never want to see him again. If he is gone, good riddance.'

He considered the words. 'Thing is, I don't know if I believe that. And Thomas Saint John certainly don't. 'Cause Sammy said he was going out to meet your little friend there, Miss Nailer...' Emmy shrank at the sound of her name, but didn't make a sound. '...And he never came back.' Beaumont breathed labouredly again, the cigarette smoke on his breath acrid in the closeness of the car's interior. 'And seeing as you three are pretty much attached at the hip, I think that makes for some pretty good evidence that you know something about this.'

'I think it makes pretty good evidence that Sammy Saint John is a liar.' I had to keep my cool, but I was struggling to. 'We were at the movies last night. Then the diner. Just the three of us. Ask anyone.'

'Oh, I intend to,' Beaumont said. 'Sammy was—'

But he didn't get to finish.

His door was ripped open and suddenly Pop's face was in the gap, moustache bristling, face red like he'd been running. 'What the hell d'you think you're doing, Beaumont?'

'Following orders.'

'Not my orders.'

'I'm only having a little talk here with the kids,' he answered dryly, 'doing my job.'

Pop stood straight, hands on hips. That was a slight. As though Pop hadn't done his job for Thomas Saint John, so Beaumont had to pick up the slack.

'Jesus Christ, Beaumont,' Pop muttered, stepping away from the car. 'Do you even know the fucking law or are you just that stupid? Anything you said, anything they said, none of it's on record, none of it is admissible! It's your word against theirs,

25

and if they did have anything to do with this, you just… you just…' He grunted, unfastened his hands from his hips, and came towards the back door, pulling it open. 'You three,' he ordered, 'out, now. In the station, go.'

'You wanna watch yourself, Pop,' Beaumont said, not bothering to even unbuckle. 'That badge on your chest don't mean as much as you think it does.'

We all climbed out and headed for the front door, but I could still hear them talking.

'Whether the Saint Johns run this town or not, we still got a job to do, and any judge, any lawyer will shred you in court for what you just did. You *fucking* idiot.' Pop slammed the back door closed.

Beaumont harrumphed. 'Yeah, if it ever gets that far. Problems in Savage Ridge have a way of sorting themselves out, remember?'

Pop stood there, a statue beside Beaumont's car. His eyes slowly turned to us, but his words were still for Dickie Beaumont. 'Get the hell out of here.'

Beaumont pulled the door closed wordlessly and peeled away from the curb, heading for the hills and his master's feet.

Pop walked towards us slowly, the heat of a maturing morning building around him. 'Go on inside,' he said then, motioning us in with a sigh, 'I'll call your parents.'

'What're you going to tell them?' Pete asked then. His father could be scary. Mine could, too.

'Honestly,' Pop said, holding the door open for us to enter the Savage Ridge police station, 'I don't really know.'

Chapter 6

Ellison Saint John

The front door opening could be heard through the house. The thudding of the lock, the creak of the huge hinges, the clipping of the maid's shoes on the tiles as they went to it.

Dickie Beaumont's heavy breaths were a dead giveaway as to who was calling, even as Ellison stood on the gallery landing, out of sight, above the split staircase.

Beaumont advanced into the house, turning right. Father's study, Ellison guessed, coming closer to the rail. Beaumont knocked, then entered.

Expected, Ellison surmised, waiting for the footsteps of the maid to subside before he went any further. He slipped his shoes off at the top of the stairs and padded down in his socks, staying quiet.

He looked both ways at the bottom step, then headed for his father's study door. It was solid oak, like the rest of the doors in the house. But Ellison found if he held his ear to the corner, next to the hinge, he could hear clearly enough.

He approached slowly, the voices growing from nothing to a muffle. The wood was cool to the touch against his clean-shaven face. Ellison did his best to control his breathing, but it was difficult to keep it even, his heart beating fast.

Sammy had been gone all night, and though they weren't close, it had still rattled him. He'd never seen his father like this.

As his ear touched the jamb, the words reached clarity.

'—and I want him found now,' his father said.

'I'm working on it,' Beaumont replied, out of breath from the walk in, it seemed.

'Working on it?' His father scoffed. 'That fills me with confidence. Between you and Poplar, there's not a spare brain-cell. And don't get me wrong, your predictable ineptitude has its advantages, but when required, actual police work isn't one of them.'

Beaumont huffed a little, but didn't dare speak.

'I thought between the two of you, you might be able to keep some sort of peace here, but I was clearly mistaken. This is already out of your hands, I'm sure you'll be glad to know.'

'I had the kids in my cruiser. I woulda squeezed them, like you wanted, but then Pop showed up, and—'

'And what?'

'Interrupted us. Five minutes, and they would have been singing.'

'And why would he do that? Hmm?'

'I don't know. He was saying something about inadmissible-ness, and—'

'Inadmissibility,' Ellison's father corrected him. 'Don't tell me you were stupid enough to question them together?'

'They were in the back seat, outside the station—'

His father laughed incredulously. 'Jesus fucking Christ! All you had to do was pick up the Pips boy, get him to talk, and then the others. One by one. I didn't think I needed to explain the necessity of that simple task. But sure enough, wrong again.' Ellison's father got up and walked around. 'It sounds like Poplar did you a favour. Maybe he does have a modicum of sense,' his father muttered. 'If this does ever need to see the staleness of a court room, then we'll likely be thankful he had the good sense to interrupt you.'

'I can do it,' Beaumont said then, louder now. 'I can make them talk.'

'No,' his father said cuttingly. 'We need this handled quickly, and competently. Two attributes that don't apply to you. I've arranged for a senior investigator from the State Patrol's CID to handle this personally. He'll be here by the end of the day, and then we'll find out where Sammy is.'

Beaumont was quiet for a moment or two. 'He's fine, Mr Saint John, I promise—'

'Your promises mean nothing to me,' he said. 'Find Sammy, and you'll prove yourself worthy of wearing that badge, if nothing else. And if you don't… well, things that are done are just as easily undone.'

Ellison didn't know what that meant, but he knew a threat when he heard one.

'That's all. You know your way out. And close the door behind you.'

Ellison pulled away from the wood and made for the corner of the hallway. He didn't make it.

The door opened and Beaumont sidled out, stomach straining at the buttons of his khaki shirt.

He pulled the door to the jamb, pudgy hand still around the handle, and stopped, looking over at Ellison, white socks on tiles, mid-stride on the way to safety.

Beaumont looked at him, bunched his lips, as though deciding whether to rat on him or just keep walking.

He decided after a second, turned his eyes to the front door, sour-faced, and headed for it.

Ellison waited until he was gone before he turned back and crept towards the stairs once more. He was supposed to be studying, after all.

But he couldn't resist taking one last glance through the crack, trying to spy his father, to see, to just glimpse what a man who'd lost his son might look like.

For a moment, he thought he was hunched over the desk, weeping. But as his father turned the page on the file he was reading, he realised he was not crying.

He was working. His father always said, a day's work is never done for a Saint John.

Ellison looked away, teeth gritted, then started for the stairs, hands curling at his sides.

Chapter 7

Nicholas Pips

Pop stared across at me, head tilted forward so that his eyes were out of the bright light hanging above us. His cheeks were shadowed, brows lowered, expression stern, hands flat on the table in front of him.

The walls were covered in brown polystyrene tiles, the ceiling covered in white ones. There were no windows, and just one door. He'd called it an interview room when he'd walked us into the station, sat us in the corridor, and brought us in one at a time. Pete first, then Emmy, then me.

Pop had one of the officers at the desks call our parents in turn. They all arrived pretty much together, asking what the hell was going on.

'Samuel Saint John is missing,' Pop had said calmly, hands on his belt. He took the time to look each of them in the eye as he spoke, while we remained quiet on the chairs behind him. 'Now this isn't how I wanted to do this,' he assured them, 'but my hand's been forced here, and for that, I'm sorry. Now, I know these three kids aren't guilty of anything except giving a damn about each other, but we have our due process.' He enunciated at a speed and in a tone that told our parents not to interrupt. 'With the pool incident still in recent memory, and with what was said at the time...' Pop turned and cast an eye at me '...threats that were made—'

My father interjected, 'You can't hold that against him! It was in the heat of the moment, and you know what Sammy is like, what he did—'

'Nevertheless,' Pop cut in sharply, staring hard at my father.

My mom squeezed his elbow and he fell silent, nostrils flaring.

Pop cleared his throat and took a breath. 'Nevertheless, with that still lingering at the forefront of our minds—'

'Thomas Saint John's mind,' Pete's father muttered.

Pop kept going. 'And the fact that Ellison Saint John swears that Sammy told him that he was meeting Emmy – and he mentioned her by *name*, mind you,' Pop raised his hand to sway Emmy's mother from protesting before she could speak, 'those factors all mean that I wouldn't be doing my job unless I questioned them. Now they're all over the age of eighteen, which means I called you down here as a courtesy. They're not under arrest, or even suspicion of anything right now. This is not even an official investigation yet, as we've got no reason to suspect any sort of foul play here. Sammy's been out all night before, it's not impossible to think that he'll come walking through his father's front door at any moment. But saying that,' Pop added, taking another breath, looking at them all again, 'I'm reacting to a plea of a parent whose child left the house yesterday afternoon and didn't come back. His phone is off, no one has seen him, and no money has moved from his bank account. And if any of you called me and told me the same thing about your kids—' Pop gestured to us, but didn't look over '—I'd react the same way.'

Emmy's mom snorted and shook her head.

Pete's dad closed his eyes, sighed.

My father just scowled. 'You came to my house, Barry. You asked me a question; I gave you an answer. You took my word, and then you shook my hand. And then you picked him up anyway.'

Pop considered that for a moment, lips pursed. 'Nicky wasn't at home when we picked him up, Gene, and it wasn't me that did it. And if I hadn't stepped in when I did, then your kids would have gone through something totally different, and a whole lot worse.'

'So, I should thank you? That's what you're saying?' My dad shook his head.

'You should let me do my job. And I'll make sure it's done right, that your kids are treated fair, in accordance with the law. And if they've got an alibi for where they were yesterday afternoon, then we can get this all straightened out, have them home for dinner. And once that's done, it's done. And that's it.' He clapped his hands and dusted them off for effect, then held them up. 'Alright? Good. If you want to wait, you can, otherwise, the kids can call you when we're finished.'

Our parents looked at each other, then answered together. 'We'll wait.'

Pop just nodded, turned, walked towards us, and motioned Pete to his feet. 'Come on, Pete, you first.' He clapped him on the back, walking him towards the interview room. 'You want a soda or something?'

Pete didn't answer, just looked back at us.

Emmy and I were both careful not to move a muscle, not to do anything. We just stared back, and as I laid my hand on the bench next to Emmy's, she drew it up onto her lap.

Between that moment and the one where I was sitting in front of Pop, staring across the table, time seemed to lurch forward. Between flashes of darkness, moments drifted in front of me like polaroids. The door closing after Pete. Emmy getting called in. Pete's father shaking my father's hand and then walking Pete out the door. Emmy coming out, walking into her mother's arms. Pop repeating my name from the doorway, beckoning me in. My father staring at me, nodding to me in silent support. My palms sweaty as I pushed to my feet, walking towards Pop, wondering if he was going to ask me the question I was dreading: *Did you kill Samuel Saint John?* And me, having to lie. *No. No, I didn't kill him. I didn't beat him to death with a shovel and I definitely didn't bury him in the woods. I did not do those things.*

'Nicky?' Pop snapped his fingers and my eyes refocused on his hand on the table in front of me. His left hand, lined, spotted a little, hairier than I'd noticed before. There was a wedding band on his ring finger, cutting into the flesh. Pop was probably forty, the second of the Poplar line to be sheriff in Savage Ridge. His father held that station for a lot of years. I didn't know him, but my father swore he was a good man.

I looked up at Pop, and wondered if he was, too. Or if Thomas Saint John had enough money to buy Pop's honour as well as his loyalty.

'Did you hear me?' Pop asked.

I swallowed. 'Sorry, I'm just… tired. This is…'

'I know,' he sighed. 'I don't want to keep asking you the same questions, but I need it on record, alright?'

An old-fashioned tape recorder sat at the corner of the table, wheels turning slowly, a foam-tipped microphone sitting in front of it.

'So again, tell me, from the beginning. Yesterday, where were you?'

I drew a slow breath. 'It was a normal Sunday,' I said, reciting the line I'd practised a hundred times in the last week. 'I woke up, ate breakfast with my folks, played some video games—'

'What games?'

'Call of Duty,' I said, 'A little Madden at the end. With Pete.'

Pop watched me closely, unmoving.

'Online,' I added. 'We quit out around three, I guess. I had a bite – Mom made me a sandwich. Tuna salad.' I shook my head. 'Then, at around 4:15 p.m., maybe a little later, my dad drove us to the movie theatre. He picked Pete up on the way, Emmy's mom dropped her off. She was there when we arrived.'

'What time was that?'

'4:30ish, I guess?'

'What time'd the show start?'

'Uh, 4:45 p.m.?' I shrugged. 'But I guess the movie didn't roll until nearly 5 p.m. Previews, you know?'

'What'd you see?' Pop glanced down, making notes of the times on a little pad in front of him using the ball point that was tucked in his top pocket.

34

'*Inception*.'

'What's it about?'

'Dreams, it's weird. It's, um… does this matter?'

Pop looked up. 'You tell me?'

I drew a breath, clenched my fists under the table and wiped them on my jeans. 'It was good. These guys, um, they go into people's dreams to convince them to, um, do… things. But, it's… um, it's…'

'You don't know what the movie was about?' Pop's eyes narrowed, moving minutely across my face. I resisted the urge to look away, to wipe the sweat from my face.

My voice was quivering, I tried to keep it firm.

'I do,' I said, 'but it's… it's hard to explain. You should see it, you'll understand. It's crazy. There's this one scene where they're in a van, and um, it goes off a bridge, but they're inside someone's dream who's in the van, and it's, um, like flipping through the air, so, um, inside the dream of the guy in the van, the whole world, it's like…' I used my hands to mimic a turning motion '…spinning, around and around, and the scene, in the hallway, in the hotel, it's rotating and it's—'

Pop cut me off. 'And how long was the movie?'

I exhaled, realising I'd been rambling. Shit, I'd memorised that entire movie's plot and about fifty reviews, studied every trailer, every clip I could find. We couldn't risk going to see it before yesterday, in case they found out. We had to be careful. And we were. But was it enough? 'It was two hours, a little more.'

'Two hours,' Pop said, noting that down. 'Snacks?'

'What?'

'Did you get snacks?'

'Popcorn. Emmy got M&Ms, I think. I had a Sprite. Pete got a Coke.'

'And Emmy?'

'What about her?'

'What drink did she get?'

35

'I, uh…' I stumbled. *Jesus, what did she get? I was standing next to her while she ordered it! Jesus Christ.* 'Uh…'

Pop shrugged. 'Not import—'

'Orange soda!' I said, probably a little quickly.

'This isn't a test, Nick,' Pop said slowly. 'I just want to know what happened. Where you were. Take a breath, alright?'

I nodded, but couldn't ignore the feeling that Pop was in full control of this, was driving the conversation whichever way he wanted it to go. Was he just waiting for me to trip myself up?

'So, the movie finished at 7 p.m.?'

'A bit later. Previews,' I said. 'Maybe like 7:30 p.m.?'

'Maybe *like* 7:30 p.m., or 7:30 p.m.?' He lowered his head again, pen hovering over the pad.

'7:30 p.m.,' I said, trying to be a little more decisive.

He noted it. 'And then what?'

'We walked down Main, to the diner.'

'Straight there?'

I nodded.

'Words, Nick, for the tape.'

'Yes.'

'You eat?'

'Just milkshakes.'

'You weren't hungry?' He raised an eyebrow. 'Dinner time.'

'Popcorn.' I nodded. 'We filled up on popcorn. Got a large. Cheaper than burgers.'

Pop smiled. 'Ain't it just.' He jotted more down. 'Inflation. Nowhere's safe, not even Savage. What flavour'd you get?'

'Popcorn?'

'Milkshake.'

'Chocolate.'

'Partial to vanilla, myself,' Pop said with a little shrug. 'Though the wife thinks that's boring. She likes pistachio, though I can never get over the colour.' He tapped the pen on the page, sighed. 'Anyone else at the diner?'

'Darlene,' I said. 'The waitress?'

36

'I know her.' He gave me a weak smile now. 'Anyone else?'

'I didn't recognise them.'

He nodded. 'Alright. And how long were you there for?'

'Until 10:30 p.m., I guess? Something like that.'

'Late for a Sunday. Diner closes around then, huh?'

'I dunno, we were talking about the movie. Lots to discuss.'

'Must have been good.'

'You should see it.'

'Maybe I will. You walk home?'

I shook my head. 'Pete's dad picked us up. Dropped Emmy off first, then headed to his place. I walked from there, it's right down the street.'

'I know it is,' Pop said, 'I've known you since you were in diapers, and your dad a lot longer. I remember watching him play football in high school. I was only a kid back then, but your dad was a hell of a running back, and my dad never missed a game. He loved Savage Ridge, 'til his last breath.' Pop closed the notebook. 'And I do too.'

I didn't know what to say to that. I didn't know what game Pop was playing or where he was going with this. All I knew was that I had to keep my mouth shut, had to stick to our story. Our alibi was solid. It was airtight. We knew that. Pop was just… he was just doing his job. Pressing me to see whether anything squeaked out.

'You know, Nick,' he said, speaking slowly, leaning in, 'I know you hate Sammy Saint John.'

'I didn't—'

'Don't lie, Nick. I know you hate him. And if anyone would want to see him out of this town, it'd be you.'

I didn't reply.

'But that doesn't mean that you had anything to do with this, or that you know anything about it.' His gaze burned into my skin, unflinching and sharp. 'I'm going to look into what you said today. I'm going to go to the theatre, to the diner, I'm going to watch the security tapes, question witnesses.

I'm going to make sure everything checks out, the times, the places, everything. And even then, I'm probably going to call you back in here, have you tell me again. And again. Unless you know where Sammy is or you know anything about his disappearance?'

'I… No. I don't.'

'Then why did he name Emmy as the person he was meeting?'

'Emmy would never,' I said, practically spitting the words. 'You think I hated Sammy? Emmy couldn't stand him. She'd never speak to him, let alone meet him.'

Pop drew back a little. 'I'll be checking that, too. She already showed me her phone, and there was nothing on it to suggest she'd had any contact with him. But then again, texts can be deleted, call logs erased.' Pop exhaled, put the pen back in his top pocket. 'We'll look into it all, turn over every stone. We'll pull apart your life, Pete's life, Emmy's life. We'll go over what you told me here, and everything else, going back as far as it takes.'

'Everything?' I asked, trying not to sound scornful.

Pop measured me. 'We'll find Sammy, Nick. Today, tomorrow, eventually we'll find him. And this won't stop until we do. Do you understand?'

I didn't know what to say, so I said nothing.

'It's not going to stop, Nick. Not until Sammy is found. Say something, Nick.' He nodded towards the tape recorder.

'I understand.'

'So, do you have anything to tell me? Anything at all? If you do, and you tell me now, it'll be better. For everyone.' He kept his eyes fixed on mine. 'Do you know where Sammy Saint John is?'

I drew a slow breath, clenched my hands in my lap, and stared right back. 'No, I don't.'

Chapter 8

Lillian Dempsey

The sun was setting over the western rise by the time Lillian saw the words 'Welcome to Savage Ridge'.

The evening was cloudless and pale yellow, a haze of distant wildfire smoke blurring the barrier between earth and sky. Her satnav took her along the fir-lined highway, hugging the cracked yellow line in the middle. A house half hidden by trees appeared ahead, and then another, and another, and then suddenly she was plunged into town, the sidewalks quiet, the traffic lights changing at the intersection ahead for no cars.

Lillian slowed towards a red and looked around. A rundown-looking dive bar was the only thing showing life, a neon sign in the window saying 'open', an unlit metal sign over the door saying 'Rockefeller's'. The first E and the second L were missing, but she pieced it together. A guy stood outside smoking. He was thin, with long black hair and a leather waistcoat on. He stared at her, narrowing his eyes through the blue of his cigarette smoke. He recognised the Ford Crown Victoria; black, silver capped wheels, long-range aerial spiking from the trunk. No one that didn't know would look twice at the thing, the most boring sedan on the road. But to those who knew, a plain clothes cop car was as visible as a liveried one.

And this guy knew.

Lillian pulled her eyes from him at the green and drove on, following the route on her navigation. She hung a left and headed out of town, passing through blocked suburbs rising up the slope towards the mountains, and then hooked onto a single lane highway that climbed ever higher, snaking towards the house on the hill. When she'd first received the address where she was heading – a private residence, not the local police station – she'd looked it up. From the satellite view alone, she could tell she was headed for a walled-in mansion. The abode of this Thomas Saint John.

She'd looked him up, too. Granddaddy's money. He bought the whole town before there even was one, logged the valley floor around the river, flattened it, sold it off to developers and other logging companies just before the wood ran out. Despite butting up to native reserves and public land, there was still plenty of logging left, and the other companies were salivating at the thought of biting off a piece of the Saint Johns' bottom line. Only old Mickey Saint John failed to tell them that the only reason that land hadn't been logged already was because the ground was liable to tear away under the machines the second there was weight on the earth. The first few machines to come tumbling down the mountainside were collateral, the next few were a wake-up call. The companies mitigated their losses when Mickey bought the land back, at ten cents on the dollar, of course.

That gave him enough cushion to jumpstart the town, the local economy, open a huge mill in Savage, dam the river and put together a big float operation. *He who controls the water controls life.* That was what was written on Mickey Saint John's grave stone. As though his being a massive asshole was a badge of honour. Though by the way his son, Kenneth Saint John, continued to mould his father's estate, screwing over people left right and centre to get ahead, throttling businesses and then chomping up their assets to expand the Saint Johns' empire, Lillian thought that Kenneth probably *did* think that. And wore the badge with pride.

Thomas Saint John, current asshole-in-chief, on paper, was no different. A quick Google search revealed wholly negative press. Though no one gave much of a shit about a jumped-up tycoon operating in the far reaches of the Pacific Northwest. That wasn't totally true, though. Lillian figured that the locals here probably gave a shit. Which begged the question: what exactly was she walking into? And with barely twenty-four hours passed since Samuel Saint John had walked out the front door, the world at his fingertips, a bottomless bank account at his disposal, what exactly had Thomas Saint John so worried?

Dempsey pulled up to the black iron gates and wound the window down. It was cool inside the car, but now the heat and smoke of the waning day pressed in on her, made her throat tight.

She took her first real, pine-heavy breath of Savage Ridge air, and pushed the call button.

'Saint John residence,' came the stiff reply.

'Lillian Dempsey for Thomas Saint John.'

'One moment.'

Nothing happened for almost an entire minute, and then the gates began to swing open in front of her, revealing the mansion behind the golden SJ.

She rolled up the gravelled drive and parked in front of the main doors. As she got out, heels crunching on the stone, pantsuit pulling and clammy in all the wrong places, the last of the daylight was fading from the sky.

Lillian climbed the steps in twilight and was received at the front door by a maid, black dress with a white collar, white half-apron. She curtsied a little and Lillian couldn't help but fire her a questioning glance. She stepped inside, hands in pockets, and looked around the cavernous entryway.

There was a boy on the stairs, staring down. Blonde hair, blue eyes, youthful in his face. Thomas Saint John's other son, Ellison, she figured. Smart boy, a good sportsman, played lacrosse at college, got good grades. Had everything going for him. And yet there was a sadness there. No, not sadness, more like... submissiveness. Browbeaten – yeah, that was the word – written all over him.

41

'Dempsey?'

She turned at the sound of her name and watched as the man she guessed had to be Thomas Saint John approached. He was broad, his belt cutting into his stomach, leather loafers squeaking as he walked. He was wearing a grey knitted sweater with a zipped collar, a shirt and tie under it. The man looked stern, his sagging face and lined eyes giving away his age, but not betraying his sharpness. He was turning his glasses in his hands as he walked.

When he got within six feet, he stopped, held his shoulders back, inspecting her like she was a racehorse.

'Dempsey?' he repeated, the tone already impatient, as though he were instantly annoyed to have to repeat it.

'Lillian Dempsey,' she replied, extending a hand. 'Washington State Police, Criminal Investigation Division.'

He looked down at it, then stopped turning his glasses, shook it quickly and firmly, and then dropped it just as fast. 'I was expecting…'

'A man?' She looked at him like she looked at all the other men who started that sentence but never finished it. Though it was immediately apparent that Thomas Saint John wasn't like other men.

'Exactly. I asked for the best they had.'

'I am the best.'

He stuck out his bottom lip, looked her up and down, and then hummed. 'We'll see. Come,' he ordered her, turning and walking back down the corridor towards what she guessed was an office.

He went through the wooden door and around to the far side of his sprawling desk. By the time Lillian crossed the threshold he was already leaning on it, hands wide, face lowered, papers spread out all in front of him.

'Close it,' he said.

Lillian stared at him, then reached back with her heel and nudged the door closed.

Thomas Saint John's jaw flexed under his jowls. 'That's a fifteen-thousand-dollar door.'

'Then I'd say you overpaid.' Lillian pushed her hands into her pockets. 'You want to tell me why I'm here and not at the station speaking to a Sheriff Poplar?'

'Because Poplar is an imbecile, as are the rest of the police officers in this town, and I can save you the trouble.'

'Oh?' She feigned surprise.

'Nicholas Pips. He threatened Sammy a week ago.'

Lillian just waited for him to expound.

'He had something to do with Sammy's disappearance. If he and his friends didn't kidnap him, they know who did, and why.' He sucked in a deep breath, then exhaled hard, glancing down at the papers in front of him. He collected his thoughts, then stood upright. 'That's all. You can go.'

'That's all?' Lillian really was shocked. 'You want to tell me why you think this Nicholas Pips—'

'I don't *think*. I know.' His voice was as barbed as his gaze. 'They're classmates, and the Pips boy has had it out for Sammy for months now. So, pick him up, make him confess, and then find my son.'

Lillian just stood there. 'This Nicholas Pips, one of Samuel's classmates, abducted your son. That's what you're telling me?'

'And I hope I won't have to tell you again.'

'So, if you're so sure, then firstly, why isn't Pips in custody?' She blinked, taking her hands from her pockets and offering them in a mild shrug. 'And secondly, why am I here?'

'You'll have to discuss the first thing with Poplar, because he let him go this afternoon. And the second thing, I'm beginning to ask myself the same question.'

Lillian's mouth curled into a little smirk. 'Why don't you tell me *why* Nicholas Pips has it out for your son, and then I'll see about speaking to Poplar about the next steps.'

Thomas Saint John grunted impatiently and stood straight. 'A week ago, there was a party. Sammy was in attendance,

43

along with a bunch of his classmates. It was a pool party. Not uncommon among their age group, so I hear. Pips was drinking, heavily. Sammy was talking to a girl by the name of Emmy Nailer – the same girl he went to meet yesterday afternoon.'

Lillian listened carefully, embedding the names, the details in her mind.

'Pips and Nailer have supposedly been friends for some years. He decided he didn't like her speaking to Sammy. Jealousy, I suppose. Not surprising.'

'No, there's probably not a person in this town who isn't jealous of your family.'

Whether he knew that was an insult or not, Lillian couldn't tell. Thomas Saint John went on regardless. 'Pips came over, and told Nailer not to speak to Sammy. He put hands on her. Was rough, apparently.'

'Rough?'

'Grabbed her. Manhandled her. Whatever you like, it doesn't matter.'

'It does matter.'

He pressed on. 'Sammy intervened, protecting Nailer. Pips shoved Sammy, Sammy held his ground, and then Pips swung for him.'

'Punched him?'

Saint John nodded. 'Sammy stumbled, fell into the pool. And when he climbed out, Pips pinned him down, threatened to kill him.'

'For talking to… his friend?' Lillian lowered her head slightly, watching Saint John closely.

'The boy is unhinged, what can I say? Like his father. He used to work at the mill, but was laid off years ago. Problem after problem with him.'

'Why was he laid off?'

'That's of no concern to my son.'

'I'm just trying to form a picture here. Is this a personal grudge, or a family feud?'

Saint John snorted. 'The Pips? They're nothing. To be crushed beneath the boot heel of industry. But if the boy is like his father, he's the swing first, think second type. And that's all the more reason to have him arrested. Before he hurts anyone else.' Thomas Saint John's finger came down heavily on the top of his desk. 'Immediately.'

Lillian took stock of that for a few seconds. 'You said Samuel left the house yesterday afternoon to meet this Emmy Nailer?'

Thomas Saint John nodded. 'Yes. Around five in the afternoon.'

'You saw him?'

'I was told.'

'By who?'

'My staff. My son. Confirmed by the security footage.'

'I'll need to see it. Speak to them. And your son.'

'There's no need.' Thomas Saint John cut the air with his hand. 'He doesn't need to be involved. And he doesn't know anything. He's been away at school. He only got back a few days ago.'

'There's always a need to question everyone about everything,' Lillian said pragmatically. 'It's the nature of an investigation like this.'

He stared at her, temple vein bulging. 'Nicholas Pips.' The name hung in the air. 'That's all you need. Now prove it. That's why you're here. I trust you can see yourself out.' He returned his attention to the papers in front of him, pushing his reading glasses onto his face with one hand.

Lillian lingered for a few seconds, watching him, and then turned and let herself back into the hallway, closing the fifteen-thousand-dollar door behind her.

She walked slowly through the empty house, the checkerboard tiles on the floor stinking of good money and bad taste, listening to the silence. Everything was clean, the frames of the expensive paintings, the vases and ornaments, the doorknobs that led to umpteen rooms populated by furniture that was

45

never used, positioned in front of bookcases that would never be read from, lit by windows that gave stunning views of manicured grounds that would never be enjoyed.

Two children grew up here, but she doubted that laughter ever echoed in these halls. When she reached the bottom of the stairs she looked right, knowing she'd see Ellison standing there. Twenty, and a man everywhere except in this house.

'Ellison,' she said, nodding to him.

His eyes widened slightly at the use of his name. 'Are you… are you going to find my brother?' he asked, like a child.

She resisted the urge to nod, to reassure, as she usually would. 'I'm going to try.'

'Do you think he's okay?'

She just stared up at him, knuckles clenched around the bannister, his clothes expensive, face clean shaven, whole life laid out ahead of him in a series of checkboxes. 'I have to go now, Ellison,' she said, making sure to use his name again. She reached inside her jacket then, and withdrew a business card. 'But I'd like to speak to you about your brother. Soon. Would that be okay?'

Ellison's eyes went to the corridor she'd just walked from. She knew what he was looking for.

Wordlessly, she came forward, and rested it on the top of the balustrade post at the foot of the stairs. 'Call me if you want to. You might be able to help.'

'Help?' he asked, coming down just one step. 'I don't know anything.'

Her smile wavered a little. 'Everyone knows something.' She tapped the card gently and then turned towards the front door.

'I hope you find him,' he called after her.

She paused at the door, glancing back. 'I do, too.'

46

NOW

Chapter 9

Sloane Yo

Arizona in the summer is hell.

Not in the metaphoric sense, it's actually a beautiful state with great cities, kind and generous people, and lots to do and see. But in the literal sense. July and August temperatures average over forty degrees Celsius, and can swing as high as forty-five, especially in the south. Being outside is unbearable. Being inside is tolerable. But living in air conditioning for months on end and darting from one building to another was also intolerable. As such: hell. Fiery, hot, brimstone hell. Which was also supported by its nickname, the Grand Canyon State – for obvious reasons – the deepest point of which is over a mile below ground. Six thousand feet. As close to hell as you can get.

Sloane was a kid of the north. Michigan born and bred, Detroit smelted and milled into the woman she was today. One who liked snow, and cold, and rain. She'd never realised how much she missed rain until she came to Arizona.

Though she wasn't here for the parks and the people. Well, that wasn't true either. She was here for someone. Just one person, who'd fled Washington and gone as far south as they could. Another hundred miles and they'd be out of the country altogether. And if that didn't stink of someone running from something, she didn't know what did.

Sloane sighed, arms folded, and tapped her foot. She was in a white T-shirt, rolled to the shoulders, exposing her tattooed arms. Sweat was running down her neck despite the coolness of the cafe. Though it wasn't nerves making her perspire. Rather, the heat coming off the espresso machine six inches from her back. She was leaned against the counter, watching Emmy Nailer pay for an iced Frappuccino at the till.

They churned those out in an average of seventy-six seconds, mostly due to the fact that they made more than three hundred every day. And they served a customer every thirty-two seconds on average. So, with Sloane being inconspicuously two people ahead of Emmy, the girl didn't even clock her.

Sloane had ordered a decaf oat latte, and had told the barista that she had a soy allergy. She didn't. But she knew that they didn't wash the jugs in between steams if you didn't say that, and that doing so added an extra thirty-odd seconds to the make time of the drink. In the time it took to mill the decaf, pull the shot, wash the jug, steam the milk, and serve it, Emmy would have been served; she would have ordered, paid, and she'd be walking towards the end of the counter before Sloane even got her drink.

She figured she had less than a minute to interact with Emmy, to sow the final seeds.

Sloane didn't particularly *like* doing this, but she was good at it, and took pleasure from the mechanics of it. She'd been following Emmy for weeks. She'd sat in this cafe, making notes, for the last five days. She'd nailed down Emmy's schedule to a degree that Emmy didn't even know existed. This twenty-eight-year-old woman, who still had her brown curls, her button nose, her full pink lips. Who men gravitated towards, and who people seemed to want to care for, who people wanted to help, because, for some reason, you could just tell. You could tell she was... broken. That something was wrong, but you never asked what, and she didn't tell. This woman who'd bounced from apartment to apartment, job to job, trying to find meaning in her life after leaving Savage Ridge ten years ago.

After the mysterious, sudden, and still unsolved disappearance of Sammy Saint John.

And sure, Sloane could probably corner her here, but as a PI, her options were limited. She couldn't make a citizen's arrest or hold her in any way. And short of abducting her and tying her to a chair, there wasn't much she could do to get the truth. She doubted Emmy would talk freely, which meant she'd probably run. And if she ran, there was no way to stop her calling Peter Sachs and Nicholas Pips and giving them the heads up. And then they'd all be gone.

That wasn't the deal, though. The deal wasn't to make one of them talk, or to find the truth, finally. To prove that these three kids had killed Sammy Saint John. The deal, the job, Sloane reminded herself, was to bring them home. All of them.

'Jesus,' Sloane muttered as Emmy found the space next to her at the counter and pulled out her phone. 'It's so hot.'

Emmy smirked a little. 'This isn't even hot. Wait 'til August.'

'Don't say that. I don't know how anyone lives here.' Sloane pulled a pamphlet from her back pocket and began fanning herself with it.

Emmy didn't notice at first. 'It's a dry heat, you get used to it.'

'I don't think I want to,' Sloane replied, pushing her long, dark fringe behind her ear. The sides and back of her head were shaved, which she was thankful for just then. She couldn't imagine having hair on her neck in hundred-degree heat. 'I'm just here for work, but I can't wait to get home.'

'Where's home?' Emmy asked, more out of politeness than anything else.

'Idaho,' she lied. 'Pocatello. You know it?'

Emmy stuck out her bottom lip, shook her head and shrugged, kept scrolling.

'Hell of a lot cooler than this. Plus, I hate being away from my kid. She's with my mom right now. It's handy, you know, to have her there with me travelling for work so much. But I don't like being away from my family. I miss them, you know?'

More silence.

'You got family down here?'

'Here? No.'

'Where are you from?'

'Not here,' Emmy asked, looking up now, eyes questioning. She saw the pamphlet then, watching it move through the air like a magician's swinging pocket watch.

'You been?' Sloane asked, slowing the paper down so Emmy could read it. The title read, 'Experience the Wonder of the Pacific Northwest'. It was laid over a photograph of Mount Washington. 'Got a few weeks off when I get home,' Sloane said. 'Gonna pack up the car, take the little one on a road trip.' She stared into space, imagining it. 'Start in Oregon, head to the coast, then go north, towards the Cascades, see the whole thing.' She looked over at Emmy, who was staring at the pamphlet, taking no notice of the video playing on her phone. 'I went as a kid,' Sloane went on, speaking softly. 'My parents took me in a camper. I remember the smell of the wet roads, of the pines, so thick you could chew on it. The way they creaked outside the windows at night, swaying gently. I remember the steep valley sides, the rivers, the lakes, the snow that hung around too long at the peaks, splashes of white even at the height of summer. I remember the roads that snaked through the mountains endlessly, the vastness of it all. But mostly, you know what I remember?'

'What?' Emmy asked, voice small and hushed. Her eyes lifted to Sloane's; they were dark, her Chinese–American heritage apparent in her features. Sloane narrowed them slightly, letting her lips part just a little. She watched Emmy's do the same, mirroring her as she paused before speaking. She had her.

'I miss my parents. I lost my father,' Sloane said, knowing Emmy had lost her own when she was young. 'That's one of the clearest memories I have of him. My mom's still around, but I can't help but feel like I take her for granted, too. You never appreciate them when they're there, you just feel it when they're gone. It's not guilt, but...'

'It's close,' Emmy finished for her, clearing her throat and nodding. She stowed her phone, eyes lingering on the brochure again.

Sloane laughed lightly, shaking her head, but keeping her eyes on Emmy until she looked back at her again. 'Here,' Sloane said, offering the pamphlet. 'I've read it a hundred times, take it if you want. If you haven't been, you should visit.'

Emmy swallowed, hesitated, and then reached out.

'Hey,' Sloane said then, touching her arm. Emmy held the brochure in both hands, staring down at it. She looked up. 'I think they're calling your name, Emmy?' She blinked a few times. Sloane gestured to the counter behind her, to the young girl with braces in the visor and apron calling Emmy's name.

'Right, yeah,' she said, holding tightly onto the pamphlet with one hand while she turned and picked up her coffee with the other. She looked rattled, off balance. Before she left, she stopped, looked at Sloane, brow crumpled, words almost escaping her. 'I... I hope you have a good trip,' she said then, her face settling into a warm smile. 'I'm sure your daughter will love it.'

She gave Sloane a nod, and then headed for the door.

Sloane watched her go, ducking into the baking sun through the tinted windows. She wondered if Emmy really could have killed someone. But she supposed she'd find out soon enough. Emmy would look over the brochure that day, think about it. Think about going home, to Savage Ridge. And the final push would come tomorrow, when Sloane swung by her mailbox and pushed a 'Random Winner!' gift card through the slot, giving her $250 off any flight of her choice to selected airports with a popular airline. The random airports she'd written on there were scattered all over, but none were close to anything interesting. Except for the one that was just over ninety minutes' drive from Savage Ridge.

And seeing as the voucher was only valid until midnight tomorrow night, and that Sloane had determined that Emmy was the impulsive type – if she'd have been the sort to lay money on things – she would have bet big that by tomorrow afternoon, Emmy would have booked her flight home to see her mother for the coming weekend, if not sooner. She was barely in a job, anyway, and the 'anonymous' customer complaints that Sloane had been calling in about Emmy for the last few weeks had definitely added some friction between her and her boss. They were friends, but that didn't matter. Emmy was a liability; generally unreliable, scatter-brained, perpetually hungover, and now, she was supposedly losing them customers too.

She'd only needed a nudge to leave and take off like a rocket headed north, but Sloane had to give her a push. Well, maybe a shove.

But she supposed that was why she was chosen for the job. Because normal channels couldn't achieve this. And other investigators didn't have the vision, or she supposed the callousness, to pull this off. She didn't take kindly to the way her new employer had relayed how she had been described to him on the phone; the reason he was hiring her. But she couldn't wholly disagree. She *was* a cold bitch, when she needed to be. But the money always came thicker and faster when she was.

Someone tapped her on the shoulder then and she turned to look at the guy. He had a man bun, overly manicured facial hair, and horn-rimmed tortoiseshell reading glasses. The MacBook poking out of his satchel and his Birkenstocks and naked toes told her he was probably a budding author-cum-entrepreneur, here to write the next Great American Novel. 'You Sara?' he asked, pushing his glasses up his nose. He then pointed to her drink on the counter, the girl with braces cupping calling, 'Decaf oat latte for Sara?' over and over again.

Sloane took one glance at it. 'God, no.' Then she headed for the door, sucking in one last lungful of air conditioning before plunging into the relentless sun.

She squinted, fishing her sunglasses and phone from the pockets of her black jeans – why the hell did she only bring black jeans with her to Arizona? – put the former on, and then opened the call log of the latter, dialling the number for her employer.

He answered quickly. 'What is it?' he asked, curt, as usual.

'It's on,' she answered. 'I got Nailer.'

'Good,' he replied. 'Now get here as soon as you can. We won't have long, and I've been waiting ten years for this. We can't screw up.'

She hung up before he had the chance to. She didn't like taking orders, and she definitely didn't like being told how to do her job.

She'd already met him once in person, but she wasn't looking forward to seeing him a second time.

The Saint Johns ruled from on high over Savage Ridge, and they sure as hell acted like it too. Though if there was one thing Sloane Yo knew, it was the higher you fly, the further you fall.

And no one – *no one* – could escape that truth.

We all find ourselves face down in the dirt at some point.

The only question is when.

Chapter 10

Ellison Saint John

Ellison Saint John pulled the phone from his ear as Sloane Yo, the private investigator he'd hired to finally prove that his brother was murdered, hung up the phone. It was sudden, the click a little jarring. He stared at the screen, taken aback. People didn't hang up on him.

He'd finished talking, sure. But still, it was abrupt, and he didn't much like it.

Then again, he'd been told what she was like, that she'd be a handful. That she was liable to get the job done, whatever it took – that's why he'd hired her – but that she was unpredictable, borderline uncouth, and that she had a 'history'. He didn't much care about her life, her prior career and its derailment, or anything else. What he cared about was justice. The truth. Finally laying his brother to rest by finding out, once and for all, who murdered him. Except he already knew *who*. He just didn't know *how*.

Ellison tsked, looking out of the window over the front lawns where two men in khaki overalls were working. One sat astride a huge ride-on mower, the other was on an A-frame ladder, trimming the trees that lined the driveway leading to the front door. Here, inside the stone walls of the Saint John estate, you could almost forget you were in such a place as Savage Ridge. Where he'd pick the house up and move it to if he could, he didn't know. *Saint Johns don't deal in dreams and fantasies*, his father had always said. They dealt in lumber, real estate, and winning. And now, Ellison Saint John was finally going to win.

He stowed his phone in his chinos and turned, walking towards the top of the stairs. He often liked to stand on the landing in front of the floor-length windows and gaze out at what would soon be his. He didn't let himself smile, though, didn't let himself get too wrapped up in it before it was here. It was still his father's house – for now. And there was work to be done before he could step into those shoes.

He reached the entrance hall, the checkerboard tiles freshly buffed and polished, and looked around. Empty. Twelve bedrooms, and only one of them occupied. Well, he supposed there were sixteen bedrooms. But the other four were at the back of the house, at ground level, beyond the laundry room. The staff bedrooms. One for the live-in chef, one for the estate manager, and two for the maids.

Though despite the fact that there were four other people living here, there never seemed to be anyone around.

Ellison waited, listening. A door closed somewhere to his left and he walked that way, pace quick but still casual. Ashley, one of the maids, appeared from one of the living rooms, studies, parlours, whatever you'd want to call it. She had a dusting rag in one hand, wood polish in the other.

Ellison stopped abruptly, feigning a stumble, as though he'd been surprised by her sudden appearance. 'Sorry,' he said, grinning with perfect white teeth. 'I didn't see you there. In a world of my own.'

'Sorry. Sir,' Ashley said, hastily adding the formality, looking at the ground, bowing a little. 'I'll get out of your way.' She began to move off, but Ellison spoke again.

'No, no, it's fine,' he said, laughing. 'How's, uh, work? Everything... good?'

She lifted her eyes to look at him. She was in her late twenties, he guessed. She had a slim frame, thin wrists and hands, a cute, pointed nose, and thick eyebrows. He'd not really noticed her at first, she wasn't really his type, for obvious reasons, but now he actually thought she was quite attractive.

'Good?' she asked, unsure what he meant. 'I'm doing my best to keep the dust off,' she said, offering a polite smile, 'but the house is big, and...'

'There's a lot of dust.' He put his hands in his pockets and shrugged. 'Tell me about it. Bet it's like the Golden Gate Bridge in that way, huh?'

'The Golden Gate Bridge?' She didn't seem to be following.

'Yeah, it's so long that once they've finished painting it, they have to start all over again.'

'Oh, I don't know anything about that,' Ashley said, shaking her head. 'I was just dusting.'

'Yeah, I know, I didn't mean that you were painting, I just...' He cleared his throat awkwardly. 'You know what? Never mind. Have you ever been to California?'

She shook her head.

'It's beautiful. San Francisco is a great city. And San Diego, of course, LA... Cruising down the 1, stop off at Big Sur, see the redwoods, it's all amazing.'

'Sounds wonderful, sir.'

'Call me Ellison.'

She just nodded, eyes on the ground.

'I could, you know, show you some time?'

'Oh,' she said, looking up then, 'I, um, thank you, and all, it's just...'

He leaned in.

'I've got a boyfriend,' she answered hurriedly. 'He's in the army, and—'

'Right, yeah, of course! I didn't mean it in a romantic way or anything, I just meant that if you hadn't seen the coast, it is beautiful, you should go.'

'I don't have the vacation days, or money for something like that,' she said bashfully.

'Oh? What do I pay you? Is it not enough?'

Her cheeks reddened suddenly. 'I didn't mean like that, no, I'm happy with the salary, I am, I just, I don't know what I'm saying. I should go.' She turned to leave again.

'Did I say something to upset you?' Ellison asked, reaching out and touching her elbow. He couldn't help but notice she recoiled slightly.

'No, no, I just have a lot of work to do.' She struggled, but eventually looked him in the eye again.

He tried to hold his grin.

'Right, but, if I say it's okay to take a break…' He laughed again, but was distinctly aware that it was echoing down the halls and dying around them.

She hovered, but didn't reply, just clutched the rag and polish.

'Are you from Savage Ridge?' he asked hopefully.

She nodded.

'You have family here?'

Another nod. 'My parents, is all. And a sister.'

'Younger, older?'

'Older, a few years.'

'Would I know her?'

'I don't know, sir.'

'How old is she? I might have gone to high school with her.'

'You went to high school with me, sir,' she said, voice quiet.

'Did I?' He laughed again, cursing himself for it instantly. 'I don't remember you, shame,' he said, trying to keep it light.

She just smiled with closed lips, let her eyes fall again. 'I really have to go.'

'Yeah, yeah, right, don't let me stop you.'

He pocketed his hands again, rocked on the balls of his feet.

She turned to leave with fast little steps, trying not to look like she was hurrying.

'Oh, how's my father?' Ellison called after her, the thought springing to mind.

She slowed, but didn't stop, cast a glance back at him. 'The same,' she said. 'Do you want me to call the doctor?'

He just shook his head, opening his mouth to speak but not finding the right words.

Ashley pulled open a door that led down to the laundry room, pausing to hear his answer, something in her eyes telling him she was willing him not to.

He closed his mouth instead, then lifted a hand, waving to her.

She disappeared, the door shutting behind her, and Ellison was once more alone in the Saint John house.

He walked slowly towards his father's office, thinking about Ashley, trying to remember her from school. But for the life of him, he couldn't. And that thing about her boyfriend was total bullshit, too, right? Had to be. He tsked, shook his head. Why was everyone so intimidated? He was just like them. He'd find out more about her. They must have records somewhere in the house, her resume, her details. It wouldn't be tough to see what was true and what wasn't. He could ask the estate manager, Frank, no Fred… something with an F, about her. See what he knew. What she was being paid. And if she was lying…

His hand was locked around the handle, but he was reluctant to open it.

No, no. He shook his head. If she was, he didn't think he wanted to know.

Because if he did find out, and he was right…

Ellison swallowed that thought – and the lump in his throat – pulled back his shoulders and held his chin up high, and then stepped through into his father's study.

'Father,' he announced, walking towards the hospital bed and IV stand, 'the PI came through for us. Pips, Sachs, and Nailer. They're all coming back to Savage Ridge.' He circled around the oxygen tanks and heart monitor, staring down at his decaying father. Thomas Saint John stared out of the window vacantly, an old, rich man clinging to life. But no amount of money in the world could buy immortality.

'Did you hear me?' Ellison replied. 'We got them. And we're finally going to prove it. I'm finally going to prove that they did it. That they killed Sammy.'

His father's heart monitor beeped a little more quickly, the tracheal tube in his throat, feeding oxygen straight into his lungs, bobbing in time with his pulse.

Ellison let a smile play across his lips. He'd always looked up to his father, but had never taken pleasure in looking at him. And he didn't now, either. But what he did feel was pity. A man so mighty, laid low like this. If he could only see himself. He would be ashamed. Disgusted.

Ellison stepped forward, laid his hand on his father's shoulder. 'I'll make sure it gets done, don't worry. Just rest. I'll take care of everything.'

His father looked up at him, stinking of the medicated cream the nurse rubbed on his bedsores and the stale urine soaked into the fibres of his silk pyjamas. It hurt terribly for the old man to speak, so he said nothing, just let his eyes rest on his son for a few seconds more, and then lowered them to the window, looking out over the grounds he'd never walk again.

Grounds that, Ellison thought, as he pulled his grasp from his father's withered shoulder and headed for the door, would soon be his.

It would all be his.

He was going to make sure of it.

And yet, as he stepped into the empty hallway and made once more for the stairs, footsteps echoing around him, the thought brought him little comfort.

Chapter 11

Nicholas Pips

By the time the seatbelt sign clicked on, I was feeling like a bag of dog shit someone had stomped into the gutter.

I reached up, touched the call sign and waited for the stewardess to find me.

'Can I get another?' I asked, raising my little plastic cup full of ice.

'The fasten seatbelt sign has been turned on, sir,' she said, all smiles. 'We're beginning our descent.'

'So that's a no then?'

Another smile. Then she walked away.

I sighed, drummed my thumbs on the armrest, waiting for the sickness to fade. It was part hangover, part dread. It didn't feel like coming home.

And then the plane was landing and I was whipping through customs, teetering on the edge of an anxiety attack. I hopped a cab to the train station, and two hours later, the train squealed and slowed into Savage Ridge. It was a decent enough place, quiet, forgotten, like most lumber towns. An old mill still belched smoke into the sky above the greened river, but beyond the rough din that echoed out of that metal-sheet fortress, the town was almost silent. Sleeping. Waiting for a wake-up call that would never come.

I stepped onto the platform with just a duffle in hand, and watched as the train moved on through the valley towards the next little nothing town. The two other people who got off both headed for the parking lot. My car was parked back in Portland, the city I'd called home for the last ten years. Back then, cabs used to be lined up at the station step in Savage. Now there was just an empty road.

I checked my watch, sighed, then slung my bag over my shoulder and started walking. It wasn't far to my parents' house, and they didn't even know I was coming. I hadn't been home in a long time, and I wouldn't be now if it wasn't for my mom.

Dad said she was getting worse.

It was late in the summer and the place still felt almost the same. The blacktop road was still cracked, the grass on the verges still creeping on to the asphalt. The crickets still roared and clicked in the undergrowth, and the trees still stood sentinel throughout the town, shading it, tiger striping every inch of the place. I couldn't help but soak it in, drinking the pine smell, letting the gentle creak of the alders and firs guide me home.

It was thirty-five minutes later that I turned the corner into my street, eyes already looking for my house. Eight down on the right.

The trees here, cedars and maples, seemed smaller than I remembered. I slowed, glanced left at Pete's old house, saw his dad's old C10 still in the driveway. But parked behind it there was a sleek black Mercedes. For a second, I paused, checking the thing out. Pete's dad had always worked at the mill. I doubted he'd be able to afford a car like that.

I sighed, stuck out my bottom lip, and hiked on. I was here to see my mom, not gawp at Pete's old house. I shook off the memories and climbed onto my porch. The steps still creaked like I remembered them. Guess that was something. But the driveway sat empty now. I knew Dad had to sell the car to pay for some stuff. Repairs to the house. Medication. Medical bills. Medical bills. Medical bills. It was the reason I had ten grand in cash in my bag and the house had a mortgage for more than it was worth. Dad never liked cheques or money orders, but he'd take the cash. Not willingly, but he would. He needed it.

Dad was as stubborn as they came, a real old man even when he was young, the kind of guy that thought doctors were working an angle when they told you something was wrong, that'd sit around a week with a nail in his foot before he finally accepted it was probably not gonna just 'work its way out when it was ready'. I grinned at that thought. It had really happened, and was the reason Dad had eight toes now.

I pulled the outer screen door and rapped on the peeled wood. It'd be open, but I don't know… after ten years, walking in just seemed… I sighed again, rubbed my face, and waited.

It opened after a second and he was standing there, faded denim shirt, white vest underneath, boots with the toes worn down to bare steel.

He said nothing, just smiled, then opened his arms, let me walk into them.

'Dad,' I said.

He was silent, just held me, clapped me on the back, then beckoned me inside. 'Glad you came, Nicky.'

'How's Mom?' I asked as he took my bag, tossed it onto the stairs. I looked at it, imagined the ten grand sloshing around, then lost sight of it as he led me deeper into the house, just the same as it was when I'd left.

'Not so good,' he replied. 'She'll be glad to see you, though.'

'What did the doctors say?'

He pushed through into the kitchen, towards the sunroom he built twenty years back. 'Nothing good. But what do doctors know, anyhow?'

I was the one who was silent then.

Mom came into view, sitting on a green suede couch with yarn and needles in her hands, facing the backyard, a little square patch of grass that used to be lined with flowers, all surrounding an ornate wrought iron bench that she always kept painted white. It was rusted now, the paint flaking. Weeds stretched out and touched it from all sides, threatening to drag it under.

I sat next to her, but she didn't look up from her knitting. Her hands moving on autopilot, her eyes fixed on the flat grey sky.

'Hey, Mom,' I said, 'it's Nicky.'

She stopped for a second, then carried on, didn't even look over.

Her hair had thinned out to the point you could make out the individual strands. I could see every sinew in her neck, the bright red scar running from behind her ear around the base of her skull, a reminder of the failed surgery from two years before.

Sometimes it goes well, the doctor had said. Sometimes they don't get it all. And if they don't…

I bit my bottom lip. What do doctors know, anyway?

'I'm gonna be here a while, Mom,' I said, quiet. As I reached out, she pulled her hand away so I couldn't touch it. Suddenly, a part of me was glad. I felt sick instantly, a deep shame closing its fist around my throat. Repulsed by my own mother.

Dad was pulling me away then, guiding me into the kitchen again. 'It's alright,' he said. 'She's just having a bad day. She's in and out like that. Don't take it personally.'

I was choked. 'How else am I supposed to take it?' The words were bitter on my tongue.

Dad sighed. 'Head upstairs,' he said, 'unpack. I'll talk to her, see if I can get her thinking about you. It's been a long time, Nicky. Ten years… and she's not been right for a while now. It'll just take time. I'll fix some tea, and then we'll try again.'

I felt the pang on the sides of my tongue then. 'No,' I said, 'I need a drink.' I wasn't a drunk or anything. In fact, I didn't do a whole lot of it. But right then, it was all I wanted in the world.

Dad just nodded, hand on my shoulder. 'Okay,' he said, 'I'll take your bag up in a while. Be safe.'

He let his hand slip, and I was already going towards the door.

'And Nicky?' he called.

I looked back.

'I don't know if you two still keep in touch these days, but your friend Pete?'

'Yeah,' I said, my hand tightening on the frame. 'What about him?'

'He's in town, too. Wasn't sure if you knew.'

I licked my lips, met his old, watery blue eyes, rough hands kneading themselves in front of his over-tight brown belt.

'I didn't know,' I said.

'You two fallen out of touch?'

I sighed, swallowed, heading out into the pale afternoon light. 'Yeah,' I muttered to myself, 'something like that.'

'Nicky?'

The voice rang across the quiet street. I hadn't heard it for a decade, but I could never forget it.

'Pete,' I said, more to myself than him. I turned, looking across the roof of the shiny black Mercedes. I watched as my old best friend stepped slowly down off his porch, looking lean and scrubbed in a smart suit, grinning at me. He was tall, with soft, dark eyes and curly black hair that held around his head like a halo. The kid had always been an angel.

He had his hands up in front of him and was turning a class ring around his finger, a gleaming silver watch with a pearl inlaid face glimmering from under the tailored cuff of his white dress shirt. He wasn't showing off, but I couldn't not notice.

He approached cautiously. 'I thought that was you,' he said, keeping his voice low. He stopped at the end of his drive so there was half a street between us. We were strangers in that moment. Strangers who knew everything about each other, our darkest secret. 'I saw you walk by earlier, didn't get out in time,' he said, glancing back at the house.

I lifted my chin. 'Nice car,' I offered. 'Life worked out okay, then.'

'Yeah, you could say that.' He laughed a little, then looked down.

I didn't mean it to come across like that. 'Not moving back home, are you?'

He shook his head, glad to be past it. 'No, no, just some family stuff, you know?' He hooked a thumb at the house.

'Yeah, I know,' I said, nodding my head back towards mine.

'So...' He swung his arms wide, clapped. *So...* The swansong of a dying conversation.

'So.'

'Where you headed?'

'Rock's.' I looked towards the end of the street. 'If it's still there.'

'It is,' he said, smiling now. 'I drove past it on the way in. Still a dump. Remember that time we stole that keg from the loading dock and Pop chased us for three miles up that logging track before he beached his truck on that old run-out?'

I returned the expression now. Barry Poplar. Sheriff Pop. I could still picture him clearly. 'Emmy twisted her ankle, we had to carry her back.' I chuckled at the memory. 'And we never did get to drink that thing.'

'You rolled it into the river.'

'You dropped your end, I couldn't hold it,' I laughed. 'Hell, is Pop even still sheriff?'

'Probably,' Pete said. 'Waiting for us to come back so he can finally bust us, probably.'

My back stiffened and I met Pete's eye.

'For the keg, I mean,' he added quickly. 'Not for...' He trailed off, cleared his throat. 'Hey, you want some company? I could use some breathing room from everything here.'

I thought on that for a second. We promised ourselves we'd never be in the same place again. Promised each other. But ten years had passed now. Was it safe? Was it finally safe?

'I... sure,' I said. 'That'd be cool.' I lifted my chin at his Mercedes again. 'But you're paying.'

He laughed. 'Shit, Nicky, and here I was thinking maybe you'd changed these last few years.'

I welcomed him in with a clap on the back and then we were walking down our street again. 'Yeah, fat chance there. Some things never change.'

Rock's was a rundown old bar on Main. It was short for Rockefeller's, as in, John D. Rockefeller. It was a pretty ironic nickname. The place had a wood and stone exterior and black marks all up and down the sidewalk outside from where people had ground out a million cigarettes under a thousand boots. It had no windows and a nondescript door that begged to be walked by.

We pushed inside, a little pang of nerves scratching at me. We'd never been inside legally before. We all blew out of Savage the end of the summer after high school and never looked back.

'You still drink Miller?' Pete asked. Before I could answer, he spoke again, snapped his fingers. 'I know, I know, some things never change.'

Miller was my dad's brand, and we used to sneak them out of the basement refrigerator. I seemed to keep the tradition alive. Whether I'd realised it or not.

I spotted a little table near the wall and aimed for it – the place was empty, or as good as. It was still pretty early in the afternoon. Though by four or five it'd pick up if history was anything to go by, and there'd be a good crew of regulars set to close the place out.

My shoes stuck to the old floorboards as I walked through the dim interior, posted up at the table on a stool, and risked putting my elbows down on the surface. This shirt was old anyway, faded red plaid to go with my faded black T-shirt, my faded jeans, and faded boots. I guess that word was as good as any to describe me. Faded.

The sheen taken off.

I scoffed a little as Pete came over looking like the kind who'd stand up against my kind in court and plead down to misdemeanour on account of ignorance.

The beers hit the table and my hand was around the glass in a second.

I figured the conversation would be sparse until we sank a few, and I was right. Though even once it picked up and we got to talking about how Pete was now a tax consultant living in Sacramento – a good one – and about how I'd bounced around until I found a small town just outside Portland, got my realtors licence and found myself a reasonable little chunk of business that kept me going, we still only had one topic on our minds. One we could never talk about.

When Pete went to piss it was even worse. I was three beers down, him two, and the thoughts of Mom and Savage-fucking-Ridge were beginning to get darker. More invasive.

The thing really bugging me, though, was the woman in the corner watching me. Sitting there on her own, arms folded, cup of coffee in front of her.

I didn't know what was weirder, the fact that she was just staring at me, or the fact that she'd ordered a coffee at Rock's. Hell, I didn't even know they served coffee.

And then, after a few seconds of us looking at each other, she got up and headed over, making a beeline right for me. The way she walked, the way she looked, the way she held her chin up, eyes not moving from mine, only one thing came to mind: she was a goddamn cop, and this day was about to get a whole lot worse.

Chapter 12

Sloane Yo

Sloane pulled the old pickup off the road and let it idle at the gate. She rolled the window down and reached out, pushing the intercom button.

The stone wall and black iron spikes told her that the Saint John family didn't much like visitors. But the giant golden 'SJ' on the metalwork told her that despite that, they still wanted everyone to know who lived in the mansion on the hill.

'Saint John residence,' came a falsely regal voice from the speaker box. 'How can I help you?'

'Sloane Yo for Ellison,' Sloane said, elbow on the sill, hand on her forehead.

'Mr Saint John is very busy,' the woman said. 'Do you have an appointment, Ms…?'

'Yo,' Sloane repeated. It was two letters. How hard was that? 'No, I don't, but tell Ellison I'm here and I have news. I'm sure he'll want to make time in his *very busy schedule*.'

There was silence, then, 'One moment please.'

The woman went quiet, and a minute later, the gates swung inward and Sloane trundled up the gravel drive towards the stone manor. It was an old place, as old as Savage Ridge. The first house built here, back when the Saint Johns owned everything. The reality now wasn't much different. Most everyone who rented here rented their houses from Ellison Saint John's father. And would soon be renting from Ellison. His father wasn't in the best of health. Lung cancer. Stage four.

Ellison was okay, Sloane thought, as she rolled to a stop in front of the big house. Especially for a rich kid who grew up behind stone walls, with a dad like he had. Especially for a rich kid whose little brother disappeared.

The official story said runaway.

The facts said otherwise.

The conspiracy said murder.

And Ellison said it was finally time for the people responsible to pay for it.

Sloane killed the engine and stepped out. With her short black hair shaved on the sides and her black skinny jeans, jacket and leather boots, no one would have looked more out of place walking up the front steps, except maybe a rodeo clown.

But that didn't stop Ellison Saint John inviting her inside. He came to the front door, all solid oak and glass, and opened it. He was tall, broad, blonde, wearing a polo shirt and chinos. The shirt was at least one size too small, showing off his sculpted chest and arms. Though his skinny calves poking out from the ends of his chinos, diving down into boat shoes, told her that he hit the gym purely for the looks, and made sure every exercise involved a mirror.

'Ms Yo,' Ellison said without the offer of a handshake, pushing his hands into his pockets to showcase his arms, as well as the tautness of his trousers. 'You're late.'

'I didn't realise we'd put a timer on it,' Sloane said, reaching the top step.

'You're a *week* late, in fact,' Ellison replied.

'I told you these things take time,' Sloane replied coolly. 'I'm not a miracle worker.'

'No, but you do work for me. And when you took on this contract, you said you could get it done. And when an employee agrees to do something, I expect it to be done quickly.'

'So shall I just fuck off then?' Sloane asked, stepping back down again.

'You said you had something?'

She paused. 'I'm not here socially.'

'And you deigned not to call?'

Deigned? She restrained a smirk. 'What you had me do wasn't exactly legal, Mr Saint John,' Sloane said, ignoring the sudden fire in his eyes and the way he was motioning her to keep her voice down. 'Getting two people to the same town at the same time is one thing, but getting three? Money doesn't solve everything.'

'So then why have you spent so much of mine?'

'A drop in the bucket, I'm sure. But in any case,' Sloane added, 'we had to wait for the time to be right. Sachs' grandfather kicking the bucket was our cue, but Nailer took time. That needed finessing. Pips was the gimme. And he just got into town about...' Sloane checked her watch, 'Twenty minutes ago.'

Ellison Saint John drew a slow breath, balled his fists in his pockets.

Sloane kept her eyes on his. She didn't know if he was flexing for her or that was just his default. But either way, she'd eat him for breakfast. Not that he'd ever get within a hundred miles of getting to spend the night.

'You have anything else for me?'

'No, my liege,' Sloane said, feigning a bow.

'Watch it,' Ellison growled.

'You watch it.'

He ground his teeth. 'You know, I had my doubts about hiring you. People warned me what you were like. Maybe I should have listened.'

Sloane smirked. 'Maybe. But it's too late now. Try and screw me, and I've got enough shit on you to make your life real difficult.'

'Is that a threat?' He spoke with the confidence of someone who commanded a legion of lawyers.

'No,' Sloane said, 'it's a reminder. That *you* found *me*. You asked me. You hired me. And I don't appreciate being jerked around. So, either pay me what I'm owed and I walk away and forget about you Saint Johns and this nowhere town, or let me do my job.'

He kept her gaze for a few seconds, then lifted his chin towards the gate. The conversation was over, and she didn't see him reaching for his wallet.

Sloane turned and headed back down to her truck.

'They killed my brother,' Ellison Saint John called after her. 'Remember that.'

Sloane Yo climbed into her beat-up old Ford F250 and closed the door with a dull, metallic thunk. She looked at Ellison as she cranked the engine and pulled away, the conflict in his eyes. He really believed it. That Nicholas Pips, Peter Sachs, and Emmy Nailer killed his brother.

No one had seen or heard from Samuel Saint John for ten years. And Sloane had dug. She'd dug hard. If you had enough money, you could disappear. That much was fact. But Samuel 'Sammy' Saint John had barely turned eighteen when he dropped off the face of the earth, and not a cent had moved from his accounts. Which probably made Ellison Saint John at least half right – Sammy Saint John was dead.

But was he murdered?

That's what she was here to find out.

Sloane parked at the end of Pips' and Sachs' street and waited. By now Pips would have gotten home, and seeing as Sachs had been in town for a few days already, she figured it was only a matter of time before they crossed paths.

And she was right. It wasn't long before Pips came out and met Sachs. She was too far away to hear what they were talking about, but she figured the first words they exchanged in ten years wouldn't be, 'Hey, remember when we killed Sammy Saint John?'

She watched them walk past, waited until they were a way away, then let off the handbrake and started the engine, easing forward, keeping out of earshot, tailing them from a distance. She was good at this, didn't get nervous, didn't get guilty over it. Though her hands took a pounding when she was on the job. She'd already torn into the side of her thumb with the nail of her index finger, peeled the cuticles down to raw red. She'd start chewing next. Nails, skin. Whatever. The pain felt good, kept her straight.

Nicky Pips was twenty-eight, same as Sachs and Nailer. He was a realtor out of a little town a bit outside Portland. He did okay, but the word that kept coming to mind as she was looking into him was 'unremarkable'. He made ends meet, didn't drink much, didn't get around with women. He had a clean record. Kept his nose clean. Hell, he didn't even smoke pot, which was saying something considering Oregon was the pot capital of the damn world these days. It was almost as though he was trying to keep himself quiet. Which was interesting, but not incriminating.

Sachs had done a little better, went to college in California, and now he worked for a corporate tax consulting firm in Sacramento. He pulled down solid six figures, owned a place on a quiet residential street, ran five miles every morning. He wasn't married, but he did well with women. Owned a Labrador-cross-German wire-haired pointer named Seamus. Seamus was with a neighbour while Sachs was in town.

Nailer was the most interesting of the three. She had pinballed around the south-west for a few years, been married twice already, but no kids. Both had been whirlwind romances, divorced inside a year. She'd been arrested twice for drunk driving, once for public disturbance. She worked at a high-end restaurant owned by her best friend's husband. She was the part-time maître d'. Worked day shifts in the week, Sunday mornings. She rented a little place around the corner, held it together, barely.

Sachs had brought himself home on account of his grandfather. When Sloane had started looking at them, she knew that'd be the way to do it. That when Sachs' grandfather passed away, she'd have to bring the others back at the same time. It was Ellison's singular, seemingly impossible request. That they all be in town, and that they all be arrested for killing Sammy Saint John at the same time. Under no circumstances were any of them to slip through the net.

They all had to pay.

And he was willing to cover whatever costs made that happen.

Pips seemed like he was going to be tough at first. But he'd caved easily enough. Sloane hoped it'd be the same when she cornered him in town and started asking questions. He'd been putting off seeing his mom for months now. And Sloane thought nothing would bring him back, it seemed like it was out of sight, out of mind. But with just a little digital coercing, she'd managed to get him looking at flights. Some tailored ads, some leaflets about funeral planning and palliative care through the door to plant the seed. Then she'd slipped into his place while he was at work – the sliding door on his deck wasn't even locked. She cracked his laptop with the military-grade decryption software she'd snagged from a Chinese retailer on the dark web, and then searched enough stuff on Google to get his ads to start showing him things to make him feel guilty enough to come back.

When she knew that she had Nailer on the hook, she ramped it up, hacked his Netflix account and started giving thumbs-up ratings to movies about families and death so more of the same would be suggested. She was worried for about a minute that he'd hold his nerve. But he crumbled just when she was beginning to think he wouldn't and booked a flight. He was living up to her original unremarkable judgement.

Nailer took the most time. Because she was the most afraid to come home.

Sloane tailed Emmy, learned her routine and everything else about her. It took a while to put a plan together, but once

Sloane had, it had gone off flawlessly. She'd not even needed to meet Pips, but Emmy had resisted. She needed that final nudge in the coffee shop. The mention of a mother away from her child, the stoking of homesickness for the PNW. From the outside looking in, her job probably seemed like manipulation, coercion, and a bunch of other things that judges didn't look too kindly upon. But in reality, it was a fine fucking art. It was masterful, what she'd done. And no one would ever know. And though Ellison was footing the bill for all her hard work, it somehow didn't feel like enough. But then again, she wasn't a PI for the gratitude, she was a PI because she wasn't a cop anymore, and because she was damn good at it.

But getting them all here was only the first half of the battle.

Now was the hard part. And that was nailing them to the wall for a murder they'd all been proven to have no involvement in ten times over. Local police, state police, a handful of other PIs that Sloane was aware of, and even a few white and black hat hackers had all come to the same conclusion: despite the pool incident and the threat made by Nicholas Pips against Sammy Saint John's life, and Sammy supposedly naming Emmy Nailer as the person he was going to meet on the day he disappeared, there was no hard evidence to support their involvement in any wrongdoing. And plenty of evidence to support the fact that there was *no way* they could have had any involvement at all. An airtight alibi and more than twenty confirmed witnesses all put them in the movie theatre at the time Sammy left the house to meet Emmy, and there was undisputed security video and traffic camera footage that showed them leaving the theatre and heading straight to the diner afterwards.

Now, Sloane hadn't seen it herself and hadn't spoken to the witnesses. But she wasn't so arrogant to think that everyone that had walked this path before her was so inept that they'd overlooked something truly obvious.

But there *was* something obvious, she thought, that Ellison Saint John was overlooking. And that was the fact that if Sammy was murdered, then it probably wasn't Nicholas Pips, Peter Sachs, and Emmy Nailer that did it. And that with all the focus being put on them, someone else had gotten away with murder.

Sloane couldn't ignore three lifelong friends going their separate ways in the wake of the case, blowing out of their hometowns, and never speaking to each other again, but she didn't know if they had done that out of guilt, or because they just couldn't live with the Saint Johns' vendetta hanging over their heads. The scrutiny, the pressure, the endlessness of their crusade to prove the unprovable... it'd be enough to push anyone to leave.

But finding who might have actually killed Sammy Saint John wasn't her mandate. Not yet, at least. Her mandate was to get under their skin, to probe deeper, more invasively than anyone had before. To leave ethics at the door and to wring the truth out of them. Because even if they didn't kill Sammy, they probably knew something about it. Ellison Saint John wasn't unintelligent, and he was certain they were responsible. And from what she understood, Thomas Saint John was, too.

So, until she was absolutely sure they were wrong – or until Ellison decided to stop paying her fee – she would probe. She'd peel, and scratch away at them until everything was laid bare.

She thought Nailer was the easy target, the one liable to crumble. But she was also going to be the one who was easiest to spook. The one who was most tightly wound. The one who was a flight risk. So, she'd have to tread carefully, choose her moment. Especially as Emmy would recognise her from Arizona and know something was up.

Sachs was going to be the toughest. He had the most to lose. A great job, a good life. And he knew his way around tough conversations with guys who talked at you and not to you on account of his job. She'd struggle to find a crack to sink her fingernails into there.

Which left unremarkable little Nicky Pips. Small-town boy, chronic underachiever. Sloane chewed her thumb, watched him in the distance, walking with Peter Sachs, heading for the only bar in town. He was lonely, he was coasting through life. The more she looked at him, the less at ease she felt. The FBI taught courses on how to spot bad guys who were trying their best to remain undetected. And usually, they didn't live in off-grid cabins in the middle of the woods. They hid in plain sight, worked normal jobs, lived in normal towns. Lived unremarkable lives.

Just like Nicky Pips.

Sloane cut the engine once more, let the old Ford roll to a stop down the street from Rockefeller's. She pulled up the handbrake and watched Sachs and Pips go in, and waited for a bit. Then she got out, crossed the street, and went in after them.

Chapter 13

Nicholas Pips

I'd never been arrested.

And the three of us were never arrested, either. Not for Sammy Saint John or anything else. We were questioned, sure, but our alibi was rock solid. We made sure of that. At least a dozen people saw us go into the movie theatre.

So, when Ellison Saint John came forward and said that Sammy had gone out to meet Emmy that afternoon, we all said that he must have been mistaken, that Emmy was with us. That we were all in the movie theatre from 4:30 p.m., and afterwards we were at the diner on Main, where we stayed until gone 10:30 p.m. Then, Pete's dad picked us up. He dropped Emmy off first, then Pete. I walked home and was there two minutes later. Mom and Dad confirmed that. There was nothing out of the ordinary to that story. And nothing they could pick apart. We walked into the theatre at 4:30 p.m., we walked out at 7:30 p.m., and that was that. For all anyone knew, we were in there the whole time. That's how we'd planned it.

Hell, we'd even joined in the search for Sammy. On the side of town where they found one of his shoes.

The other side of town from where his body was buried.

We'd been so fucking careful. And the investigation ended as fast as it started. The Saint Johns even brought in private investigators, outside help, petitioned the state police, but none of them found a damn thing.

The perfect crime.

And yet, every time I saw a cop, every time one looked my way, my throat tightened, my balls shrivelled up close to my body, and my hands got slick with sweat.

And now was no different.

She was tall, lean. Asian—American, I guessed. Pretty, in a kind of androgynous way. The kind of woman you'd walk past without noticing, but then look at for a second time and see it. But she looked mean, too, striding fast, not wasting time.

And definitely not heading to a different table.

She approached, stopped abruptly, and reached inside her jacket.

I tensed.

Then she laid a leather billfold on the sticky top, thumbed it open so I could see it. 'Sloane Yo,' she said flatly, 'licensed private investigator.' She retracted the wallet, stowed it. 'Are you Nicholas Pips?'

I swallowed, tried to hold my voice. 'I feel like you wouldn't be here if you didn't know I was.'

She smiled briefly, then it faded, the meanness returning. 'I'd like to speak to you if I could.'

'About what?' I asked, wondering if lifting my arm above the table to reach for my beer would give away how much my hand was shaking, stopping myself from peering around her towards the bathroom, hoping Pete was on his way back to interrupt.

'About Ellison Saint John. And about why he seems convinced that you killed his brother, Samuel.'

I'd practised this face in the mirror a million times, but it still felt wobbly. My brow crumpled in concern and confusion. 'I'm sorry,' I said, 'I don't understand… Sammy disappeared ten years ago? What does this have to do with me?'

'That's good,' the woman — Sloane? — said. Sloane Yo. 'Practise that a lot?'

'No,' I lied, then regretted saying anything. I cleared my throat, rubbed my hands on my thighs. 'Look, I don't know what Ellison has said, but… we never really saw eye to eye.

80

It's not uncommon knowledge that I thought the guy was a massive douchebag. Hell, I still do, unless he's changed in a big way. But I guess you already know that if you're working for him.' I watched her reaction. She didn't have one. But she was scratching at the side of her thumb with her index finger. It looked sore.

'Look, Mr Pips,' she said after a second, 'I'm not the first investigator to look into this. And I'm sure I'm not the first to dig into your life.'

I squirmed.

'But Ellison Saint John is insistent, and he's happy to keep the meter running until my investigation is done. Now he's pretty set on the fact that you, Peter Sachs and Emmy Nailer are the ones responsible for his brother's death. So, you've got two options here: either you help me out, we get this conversation done and dusted and I can move on to the next name on my list, finally crossing off Nicholas Pips – or you can sit there with that dumb look on your face, and I'll peel back your life, layer by layer, until I know everything about you. And I mean *everything*.' She kept talking. 'If you didn't do it and you have nothing to hide, then you'll speak to me. If you don't… Well, I'm currently on the fence as to whether you're even capable of something like that. Are you?'

She'd machine-gunned me. And I was stunned, poked full of holes. My brain reeled, my eyelids stuttering. Which I feared told her more than my words would.

'Hello? Can I help you?'

Pete. Thank God.

Sloane Yo turned to watch Peter Sachs approach, his pace quickening. He slid into the space between the table and Sloane, blocking her from me.

She held her hands in her pockets. 'Sloane Yo, licensed private investigator. I'm here on behalf of Ellison Saint John, looking into the murder of his little brother, Samuel.'

'Murder?' Pete said fluidly. 'I didn't think it was ever confirmed as that. Last we heard Sammy just up and disappeared. Trouble at home was the story.'

Sloane Yo didn't hide her widening smile. 'Right. Yeah, that was the story, huh?'

'You'll forgive me if I ask to see some identification,' Pete went on, cooler than I'd ever known him. The nervous kid that always got made fun of for giving a damn about school was all grown up. He didn't need me to protect him anymore, that much was for damn certain.

Sloane lifted her chin then, at me. 'He's seen it. He'll tell you.'

Pete looked over his shoulder at me, and then they were both staring at each other. He held his hand up, as though to bar any more questions. 'The police spoke to us ten years ago. We had nothing to do with it. We were at the movies that night. It's all in the reports, I'm sure.'

'I'm sure.'

What was she, a goddamn parrot?

Pete stood a little straighter. 'I'd like to get back to having a beer with my friend now, so if you don't mind?'

Sloane grinned a little, nodded. 'Sure thing, Peter.'

Pete twitched at his name. He hadn't given it. But she knew exactly who he was.

She walked backwards, still watching me. 'We'll speak soon, Nick,' she said. 'See you around.'

And then she was out the door and Pete and I were alone.

He waited a few seconds, then turned, came close, hissed at me, eyes fire. 'What the hell was that about?'

My jaw was set, eyes fixed on the door, mind turning again. 'She blindsided me.'

'I could see that. What did you tell her?'

'Nothing.'

Pete sighed, closed his eyes. 'Goddamn Ellison Saint John.'

I felt like saying, *well, we did kill his little brother.* But instead, I just sipped my beer.

'Look,' Pete said, 'we keep our heads down, we stay quiet, we stay away from each other, and we get out of here as fast as we can, okay? But not too quickly, or that'll look suspicious. When's your flight out?'

'Tuesday.'

'You're here a week? Shit.' He sounded surprised.

'Five days. What about you?'

'Open-ended, not really sure when it is.'

'When what is?' I asked, watching him.

He looked up at me, sad then. 'My grandfather – his funeral. He died, Nick.'

'Shit, Pete. Why didn't you say? Grandpa Bill? Jesus. Look, I'll come by later and—'

'No,' Pete said decisively. 'It's not safe, we can't be seen together, alright? Can't be seen talking, or—'

'Won't that look more suspicious? If I don't come by? If we *don't* talk?'

Pete searched my face. 'Honestly, I don't know. But anyway, why are you in town? Thought you'd never come back.'

'It's my mom,' I said. 'She's not doing so hot.'

'Yeah, my mother said, sorry to hear that.'

I shrugged. All I could do. Then it hit me. 'Don't you think it's weird we're both here at the exact same time?'

'My grandfather died,' he said, a little bitterly, 'didn't have much of a choice.'

'But I did...' I muttered. 'And yet here we are together.'

'What are you saying, Nicky?'

'You still keep in touch with Emmy?'

'You know I don't. We promised.'

I swallowed.

'What is it?'

I grabbed my coat off the back of the chair. 'Come on,' I said, draining my beer and heading for the door. 'I want to see something.'

'Nick... Nick? Where are you going? Fuck...'

I heard his footsteps behind me as I reached the door and pushed out into the dusky sunlit streets of my childhood.

It was not good to be home.

Chapter 14

Ellison Saint John

Ellison slid into the dark room, the only light the thin rays bleeding through the blinds.

They cast a dim glow over the bed, the old man lying in it. The sound of a respirator moving up and down, gently forcing air into his father's lungs, cut the silence between the slow beeping of the heart monitor.

The room stank, like two-day-old urine and shit. But that wasn't surprising considering his father hadn't moved in nearly a month. The doctors said that this was it. The end. That all those cigars had finally caught up with him. He could no longer breathe on his own, and now spent his hours facing the window, trying to remember how the pines smelled. Or maybe he didn't. Ellison didn't know what was going on inside the old man's head. It had always been a skill that escaped him.

'Dad?' Ellison said, approaching slowly.

The old man did not look up. Thomas Saint John was a cantankerous man. Always had been. And even in death, he remained the kind of person it was impossible to like. He didn't have friends, he had associates. No one chose to spend time with him. No one could stand to. He was a ruthless, emotionless man who'd slit your throat without a second thought if he even had an inkling it would benefit him.

Ellison, like any son in his position did, idolised and despised him in equal measure. When the old man's heart finally gave out, Ellison would be the final Saint John. But despite the clear succession, one loose end still remained. What would happen to the estate? The house, the business, the money, the empire. Everything.

It was not coming to Ellison.

Not yet, at least.

He knew why his father didn't want to leave it to him, that he thought Ellison young, hot-tempered, rash, ignorant, arrogant – and that wasn't conjecture, it was quoting the old man verbatim. A good father he was not. Which made it all the more strange that he'd kept Ellison and Sammy when he drove their mother away. Ellison couldn't even remember her. His father never spoke of her. But Ellison had no doubt that he and Sammy stayed with him not because their father wanted them, but because it was a way to hurt his mother. It was either that, or accepting that she just hadn't given a damn about them. And believing that they were used as pawns to inflict pain was somehow easier to bear.

Two boys who had everything except love.

'Dad?' Ellison said again, stepping into the dim light. The dark, regal, wood-panelled study, lined with old books and hunting trophies hung around them like a heavy cloth, dragging Ellison's shoulders into a sagging hunch.

The old man kept his eyes on the window, didn't reply. Couldn't, with a tube in his throat. The morphine drip did its work next to the bed.

'They're here,' Ellison said, keeping a grimace on account of the smell. 'She did it, the investigator I hired. She got them here. This is it, Dad. We're finally going to prove it. Prove what they did.'

Ellison watched as his father's hand slowly curled into the bedclothes next to him.

'She's different from the others,' Ellison said. 'She's an ex-cop, but she's different, does what she needs to. Whatever she has to. She gets things done, and she's already found out more than any of the others.'

The heart monitor quickened slightly but the old man remained still.

Ellison did his best to keep the quaver from his voice. 'Pips, Sachs, Nailer. They're all back. For the first time since...' He trailed off, exhaled slowly. 'We'll find him, Dad,' he said, voice growing harder. 'We'll find out what they did to him, where they put him.' His own fists curled now. 'And then we'll make them pay.' He swallowed. 'We'll make them pay.'

Ellison left the room, his father still silent, eyes glimmering in the pale light.

Chapter 15

Nicholas Pips

I shoved my way out into the afternoon sun and hung a right. If Emmy was here, she'd be at home.

Pete caught up with me and we walked the sidewalk in silence, skirting around the odd person ambling along. No one recognised us anymore, but there would have been a time when every person we passed said hello, asked how our folks were. Savage seemed altogether more worn out now. Like the weight of what happened here crushed the life out of the place.

We both wanted it to be a coincidence that we were back in town at the same time and nothing more, but as we turned into Emmy's street and started towards her place – the old white house with the overgrown garden, the bowed and rotting wood siding – we both couldn't help but slow down, neither of us looking forward to knocking on that door.

As we climbed the steps, I thought about the last time we'd done it. The afternoon we'd killed Sammy Saint John. Sure, I could call it something else, refuse to face up to what we did: murder. But what was the point? There was no getting away from it. We planned, and then carried out a murder. We killed someone.

Bile rose in my throat as I lifted my knuckles to knock.

I killed someone.

I slid down that slope towards Sammy Saint John, came up behind him as he tried to crawl away, one arm, one leg broken, crying, sobbing, begging, eyes fixed on the hole three feet to his left.

And then I raised that shovel, gritted my teeth, and hit him. Hard. As hard as I could. Not with the flat side, with the edge. Watched as it cleaved his skull, as he fell still.

Pulling it out was worse.

Then I rolled him into the grave with my foot, and started pushing dirt over him, his dead eyes fixed on the sky until he was swallowed by the earth.

Pete joined me, to help fill in the hole, to help cover our tracks. But I was the one who hit him.

And I'd have to live with that for the rest of my life.

The door opened in front of us and Emmy's mom filled the frame. Cynthia Nailer. She was short, a little dumpy, with curly gold hair. Dye job.

'Well, I'll be,' she said, grinning, then laughing. 'Am I seeing ghosts or are little Nicky Pips and Petey Sachs standing on my porch?'

'Hey, Mrs Nailer,' I said, looking at my feet. 'Been a while.'

'Must be going on ten years,' she said, laughing again. 'Wow, I'd say you haven't aged a day, but…'

'Well, you recognised us, so that must be a good sign.'

'You two practically lived here as kids. Be hard to forget you! And harder to forget how much my weekly food bill dropped once you two cleared out of Savage.'

I kicked my foot nervously, feeling sixteen again. 'Sorry, Mrs Nailer—'

'I think you can call me by my first name, now, Nicky.'

'Uh-huh, um…' It felt weird, so I didn't call her anything. 'By any chance, Emmy's not here, is she?'

'Emmy? No,' Mrs Nailer said, shaking her head.

Thank God for that. I was damn near going out of my mind. If she was in town, I was going to lose my—

'You just missed her.'

'What?' My eyes shot up, meeting Mrs Nailer's. 'She's here?'

'She just ran down to the store for me. She'll be back in a few minutes. You want to come in and wait?'

I could practically hear Pete's teeth grinding next to me.

I swallowed. 'Uh…' I shook my head, thrown. 'Yeah, I mean, sure, that'd be great, thanks.'

We stepped inside. I didn't want to see her. Didn't ever want the three of us to be in the same place ever again – that's what we promised each other. But if she was back in town, and there was a PI sniffing around, then we needed to see her. Needed to warn her. If it wasn't too late already.

Emmy got back fifteen minutes later, stepped in through the door and dropped the plastic bag of groceries. Whatever jar was inside smashed and the blue bag filled with a dark liquid.

'God, Emmy!' her mom yelled, jumping up off the couch and rushing over.

We stood up from the other couch, Pete and I, shoulder to shoulder, and looked at her.

Emmy was five-three, tanned, with long, ringleted brown hair and close-set eyes. Her mouth was hanging open in shock.

'Emmy!' her mother said again, stooping to pick the bag up. 'Look what you did! My God, girl, close your mouth.'

Emmy blinked a few times, stepped to the side as her mother pushed her out of the way, scooping the bag up off the ground. Her mother went to the kitchen then, leaving Emmy, Pete, and me standing in that tired living room.

Pete spoke first. 'Emmy…' he said.

She ran over, threw herself at him, arms around his neck.

He stepped backwards, looked at me through her hair, then took her in his arms and squeezed.

She let go after a few seconds, and hugged me. With noticeably less energy. If anything, it felt stiff – token, almost. I hugged back, out of politeness. Habit, maybe.

Emmy stepped back, wiped off her eyes, smeared the little mascara she was wearing across her cheeks. She was in an old, worn-out grey track hoodie. 'What are you guys doing here?' she asked, keeping her voice low. She looked from one to the other. 'I thought we were never gonna be, you know… in the same place again? Or is… is something wrong?' Her eyes widened a little.

I swallowed.

Pete spoke. 'Why are you here, Emmy?'

'This is my house?'

'No, I mean in Savage.' His tone was direct, not warm.

'I, uh… I dunno. Just felt like I hadn't been back for a while. Missed my mom, needed to see her.'

Pete bit his lip. 'My grandfather died.'

'Jesus, I'm sorry,' she said, shaking her head. 'I didn't know.'

'That's not what I meant,' he said quickly. 'I had to come back, for the funeral. Nicky,' he went on, 'is back to see his mom too, she's not doing too good.'

'Shit,' Emmy said again. 'I'm sorry guys, if I'd have known…'

'Don't sweat it,' I added, waving it off.

Pete kept going. 'All I'm saying is that all of us are back at the same time, together. And with this PI showing up—'

'Sorry, did you just say PI? A private investigator?' She practically hissed it.

Pete and I nodded in unison.

'What do they want? Have you spoken to them? What did they say? What did *you* say?'

'Nothing,' Pete said, firing me a little sideways glance.

'What was that? You looked at him,' Emmy said. She looked at me then. 'Did they speak to you? What happened?'

I shook my head. 'Nothing. Like Pete said, she came over, out of nowhere, in the bar. At Rock's. She told me she was a PI, asked about Sammy Saint John.'

'Jesus fucking Christ. She knows.' Emmy started shaking, collapsing down into a crouch, leather boots creaking. She held her hands in front of her lips like she was praying. 'She knows. Who is she? Did you get her name?'

'Uh, Sloane… something.'

'Yo,' Pete finished. 'Sloane Yo.'

'Yo?' Emmy looked up at us. 'What's she like?'

'Mean,' I offered. 'She didn't seem like the type to pull punches.'

'I meant what does she look like?'

I tried to picture her. 'Thin, I guess, Asian, black hair, shaved sides—'

Emmy paled a little, cutting me off mid-sentence. 'Dark eye make-up, tattoos on her arms?'

'She had a jacket on,' I answered, my voice a little quieter, my blood running a little colder. I wound my mind back to when she'd pulled that badge. Had I seen tattoos? I think so, maybe, poking out under her sleeve. My heart hammered.

'Shit, it's her,' Emmy said then. 'It has to be.' She shook her head, scoffed. 'That fucking bitch!'

'Wait,' Pete jumped in. 'You met her? Here, in Savage? What did she say to you?'

'No, not here,' Emmy said, nostrils flaring. 'In Sierra.'

'Arizona?' Pete sounded surprised.

I didn't recognise the name of the town where Emmy lived, but apparently Pete did.

Emmy nodded. 'Yeah, in my coffee shop. Chatted me up while I waited for my drink.'

I closed my eyes, taking that in. 'So, she went all the way to Arizona to talk to you in a coffee shop? What did she say? Did she ask about Sammy?'

Emmy shook her head, looking like she was trying to remember. 'No, no, just some bullshit about her mom and her kid, and… and taking a trip through the PNW.' Her eyes widened, realisation seemingly dawning. 'Jesus Christ, the coupon.'

'You've lost me,' Pete said, folding his arms.

'The next day,' Emmy said, 'after seeing her at the coffee shop, there was a coupon in the mail for a discount on flights. That was her, too. I booked a flight that day!'

Pete drew a slow breath. 'We can't jump to conclusions here,' he said pragmatically, but I could tell he was seething. 'You and Nick could have met different people. This could just be a big coincidence, and we need to—'

'It's not,' I interjected, struggling to muster the words. 'It's not a coincidence. She screwed with me, too. Flyers for cancer care centres, weird ads popping up online, even my goddamn Netflix suggestions got all screwed up, started showing me weird fucking shit: *The Fault in Our Stars*, other sad movies. Fucking hell, *Homeward Bound*, even!' My heart sank. I felt sick. 'That's why I came. Guilt.' The word stuck in my throat.

Pete looked from one of us to the other. 'Well, I never saw anything weird,' he said. 'I came because of my grandfather.'

'Because she knew he wasn't well,' I said slowly. 'She knew you'd come for the funeral. But we needed some convincing.' I tried to meet Emmy's eyes, but she was looking every which way but at me.

Pete opened his mouth to argue logic, but there was none. We just stood there in silence, in Emmy's lemon-yellow living room.

'So, she brought us all back here,' Emmy said, her voice a whisper, eyes beginning to glisten. 'And she knew that you were at the bar?'

I could see where she was going with this.

'She followed you.'

Pete and I looked at each other and we all three rushed towards the window, looking out through the blinds.

'Shit, I don't see anything,' Pete said.

'Check the cars,' Emmy added.

'Do any of these look out of place, Emmy? Any of them not belong to neighbours, or—'

'How the hell should I know? This is the first time I've been back in ten years!'

Pete pulled away first. 'Fuck!' he yelled.

'Language!' came an echo from the kitchen.

'Sorry, Mrs Nailer,' Pete called back.

Emmy and I peeled away from the glass too, looked at each other for a second, then she looked away, hiding a grimace. I didn't think she'd ever look at me the same after what we did. After what *I* did.

'So, she knows,' Emmy said then. 'She must know – this Sloane person – otherwise, how would she know to follow you guys? And you brought her here, too? To my house?'

'We don't know that,' Pete said.

'It's a safe bet,' I interjected, 'that if she does know—'

'*Thinks* she knows,' Pete corrected me. 'If she knew then we'd be in cuffs already. Remember that. She doesn't know shit. She doesn't have shit.' He lifted a finger to illustrate that to us, but I wasn't buying a word of it. 'She's just fishing, that's all. We just need to keep to our story. Alright?'

I let out a long breath. 'Right. She doesn't know anything right now, she's just fishing.' I repeated his words, mostly to convince myself. It didn't work. 'We were cleared of all suspicion. Our alibi is solid, there's no evidence—' I dropped my voice lower '—no body. Nothing. The only thing tying us to Sammy is that he told Ellison that he was meeting you that night, right?' I looked at Emmy. 'But that's it. There are no phone records, no texts, nothing to say that was what happened.'

'Right,' Pete chimed in, nodding, as much to himself as to us.

'So, she can't have shit – except what Ellison Saint John has told her.' I began to gain a little momentum. 'And if he's paying her to look at us, then she's going to be looking at us. But the more she does, the more she'll see that there's no way we could be responsible, and that the likely truth is that Sammy Saint John wanted to escape his abusive piece of shit father and giant gaping asshole of a brother. That he got some cash together, and disappeared. The fact that your name came up at all was just coincidence, right? You were the first person that came to mind. He had a crush on you, that much was common knowledge –

94

turned up in the original investigation. And yeah, we'd be in the spotlight because I punched that little prick in his stupid mouth the week before. So, it's not surprising that Ellison Saint John still has a rod up his ass about us. But again, if they had anything, we'd already be in jail.'

Pete kept nodding, but Emmy just looked on, about ready to throw up.

'So, all we have to do is keep our heads down, visit our folks, then catch our scheduled flights out. We hang out as much as possible in the meanwhile, stick together, don't let ourselves get cornered.'

Emmy nodded at that now, too.

'We're just three old friends catching up, making the most of seeing each other again. We've got nothing to hide. No reason to run or stay apart. We know our story, it's the same as it was then. So just stick to it, don't say anything else. And we go our separate ways when the time is right. Sound good?' I looked at each of them in turn.

Pete looked solid. As a fucking rock.

Emmy was shaken. But she swallowed and then gave a little nod.

It wasn't surprising. It'd destroyed her then. She'd barely held it together. We damn near had to shove her on that bus to the airport. And now, she didn't look to be much better. I exhaled shakily. Jesus. How did we get ourselves into this?

None of us said anything more.

A few minutes later, Mrs Nailer came in with a plate of sandwiches, crusts cut off, just like Pete used to like them.

We all thanked her, sat, and ate in silence.

Mrs Nailer looked at us quizzically, then spoke. 'You kids haven't seen each other for ten years, you don't have anything to say?'

We exchanged nervous looks.

No, it didn't seem like we did.

95

Chapter 16

Sloane Yo

Sloane watched Nick and Pete exit the bar and make a beeline for Emmy's. Just as she knew they would. She followed them for a while, sat outside Emmy's house, watched from up the street with the little monocular she carried with her as they came to the window and peeked through the blinds. She cracked a smile at that.

At 4:00 p.m., she cranked the engine and backed up, wheeling into a driveway, and then headed out. There'd be no way to tell what the three of them were talking about, but she didn't need to have Emmy Nailer's house bugged to know that they'd be shoring up their story, going over the 'facts' of what happened ten years ago. Gentle encouragement to get them back in town was one thing – and she could maintain plausible deniability about all of it. But breaking and entering and then illegally recording conversations? Even if Washington wasn't a two-party state, that wouldn't hold up in court. And that's where Ellison wanted to nail them.

Sloane had heard a lot about Sheriff Barry Poplar from Ellison, and had read a lot about him in the reports, too. But that didn't stop her doing her own due diligence either. She was headed to meet him now, and had no intention of going in half-cocked.

He was an average height forty-nine-year-old with grey hair cut flat on top like he'd walked under a low-hanging weed wacker. He had dark eyes, a uniform that was good and tight, and a hand that always stayed clamped around his belt, no more than six inches from the safety catch on the holster of his Glock 17 even though he'd only ever discharged it twice while on duty in the twenty-five years he'd been a cop in Savage Ridge.

The place was quiet, pretty much crime free. And his record reflected that. No recorded murders – unless you counted Sammy Saint John. The first time he'd fired his weapon, it was because a local drunk pulled a revolver at a gas station because he'd forgotten his wallet and the clerk wouldn't serve him a pack of cigarettes. Pop hadn't shot at him, though, had just parked outside, and fired into the air to get his attention. The guy dropped the gun and surrendered peacefully, until Pop told him he couldn't go back to Rock's for another drink. Then he got a little angry, and ended up defecating in the back of Pop's cruiser. It was unclear if it was intentional as an act of protest, or he was just drunk off his ass. The jury was still out.

The second time he fired his gun was when a brown bear appeared at the high school during a food drive and chilli cook-off. Pop didn't hit it, but he did scare it away, got a standing ovation and several pats on the back, and then went on to win the chilli-eating contest. 2013 was a big year for him.

But despite his tenure and dedication to the safety of the residents of Savage Ridge, he had not appreciated the call from Sloane or the idea that she'd be looking into the Sammy Saint John case. But they both knew she wasn't the first PI to come poking around, and if he refused her his time, she wouldn't be the last. Over the years, Thomas Saint John had reminded Barry 'Pop' Poplar that he pretty much paid his salary, or at the very least paid for the renovation to the police station they did in '02 as well as the Chevy Tahoe truck he was driving. As such, Pop didn't really feel like he could say no – Sloane got that much from the tone of his voice. She hadn't even needed to say that the Saint Johns would appreciate his cooperation.

It was also Pop who got the rap for failing to solve the case the first time around. And Thomas Saint John had never let

97

him forget that fact. Pop had taken the lead on it alongside an investigator from the Washington State Police. He'd been sheriff for just two years at the time, an office he assumed at just thirty-seven years old. So now a portion of his time was dedicated to repeatedly walking investigators through his incompetence – Ellison Saint John's words, not Pop's. Sloane was sure he had his own version of events. And she was keen to hear it.

So far, she'd scoured the reports from the other PIs, as well as the state police investigator, and had Ellison's side of it – that his little brother was a sweet kid, smart, ambitious, handsome, that girls wanted him and guys wanted to be him. That Emmy Nailer had a thing for him, and Nicholas Pips and Peter Sachs were jealous of that. That the three of them had a weird friendship with both Pips and Sachs vying for her attention romantically. That a week before Sammy disappeared, Nicholas Pips took a swing for him at a party because Sammy and Emmy were flirting, and then threatened to kill him.

Sammy left that party, and then, a week later, he walked out of his house to meet Emmy Nailer for a date. And was never seen again.

Except the official investigation report, compiled by Sheriff Barry Poplar and one Lillian Dempsey, senior investigator with Washington State CID, along with more than two dozen different eye-witnesses, put Emmy Nailer, Peter Sachs, and Nicholas Pips in the Savage Ridge movie theatre between 4:30 p.m. and 7:30 p.m. The kids saw *Inception*. The movie had a two-hour and twenty-eight minute run time. They were seen entering, and they were seen leaving, at which point they walked down Main to a diner, sat, had milkshakes, and left after ten.

Sammy Saint John left his house at 5:00 p.m. that afternoon. Supposedly to meet Emmy.

Other investigators had done the leg-work. They'd checked with Pips', Nailer's, and Sachs' parents. They all confirmed that the kids left their respective houses in time for the show.

Gene Pips, Nick's father, drove the boys. Emmy Nailer's mom, Cynthia, dropped her off.

Pete's father picked them up from the diner after 10:00 p.m. No stops, no deviations.

It was only Ellison that saw Sammy leave the house, too. Security cameras showed him walking down the front driveway and slipping through the front gate. Then he went out of frame of the intercom camera.

There weren't any neighbours on the road leading to that gate, so those final frames of Sammy, recorded at 5:04 p.m. on Sunday afternoon, were the last time anyone knew where he was, and the last time anyone saw him alive. Or at least admitted to seeing him alive.

Someone knew something. They just weren't talking. Yet.

The three kids were at the movie theatre. That much was fact. And even if they weren't they had no vehicles. No way to get to Sammy or anywhere near the Saint John House. Which was a long way from town on foot. A hell of a long way. Too far to walk.

But while they were stuck there, Sammy was supposedly meeting Emmy Nailer – which she flatly denied on account of her being at the theatre. And even if she wasn't, she said, she wouldn't go within a hundred miles of him because he was a massive goddamn creep.

Sloane had read that interview transcript. Nailer was insistent on the creep thing, too. It hardly needed to be inferred. She used the word three times in twelve seconds. Which didn't really match up with Ellison's perception of their whole relationship, further undermining his testimony and belief in what had happened. Because he had exactly no evidence to support his theories. While there was plenty of evidence to support the kids' story.

Emmy Nailer had even willingly turned over her phone for inspection too, which showed no communications with Sammy Saint John. Sammy's phone was active until he left his house,

99

but then it turned off about a hundred metres from the gate. And that was it. He was gone.

She'd asked Ellison for copies of Sammy's call logs, for his texts, his online activity. Which were missing from the three boxes of reports and notes that he'd given her when she took the job.

He said he'd get them. But she wasn't confident. She guessed every investigator so far had asked for them. So, if he was going – or even able – to get them, he'd already have them. Why they weren't available and what they showed, Sloane could only guess at. But she figured that whatever it was, it likely contradicted the Saint Johns' theory that the three kids had killed him.

But she'd been spun a narrative before. And she'd figure out the missing parts for herself.

Sloane drew a slow breath, waited at a stop light, then crossed the main intersection in town and swung into the parking lot next to the diner that didn't seem to have a name other than the 'Main Street Diner'. The sign above the door just said 'Diner'. She guessed there probably wasn't much competition here.

The black and white Chevy Tahoe was already parked, and she could see Barry Poplar in the window, sipping a coffee. She knew he took it with cream, two sugars. She also knew what football team he supported, what church he went to, that he and his wife were divorced, that he couldn't have kids – low motility – which was also the reason his wife left him. Sloane knew what brand of beer he drank in the evenings after work, that he'd once begun training to run a marathon, and then backed out because he got bad shin splints. That he was a local kid whose dad was sheriff before him. That he'd done okay in high school, been a running back, but not one good enough to ride a sports scholarship out of Savage. So here he was, thirty years later, his father reincarnate. High cholesterol and all.

She thought about all that as she climbed the steps, walked into the diner, pushed her hair back over her head. A late afternoon mist had come down over Savage and made everything damp, including her clothes. The trees sighed with the waning sun and the humidity grew, a natural cycle of breathing that made the whole valley feel alive. The air thickened, the wind dying. And then the fog came.

Pop got up, straightened his belt, shirt buttons straining at his little paunch. He seemed to recognise her. He gave a nod, extended a hand. She figured she didn't look like she was from around there.

'Barry Poplar,' he said as she approached, smiling like he was afraid she'd tell Ellison Saint John if he didn't. 'People call me Pop.'

'Sloane Yo,' Sloane replied, shaking it briefly.

'Yo?' he asked, raising an eyebrow. 'Like, *Yo, wassup?*' He grinned at her.

Small town humour. Borderline racist.

She set her jaw. 'No, not like that,' she said flatly. 'You mind if we get on with this?' She gestured to the table.

He cleared his throat, realised what he'd done, then sat. 'Apologies, we don't get many tourists here.'

'And when you do, you feel it's your duty as sheriff to insult them?'

He sat, clasped his hands, laughed nervously. 'Look, sorry, alright? I didn't mean anything by it. You want some coffee or something?'

'I'm fine,' Sloane sighed. 'Can you tell me about Sammy Saint John?'

'Right to it, of course,' he said, taking a long breath. 'I know this story off by heart now. You want the long or the short version?'

'How about both?'

He slurped some coffee, did a strange exaggerated nod, bottom lip extended. 'I heard the old man is sick – supposedly pretty bad. You see him?'

'Thomas Saint John?'

Another nod.

'I don't know anything about that. Ellison's my client.'

'Client?' he laughed. 'All business, aren't you.'

'When the state doesn't pay your salary, you have to be. I get paid by the case. If I waste time, it's my own.'

'What's that supposed to mean?' he asked, defensive.

It wasn't a jab at him, but it told her plenty about how he viewed himself that he took it that way.

'It's supposed to mean that this isn't a social call, and that I've got other leads to follow. So, if you want to just get on with your stories – short, then the long version – I'd much appreciate it.'

He scowled. 'You don't want a notepad or anything?'

'I think I'll manage.'

He sighed out a stream of sour coffee breath, then started speaking. 'I don't know what Ellison's told you, but Sammy Saint John was...'

'You don't have to be bashful. This stays between us. Ellison Saint John pays my rate but I already have my assumptions about what kind of kid Sammy was. And they aren't good.' She met his eye. 'You can talk freely – in fact, I'd appreciate it. Believe it or not, I do give a shit about justice. If Sammy Saint John was murdered, I'd like to find out who did it – and whether he deserved it or not.'

'Jesus,' Pop muttered, shaking his head. 'Alright then. Sammy Saint John was... he was troubled. Angry. At the whole world.' He took a moment to consider that, shook it off and carried on. 'Now, for all of Ellison's arrogance, he was a breeze. Never did anything except look down his nose at people. Harmless enough. But Sammy, he was a chip off the old block. Thomas Saint John's son through and through. A kid who thought he shit solid gold. You ever seen a fourteen-year-old kid threaten to get his teacher fired after being sent out of class for yelling the word "boring"?'

'Not first-hand.'

'Well, that's the kind of kid Sammy was. He thought Savage Ridge, and all the little people who lived here, were his birth-right.'

'I thought this was the short version.'

'I'm getting to it.'

'So, get to it.'

He eyed her. 'So, you know Sammy disappeared, obviously.'

'Obviously.' Sloane folded his arms. 'What do you know about it?'

'Same as everyone, I guess. First I heard about it, Thomas Saint John called me, told me he didn't know where Sammy was. I suggested that he might be out with friends. Thomas Saint John quickly reminded me that Sammy didn't have any.'

His own father? Brutal, Sloane thought. She also noted how everyone seemed to refer to the Saint Johns by their full names.

'Sammy'd only been gone three, maybe four hours by that time.'

Eight, nine p.m., Sloane noted in her head, not interrupting.

'And I told him that it's usual to wait longer before making any sort of assumptions, but...'

'He didn't like that answer.'

'See, I made the mistake of thinking that he was making a request that I go up there. But I caught on pretty quick and got up there as fast as I could, at which point he told me that Sammy wasn't answering his phone, which he always did.'

'And that was enough to make Thomas Saint John think something was seriously wrong?' Hell, even she was doing it now.

'I guess so. He demanded that I bring in Nicholas Pips, Peter Sachs, and Emmy Nailer immediately. He wanted them arrested.'

'Why was he so hung up on the three of them?' Sloane wanted this part from the horse's mouth.

'Gene Pips, Nick's father, never much liked the Saint Johns. His father was the first one to start that feud. They were mill-wrights, the Pips. Nicky's grandfather, Henry Pips – Hank to his friends – rest his soul, was a foreman at the mill here in town.

One of his guys got injured, pretty badly, back in, oh, sixty-something, got crushed by a falling log. And Kenneth Saint John, Thomas Saint John's father, fired him. His wife wasn't working, and they had two little ones, a third on the way. He was turning the family out onto the street. It was Nicky's grandfather, Hank, that unionised them, staged a walk-out until Kenneth Saint—'

'You can just call him by his first name.'

Pop's brow furrowed. He was immune to it, deaf to it. Sloane wasn't and it was grating on her. These were just people, nothing more. No matter what this town thought.

'Kenneth…' Pop hesitated, as though it was strange not to say it. 'He didn't like that, at all. Tried to bring in scabs, but Henry Pips was a good man, a good foreman, and people respected him, wanted justice for the worker's family. The mill was shut down for over a month before Kenneth caved, paid the family, and asked everyone back to work. But Hank wanted more, pushed for insurances, health cover, the basics, nothing unreasonable. Except Kenneth Saint John – sorry – wasn't what you'd call a reasonable man. He was always looking for a way to get rid of Hank, but he never could. Hank passed a while back, must be going on twenty years. Dropped dead of a heart attack, his wife moved back with her sister near the coast after that.'

'And this is the short version?' Sloane sighed. Maybe she did want that coffee after all.

'Right, right,' Pop said, hurrying himself along. 'Gene, Nick's dad, also worked at the mill. He never made it to foreman, of course. Guess Thomas Saint John knew all about the trouble that Hank caused his father, so despite Gene being the best man for the job, a great guy, a great millwright, he was never allowed to move up. And that stung, you know? Not that Gene ever did anything about it, but to know that you'll never make anything of your life because someone else is keeping you down…' Pop clicked his teeth, slurped some more coffee.

'It doesn't sit well. So yeah, I guess you could say that the Pips and the Saint Johns never really saw eye to eye.'

'And that's why Thomas Saint John thought Nick killed Sammy?'

'Well, that and the pool incident, I suppose. You know that a week before, Sammy got into a fight with Nicholas Pips at a party?'

'A fight? I heard it was one punch and then Sammy left.'

'You know why?'

'He was coming on to Emmy Nailer.'

'Right. Ellison tell you that much?' Pop raised his eyebrows.

'I read the investigation reports.'

'The reports? You didn't requisition them from me.'

'But the other investigators did.'

'They weren't supposed to make copies,' Pop said, fist clenching around his coffee cup.

Sloane shrugged. 'I sure as shit didn't Xerox them, what's the difference? Ellison's got stacks of it. All I did was read. If you want them back just ask him.'

Pop ground his teeth.

'What's your version?' Sloane asked. Ellison maintained that Sammy was flirting with Emmy. The kids' own recollection of it was pretty vague: that Sammy was coming on to Emmy, and that Nick got between them. They maintained that Sammy swung first. Ellison's story was the other way around. Sloane figured that the kids knew better than to try and throw a Saint John under the bus, so they didn't.

'We got a call to go out and break that party up, from a neighbour. It was the middle of summer, the folks who owned that house had a pool. Usually with these kinds of things it's just a couple of kids, nothing serious, you know?'

'So, what was different about this time?'

Pop took his time with his answer, took another sip in the meanwhile. 'Sammy Saint John wasn't the kind of kid that got invited to parties much. No one really liked him. And don't get me wrong, I'm not saying the kid had whatever happened to him coming, but he didn't really behave in his own favour, you know? He spoke to people like shit, treated them like shit. And he used to show up to these parties, uninvited, in his BMW or Mercedes—'

'His *father's* BMW or Mercedes,' Sloane interjected.

'Right, the kid had never earned anything for himself. So, this one evening he shows up to this house, already drunk. He gets out of the car, swaggers inside, liquor bottle in hand.'

'At eighteen?'

Pop nodded. Another sip of coffee, eyes squinting over the rim. 'Like I said, the kid thought he was untouchable.'

'And you never did anything about it? Knowing he was drinking, driving drunk…'

Pop just licked his teeth. He didn't seem to like her insinuation, and she was pretty certain that arresting Sammy would have cost him big, one way or another.

'What happened next?' she asked.

Pop went on after a few seconds, again considering his words, eyes falling to the table between them. 'This is where things get hazy. He came into the street fast, music pumping, mounts the curb, knocks down a mailbox, leaves the car half on the neighbour's lawn.'

'The neighbour who called this in?'

'Yeah, saw Sammy come, park, get out, bottle in hand – I know the guy, name's Jerry, he's an insurance broker, lives over on—'

'Short version.'

'Right, right. So, like I said, this is where things get hazy. Sammy lets himself inside, heads through, out back. The kids weren't exactly forthcoming on details. They were all drinking, smoking, probably into a little bit of the old nose candy, if you know what I mean?' He put a finger against his nostril to illustrate.

'I do,' Sloane answered quickly. 'Go on.'

'By all accounts, he goes out into the backyard, and that's when Pips spots him. He supposedly heads over, stops Sammy, tells him to leave. Sammy pushes him away, shoves the bottle into his chest, tells him to take it easy, have a drink. Then he pulls off his polo shirt, and jumps in the pool.'

'That doesn't sound like a fight.'

'I'm getting to it.' He shook his head again, as though finding his train of thought. 'Now, there are some girls in the pool, and apparently Sammy decides to try his luck. They all get out pretty fast. He was yelling about them being fucking sluts or something.' He waved that off. 'The truth is no girl wanted anything to do with him.'

'Funny how that makes them sluts.' Sloane folded her arms.

'So, Sammy starts ranting, people are yelling at him to get out of the pool – Jerry has come outside at this point, is watching through the fence, so we have this much on good authority, right? Sammy starts yelling back, thinking it's all fun. He pretends to swim around like he's having the best time in the world. Then he gets on his back, starts doing the back stroke.'

'And then throws up.'

'You did read the reports.'

'Didn't have to, to see that coming.'

He looked out the window for a second, then carried on. 'So, at this point, he does get out, everyone's shouting at him to leave. So, he heads over for Nicky Pips, demands his bottle back. Nicky Pips refuses, tells him to go home. Then Emmy Nailer gets between them to try and calm things. Then he takes a swing.'

'Nicholas Pips.'

'Sammy Saint John.'

'Sammy swung first?' Sloane confirmed.

Pop nodded. 'Yeah, Thomas Saint John was pretty insistent that was left out of the official report. Threatened to sue me if I put it in there.'

'You tell the other investigators this?'

'Some,' Pop said. 'But it never seemed to matter. The investigators were never paid to find out what happened at that party, but to get to the bottom of what happened to Sammy a week later.'

'So, Sammy took a swing for Nicholas Pips?'

'Or Emmy Nailer, maybe – details are vague. Jerry couldn't see. None of the kids wanted to speak out against Sammy. They thought he was a little prick, but they knew who his father was. But Emmy got shoved out of the way by Pips. Sammy misses his punch. Then Nicky socks him. Not hard. But hard enough. In the mouth. He stumbles back, falls into the pool again. He gets to the side, starts screaming about how Nicky is finished, is gonna go to prison, how Sammy's father is going to buy his house, get his father fired, turn his whole family out onto their asses, says his mother will be sucking dick on a street corner by the end of the week.'

'This kid sounds like a real charmer. So, what happened then?'

'Nicky goes over, drags Sammy out by his collar, throws him to the ground, presses his face against the concrete, tells him if he ever talks about his mom again, he'll kill him.'

'And that much is confirmed?' Sloane asked.

'Yep, the kids weren't bashful about quoting that one. Everyone heard him. Plain as day. Nicholas Pips hit Sammy Saint John, then threatened to kill him. A week later, poof.' Pop snapped his fingers. 'Sammy Saint John is gone, and Thomas and Ellison are only pointing their finger at one person.'

'Nicky Pips. Except his alibi is airtight. The theatre, then this diner?'

'Saw them myself. All three of them. Sitting in that booth right there.' He hooked a thumb over his shoulder.

'So why are the Saint Johns so sure?'

Pop shrugged. 'Sammy said he was meeting Emmy Nailer. Pips threatened to kill him. And Peter Sachs was never more than six feet from either of them.'

'But they have an alibi?'

'I don't know what you want me to say. They didn't kill Sammy Saint John. They couldn't have. There's no evidence that points to that. None at all. They were all in that theatre. Their phones showed that they never moved. GPS logs put them there, then here, then at home. Nowhere else.' He let out a long sigh, tapped his empty coffee cup on the table. 'I think the Saint Johns held onto the belief because the other options were too tough to swallow – either Sammy skipped town, someone else killed him, or maybe... maybe he killed himself.'

Sloane let that sit. It had crossed her mind, too. Sammy was reckless, a loner, universally disliked by his peers. His brother was absent, his father loathsome and cold.

People had ended their own lives for less. 'Was there anyone else? Any other suspects? Anything?' Sloane asked, knowing that giving that answer to Ellison Saint John would not be good enough.

Pop shook his head. 'Nope. The kid was a little prick, but no one in Savage would dare cross the Saint Johns. It couldn't have been Nailer, Sachs and Pips, but honestly... there's no one else. Not as far as we knew, at least. Though I got shut out of the investigation pretty quickly. Sammy was barely missing twenty-four hours before they brought in some state police investigator to take over. I did the initial interviews, led some of the searches, wrote up the reports and submitted them, but otherwise I was kept out of the loop on Thomas Saint John's orders. I don't think he had much faith in my ability to find Sammy.'

'The state police investigator, that was Lillian Dempsey,' Sloane confirmed.

Pop nodded. 'That sounds right.'

'And she didn't find anything, either?' She needed to be sure. The reports clearly couldn't be trusted as gospel.

'She found Sammy's shoe. But otherwise...' He shook his head. 'Nothing that pointed to the kids. And she was insistent on that with Thomas Saint John. She wanted to pursue other leads, dig into his business dealings. She thought it might have been a kidnap and ransom job, or something like that. But he wouldn't budge from Pips and the others. Which I guess is the reason the investigation stalled so quickly and Dempsey was out of here as quick as she arrived.'

Sloane took stock of that. 'The kids all left Savage Ridge pretty quickly after they were ruled as no longer being persons of interest.'

He shrugged. 'No one blamed them. The Saint Johns spread it all over town, that they had something to do with Sammy's disappearance. Guilty by public opinion – and no one would disagree with them.' He laughed a little.

Sloane narrowed her eyes. 'You don't think that's suspicious at all?'

'What? Wanting out of a town where everyone thinks you're a murderer? No, I don't.'

Sloane chewed on her thumb.

'You think different?' Pop asked.

She sat back, thought on it. 'Sheriff, if I thought the same, there'd be no point in me even being here.'

Sloane left the diner soon after and slid back into the driver's seat of her old Ford. The door closed and she sat in silence, thinking about it all.

About the pool party – how Sammy Saint John swung first, then Pips floored him. Sammy threatened his family, Pips threatened back.

Sammy was the one who showed up drunk, made a nuisance of himself, and was pretty universally disliked.

Sloane sighed.

And Ellison must have known that much, that Sammy wasn't the little golden boy he'd been making him out to be. That Sammy had swung first. That Sammy had a string of swept-under-the-rug misdemeanours by the sounds of it.

And yet he'd neglected to tell her any of that. Shocker.

She had her hand on the gear shift, chewed fingernails digging into the old leather. Sloane thought about a drink then, the feeling coming on all at once. It grabbed her body, made her shudder, made her mouth salivate.

She balled her fist, lifted it into the air, and then brought it down on her thigh with everything she had.

It rebounded off, sent a bolt of pain down her calf.

She thought about drinking again, so hit herself again, screwed her toes up, slammed her head backwards against the seat rest.

Pain came, then anger, then focus.

Damn, she hated being lied to, hated being made to feel a fool.

Sloane reached up, shoved the rear-view mirror away so she couldn't see herself, then cranked the ignition and backed onto the street at speed.

Ellison Saint John had some questions to answer. From what Pop had said, Ellison knew a lot more than he was letting on, and if he expected her to do her job, then she needed to go into this with her eyes open. And right now, she was fumbling in the dark.

Her leg ached all the way there.

Thankfully.

Chapter 17

Nicholas Pips

It was dark when we stepped down off Emmy's porch and headed for home. We walked slow, kept our voices quiet, looked out for any sign that someone was watching us.

At her corner, when we were out of eyeline of the house, Pete stopped, grabbed my arm. With a grip tighter than I thought necessary.

'What are we gonna do?' he asked, tilting his head forward and looking up at me from under his brow.

'What do you mean?' I asked carefully. I felt like we'd already decided on the course of action here, but I could see it in his eyes that his brain was working overtime.

'About Emmy.'

'What about her?'

'Come on, Nick,' he said, releasing my arm now. 'You saw that PI, she's a fucking wolf. A wolf in tight pants.'

'Didn't really notice her pants.'

'Cut the shit, Nick.'

I sighed. 'Yeah, okay, I'm shit-scared. That what you want to hear? You think I like being mind-fucked into coming back here just to have Sammy Saint John shoved in my—'

Pete waved me to quieten.

I drew a breath, glancing around the empty street, checking windshields for silhouettes. 'I don't like this any more than you, but what can we do? At some point in the next few days, she's going to come at me, and you're not going to be there. She'll come for Emmy, too. That much I'd bet on.'

'Exactly, so what are we going to do before that happens?'

'I don't know if I like where this is going.'

'We stuck Emmy on a plane once. I think we should consider doing that again.'

'That's dumb.' I shook my head. 'Sorry, but no. This PI, Sloane Yo, she's on us. And seeing as she's on Saint John's payroll then she's gonna have plenty of cash to throw around, sway over the police, and access to whatever she wants. She's ahead of us, knows who we are, where we live. And with Ellison's version of events, she already pretty much knows the truth; she just doesn't know all of it. So, if we do anything out of the ordinary, she's going to see right through us.'

'So, what's your big idea, Nicky? Because I'm not hearing any goddamn solutions here.'

I licked my lips. 'Just… just let me think, okay? I'll come up with something, a plan, and then I'll let you know.'

'Sorry if that doesn't inspire confidence in me. You basically turned into a puddle when she showed up in the bar!' He threw his hand out towards town.

I felt anger bubble in me, got up in his face a little. 'Well maybe I'd be a little cooler about the whole thing if it was *you* who'd put the edge of that shovel in Sammy's head!'

'Keep your fucking voice down!'

I shoved him. 'You keep *your* voice down.' My finger was up then, right in his chest. 'This is fucked, alright? Nothing about this is okay, but don't come at me with a *let's deal with this* look like you want to do something stupid here.'

'Stupid? I'm the only one thinking clearly. You heard Emmy in there, talking about guilt and feeling bad and all that shit. Hell, she drank a whole bottle of wine in twenty minutes, Nicky. She's coming apart at the seams. And we need to deal with it, because the second she talks, we're all going down for this.'

There was silence, then a dog barked in the distance. We took a step back from each other, drowned in the glow of a streetlight.

'Alright, alright.' I ran my hands through my dark hair. It felt greasy. 'What do you suggest doing about Emmy? We can't get her out of town, as that'll just draw more suspicion. And if she's here, then Sloane already knows about her, so she'll follow her out. Which is worse, because then she's out of our reach and totally vulnerable. And if she tells Sloane the truth…'

'Right, the safest place for her is in Savage, where we can make sure she doesn't talk,' Pete said.

'Good. So, you run interference then, make sure Emmy's taken care of, make sure that Yo doesn't get close.' I kept his eye.

'I can do that. And what are you gonna do?'

I swallowed. 'I guess I'll just wait. Yo said she'd come for me, right? I'll just make sure I'm ready when she does – I know a bit about the Saint Johns that I doubt Ellison has told her. All we have to do is turn her around long enough for us to get out of here, and then she's got nothing.' My voice strengthened a little. 'If she had enough to do anything real without us being here, then we'd have just been picked up by our local cops, right? If we're here, then she's hoping that being brought together means we'll crumble – that she can get us to talk, pick holes in our stories, that she can lean on us, and that we'll buckle, let something slip.'

He was nodding. 'Yeah, yeah, that makes sense. Why would we need to be back here if she had anything except conjecture?'

'And the Saint Johns have been pointing the finger at us for years, right? That's not news. Not to us, and not to Yo. So, all we gotta do is stick to our story, wait for the investigation to turn up nothing, and we're all good.' I forced a smile, hoping I sold it.

He bit his lip, looked at me with his dark eyes, then let out a breath, nodded slowly. 'Okay, Nick, whatever you say.'

I don't think I sold it.

He held his hand up then, and I clasped it. He pulled me in, held me for a second. 'We'll get through this,' he whispered, I thought as much to himself as me.

'I know. And it's just like before, alright, Pete? Me and you until the end. I won't let anything happen to you. I promised you that, didn't I, back then?' I pulled away, met his eye again.

They looked big now, filled with fear, but something else, too. Something that unnerved me. 'You did.'

'I meant it then. And I still do. We aren't going down for this. Not for Sammy Saint John, and not for anything else. I won't let that happen. I won't.'

He kept squeezing my hand. 'You still think much about it? About him?'

My throat tightened. 'No,' I lied.

'Yeah,' he said, taking his hand back and looking away. 'Me neither.'

–

It was just after nine in the night when I glanced up at the curved mirror in the corner of the liquor store. Designed to give the cashier a view of what was going on in the furthest aisle, it also gave me the chance to see who was walking through the door.

The bell above it rang and my eyes lifted from the label on the bottle of whiskey I was holding. It was a brand I'd never heard of. I didn't know why I was checking the label. For eighteen bucks it'd be dog shit regardless of which phoney Scottish glen it was supposedly distilled in.

Sloane Yo walked in.

I lowered the bottle a little, watched as her keen eyes swept the store and zeroed in on the mirror. She approached quickly. There was no point running. She knew I was in there before she even came in.

'Nicholas Pips,' she said, sighing like she was already tired of the conversation. 'Looks like your friend Pete isn't here to save you this time.'

I chose my words carefully, reading from the script I'd memorised. I'd been waiting for her to show up again, though I didn't expect it to be so soon. I didn't know if PIs clocked off at the end of the day, but stalking me here either meant that they didn't, or that the Saint Johns were paying overtime. Either way, I needed this shut down quickly.

'Sloane Yo,' I said back, watching her. She kept her eyes fixed on mine, her index nail doing that thing where it scratched at the side of her thumb. It looked raw as hell. I noticed she was also swallowing every few seconds, cleaning her mouth of saliva.

I didn't let on that I noticed.

'What can I do for you?' I asked.

'Not making a run for it? You're either confident or cocky.'

I shrugged, put the whiskey back, picked up another bottle. 'Or I'm just innocent of whatever it is you think I did.'

'There's always that,' she said lightly, keeping her eyes on the side of my head and off the bottles. 'But I think you and I both know that's a lie.'

I shrugged again.

'I know Sammy Saint John was no prize – I asked around.'

'That's one way to put it.'

'Pretty much everyone's in agreement that he was an asshole, a ticking time bomb.'

I looked up at her now. Her eyes became questioning. What had she said that had piqued my attention? She searched my face but couldn't tell.

I bit my lip, looked away again. A ticking time bomb? She had no idea, did she?

'No one was sorry he went away,' Sloane said then, dropping her voice. 'You did everyone a favour.'

'And what favour is that, huh?'

'Getting rid of him. I spoke to Pop, I heard what happened the week before he disappeared. The pool party?'

I paused, my brow crumpling. 'Oh yeah? And what's the story going around? I'm curious.'

She let out a long breath. 'That Sammy showed up in his dad's car, blind drunk, got in the pool, started making a nuisance of himself to some girls.'

I watched her speak, watched her lips, holding what I thought might be a poker face.

'Then he throws up, crawls out, gets in your face...' She let that hang a moment. 'Then Emmy Nailer gets between you two, he takes a swing for you, you hit him, he falls, spouts some shit...' Another pause. 'Then you threaten to kill him.'

I slowly put down the bottle of gin I was holding, hung my head. 'That what Pop said, huh?'

'About the sum of it. Him and a dozen witnesses.'

I couldn't help but laugh. 'Christ.'

'Am I close? Because it feels like you threatening him and him disappearing a week later is somehow more than coincidence.'

I turned to face her. 'Is this what you do? You invade people's lives, manipulate them, accuse them of crimes, and then what, stalk them and harass them until they blow up, get themselves arrested for throwing a punch at you?'

'Or until they break,' Sloane said coolly, not flinching.

'Then let me save you the trouble and answer your last question. No, you're nowhere *near* close.' I snatched a bottle of cheap vodka off the shelf.

Sloane did flinch at that.

'And you're right, Sammy Saint John was a colossal prick – but that doesn't mean I killed him.' I tossed the bottle into the air. Her eyes lit up.

She caught it.

'Before you get in my face, I think you should look a little more closely at the people who hired you. The Saint Johns are as dirty as they fucking come.'

Her knuckles whitened around the neck of the bottle but she refused to look down at it.

'And yeah, I had a problem with Sammy, everyone did. But you know who he hated most of all? His father. And his brother. Ever wondered why they've been searching for his "killer" for ten years? Because they can't face the fact that just being related to them was enough to drive Sammy to kill himself.' I gritted my teeth to stop my mask from slipping. 'Why don't you have a drink, huh? You look like you need one.'

I turned away just as her jaw flexed, her eyes narrowing, nostrils flaring.

But I didn't feel the bottle shatter against the back of my head, and nor did she say anything else. So, I figured I'd hit the mark.

Sick as it made me feel.

Chapter 18

Sloane Yo

Sloane snatched the bottle out of the air, barely hearing Nicholas Pip's final words.

There was just a high-pitched ringing in her ears and a wetness in her mouth. She didn't know if it meant she was about to throw up, or tear the cap off the bottle and pour five fingers down her throat.

She screwed her eyes closed, focused on uncurling her fingers from the bottle, and dropped it.

Her foot lifted, the bottle landing on her laces. She cushioned the fall, listened as the glass clinked down onto the tiles. The bottle rolled away under the shelf and she let her eyes fall open, fists shaking at her side. Her jaw quivered, stomach knotting.

Sloane turned, looked at her ghostly reflection in the beer fridge to her right, met her own eyes, saw the hatred and disgust there and stepped forward. She lifted her hand, grasped the handle, and moved in front of it, grip tightening. She leaned in, let out a long breath, closed her eyes, and pulled the door towards her as hard as she could.

It flew out, the metal frame connecting with her forehead. Pain ripped down through her face, her nose, into her mouth, and she stumbled backwards, letting out a stream of profanity. She hit the shelf behind. A thousand bucks' worth of bottles all clinked and rocked, threatening to fall.

Her head throbbed, her hands cradling it, waiting for the warmth of blood. But it didn't come. She hadn't broken skin. That surprised her.

'Miss, are you okay?' came a voice from her right.

Her eyes snapped open and went to the shop assistant in the blue vest hanging around the corner. He was tall, with thickly framed glasses and long hair.

She managed a nod, throat tight, and then headed for the door.

He watched her all the way out.

Back in her truck, Sloane got hold of herself, wound the window down and took in some Savage Ridge air.

It wasn't late but the streets were empty, the town asleep. She knew that only three police cars rolled around. Pop had three deputies, one of which was always at the station. They worked in eight-hour shifts, and between nine and five Monday to Friday there was also a desk clerk to take calls and help with paperwork. The town didn't need anything more than that.

She looked up and down the deserted main street – the only street in Savage that had stores and diners and bars on it – and thought how easy it would be to disappear without anyone seeing or noticing. She thought about what Nick had said. That her assumption was way off. That everyone hated Sammy, his own family included.

Sloane was already driving then. She had been operating on the assumption that Sammy Saint John was a beloved member of the Saint John family, but maybe that wasn't the truth. Pop obviously wasn't going to speak out against them, he cared about his position too much and the Saint Johns had a tight leash around his neck. With Thomas Saint John being incapacitated, she wondered who held the reins to his empire? Ellison was no more than a peacock in a fancy enclosure. He didn't have real power, Sloane didn't think. And yet Pop was still treading carefully. Was he loyal to them? Thankful for what they'd done for the town, for him? Maybe it wasn't a begrudged relationship he had with them. Maybe he felt like he owed them. He probably did.

And yet, he still sided with the facts, that Nick Pips, Pete Sachs, and Emmy Nailer were innocent.

So, what if Nick was right? What if Sammy had been driven to kill himself? Pop had said that Ellison was an ass, but not dangerous. Not a problem to anyone. It was Sammy that was the outlier. The black sheep. The liability. The embarrassment that needed cleaning up after. And embarrassing a man like Thomas Saint John wouldn't come without its repercussions. Cooped up in that house, no friends, no mother, just an absentee father and an overachiever brother whose shadow was long, wide, and utterly inescapable. She wondered what Thomas had done after the pool party, how he'd handled disciplining Sammy. She doubted he was the sort of man to let something like that slide.

So, what if Sammy had been running away?

But then *why* name Emmy Nailer?

And why was his shoe found in the forest? It didn't make sense. If he killed himself, where was the body? It would have been found, surely?

Sloane was missing pieces of this puzzle, and she couldn't tell what the hell she was looking at yet.

She swung onto the road that led to the Saint Johns' fortress on the hill and braked at the iron gates. She buzzed the call button until the house staff let her in, and as she drove up, another thought occurred to her.

The door was shut and impenetrable, but after a few minutes, Ellison opened it for her. She doubted he did his own door service usually. Which meant that he seemed to want to keep the staff away from her. Was he afraid she'd ask them questions that he wouldn't like the answers to? Or was it simply that he was trying to keep them from seeing Sloane altogether?

She'd find out soon enough.

Ellison was wet when he let her in. It was apparent he'd just climbed out of the indoor pool. His blonde hair was damp and tousled, his jersey work-out trousers spotting with water where he'd not managed to towel off.

He had on a T-shirt that was clinging to his well-toned body, and just for emphasis, he kept the towel in hand, running it down his forearms and around the nape of his neck as he showed her through to the same regal sitting room he'd entertained her in the first time she'd visited Savage Ridge.

There were lots of chairs and sofas but she suspected no one ever sat in any of them.

'I'm guessing by the lateness of the call you've got good news?' Ellison asked, tempering his expectations. His eyes widened then as he noticed. 'Jesus, what the hell happened to your face?'

'It's nothing,' Sloane said, keen to get to the heart of the matter.

Ellison reached out to touch her and she swerved backwards out of the way. 'Don't do that.'

'I just want to see—'

'See with your eyes,' she growled. 'You don't get to touch me.'

'Okay.' He held his hands up. 'Whatever, if it's such a big deal.'

She was disliking the Saint John family more by the minute. 'Your brother wasn't popular,' she said.

'That a question?'

'No.'

'You come out here at ten at night to tell me that?'

'I came out here to ask you why you lied to me. Nicholas Pips did threaten to kill your brother, but it was your brother who swung first. He also drove drunk to that party, destroyed property, made some inappropriate advances on some girls, threw up in a pool, and then threatened to turn Pips' family out on the street.'

Ellison stiffened but kept his relaxed expression.

'In fact, I think that his exact words were that Pips' mother would be "*sucking dick*" by the end of the week.'

'I don't know anything about that,' Ellison said, shrugging. 'All I know is that Pips is a liar and he hit Sammy.' Ellison's voice rose a little.

'You don't know anything about that? Where were you during this party? Town's not that big. School must be small.'

'I was three years older than Sammy – I was probably away at college. I went to Whitman,' he said, turning out his bottom lip and pocketing his hands. A vague attempt at displaying humility. Whitman was a private institution in southern Washington state. Ellison was smart, but Whitman required money too. And lots of it. Sloane had checked out who Ellison was before accepting the meeting.

'Probably?' She raised an eyebrow. 'You've spent the last ten years obsessing over your brother's death and you don't know if you were away at college?'

He lifted his chin. 'I was here. I was home for a few weeks,' he said, reserved. 'But I didn't go to that party. I didn't go to any parties in town.' He set his jaw, looked over Sloane's head, almost sad about it. 'My father says it isn't befitting for people like us to go to things like that.'

'Sammy seemed to disagree.'

Ellison pushed his hands into the pockets of his training trousers. 'Yes, well, he disagreed with a lot of things our father said. But that doesn't change the fact of what happened.'

'No, it doesn't change the *facts*, but what it does change is the likely story. Because I spoke to Pips, and he freely admits to putting Sammy on his ass – and I can't say it didn't seem well deserved.'

Ellison puffed out his chest, nostrils flaring, but he kept quiet.

'But Pips also said that Sammy wasn't having a good time at home. That your father and he—'

'There were no problems at home,' Ellison cut in, shaking his head incredulously. 'My father and Sammy were—'

'And how exactly would you know what they were? You're three years older than Sammy and a second ago you weren't even sure you were home from college when he died. You took a four-year degree in business. Which means when Sammy disappeared after his senior year of high school, you would have just been going into your final year. Three years is a long time to be gone, Ellison. And it sounds like things weren't as good at home as you might think.'

He sneered then. 'So that's it? One conversation with a murdering piece of shit like Nicholas Pips and you're here, accusing my family of what?'

'I'm not accusing anyone of anything,' Sloane said lightly. 'I'm just here to find the truth. It's what you're paying me to do.'

'I'm *paying* you to find out who killed Sammy. No, actually, I'm not. I'm paying you to prove that Nick Pips and his fucking friends killed Sammy!' Ellison's voice rose to a deep yell. The noise reverberated off the wood-panelled walls and died in the room.

Sloane just stared at him for a few seconds. 'You done?'

He scowled.

'You're paying me to find out what happened to Sammy. And right now, I'm not convinced he didn't kill himself.'

Ellison laughed scornfully. 'Kill himself? My God, you must be the worst private investigator in the country. I bring you here, *give* you the names of the people who killed my brother, and after speaking to Nick once, you think Sammy killed himself?'

'Well, not to point out the obvious, especially not to an esteemed Whitman grad like yourself, Mr Saint John, but if a dozen other investigators and the police looked into this, and all of them came to the same conclusion, perhaps it's the right one. Perhaps Nicholas Pips is innocent and Sammy, embarrassed and alone, shunned by his father, abandoned by his brother, finally had enough and took himself out into the woods and ended it on his own terms.'

Sloane watched Ellison's fist clench in his pocket.

'Go on,' Sloane said, glancing at them, 'see what happens.' Her mind went to the Browning 1911-380 compact semi-automatic pistol in the strapped holster in the small of her back. It sat there snugly, and was the perfect size for her small hands. She could draw it and put three close-grouped shots wherever she wanted in under two seconds.

Ellison let his hands relax.

'You want me to believe that Pips killed your brother, you're going to have to give me more to go on. Because all I have right now is a vague threat made a week before and you telling me that Sammy was going to meet Emmy Nailer that night. Except there's nothing to back that up. And I still don't have Sammy's phone records.' She narrowed her eyes at him, waiting for a response, but he said nothing. She went on instead. 'Nailer's testimony also said she thought Sammy was a creep. And on top of that, she, Pips, and Sachs all have an airtight alibi for the entire afternoon and night – corroborated by the sheriff himself. Which doesn't leave me a whole lot to go on.'

'And you don't think that's odd? That they all have such a solid alibi?'

'Do you even hear yourself?'

'Or what about the fact that they all skipped town right after?' He pulled his hands from his pockets and snapped both fingers, eyes wide.

'From what I hear, you were pretty adamant that they were responsible, and weren't bashful about saying it or putting pressure on Sheriff Poplar to get an admission from them.'

Ellison tsked and shook his head. 'You don't understand. You weren't there. You didn't see what I saw. Hear what I heard.' He put his finger on his chest and tapped it.

Sloane looked over her shoulders, then backed up and sat on one of the sofas that had never been sat on. 'Okay then.'

'Okay what?'

'*Okay then*, tell me. From the top – everything. You were home for a few weeks, from Whitman. It was Whitman, wasn't it?'

He sneered again, not appreciating the emphasis on 'whit'.

'You say Sammy was fine. You say Sammy was murdered. So, make me believe it. If you're so sure, and you saw so much, heard so much, then tell me exactly what happened. And if I think it's solid, then I'll do what you asked.'

'You'll get Pips to confess?' Ellison looked down at her hopefully.

'I'll find out what happened to your brother – whatever it takes.' She put her arms over the back of the sofa, crossed her slim legs. 'You have my word on that.'

THEN

Chapter 19

Ellison Saint John

It was raining the night that Ellison Saint John arrived home. He had a car, but didn't drive it. He had one of his father's drivers pick him up.

By the time it pulled up outside the family house, he'd gone through the half a bottle of scotch – or brandy – that was left in the chiller in the back. He couldn't ever really tell the difference. Especially not the strong, aged stuff. Which was what his father always drank. He didn't even really like it. But his father always said, 'Beer is for poor people. And don't ever let them think you're like them, son. Not for a minute. You're a Saint John. And you wear that proudly everywhere you go.'

He waited in the back seat until the driver came around, took his bags from the trunk and carried them up to the front door, then came back and opened the car door for him, holding an umbrella over his head to stop the rain from wetting his Whitman blazer.

Ellison didn't remember what the driver looked like. He barely even glanced at the guy. The only thing he did remember was how cheap his cologne smelled and how tarnished his shoes were.

The house staff opened the door and Ellison walked in, the place quiet. It must have been the evening, but he didn't know exactly what time.

His gait was languid, chest out, arms swinging, head high like he owned the place. Which he did.

'Your father is in his study,' one of the maids said. He didn't even look at her.

Ellison headed in there, leaned around the door, knocked on it, said, 'Knock knock.'

Thomas Saint John looked up over his thin spectacles, said nothing for a few seconds.

'Hey, Dad,' Ellison said, suddenly uneasy, trying to hide his outward inebriation.

Thomas Saint John sighed. 'Hey, Dad?' He dropped the papers he was holding, but didn't lift his head out of the glow of the desk lamp in front of him. 'That how you greet your father? What are you doing here and why aren't you in school?'

Ellison stood straighter. 'I thought I'd come home for a few weeks, see you.'

'See me?' He repeated it like the words didn't make sense. 'So why the hell am I paying for a room for you if you're not going to be in it?'

'Almost everyone goes home for the summer,' Ellison said, feeling small.

'Almost everyone isn't a Saint John, boy.'

'Sorry, sir.' Ellison swallowed. 'I just thought I'd get some studying done, you know? Get away, a change of scenery.'

'You think that Whitman isn't conducive to studying?'

'That's not what I meant.' Ellison faltered.

'Then what did you mean?'

'I just, uh, meant...' he started, stammering.

'I, uh, I, uh. Speak clearly, boy.' Thomas Saint John threw his hand at his son. 'Say what you mean, don't stutter. You're a Saint John, for goodness' sake. Act like it.'

Ellison took a breath, steeled himself. 'Sorry.'

'Sorry? Don't apologise.'

'Sor— I mean.' He clenched his fists at his sides. 'I have decided to spend some time at home, to remind myself what I am working towards. To remind myself of the legacy I am to live up to.'

Thomas Saint John watched his son for a moment, then looked down at the paper he'd dropped and reached for a pen. 'No one likes a suck up, Ellison.'

Ellison's jaw quivered, but Thomas didn't see. Returning to his work was as good as him telling Ellison to piss off.

It stung just as much.

Ellison shrank from the door and back into the empty hallway, the house now suddenly feeling as cold and strange as the empty halls of Whitman. He wondered whether any of the others received similar welcomes when they went home. He could text some and ask, if he had their numbers. If he had friends. His father told him Saint Johns didn't need friends. Was there a difference between not needing them and not being able to make them? Ellison didn't know.

He walked the halls. Despite the twelve bedrooms, the six sitting rooms, two dining rooms, numerous bathrooms, and the four permanent staff that worked at the house, the whole place couldn't have been more devoid of life.

Then someone walked across the top of the stairs.

'Sammy,' Ellison called out, stepping into the space at the bottom. He stared up the double-wide staircase at the boy on the gallery landing.

Sammy was eighteen. He'd turned eighteen in June. Ellison had wanted to come home, but exams were just a few weeks away. His father had told him the choice was his, but he'd be faced with decisions his whole life. And those who made enough wrong ones now would struggle to tell the difference later on.

Ellison missed his brother's birthday.

He didn't know if Sammy had even celebrated.

Ellison had got his father's blonde hair and athletic frame. Sammy hadn't. He had black hair that always looked wet even when it wasn't, and sunken brown eyes ringed with dark circles. He never tanned in the sun, just burnt, and his pink lips gave the effect that he was wearing lipstick. He couldn't have looked more different from Ellison. And couldn't have been any more different, either.

'Hey,' Sammy said, lingering at the balustrade post, wearing a pair of sweatpants and a hoodie. 'When'd you get back?' he asked, thin hands grasping at the wooden rail.

'Just now,' Ellison said. 'How are you?'

Sammy shrugged. 'Okay, I guess.'

'Just okay? You just graduated high school, you should be out – parties, girls, having the summer of your life. By fall you'll be drowning in books at Whitman, trust me.' Ellison flashed him a wide grin.

Sammy didn't return it. 'Yeah, girls, parties – I'm on the way right now, can't you tell? I just got dressed up and everything.' He gestured down at his tired clothes.

'You're telling me you want to spend your senior summer holed up in this house, alone, not out, celebrating with your friends, falling in love, having the time of your life?'

Sammy's expression changed, his brow creasing, grip tightening on the bannister. 'Yeah, that what you did?' He shook his head. 'Screw you, Ellison. You don't know shit.' He turned away.

'Hey, hey!' Ellison stared up. 'Sammy!'

'Don't call me that,' Sammy said, turning, his narrow face full of anger. 'Don't fucking call me that.'

'What, why not? What's wrong?'

Sammy met his eye, then turned his attention past Ellison.

Ellison glanced back, saw his father hovering in the doorway to his study, turning his glasses over in his hands. 'Ellison,' he called, letting them hang at his side now. 'Don't you have some studying to get on with? Stop bothering your brother.'

'I was just…' he started, but when he looked around, Sammy was already gone.

Then the study door closed.

And Ellison was left alone on the stairs, still a little drunk, his world beginning to spin.

The days in between were formless in Ellison's mind, but the day of the party still burned brightly. It was the only day he recalled being truly afraid of his father.

He was sitting in his bedroom reading up for his economics course in the fall when he saw the headlights swing into view and roll through the gates. He knew the lights, square and wide-set. It was an SRPD squad car, one of only three in town. He'd seen it come to the house enough times, but why it was coming now, he didn't know. But whatever the reason, it was something. Something was happening. And it was surely more interesting than the econ textbook in front of him.

Ellison was up and heading for the front door before the car had even gotten halfway up the drive.

He got to the bottom of the staircase and faltered at what was in front of him.

His father was standing on the top step of the porch, arms folded. One of the house staff was standing next to him, a woman. She was pulling at her apron nervously. But his father was an obelisk. Unmoving. Which wasn't normal. It was the weekend, but he was still in a suit.

Officer Richard Beaumont pulled the old Ford Crown Vic to a stop, and killed the engine.

Ellison hovered in the hall, taking a few steps forward, but afraid to go out. His father hadn't moved or made a noise, but his posture alone was enough to exert a palpable heat. Ellison's heart beat faster just watching him.

His father never came to the door either, so this must be serious. Beaumont's arrival didn't warrant Ellison's father going to the front door, so this must be something else…

Ellison spied a shape in the front passenger seat then, hunched, dark hair falling over his face.

Sammy.

It all clicked into place. His father on the step, Beaumont's car. Sammy in the passenger seat.

Something was wrong. And Sammy was in trouble.

Quiet, sweet Sammy. What could he have done that would warrant Beaumont having to step in? Ellison couldn't imagine. Hell, he'd barely glimpsed Sammy in the halls and hadn't spoken to him since he'd arrived here.

Ellison drew a shaking breath, recalling the one and only time Beaumont had brought him home. He'd tried to buy beers for some guys at the high school to impress them, told them he could get it done. But he couldn't, and the clerk ended up calling the police.

His father hadn't said a word to him when he'd come home in Beaumont's car. Just twisted the corners of his lips down into an ugly grimace, then shook his head in disgust and gone back to his office.

He hoped that his father would go easier on Sammy than he had on him, but something in his demeanour said otherwise.

No one moved. Ellison could still see Sammy in the passenger seat, head hung. Beaumont was in the driver's seat, looking straight out the windscreen at his father, unflinching.

Ellison's father muttered something to the woman at his side. Just a word.

She rushed down the steps to the car, pulled the passenger door open.

Sammy didn't move.

Ellison didn't move.

Over the sound of the idling engine, he could hear nothing.

Sammy looked up then, so he suspected his father had said something, or the maid had urged him out of the car.

He unbuckled, got out, swayed a little. The maid steadied him.

Ellison could see his face was a mess, his lip split, cheek bruised. What had happened?

Sammy approached the steps, not meeting his father's eye, and climbed.

He slowed, a step below, and then looked up.

It happened fast, his father's hand unholstering from the knot of his arms. It flashed left, then came up like lightning, the back of his hand, his knuckles, connecting with Sammy's other cheek.

The boy wobbled, fell, went to a knee, stayed there, hands on the stone steps, head down, shoulders rising and falling rapidly, shuddering almost.

Ellison started forward, to help, to do something, but felt hands on him.

He looked around, saw one of the chefs holding one shoulder, the house manager holding the other, keeping him firmly in place.

They'd been standing by his side, watching. He hadn't even noticed them.

Ellison didn't understand, but the shakes of their heads, the look in their eyes – it was enough to keep him there.

He stepped back and they let go. The three of them stood in silence as his father slowly crouched, the hand he'd struck his son with going to the back of his neck. His fingers closed around it.

Ellison could see his father's face, silhouetted in profile in the glow of the patrol car's headlights. He said something to Sammy, his expression a contorted display of rage.

Sammy remained still.

And then his father stood, lifted him by the neck, and shoved him through the open door.

Sammy stumbled and then fell forward onto the polished checkerboard tiles, sliding on his knees until he came to rest at Ellison's feet. He looked down at his brother, saw droplets of liquid spot his leather loafers. Tears.

Ellison swallowed, throat tight, unable to breathe.

He looked up just in time to see his father walk in through the door, rubbing the back of his hand, face like stone. He didn't look at any of them, just strode past, into his study, and slammed the door.

After a few seconds, the chef and the house manager steered Ellison away. He fought a little, but went, numb and dazed. He looked over his shoulder, saw the maid his father had been standing next to come in, put her hand on Sammy's shoulder.

He swatted her away and she stood, clasped her hands in front of her and just waited.

Sammy stayed on the ground, not moving, not making a sound.

And then he was gone from view as Ellison was walked around a corner.

He didn't remember anything else from that night.

–

It was a week later that he saw Sammy again. The house was big enough to hide in, and Sammy had locked himself away.

Ellison had also not seen his father since that night. He too had shut himself away – from shame, or maybe just from repugnance. Either at Sammy, or himself. Ellison may as well have stayed at Whitman for all the good being home did him.

It was around five in the afternoon when a door opened and then closed out on the landing.

Ellison had kept his open, his bedroom exposed to the empty house, hoping to catch a maid or someone else walking by, just to have the chance to speak to someone.

He was out of his chair at the sound, and on the balcony above the stairs in seconds. Just in time to see Sammy skulking from his room.

He usually looked bedraggled, wearing expensive but rumpled clothes. Now, he looked... smart. Handsome, even. His cheek, cut from his father's ring, had healed. His hair had been styled and swept back, blow dried. He was wearing a clean shirt, jeans, sneakers. He had a woven jacket on. A nice one.

He saw Ellison and froze, as though he'd been caught doing something he shouldn't.

'Hey,' Ellison said, lifting a hand. A grandfather clock ticked loudly on the landing between them as though to illustrate the size and emptiness of the house in equal measure.

Sammy stayed quiet, eyed the stairs.

'Where you going?'

'Nowhere,' Sammy replied quickly.

'You don't look like you're going nowhere,' Ellison said, trying for playful.

'Don't tell Dad,' Sammy said, eyes wide. 'Please.'

Guess he'd missed playful and landed on accusative.

'I won't,' Ellison replied. 'He doesn't know then?'

'Please, El.'

'I won't, I won't.' Ellison met his eye, made sure he knew. 'But you have to tell me where you're going at least.'

'I can't.'

'It's a girl, isn't it?' Ellison grinned at him.

'I can't, El,' he said again. 'I promised.'

'Promised who?'

'I can't tell you.' His eyes darted to the door again, and Ellison knew if he pushed, Sammy would just bolt.

'At least tell me where you're going to meet her?'

He stayed quiet.

'I don't know why you're going out anyway, you should bring her back here.'

There was surprise in his face.

'Come on, we've got an amazing chef, the house is beautiful, the grounds – the pool?' He arched an eyebrow, smirked, not knowing about the incident the week before.

Sammy swallowed. 'The pool? What about the pool? Why would you say that about the pool?'

'Nothing – I just meant… I just meant that if you bring a girl here, you guys can get in the pool and…' Ellison trailed off, reading the strange look on Sammy's face. 'Hey, are you okay?'

'I'm fine, why?'

'You just look a little…'

'What?'

'Nothing,' Ellison said, shaking his head. 'Just be safe, okay? And have fun.'

He bit his lip, looked at his older brother for a few seconds, then nodded. 'Thanks.' He moved to leave, hurrying down the stairs.

'Wait,' Ellison said, coming forward. 'You can't go yet.'

Sammy stopped on the steps, looked up at him.

'You never told me her name, this girl who got you to comb your hair.'

'I can't...' He started. 'I promised I wouldn't. No one can know.'

'Come on, just tell me her name – I won't say anything, I *promise*. I'm your big brother, you can trust me. Sammy – it's me. Okay?'

He seemed to deliberate on it for a long time, then took a deep breath. 'Emmy,' he said. 'Her name is Emmy Nailer.'

'You like her?' Ellison asked, leaning on the bannister, grinning down at his little brother.

He nodded slowly. 'I do,' he said.

'Well alright then,' Ellison laughed. 'Don't let me stop you. Go get her, Sam—' He prevented himself from calling his little brother Sammy, again. He was all grown up. Sam would do just fine.

Sammy went without another word, jumped the bottom step and disappeared through the front door.

Ellison walked back up onto the landing, standing at the window facing down over the driveway and watched Sammy shrink in the distance, moving fast. He reached the gate on foot, hit the keypad, and then slipped through the gap, disappearing from view.

Ellison stayed there, smiling after him.

And in the background, the clock kept on ticking.

NOW

Chapter 20

Sloane Yo

As Ellison finished his story, Sloane sat in silence, taking it all in.

The first thing she noticed was that the Sammy in Ellison's story was not the boy that Pop and Nick had painted a picture of. Was Ellison's view of his brother that skewed? Had he built him up to such a degree in his mind that he was completely different from reality? And if so, could anything in that story be trusted?

She knew that Thomas Saint John could probably have shed some light on it, but he was laid up in the other room with a breathing tube in his throat. But from Ellison's story, she gathered he probably wouldn't be the forthcoming type anyway.

The other thing was the mention of this Beaumont – another cop working in Savage Ridge that seemed to be at the Saint John family's beck and call. She'd noticed his name in some of the old reports, but pretty much only in passing. According to Ellison's story, he'd brought Sammy home from the pool party and hadn't done shit when Thomas Saint John had struck his son – something which, last time Sloane checked, wasn't legal.

But it wasn't that which niggled at her. It was that Pop hadn't mentioned him. She wasn't sure why, but she'd need to track him down, find out what he knew. How involved in the Saint Johns' lives he was when Sammy disappeared. What *his* version of things was. Because if he brought Sammy home after the party, that meant that Sammy hadn't driven his father's Mercedes home. Had he crashed it? Or just been too drunk to drive?

So many questions riled in Sloane's brain, but one in particular stuck out first.

'Did your brother say how he arranged to meet with Emmy?' Sloane asked then. She was piqued by the name. It couldn't have been misheard. He gave first and last. But she'd seen Emmy Nailer's phone records, and there was nothing to suggest they were even in contact, let alone setting up a meeting of some kind. No calls, no texts from Sammy's number. Nothing. Though she still didn't have Sammy's records to corroborate that, and there was always the chance she'd used a burner phone – *if* Ellison's story was to be trusted and his theory about who killed Sammy was correct.

'No, he didn't,' Ellison said, answering her question. He had his arms tightly folded. He was watching Sloane closely.

'Did Sammy leave the house at all in the week leading up to his disappearance?'

'No, he was too embarrassed about his face, from my father,' Ellison said, seemingly tired, as though these questions were totally redundant.

Embarrassed. Hmm, not the word Sloane would use. She pressed on.

'How do you know that?'

'Pop questioned the house staff after he disappeared, checked the security footage from the gate camera. There was no way he could have slipped out without being seen.'

Sloane thought on that. 'Do you believe that Emmy Nailer lured your brother from this house with the intention of killing him?'

'Do you?'

'That's not how this works,' she said, still unmoving on the couch.

'Yes.'

142

'Why?'

'I don't know.'

'You think that Nicholas Pips couldn't help but follow up on his threat, uses Emmy Nailer as bait knowing your brother was desperate for some sort of attention from girls? Gets Sammy out of the house, then kills him.' It wasn't even a question now.

'Yes.'

'How? There was nothing on Emmy's phone linking her to your brother, nothing to put any of them anywhere except where their alibi says they were. Though if you got me Sammy's phone records, I could see if there was—'

'I spoke to the phone company, I already told you that. They don't have digital records from that long ago and they've already made a requisition for the paper files. But these things take time,' he said, word for word from the last time he'd fed her that line. Sloane guessed it was also the line that Ellison's father fed the other PIs and investigators. But why there was a rehearsed line at all, she didn't know, other than to confirm her assumption that they revealed something that the Saint Johns wanted to keep hidden. 'When I have them, you'll have them.' Ellison said it sternly, as if it needed no further questioning.

Sloane watched him carefully, wondered what it was he was hiding, and whether he even knew. From what he'd told her so far, not only did he not know his brother all that well, he wasn't even here in the years beforehand. The state police had been through Savage, too. And Sloane bet they'd pulled Sammy's records directly. So, if Ellison wasn't going to play ball, she'd find out herself, make some calls. She went on, keen to follow through with her other line of thought. 'If Sammy was going to meet Emmy – somehow – it was probably to intercept her at the movies. Maybe he got abducted along the way? It seems odd to me that he'd be sneaking out of the house, and then going into town on foot considering how far it is. But I don't really see any other option here, Ellison… My only other thought is…'

'Is what?'

'Is that Sammy Saint John wasn't going to meet Emmy Nailer at all. But maybe he thought he was.'

Ellison's eyes lifted, and he stared at Sloane. 'Go on.'

'I have nothing else. It's just a thought. One I'll follow up on, be sure of that.' She pushed to her feet then. 'Do you have Sammy's belongings here? I looked through the copies of the files you gave me,' she was careful to say the copies she was given, and not the files themselves. She suspected they'd been tailored, stripped of anything that could work against Sammy. But that was a battle for another day, 'but I'd like to see his room for myself, inspect his computer if I can. I'm guessing it's all there?'

Ellison nodded slowly, clearly not keen on the idea of Sloane rifling through his brother's stuff. But she had to. Because right now, she didn't know who Sammy Saint John was – rebellious son, bashful brother, insipid little shit. Three points of a big damn triangle.

'Let's go,' she said then. 'Lead the way.'

'What, now? It's late.'

'Right,' Sloane said, heading for the door. 'And the clock is still ticking.'

They climbed the stairs and went left, towards a closed door. Ellison slowed in front of it, looked back. Sloane nodded him on. Whether it was tough for him or not, she didn't give a damn. Right now, she had a lot of evidence pointing towards Emmy Nailer not meeting Sammy that night, and that frankly, the kid made her skin crawl. So, if there was a way to prove the meet-up was a lie… well, then she'd take another look at Ellison's theory. But until then, he still needed to prove what he was saying.

He pushed into Sammy's room, the door swinging wide, and then stepped aside.

Sloane followed him, stepping slowly, taking it in.

The room was bigger than her first apartment had been. It was easily twenty feet by twenty feet and had its own private bathroom. A sprawling double bed stripped back to the bare mattress stood in the middle, while the pale-yellow walls were adorned with posters of various bands that were big ten years ago. She knew a few of them. There was a chest of drawers with an empty top, a desk on the other side with a closed laptop on it in a plastic bag. There was nothing else around, and any life or personality had been stripped from the place along with any evidence that might have once been. If the police hadn't sterilised the place on the first go around, the half a dozen investigators and other technical teams who had no doubt swept through it certainly had.

She'd find nothing in the way of forensic clues. The laptop was the only thing that interested her. She went straight across, noticed the yellow label on the bag with the username and password noted. Sloane withdrew the computer, opened it, then unwrapped the power cord and got under the desk looking for an outlet. All the while Ellison watched in silence from the threshold.

When she sat on the chair, booted the thing up, he started speaking. He sighed first. 'You won't find anything. They went through his search history, his Facebook, contacted every site he'd ever visited – even those he did in private browsing windows—'

Porn.

'—and they found nothing. No messages or interactions with anyone. Nothing of any kind. At all. At least nothing suggesting anyone had reached out to him.'

She sat, looking at the login screen. 'Who? Who went through it all?'

'Everyone.'

Sloane closed her eyes, cast her mind back to the section of the reports on Sammy's internet history. There had been Facebook messages, a few posts on some forums and that sort

145

of thing, comments on YouTube videos. All innocuous enough. He wasn't much of a social butterfly. His Facebook friend list was small. *Very* small. A lot of people blocked him, she guessed.

Though he did watch a lot of porn. She remembered that much. Nothing fazed her anymore, but she remembered thinking that it was a *lot* of porn, even for an eighteen-year-old. She bit her lip. What kind? She couldn't remember, but it mattered – it would tell her more about Sammy. She'd look it up when she got back to the motel.

Ellison had suggested she stay at the house during the investigation, but she'd declined for obvious reasons.

She stood quickly, knowing the laptop would be a bust. She was good, but that didn't mean that others hadn't been thorough. She wasn't so full of herself to think she'd catch something ten other pros had missed. No, the answer didn't lie inside Sammy's laptop.

Sloane walked towards one of the windows next to the bed, stood at it, looked down over the back garden, pushed her hands into her pockets. Below and to the right a patio stretched out. Some wide stone steps led down to an outdoor pool that was lit up in tourmaline blue with lights, an ornate mosaic showing from the bottom. It looked like a mer... man? With a trident. A merman with a crown. Poseidon? She didn't know. It looked more *Little Mermaid* than Greek mythos. But she expected it cost more than what her yearly salary at the Detroit PD used to be just to lay it.

On either side, tall well-manicured bushes stretched out like sentinels lining the stone around the pool. To either side of that, a lawn stretched into the darkness, unlit. At the far end, Sloane could just make out a stone wall covered in ivy. It was maybe eight or ten feet tall. Beyond it, she could see pines, waving gently in the darkness, and through them, down the valley, the streetlights glowing on Main. It was probably less than a kilometre as the crow flies.

'Are the lawns covered by cameras?'

'The lawns?' Ellison came forward a little.

Sloane stepped closer to the glass, looking directly down. There was a stretch of chipped stones dividing the wall from the grass. 'Yeah, the lawn, here. A camera?'

He shook his head. 'There's one over the doors that covers the patio, the pool, but not the lawns. But the whole lawn is hemmed in by a nine-foot wall. There'd be nothing to see.'

'I assume the footage from that rear camera was checked leading up to Sammy's disappearance?'

'Checked for what?'

'For anything.'

'Every minute of it for a month before, and for months afterwards, just in case Sammy came back, snuck in.'

Sloane turned, looked at him. 'And?'

Ellison shook his head, shrugged. 'Nothing.'

Sloane nodded, turned back to the glass, narrowed her eyes a little. Looking for anything out of place. Anything at all. The stone of the house was old, streaked with dark patches. The sill was large, covered in moss. A few stones littered it, along with spider webs. Nothing of interest. Too high to climb to, too high to jump from without breaking your legs.

Sloane moved the latch across, slid the sash window up, drinking in the cool evening air as it wound its way up the valley.

She stood there in silence for a long time, thinking. She could feel Ellison watching her, but knew if she turned around, he would have questions. And for now, she still had no answers.

Ellison made one final comment about Sloane staying at the Saint John residence as she headed for the front door. She shot him a look and he quietened.

He didn't watch her down to the car, just closed the door behind her.

It was past ten now and she needed some rest.

But before she reached the door to her car, her phone started vibrating. She pulled it out while she climbed into the cab of her truck, saw it was her mom.

Sloane's heart sank.

'Hey, Mom,' she said, climbing in and closing the door. 'Everything okay? Is Zoe okay?'

'Oh, so you remember your daughter's name, then,' she said, her tone as cutting and cold as ever.

'Mom,' Sloane said, deflating a little. 'I know I've been out of touch, but I'm working – it's this big case and—'

'You missed her birthday.'

Sloane froze, swallowed, couldn't shift the sudden lump there.

'It was her seventh birthday today. She stayed up as late as she could, waiting for you to call. She just fell asleep.'

Sloane's fist balled on top of her thigh, her neck burning hot as anger rose in her. Shit. 'Mom—'

'Don't even,' she spat. 'I took her in without question – I wouldn't have let her go anywhere else. But you said you still wanted to be a part of her life, you made *her* believe that. And then you do this? Jesus Christ. Does anything ever change?'

Sloane's teeth ground. Why hadn't she called sooner? While Zoe was still awake? They could have talked. 'I'm clean, Mom,' was all she could say. 'I am.'

Her mother snorted.

'I'm clean,' she insisted.

'And working.'

'Yes.'

'You heard from the department?'

'Private,' Sloane said. 'But I'm working on it.'

'Private,' her mother parroted back under her breath. 'So, no set hours, keep your phone on at all times? Do whatever you want?' She paused. 'And still can't remember to call your daughter on her birthday.' She tutted. 'How am I supposed to look a judge in the eye and say you're better, that you're ready to be a mother again when you're still pulling the same old shit?'

Sloane's eyes were closed now. She did all she could to keep her voice together. 'I'm not, I'm not... I'm clean, I fucking swear.'

'You know what Zoe asked me before she fell asleep? She asked, *does Mommy still love me?*'

'And what did you tell her?' Sloane squeezed out, her throat aching. She was hunched over in the seat now, fingernails cutting into her palms, she was clenching her fists so hard.

'I told her the truth,' her mother said. 'I told her I don't know.'

Chapter 21

Nicholas Pips

I was asleep when my phone started ringing.

I pulled my head from the pillow and squinted at it. 'Pete?' I asked, answering it and squeezing my eyeballs with my forefinger and thumb.

He was panting into the mouthpiece. 'Nicky, get up,' he said.

The tone in his voice was enough to rip me from bed. 'What's wrong?'

'It's Emmy,' he said grunting a little. I heard something click over the phone, heard him jostle, and then there was a loud thud. The noise echoed from outside my window and I stood, walking across my childhood bedroom and looking out into the street.

Pete's porch light was on, and then the lights of his Mercedes came to life too. 'What happened?' I asked, suddenly alert.

'She's gone, Nicky.'

'Gone?' I asked, turning, looking for my jeans. Shit, where were they? 'Gone where? What time is it?' I looked over at the old digital clock on my bedside table and answered my own question: 1:12 a.m.

'Her mother called my house just now. She said Emmy went out earlier, told her she was meeting us, never came back.'

'Fuuuuuck,' I said, pinning the phone with my shoulder, grabbing my pants off the back of the old desk chair, wriggling into them.

'I told her she was with us,' he said. 'I'm outside.'

'Gimme a sec.' Boots. Where were my boots?

'We gotta find her, Nicky – if she's out, drunk – *fuck* – if that investigator got to her?'

'Yeah, yeah,' I said, heart pounding. 'Okay, I'm coming.' I ran down the stairs, shoved out into the cool night air, and jumped the steps down onto my walk.

Pete came reversing up the street and stopped abruptly at my mailbox.

I pulled the door open, climbed in, and then he was accelerating.

We drove in silence, moving fast. The cabin was plush, the seats leather, the dashboard home to a huge HD display. The engine hummed quietly with a growl that said it had plenty of guts. This was a high-end model, there was no doubt about that. Pete had done well for himself.

Neither of us asked the other where she'd go. Only one place was on our minds, and I think we both hoped we'd get there to find nothing. That Emmy would be anywhere else.

Pete looped around town and out towards the highway.

'Where are you going?' I asked as he joined the road, planted his foot. 'It's back that way—' I glanced over my shoulder.

'I know,' Pete cut me off. 'I'm just not taking any chances,' he said as I was pinned against the seat, the engine howling. 'If that investigator is still tailing us the last thing I want to do is lead her to Sammy.'

He looked across at me, the whites of his eyes burning in the darkness, his expression wild, nothing but silhouetted wrinkles in the glow of the dashboard.

The speedometer continued to climb until we were well above a hundred and probably a mile away from the on-ramp. There wasn't another car on the single-lane highway. There was no one following us.

Pete watched the rear-view mirror incessantly, and then decelerated suddenly, swung the car off the road and turned in to a gravel lay-by, spraying stone into the trees before getting back on the tarmac and burning rubber in the other direction.

We came up to the exit we'd joined at and kept going, now closing ground on our destination.

Two minutes later, we turned off onto another road that ran behind the old logging mill, and then off that one and onto a dirt track. It descended to the river, to an old bridge that had fed the logging sites. We crossed, the tyres fighting for traction, the bright LED headlights drowning everything in ghostly white.

The last time I'd driven up here it had been the three of us. We'd bounced around in that old Impala, the shovels rattling in the trunk. I was driving. Emmy was in the back, shaking. Pete was next to me, pale as a sheet, eyes vacant and sunken, soul heavy with the reality of what was about to come. We drove this exact road, following the river around far enough so we were out of sight of the mill. And then we stopped, and got out, all grabbed a shovel, and plunged the blades into the loamy, needle-covered dirt.

And we dug a grave.

I leaned forward now, looked out of the windscreen at the bank rising to our left.

The road up there was the one that Emmy had driven up with Sammy Saint John in the passenger seat, looking for a quiet place where he thought she'd unzip his pants, lean over, and put his ugly little cock in her mouth. He'd been grinning to himself as they approached – Pete and I had watched from a spot behind a rock. Emmy pulled the car to a stop, windows down.

Sammy said, 'So…'

And then we jumped out, circled behind the car, opened the door, grabbed him by the neck and dragged his wailing ass onto the track, hoisted him to his feet, then to the edge, and then for a split second, Pete and I locked eyes. And then we fucking shoved him. And he went over, quietened immediately, soon as he hit that first tree, and tumbled down, down, down like a rag doll, churning and carving through the undergrowth until he hit the bottom, ten feet from his readied grave.

'Nick,' Pete said suddenly.

My eyes snapped to attention, my hand moving to my face, knuckles pulling themselves across my cheeks. I cleared my throat, blinked myself clear, and saw what Pete was talking about.

Emmy.

She was alone.

Thank God. Even so, my heart wouldn't quit beating out of my chest.

Pete stepped on the brake, sending the car into a juddering slide. Emmy was on her knees, bathed in white, and thew her hand over her eyes to shield them. There was a bottle of what looked like gin clutched in her hand. Dust sailed into the air and drifted away over the water.

Pete was already out of the car by the time I unbuckled.

He had Emmy by the arm by the time I rounded the bumper.

He pulled her to her feet, protesting wildly, and swung her onto the road, making her stumble up into the headlights.

She fell into me, then pushed me off and stood straight, wiping the dirt and pine needles off her jeans. 'Christ, Pete, what the hell?' she yelled, slurring.

'Keep your voice down!' he ordered.

Jesus, I'd never seen him so angry. Didn't know he was even capable of it.

'What the hell are you doing out here?' he snapped.

I looked at Pete, then at his feet – at his nice leather shoes. It took me a second to get my bearings in the dark. Was this the place? I couldn't be sure. Close if not. Hell, if it was, then I was pretty sure Pete was standing right on top of Sammy's grave.

Emmy tried to speak, couldn't find the words, just shook her head instead. I saw tiny little dots shine on the pale ground, tears flicked from her cheeks.

'Are you fucking stupid?' Pete spat, tapping himself on the temple. I couldn't help but notice he'd made his hand into the rough shape of a gun. I didn't know if it was intentional.

'Stupid?' she croaked. '*Stupid?*' She laughed then. 'Stupid! Yeah, I'm fucking stupid. That what you want to hear? Because that's the only option, isn't it? Smart or fucking stupid. I'm here, fucking stupid because *I give a shit!*' She screamed and her voice bled through the still pines, washed away on the rush of turbulent water at our backs. 'You think I'm stupid because I care? Is that it? And you're smart because you don't?'

Pete came forward and Emmy shrank from him, backed up into me, turned, met my gaze, then stepped away from us both. There was fear in her eyes.

'No, no, no! Okay?' Pete motioned her to stay still, holding his palms out. 'Let's just think about this, okay? We could have this conversation anywhere, just not... not here, please? Get in the car, alright?'

I spoke then. 'What are you even doing out here, Em?'

She looked at me. 'What do you think?' Her eyes went to the ground behind Pete.

'I know what's here,' I said. 'But why come? What for?'

Her jaw quivered. The air was cool and her bare arms were raised in gooseflesh, the baggy T-shirt with cut-off sleeves, tucked into her jeans, doing little to insulate her from the night. Had she walked all the way out here? It would have taken an hour, probably more. And she'd just hiked it, in the dark, alone. With a bottle of gin.

'To... to see,' she said after a few seconds. 'To see how it looked.'

'And how does it look?' I tilted my head forward to catch her eye.

Pete watched me fiercely. I think he would have preferred if we'd just grabbed her, wrestled her into the car, driven away. But he knew if he made a grab for her, she'd run.

'I don't even know where we buried him,' she said then, turning to the dark. 'I just started walking and... and I thought I'd know, when I got here. I didn't think I could ever forget.' She turned back to me, then looked at Pete. 'Don't you... doesn't it bother you? Don't you think about it? All the time?' The gin sloshed in the half-empty bottle. Her words were clear but her eyes were hazy.

Pete stayed quiet.

I didn't. 'Yes,' I said. 'I do. All the time. And every single time something good happens, it makes me feel like shit.' My voice shook.

Emmy's face told me she felt the same way.

Pete was shaking his head. 'Okay, great, you both feel like pieces of shit. Can we get in the car now?'

'What about you?' Emmy's voice was calm then, cold. 'Don't you feel any guilt, Pete?'

I couldn't help but notice the emphasis on his name.

He stared at her for a few seconds. 'Of course I do,' he said. 'But that doesn't change the facts.'

'And what facts are those?'

'That we did it. That it's done. That he got what he fucking deserved. And when I do think about it, and I do feel guilty, I remember that. And then I think that if I had the chance to do it over, I'd do the same damn thing.'

I stared at Pete, saw a man in front of me, but couldn't help remember the boy who'd made us pull over to empty his stomach. The boy who had looked at me scared to death when Sammy started crawling. The one who didn't reach for the shovel, the one who didn't bury it in Sammy's skull. The one who let me do that. The one who, if I had waited another second, would have pleaded we save him instead of finishing him.

But then Pete said, without a hint of remorse, 'Sammy Saint John deserved to die.' He was not the same boy I knew. 'And the fact that we were the ones to do it doesn't keep me awake at night,' he went on. 'And it doesn't make me want to come out here blind drunk, and stumble around in the dark looking for his grave. It doesn't make me want to tell anyone, or confess, or absolve myself of my goddamn sins.' He looked from Emmy to me and back. 'It doesn't make me want to go into the damn mountains and live like a monk, or drink myself to death, or shoot fucking heroin into my veins. But do you know what it does do? It makes me want to make my life worth it.'

Emmy's jaw was clenched, knuckles white around the bottle.

'It makes me want to wake up in the morning and work hard. It makes me want to earn the things that Sammy Saint John was given for free.' He beat on his chest with his fist. 'Now, if you want to talk about what happened, fine. Great. Let's all pour our hearts out over poor innocent Samuel Saint John. But let's do it in the fucking car, a thousand miles from here. Alright?' He walked over to the car then, opened the door. 'Emmy?'

She swallowed, lifted her chin, and then strode towards him. She stopped short, narrowed her eyes. 'I'll walk,' she spat, and then stormed past.

Pete closed his eyes, drew a breath. His nostrils flared, then he turned, snatched her wrist, and yanked her towards him.

She tried to hit him with the bottle.

He took her other hand out of the air and she fumbled it. It bounced into the verge and emptied its contents onto the dry earth.

Emmy yelled, fought. Pete wrestled her without care, then shoved her into the back seat, slammed the door.

She opened it and he shunted it closed. There was a dull crack – the glass of the window hitting Emmy in the forehead.

She moaned, slumped backwards, swore, then sobbed.

Pete stared across the car at me, fury in his eyes. 'Don't make me ask, Nick.'

I swallowed, clenched my shaking fists, and didn't.

I got in, met Emmy's reddened, hate-filled eyes in the rear-view, and then felt the pull of the engine as Pete spun us round and accelerated back towards Savage Ridge.

I wound the window down after a minute, let the cold air numb my face, and rested my cheek on the sill, feeling the roughness of the road through the leather, listening as the engine rose and sank, thinking about the look in Pete's eyes. Wondering if he was still the same kid we'd known ten years ago. And knowing deep down that he wasn't.

Chapter 22

Sloane Yo

It was 8:00 a.m. and Pop wasn't thrilled to be up at this hour.

They met at the diner again. Neutral ground. She didn't want Pop feeling anything except comfortable and forthcoming. And she also didn't want him to be without coffee this early on.

She arrived first this time, chose the same booth, the same seat as she had before. She had her back to the door, but that didn't bother her because Pop would choose the other side to be facing it. That was his default, and she had no intention of throwing him off. Frankly, she needed his help.

Sloane picked at her nail, her hands throbbing and raw. Her forehead was bruised and tender, and her leg was still sore from where she'd punched herself. She didn't like working cases. In fact, she pretty much hated it. But it was just about all she was good for, and good at. She didn't think job hunting with her history was going to be any fun. And at least this paid well enough and kept her moving. She got angsty if she stayed in one place too long and Savage Ridge was already starting to get under her skin.

The bell rang behind her, she didn't turn. Pop's leather boots and tightened belt groaned as he approached the booth and slid in. The waitress, an older woman with purple eyeliner, red lips, and gum lodged between her molars, poured a cup of coffee for Pop without asking, and then put down a jug of creamer. She looked at Sloane, said nothing, just kept chewing.

'I'm fine, thanks,' Sloane said, not even looking up.

Pop smiled at her and nodded. 'Thanks, Darl.'

Sloane didn't know if that was short for 'darling' or 'Darlene' or something else entirely. She didn't bother to ask. 'Who's Beaumont?' she said instead.

Pop's hand stopped halfway to his cup and he looked up at her now. 'Well good morning to you, too.'

'Yeah, just peachy.' Sloane kept his eyes, even when they went to the bruise on her forehead.

'Beaumont...' he said slowly, topping his coffee off with creamer and reaching for the sugar. 'Beaumont, Beaumont, Beaumont. Now there's a name I haven't heard for a while.' He dumped at least two teaspoons' worth in to his cup, then lifted the concoction to his lips, slurped some off the rim, and looked out of the window. A flat and straight main street stretched out, the buildings square and brown. Above, steep valley sides rose, furred with pines laced in morning fog. The sky overhead was a slow-moving grey sheet.

'Beautiful, isn't it,' he said. It wasn't really a question.

'Like a fucking postcard.' She didn't even bother to try and keep the sharpness from her voice.

'So, where'd you hear the name Beaumont?' Pop asked.

'Ellison Saint John.'

Pop nodded.

'So, are you going to tell me anything about him? I'm guessing he was a cop here, and by the sounds of it, was pretty close with the Saint John family. I didn't look into him as I wanted to extend you the courtesy, with this being your town and all. And this being your investigation.'

Pop smiled, looked at her. 'I appreciate that. There's nothing to hide, and not much to tell, either. Dickie Beaumont was an officer here in town. He's gotta be in his seventies now, retired just after Sammy went missing. Well, the year after. Guess Thomas Saint John didn't really have much faith in him after that.'

'So, he was working for the Saint Johns?'

Pop smirked a little, drank some coffee. 'We're all working for the Saint Johns one way or another.'

'Poetic. Tell me about him.'

'Richard Beaumont. Dickie to his friends. He never rose above officer – not that there was anywhere to rise. He needed an operation back in '04… '03 maybe. He drank a bit, ate a bit, you know? His father died young, too, heart attack. High blood pressure ran in the family. He had a minor attack, needed a bypass. It didn't take, needed another, then a shunt. Was a whole thing,' Pop said, waving his hand and taking a mouthful of what Sloane only assumed was a sweet brown syrup by this point. 'Anyway, the insurance from work covered the first, but the bills stacked up, the aftercare, you know how it goes. And his wife, Clara, sweet lady, don't get me wrong – never worked a day in her life, you know? So those bills, when they started coming thick and fast, well, they crushed them. They re-financed the house, to the hilt. But it wasn't enough.'

'Enter Thomas Saint John.'

Pop made a finger gun at Sloane, clicked his tongue.

'He paid off Beaumont's medical bills and in return got an on-call Savage Ridge police officer.'

'I mean, we didn't like it – but what could we do? He only ever used Beaumont when it came to Sammy, really. Picked him up when he got a little out of hand, quelled some people when they got a little riled, swept a few things under the rug.' Pop shrugged.

'Like when Sammy Saint John totalled his father's Mercedes after the pool party?'

Pop stopped drinking mid sip, looked up at Sloane. 'Now who told you that?'

'Just a wild guess. But it's the truth, isn't it?'

He put the cup down, sat back in the booth. 'All I know is that come morning, there were fresh tyre tracks off the side of the highway, a broken crash barrier, and a brand-new German-manufactured cube at the wrecker's yard.'

Sloane wanted to see it. The cube. Talk to the person who crushed it. Fill in the blanks a little more. 'Beaumont did all that? Collected Sammy, had the car towed and destroyed?'

Pop shrugged again. 'You'll have to ask him.'

'I intend to.'

'I bet you do.'

'You gonna tell me anything else?'

'Not much else to tell.' Pop sighed, leaned forward, rested his elbows on the table, shirt straining at his stomach and shoulders. 'Look, Thomas Saint John's not a dumb guy, alright? He kept me and Beaumont separate. That way, we never knew everything that was going on. Was safer that way.'

'Safer for who?'

'For him and his family. He relied on me to keep the town clean, and to keep him informed of anything that might interest him.'

Sloane didn't even want to know what that meant.

'And he used Beaumont for the more... delicate matters.'

Ones which required the sort of leverage Thomas Saint John had. Ones which Beaumont probably didn't want to 'fix', but couldn't say no to. 'And where is Beaumont now?'

'I expect up at his house. He doesn't get around much. 'Specially since Clara passed.'

'And where is that?'

'Up on Pinewood Drive. Number 122.'

Sloane memorised the address. She was about to slide out of the booth when something else occurred to her. 'One last thing,' she said.

Pop's eyebrows lifted, the coffee cup tilted at his lips. He swallowed and put it down, offered a hand to welcome another question.

'What do you think of Ellison Saint John?'

He chuckled a little. 'That's a loaded question, huh?' He let out a long breath. 'You want the official statement, or the just between you and me answer?'

160

'What do you think?'

He smiled at her. 'Ellison's alright. He's a kid playing at being a man, a boy wearing his daddy's shoes. Clomping around, trying to make himself known.' Pop lifted his hands and moved them up and down animatedly to illustrate the aforementioned clomping.

'How smart do you think he is?' Sloane asked, narrowing her eyes a little.

'Smart?' Pop seemed a little thrown by the question. 'He may be strutting around that big house, but he doesn't have the brains, or the stones, that Thomas Saint John had. Jeez, if you'd seen him in his prime. Phew,' Pop laughed. 'I'm not saying I'm glad he's bedridden, but if you want to talk about someone you *don't* want to get a phone call from, day or night, it's Thomas Saint John. But Ellison? He's a pussycat in a tight T-shirt.'

'You noticed that too, huh?'

'That he wears children's clothes to show off his bulging biceps?' Pop smiled. 'Hard not to. What you see is what you get with Ellison Saint John. You'll have no trouble navigating him, of that much I'm sure.'

'You think he's dangerous?'

'No.' Pop answered pretty firmly to that one. 'He's impetuous, stubborn, got a damn big chip on his shoulder. But dangerous? No, I don't think so. I've known the kid since he was yay big.' He held his hand out to the side of the booth. 'I'm not sweating Ellison Saint John.'

That eased Sloane's mind, somewhat. Her assumptions had likely been true. That Ellison wasn't skewing the facts on purpose to deceive Sloane. It sounded like he wasn't even capable of that. Just an after image of his father, a pretender to the throne. Ambitious but inert. 'Thanks Pop, you've been helpful, as always.'

He leaned back, tapped the badge on his chest. 'To protect and serve.' Then he lifted his coffee cup and the waitress with the purple eyeliner came back over.

By the time she started pouring, Sloane was already out of the booth and halfway to the door.

Sloane started her truck and wheeled onto Main, her phone guiding her to Pinewood Drive. She climbed off the main drag and onto a curving road that plunged into the pine forests bordering the town. A few minutes later, she rolled to a stop outside 122. It was a small, pre-fab house with white cladding, a rotting lawnmower on the overgrown front lawn, and algae climbing over what was left of the paint.

Sloane went up the bowing wooden steps, feeling them creak under her heels, and pulled open the fly mesh storm door, knocking on the faded wood behind.

There was no answer.

A beaten-up old Saturn sat on the drive.

Sloane knocked again. 'Richard Beaumont,' she called through the jamb.

There was rustling inside.

'Mr Beaumont,' she repeated, a little louder, 'my name is Sloane Yo, I'm a private investigator here under the employ of the Saint John family, I was hoping I could ask you a few questions—'

The door opened in front of her and a large man filled the frame. He was overweight, one arm resting on a walker, the other on top of an oxygen tank. A tube ran up over his arm and fed into his nose.

His face was square, his jaw merging into his neck fat seamlessly. His skin was blotchy, red, dry, scaly almost, and his eyes were yellowed. He looked absolutely miserable, and the smell coming off him told Sloane that showering wasn't a daily occurrence.

'Mr Beaumont,' she said, not extending a hand. 'Sloane Yo. I'm here on—'

'I heard ya,' he said, rasping. 'Whaddya want?'

'I was hoping I could ask you a few questions.'

'About what?'

'About the disappearance of Sammy Saint John.'

'Don't know anything about it – usually the nature of unsolved cases.' He breathed labouredly then hacked and coughed.

'The week before, you picked up Sammy Saint John from the side of the road. He'd just totalled his father's Mercedes, drunk. You arranged for it to be cleaned up and then dropped him off home.'

He wheezed a few times. 'That a statement or a question?'

'When you got back to the Saint John house, you sat outside with Sammy for a minute or two before he went inside. What did you talk about?'

He narrowed his eyes. 'Thought you were working for the Saint Johns?'

'I am,' Sloane said, producing her ID automatically.

He didn't even look at it. 'I don't know,' he said. 'Probably nothing.'

'Did Sammy say anything to you? At that party, he got into an argument with someone. Someone who threatened to kill him.'

Beaumont nodded slowly now. 'The Pips boy.'

'That's right. Do you think there was any credence to that threat? Any credibility to the accusation that he had killed Sammy?'

Beaumont's hand left his walker, scratched at the rough stubble on his face, then leaned on the doorway. Past his elbow and sweat-stained armpit, Sloane could see a ratty brown carpet littered with old envelopes and beer bottles. 'Not sure. No hard evidence to suggest it – suppose that's the reason you're here. But Sammy was…' He trailed off.

'A problem. I won't take what you say back to the Saint Johns. You have my word.'

''Scuse me if your word don't mean shit, lady,' he said then, sighing heavily. He struggled to refill his lungs. 'Sammy was alright, just mixed up. You grow up with a father like his, no surprise, really.'

She let him go on. He seemed to have realised that he wasn't getting rid of her.

'Sammy had some trouble making friends – no one much liked the kid. He was strange, sure – but not all bad.' He paused, chose his words carefully. 'Suppose what happened with that girl was the thing that did it.'

'What girl?' Sloane asked, narrowing her eyes at him. 'Emmy Nailer?'

He wheezed, licked his lips a little, suddenly reluctant to talk.

'Did something happen with Emmy Nailer the day Sammy went missing? He was going to meet her – that's what he told his brother.'

'I gotta make a phone call.' He made to close the door.

'Wait,' Sloane said, hand slapping against the wood. 'Tell me what happened.'

He strained to close it, but didn't have the strength. 'It wasn't me, alright? I didn't do it – he had his lawyers sort it all out.'

'Who, Thomas Saint John?'

The tiniest of nods. 'Covered it up, alright? We couldn't ever prove anything when he disappeared, but we never got the opportunity, hamstrung, really. Had to keep certain things out of the investigation. But I won't say no more.' He hung his head. 'For all his troubles, I liked the kid. Honestly… he never had a chance.' He tried to shut the door again. 'I won't say nothing else for now – gotta make a phone call.'

Sloane stepped back a little. 'Can I come back later?' she asked, reading the situation – he wanted to talk to someone before he said anything else. Maybe his own lawyer. To make sure that he wasn't going to incriminate himself.

She watched him closely.

He nodded again. 'Later.'

He shut the door then and Sloane stepped back. She couldn't push too hard. She knew how this worked.

So, Sammy had a run-in with Emmy – something happened. Something bad. Bad enough that there was a cover-up. A legal cover-up.

Sloane thought back to Pop's story of the party, of Emmy getting in between Nick and Sammy. Of Nick telling Sloane she was way off with what she thought.

Ellison had been absent the entirety of that year. He didn't know shit.

But it seemed that Sammy and Emmy's history ran deeper than she'd thought. Than she'd been allowed to find out.

A legal cover-up... that meant payoffs, NDAs... Jesus, what the hell had Sammy done that he needed saving like that?

Sloane stepped down off the porch and headed for her car, mind working furiously.

All around, the pines creaked softly, watching her to the curb.

The sun was weak through the branches, the air cool and soft with the mountains.

If only they could talk, she might find the truth.

THEN

Chapter 23

Nicholas Pips

Savage Ridge High School wasn't big. It was an old building, built in the Forties, when neo-Georgian was all the rage and brown brick and concrete seemed like a choice that'd never go out of style. Except the stone was stained and the white paint on all those crisscrossed windows was a lot of upkeep for the poor bastard who had to paint them every year.

The sheer number of windows meant that replacing them all was an astronomical cost, so they remained single pane, slick with condensation in the winter, doing nothing to stem the cold, and utterly annoying in the summer when the sun streamed in through them so violently that you had to squint almost the entire day.

The place was tired, empty on account of the summer, but the steps were still lined with flowers, candles. A memorial smeared across it that didn't tell the truth of what had actually happened. That romanticised the whole goddamn thing. 'Gone but never forgotten'.

I walked along the cement slabs between the stretches of grass that separated the school from the street, looking at the flowers, stark white against the gum-stained ground. But I couldn't take my eyes off the two people in front of them.

Emmy.

Pete.

Shoulder to shoulder, the pinkie fingers of their hands touching but not locked.

I clenched my jaw, swallowed the bile rising in my throat, and jammed my fists deep into the pockets of my hoodie, quickening my pace.

The forecourt was empty, but I still didn't call out.

Didn't need to, though, they heard me coming, broke apart, and then turned.

Pete looked grave. He hadn't slept in a week. Neither had I.

Emmy's eyes were full and shining with tears. The first rays of light were yet to break over the trees of the eastern ridge, so she was bathed in a soft, pale glow that let the redness of her cheeks shine brightly. She was crumbling.

'Why are we here, Nick?' Pete asked, voice shaking.

'I hate this place,' Emmy muttered, turning her head slightly so she could look at the memorial out of the corner of her eye. Sammy Saint John had been dead for eight days, and we couldn't help but feel like the net was closing in.

'Why wouldn't we come?' I said in response, pulling up short of them. 'Why wouldn't we pay our respects? Avoiding it would be more suspicious.'

'It makes me sick.' Emmy clutched her stomach, spat the words. 'Fucking sick.'

'I know,' I said, glancing down. I couldn't look at her. 'But it's an open space, no one to overhear us.' I took a breath. 'How are you doing?'

'How do you think?' Emmy's voice was acid this morning.

'Holding it together,' Pete answered slowly. 'But my parents are freaking out. They've been called in twice already.'

'Mine too,' I said quickly, glad to engage Pete before Emmy peeled away any more layers of my skin. 'But it's fine, they don't know anything,' I reassured them, risking a quick look at her. 'No one knows anything, right? We're tight. We're safe.'

'Safe,' Emmy snorted. 'You know they brought Josie in, too? That girl who works at the theatre?'

'And she'll say she sold us our tickets, watched us walk into the theatre, and then watched us walk out the front door three hours later.' I looked right at her now. 'It's fine, Emmy. Trust me.'

I tried to ignore her muttering those words back under her breath, dripping with derision.

'I haven't seen Pop,' Pete said then, chewing his thumbnail.

'Me neither,' I said, truthfully. He was always buzzing around town, but Pete was right, I hadn't seen him in days.

'Or Beaumont,' Pete added. 'Not since he picked us up, at least. Guess he's off somewhere, doing Thomas Saint John's dirty work. Probably trying to fabricate some evidence to frame us.' It sounded like a joke at first, but I don't think it was.

'Pop put him in his place at the station,' I reminded him. 'They don't have shit. And as long as we stick to our story, they won't ever have shit, alright?'

'And what about the investigator?'

That one blindsided me. 'What investigator?' My mind reeled all of a sudden – FBI, PI, what was he talking about? Was there someone else in town looking into this already? Jesus, were we fucked? Did we miss something? No, no, we'd kept our heads down, our stories straight. There was no physical evidence. All our digital interaction simple, innocuous, not discussing anything we wouldn't usually. Video games, TV, dumb shit to buy off Amazon. We were safe. Right?

I waited for Pete to speak. 'I don't know who she is,' he said, 'but she's around.'

'Who is *she*?' I urged him. 'I haven't seen anyone around, at least, I don't think I have…' I racked my brains but nothing stuck out. Had I been that blind?

'Tall woman, red hair, pale skin, wearing a greyish suit thing when I saw her.' He ran his hands up and down his body to illustrate the clothing.

'How do you know she was an investigator? Who was she with?' I asked. Emmy had fallen quiet now.

'It was pretty fucking obvious,' Pete scoffed. 'I *think* I caught on when she knocked on my front door, flashed her badge and said my name's fucking-whatever, and I'm a senior investigator with the Washington State Police!'

'You spoke to her?' The words caught in my throat. I could feel my palms slick in my pockets.

He shook his head. 'No, she spoke to my dad,' Pete said. 'I was in the kitchen with my mom. He turned her away at the door.'

'What happened?'

'He turned her away at the door,' Pete repeated, more emphatically.

'Yeah, but like, what did she say? What happened?'

'He turned her away at the door!' He almost yelled it now. 'What do you want me to say? She came to my fucking house, she knocked, my dad answered, she asked to come in, to speak to me, my dad said no. He said they'd already spoken to me, she'd have to contact our lawyer if—'

'Wait, wait,' I cut in, 'you got a lawyer?'

'No, well, my dad, he—'

'We said no lawyers, we agreed—'

'It wasn't me! It was my dad, man,' Pete said, arms beginning to flail, voice rising. 'After the second time, he reached out to an old friend, and—'

'Jesus, Pete!' I felt rage rise inside me. This wasn't the plan. 'We said no lawyers! We agreed! If we get lawyers, it looks like we have something to hide. We need to be open, and—'

'And what the hell am I supposed to say, Nick? Sorry, Dad, we can't get a fucking lawyer because we're trying not to look like we—'

I didn't know if he was going to say it, but before he said another word, something inside me snapped. I launched forward, slamming my open palm against his mouth, gripping him by the collar. He stumbled backwards, and I almost went with him. His eyes widened, his fists finding my hoodie. Emmy called out, cried out, she grabbed at us, pulled at us as we wrestled each other around.

Pete ripped my hand away, my elbow hit something, either Emmy or Pete, I didn't know.

He shoved me away, breathless, and I staggered backwards, going to a knee.

Emmy was between us, doubled over, hands clasped awkwardly in front of her, elbows against her hips, sobbing. Her hair looked greasy and unwashed, her skin tired. We were all on the ragged edge.

Pete regained himself, wiped off his mouth with the back of his hand.

He looked at me for a few seconds, then tugged his shirt straight, looked at Emmy, who looked back, and then turned and strode away, quickening his pace into a run.

When he was gone, I got up, walked forward, reached out to help Emmy up.

She swung at me. Not a punch, but a wild arm that meant get the hell away. I stepped back, hands raised.

She didn't say anything, couldn't between the raking, seizing sobs.

'Em…' I said, voice soft.

She moved backwards, tottering almost, her legs not her own, and collapsed down onto the steps of the high school, surrounded by the white flowers of death.

Gone, but never forgotten.

She drew her knees to her chest, wrapped her arms around them, and laid her forehead against her thighs. She cried silently, and I looked on, heart beating out of my chest, pins and needles pricking at my fingertips, and a deep, twisted sickness gnawing at my guts.

My eyes drifted from Emmy to the memorial, a stark and constant reminder of what we'd done. And more importantly, why we'd done it.

The flowers would wither and die, but I don't think the image of Sammy Saint John's body flopping down into that grave, bent and broken, ever would.

173

Chapter 24

Lillian Dempsey

Lillian Dempsey exited the only motel in Savage Ridge, the Rushing River Inn, and stopped dead in her tracks.

Of all the people she thought would be leaning against the hood of her car at 8:00 a.m., Ellison Saint John wasn't one of them.

She approached slowly. 'Mr Saint John,' she said formally, nodding. 'To what do I owe the pleasure?'

The boy, no more than twenty-one or twenty-two, Dempsey thought, lanky, with tousled blonde hair, blue eyes, and a chin that never seemed to lower, pushed off her dusty Crown Vic, looking proud, and stood with his fists at his side. She figured the kid was going for assertive, but wearing a Ralph Lauren polo shirt and boat shoes, it was hard to make the case.

'My brother,' he said.

'I told your father, and Beaumont, and Sheriff Poplar, that I'm doing everything I can. As soon as I have anything, you'll be the first to—'

'No,' he said, cutting her off and stepping forward.

She lifted her hand to motion him to stop. Kid or not, she didn't like anyone advancing on her like that, and her Glock 17 was only a safety clip away.

He slowed. 'I want to help.'

She measured him. 'If you've told me everything you know, then you've helped all you can. I need to get going, alright?'

'You don't understand.'

She didn't seem to understand a lot by the reckoning of the family members of victims. The thing is, they wanted a miracle, and she dealt in facts. And right now, they weren't adding up. Though she didn't think Ellison would be the missing link.

'Okay, Ellison, what don't I understand?' she asked, humouring him. It was the fourth day of searches today, and she wanted to be there.

'My father,' he started, growing a little less puffed. 'He's...'

Lots of words came to Dempsey's mind.

'He's angry.'

'I'm sure he is,' she said.

'No, he's angry you're not making progress.'

She didn't think there was any point in telling him she sort of gleaned that. But she found it interesting that Ellison thought she thought he'd just meant in general. She didn't much like Thomas Saint John. And she got the feeling a lot of people shared that notion, and that he didn't give a shit about any of them.

'Okay.'

'He's...' Ellison seemed reluctant to speak now. 'He's in a rage.'

'A rage? What kind of rage?'

Ellison stopped speaking.

'Is he hurting people? Staff? You?' She stepped forward.

'What? No, no, he's never done anything like that, never hit us, or—' He cut himself off mid-sentence, eyes widening slightly. Then he regained himself, cleared his throat. 'No, he isn't. He's just angry, and he's... he wants Sammy found. He *needs* Sammy found. And maybe I can help.'

'Help your father?' She raised an eyebrow carefully.

Ellison nodded quickly.

Interesting. That Ellison didn't want to help find Sammy, but rather help his father feel better about it all.

'How do you think you can help?'

'I could come with you! Talk to people, help you interview them, and… I could spot something you might miss.'

'You've thought this through, clearly,' Dempsey said, sighing a little. 'Look, Ellison, I know you want to help find your brother, but unless there's something you can tell me that I don't already know, then I don't really think you riding along with me for the day is going to be appropriate.'

'I might have information,' Ellison said then. 'Things I don't know that I know.'

The kid was desperate. Just a boy trying to do something, anything to prove his worth. She could throw him a bone.

'Alright,' she said, finally, knowing there'd be no getting rid of him. 'Get in.'

He headed towards the passenger seat and waited for her to unlock the door.

'Where are we going?' he asked across the roof.

'The station,' she replied.

'Why?'

'I need some answers.' She climbed in.

'About what?'

She wondered what she could, and should tell him. 'Do you know anything about any legal troubles that Sammy might have had?'

'Legal troubles? What kind?'

She weighed her options. 'I don't know,' she answered then. 'Just some rumours I've heard. People seem pretty reluctant to talk about your family in this town.'

'That's not surprising,' Ellison laughed. 'I wouldn't want to cross my father.'

'No,' she said, smiling sardonically and cranking the ignition. 'I suspect you wouldn't.'

Chapter 25

Ellison Saint John

Ellison talked a lot on the ride. Dempsey just listened, probing gently when she felt she needed to. But he gave her a lot of information, so he wasn't sure she took it all in.

Still, if she wanted him to reiterate, he would do. The more she knew about Sammy, the better, really. And he hadn't changed much, Ellison figured, from when he was home before he went away to school. Sammy would have been what, fifteen when he went to college? Not that much changes in three years. Ellison was still the same.

The car slowed outside the station and Dempsey opened the door.

Ellison began to unbuckle, but her hand appeared in the air between them, her smile easy. 'No, it's okay, you stay here.'

He paused, not really knowing what to say. He looked over her, at her pale skin, the freckles across the bridge of her nose, her long, wavy red hair. She was slim, with an angular jaw, high cheekbones. Not usually his type, and old, but she was attractive, he couldn't deny it. And they'd had a good conversation, on the way here. And she'd let him into the car as well. So maybe she thought the same thing. For now, he'd just play it cool.

'Okay,' he said, shrugging and sitting back in the seat, lacing his hands behind his head. He spent some time in the gym at Whitman. Did she know he went to Whitman? He'd slip it into conversation casually. 'I'll be here.'

'Great,' she said, grinning. 'Back soon.'

He just nodded, barely looking at her.

She closed the door and headed for the station. It was still early but the day was heating up. Clear skies hung overhead, impossibly blue with just a tinge of yellow around the ridge. Like a crown.

Ellison soaked it in, feeling good. He wondered how long this was going to take?

She'd been gone five minutes now. How soon was soon?

He sighed and leaned forward, drumming on the dashboard with his hands. Where was she? They could be out, looking for Sammy. They could be solving this thing. And then his father would see. He'd see that Ellison wasn't a kid anymore, what he was capable of. The old fuck. Why was he such a prick, anyway?

Ellison was getting warm. The air was thickening, the day shaping up to be hot. He couldn't just sit here. He needed to do something.

The street outside the station was empty as Ellison stepped out of the car and looked around. Nothing moved, the whole town still gearing up for the day ahead. Slowly, it seemed. He checked his watch. It was half past eight already. Why the hell was everyone so lazy in this goddamn town? It's no wonder his father was able to run it like he did. No one else here had any ambition, Ellison thought as he circled around the front of the Crown Vic, running his hand along the dirtied, bug-splattered paint, leaving long, dark lines in the dust. No one else here had any sort of hard work in them. No vision. No desire to rise above their station. He tsked as he approached the front steps, slowing only as he crossed the curb and reached the rail.

But he didn't want to embarrass her, did he? Didn't want to walk in there to help hurry things along for her. Sure, his name carried sway in this town, but this was her investigation, still.

Ellison thought, then decided it was probably best to try to get a sense of the situation first, and then jump in if she was struggling.

He looked up at the building, brown brick with stone doorframes, small windows. He bet it got hot in the summer. That they opened the windows. He bet that the place was small inside, too. He'd never been inside, but even through the glass doors in front of him he could make out a front desk, a small bullpen behind it, a few offices at the back, nothing special.

He came away from the step and moved right, towards the corner of the building. An alley ran down the side, giving access to a small parking lot at the back. But Ellison only needed to make it as far as the trash cans before he heard their voices.

'…hey, hey, I understand your frustration,' a guy said. Ellison took a few steps backwards so he could see over the raised sill. He could just make out the flat top of Sheriff Poplar's haircut. Ellison stayed quiet and came closer, listening intently.

'Frustration?' It was a woman's voice, Dempsey's voice. She scoffed. 'I'm not frustrated, I'm livid,' she said, though she didn't sound angry. Her voice was barbed, but calm almost. Assertive. 'You intentionally withheld information vital to this case from me.'

'Look, it's not as simple as it seems, alright?' Pop urged her.

'It is, Sheriff. How the hell am I supposed to do my job if you're not giving me the whole story?'

'I'm surprised it didn't turn up in your initial inquiry, considering your fancy credentials and everything,' he said with a sigh, leaning back against the desk Ellison suspected. There was a little shuffling of wood on tiles. They must have been in his office. Having this conversation behind closed doors. But what information had he withheld from her?

'Thomas Saint John did his damnedest to bury it, didn't he? Paid off enough people. That much my investigation did turn up. The paper trail is a mile wide!'

'And a paper trail that big tells you that there's lots of paper, doesn't it?' Poplar said. 'Moving through the hands of lots of lawyers. And by now I suspect you saw what he had her sign, or at least, you can take a guess.'

'It's sick,' Dempsey spat.

Poplar didn't reply right away. 'It was never a criminal matter. No charges were ever filed. And everyone signed NDAs. Now, if I go splashing that information around, you think that Thomas Saint John is going to be shy about coming for my head?'

Dempsey laughed. 'Great, so you're more worried about your job than the girl?'

'We don't exactly know what happened between her and Sammy.'

Sammy? Ellison's ears pricked up. They were talking about Sammy. And some girl. No charges filed. NDAs. Money changing hands. A cover-up? He kept listening.

'I think we know,' Dempsey said. 'I've only just started digging, and I'm already getting a clear picture of who Sammy Saint John was.'

'Is.'

'Excuse me?'

'Is,' Pop repeated. 'Who Sammy Saint John *is*. We don't know where he is, yet, or what happened to him.'

Dempsey didn't seem to like that answer. She took her time to respond. And then did, sharply. 'The Saint Johns tried to bury this, and it directly relates to this case. Hell, it's motive if I ever heard it. I bet there are lots of folks in this town who'd like to see Sammy Saint John hang for this.'

'Not a lot of people knew. Thomas Saint John and his fleet of lawyers made sure of that. Quashed it before it ever got out.'

'I bet Nicholas Pips and Peter Sachs knew. They are her best friends, for fuck's sake!'

Ellison's breath choked in his chest. Nicholas Pips and Peter Sachs. Their best friend, Emmy Nailer. Sammy was going to meet Emmy that night. His father was right! She'd come on to Sammy, she must have, and then got cold feet, or maybe something happened and she was claiming that Sammy... did something to her. Trying to extort him. She only had a mother, no father, Ellison thought. And she lived in that rundown old house. Money would go a long way for them. And his father had deep pockets.

Yeah. Yeah! That must be it.

Ellison didn't need to hear any more.

If Pop and Beaumont and Dempsey couldn't get the truth, then he would.

Pips' family had always been jealous of the Saint Johns, and it was obvious that he was in love with Nailer. They were always together, and even when Ellison was a senior in high school and they were freshmen he remembered them together. He was always up her ass, pestering her. Yeah, he must have *hated* that she liked Sammy. And he didn't know how, but Ellison was sure that Pips had done something to him. He'd already threatened to kill him! He probably threatened to do it again unless Sammy left town. Unless Sammy left Savage Ridge!

Before Ellison even realised, he was running, out of the alleyway and making a left, heading for the suburbs towards the outer edge of the town.

It was within his power to end this now, here, today.

And Ellison's father always said that power was something the Saint Johns had.

So, it was about time he put his to good use.

Chapter 26

Nicholas Pips

The walk back from the school was long and quiet.

I'd not dared leave Emmy on the steps like that, but she'd been immovable for what seemed like a long time.

Something that I hadn't expected, though, was for Pete to come back.

He approached wordlessly and I didn't even notice him until he was right there.

'Pete,' I said in surprise.

His shirt was still crumpled from where I'd grabbed him, and he still looked angry, but instead of raising a fist, he raised a hand.

I took it and he pulled me in. I did the same. He put his hand on my shoulder, held our faces close together. 'We can't break now,' he muttered into my ear. 'We have to stick together.' He looked me in the eye. 'For us. For her.'

He released me and turned, kneeling next to Emmy.

'Don't…' I started, expecting her to shove him off. But she didn't. Instead, she looked up, cheeks wet with tears, and then opened her arms and threw herself onto him.

Or at least rocked forward and collapsed into his body.

I shifted from foot to foot, looking around. Wondering how this would look. Wondering how it did look. What was I looking at?

He whispered something into her hair, holding her like I'd never seen him hold her. Gently. Tenderly.

Pete had always had a crush on Emmy. I guess we both had. But we decided long ago that neither of us would pursue anything, and Pete, well, Pete never had the balls to do anything about it. Hell, he was still a virgin. He always had his nose in a book, head in the clouds, not on girls. Eighteen and a damn virgin and here Emmy was, throwing herself at him. When he was the one who'd been about to back out of this whole thing. If I hadn't been the one who'd grabbed that shovel.

'Nick?'

I looked up, saw that they were standing in front of me now, still half wrapped around each other.

'You okay?'

I let the grimace fall from my face and nodded. 'Yeah, yeah, I'm good,' I said, looking down. 'Let's… let's get out of here?'

'Where do you want to go?' Pete asked.

Emmy wiped off her cheeks, but didn't let go of Pete.

'Home,' I said, shoving my hands into the pockets of my hoodie again and striding off.

We walked together, but separately. I was on the left, Pete in the middle, Emmy on the right. None of us felt much like talking, and despite whatever the hell was going on between the two of them, it didn't matter, because Pete was right. We did need to hold it together. The cops were circling, our parents were being pulled in over and over, and now some sort of state investigator was in town? This was supposed to be clean. Simple. Get rid of Sammy, bury the body, and then get the hell out of Savage Ridge.

And now they were running search parties, combing the woods, interviewing everyone in town, over and over.

My hands were tingling again. Blood rushing. Pain in my fingers. I felt nauseous, woozy. When was the last time I ate? I couldn't quite catch my breath, it was like someone was standing on my chest.

And my heart was hammering. Beating so fast I could barely keep track of it. Couldn't even count the beats.

I wasn't breathing. My feet started to drag. Losing balance. Jesus. I was going to die. Was this a heart attack? Was I having a goddamn heart attack? Heat rushed up through my body like an eruption, exploding out of the top of my head in a shower of white-hot needles, draining down over my skin.

I looked down, my tongue swollen and choking me, and saw my hands curled into gnarled claws, stiff and locked.

I was having a heart attack. There was pain, pain everywhere.

And then my name. Echoing to me. From the darkness that was invading the corners of my vision.

'Nicholas Pips!'

I stumbled, looked around, saw Pete and Emmy clutching each other, once more, wide-eyed. Had Pete called my name?

But he wasn't looking at me. He was looking past me.

I turned stiffly, and saw Sammy Saint John, rushing towards me.

My brain faltered, I wanted to scream, but couldn't.

But it wasn't Sammy. It was Ellison Saint John. His brother.

I tried to breathe, tried to gasp, to turn, to run, to do something, anything, but I couldn't.

I saw the sky before I felt the impact, his hands driving into my chest with enough force to throw me clean off my feet.

I landed square on my back, the impact hard enough to blow the last of the air right out of my lungs. I don't think I made a sound other than a strangulated little *pfff*, but I felt my eyes bulge, pain rip through me like wildfire.

'You fucking killed him!' I heard Ellison scream, the words dull and echoing.

My eyes refocused and he was standing over me, one foot either side of my legs, bent forward, face filling my field of vision. His skin was red, slick with sweat, and he was panting. Droplets ran from his eyebrows, his chin, and landed on my face. I couldn't even muster a word.

'Leave him alone!' I heard someone yell. I didn't know if it was Emmy or Pete, the words were garbled and alien.

'Shut the fuck up!' Ellison roared, pointing a finger over my head. I craned my neck to see he was brandishing it at Emmy, and that Pete was doing his best to bar Ellison's path. 'You fucking slut!' Ellison screamed.

Emmy recoiled.

'You led him on! You asked him to meet you that night,' Ellison kept going, stepping over me now, towards them, still pointing, other hand locked into a fist. 'I don't know why he bothered with some little bitch like you! He could have had anyone, he should have known better—'

But before he could finish the word, Pete launched forward, a wild, wide swing arcing up from his side, right at Ellison's face.

Either he didn't see it, or didn't expect it, but either way, the punch connected.

Pete was small, and Ellison had at least four, five inches on him, and probably thirty pounds.

Ellison didn't seem to move, but Pete pulled back, clutching at his wrist, teeth bared in pain.

I saw Ellison's arm twitch an instant before it lashed out. A straight punch, right to the mouth.

Pete staggered, blood spattering the pavement.

Emmy screamed, the sound piercing and frightened.

Pete crumpled into her and she went to the ground, cradling him between her knees as he curled up, protecting his head.

'Please, please,' Emmy sobbed. 'Please, just leave us alone!'

'Tell me what you did to him! Tell me!'

I saw flashing lights then. At first, I thought they were inside my head, but a second later, tyres screeched to a halt next to the curb and Ellison picked his head up, eyes mad.

I managed to roll onto my side, enough to see Dickie Beaumont's fat face hanging out of the driver's window of his patrol car. 'Ellison,' he called, 'get in the car, right now.'

He hovered, looking at the three of us for a second. And then he went wordlessly, stepping over me and climbing into the back.

Beaumont didn't bother asking if we were okay, or saying anything else. He just floored it, leaving black marks on the road, and drowning them in a cloud of exhaust smoke.

I watched the tail lights zip around a corner and out of view, struggling onto my stomach, trying to get my hands under me.

When I looked around, heart still hammering, breath still seized in my chest, coming in short, sharp, useless gasps, I was alone.

It took me a few seconds to get my bearings, but by the time I did, and homed in on Emmy and Pete, they were already twenty yards away and moving quickly. Pete was stumbling, Emmy supporting him.

And all I could do was watch, struggling to my knees, fighting for air, feeling like I was suffocating under the weight of it all.

Chapter 27

Lillian Dempsey

Dempsey did her best to keep a lid on her anger. 'I bet Nicholas Pips and Peter Sachs knew. They're her best friends, for God's sake!'

'Well, we don't know what we don't know,' Pop said from his position leaning against his desk, a cryptic way of admitting he didn't have a damn clue what was going on in this town. Or with the Saint Johns. But Dempsey suspected that was the point, that Thomas Saint John had installed him as sheriff so he'd be the clueless, ignorant figurehead of this sleepy town while the Saint Johns did whatever the hell they pleased.

'That's really helpful, Sheriff,' Dempsey spat. 'But it does mean that—' She cut herself off, the crunch of gravel outside the window of Pop's office and the sound of receding footsteps enough to interrupt their conversation.

Pop was closest and jogged over, leaning out. 'Ah, shit,' he said, pulling his head back in and striding towards his office door, thumbs hooked in his belt.

'What is it?' Dempsey asked, moving from his path.

'It looks like Ellison Saint John is running down my damn alleyway,' Pop said, ripping the door open. 'Beaumont!' he yelled, raising a hand and snapping his fingers.

Dickie Beaumont twisted on his chair, his thighs dripping over the sides, his mouth white with the cream cheese off the bagel he was eating. He raised an eyebrow, holding his breakfast in one hand.

'Ellison Saint John,' Pop announced, pointing towards the front door. 'Go find him before he does something stupid. He was heading towards the high school.'

Beaumont looked at Pop, then at Dempsey over his shoulder, then at his bagel. He put it down, grunting to his feet and wiping off his lips. 'Jesus Christ,' he sighed, licking his fingers. 'Never a moment's goddamn peace.' He started sidling towards the door, then stopped, doubled back for his bagel, held it between his teeth, and then exited into the rising sun.

When he'd disappeared through the door, Pop readjusted his belt and shook his head.

'Real credit to the force, that one,' Dempsey remarked.

'His retirement can't come quick enough,' Pop replied.

Dempsey didn't reply, just thought on it, and then wondered where Ellison was going. She figured saying she'd brought him here wouldn't be helpful to anyone. What was the last thing he'd heard? 'Shit,' she muttered, realising.

'What's wrong?' Pop asked, stepping through the door to let Dempsey pass.

'Nothing,' she replied, picking up speed. 'Thanks for your time, Sheriff.'

'Call if you need anything else,' he replied, lifting a hand.

She gave him a brief wave, then stepped out of the station and towards her car. Pop would never speak out against Thomas Saint John. He was terrified of the man. And rightly so. Thomas Saint John held Savage Ridge in the palm of his hand. And with each finger he was plucking a different string – Pop, Beaumont, the mill, his lawyers. He was the valve that controlled the lifeblood flowing through this town. And if anyone stood up to him, he could choke the entire town of sustenance. If he shut the mill or stopped pouring money into this place, Savage Ridge would wither and die on the vine. It'd take months, maybe years, but it would be inevitable. And he probably thought that made him untouchable.

And it sort of did.

But she wasn't from Savage Ridge, and she didn't take well to men like Thomas Saint John throwing their weight around, especially when it came to her job and her department. She was on no one's leash. And he was about to find that out.

She thought of Ellison again, and felt saddened by him. By his motivations for wanting to help. The more she looked into the Saint Johns, the more she realised that none of them had a friend in the world. And nor did they seemingly want any, except for Sammy.

Dempsey glanced over her shoulder to make sure her satchel and the file inside was still on the back seat, and then took off up the road. She'd not expected Ellison to leave the car, and hadn't even thought about the bag at the time. She'd figured he was harmless, but maybe she'd miscalculated. Though he didn't seem to get a look at what was in her bag, and that was good. It was the last thing he needed. Although maybe the truth wouldn't be such a bad thing.

It was supposed to set you free, after all. But if she did set that particular truth free, she knew she'd be putting herself in the crosshairs of the Saint Johns, not doing them a favour. And whether she disliked how Thomas Saint John did business or not, she couldn't ignore his reach, and the power it had. She was here, after all, despite her best efforts not to be.

The golden SJ stared down at Dempsey as she waited at the gates to be let in. It was the same rigmarole as before. Pull up, buzzer, asked what she wanted, tell the estate manager, be told to wait, then finally be received. What was Thomas Saint John so afraid of that he needed impenetrable gates, anyway? A mob with pitchforks?

The gates swung open and Dempsey drove up, parking in front of the house. This time, she didn't forget her bag, and instead strode into Thomas Saint John's house with it on her shoulder. The door was opened by a maid and she gave her a quick thanks before heading for the study. She knew the way.

Dempsey had been in possession of Sammy Saint John's phone records for two days now, and when she saw what was in them, it didn't take her long to discover the thing that Thomas Saint John had worked so hard to bury. What Sammy had done.

She didn't bother knocking on the study door before she entered.

Thomas Saint John looked up from his desk, dropping the papers in front of him. 'Come in then,' he said, condescending as ever.

'Sammy's phone records came through,' Dempsey said, pulling the file from her satchel and dropping it in front of his father. 'You care to take a look?'

'I'm sure I already know what's in there,' he said, leaning back, chair squeaking. He laced his hands across his stomach. 'Now do you want to tell me why you're here and not out there searching for my son?'

'You've got some nerve,' Dempsey laughed. 'You knew about this and you intentionally withheld it. What, did you think I wouldn't find out?'

'Frankly, I didn't give it much thought at all. Because it doesn't change the fact of the matter: Nicholas Pips killed my son, the reason is inconsequential.'

'"Inconsequential",' Dempsey mouthed. 'Right. What Pips supposedly did is a crime, but when Sammy hurts someone, it's just a, what, misunderstanding?'

'An unfortunate incident,' Thomas Saint John corrected her.

She nodded, feeling sick at the sight of the man.

'There was no malice in it,' he said carefully, 'and for that reason, we were able to straighten things out amicably.'

Dempsey snorted now. 'Amicably? You're a fucking cancer.' She spat the words at him. 'In this town, and on the world.'

His eyes flashed. 'Watch yourself. This is my home, and you work for me.'

'I might be the only person in this town who doesn't,' Dempsey snarled.

He smiled as though he were in on a joke she wasn't. 'Is that all? I've got work to get on with.'

She stood, seething for a moment. 'You know your son came to see me this morning. Ellison.'

He raised an eyebrow, almost uninterested.

'It didn't take me long to figure out the kind of kid he is – and I'm surprised.'

'Surprised?' he said tiredly, shaking his head.

'Surprised that he turned out as normal as he has. But Sammy? It's not surprising he thought the world belonged to him, growing up here, with you as a role model.'

'The world *does* belong to him,' Thomas Saint John said. 'It belongs to him, and Ellison, and to me. And people like me.' He pushed himself to his feet now. 'Because people like us own things, run things, make things happen. And then there are people like you, who can't. Whose lives are only made possible by people like me. The money that pays your state salary? Where do you think that comes from? Taxes. And who pays the most taxes, hmm?' He took off his reading glasses now and dropped them in front of him. 'So, whether you think you work for me or not, the sad truth of your life is that you do. And you took an oath to protect and serve the people of this state, didn't you? And last time I checked, that includes me. And my son. So, before you deign to condescend to me about how my family is the problem, why don't you go out there and find my son?'

She swallowed the bile rising in her throat. 'I don't think he wants to be found,' she said. 'I think that he realised what kind of man you are, and what kind of life lay ahead of him, and he ran. Far away. As far away as he could.'

'He has nowhere to go.'

'Anywhere is better than here.'

'Just do your fucking job.'

'Oh, I will,' she said, drawing a slow breath. 'I'll find Sammy, and in the process, I'm going to tear his life apart. And yours. Piece by piece. I'll expose everything you've done, in this town, and beyond, and lay it out for everyone to see. You want me to find your son? I will. But are you ready for the world to see what else I find out along the way?'

He narrowed his eyes at her for a moment, though she didn't see a shred of apprehension in him. 'Do that, and I'll end your career. Right here. Right now. One phone call from me, and you'll never work another day in your life. I'll make sure of it.'

She scoffed, lips closed, incredulous. 'It's true what they say, I suppose,' Dempsey said, turning and walking towards the door. 'Money doesn't solve anything.'

She heard Thomas Saint John's chair slide backwards as he stood, his words echoing down the polished wooden corridor behind her. 'You just clearly don't have enough money.'

Chapter 28

Nicholas Pips

It took me a long time to peel myself off the ground.

I don't know how long it took for my heart to calm down, for my body to stop sweating, and for the impending sense of doom to recede from the corners of my mind. But when I finally got to my feet, I was exhausted.

Pete and Emmy were long gone, and I walked towards home alone. By the time I turned the corner onto my street, it was probably late morning. I couldn't really think about much, I just wasn't able to. All I wanted was to crawl into bed, pull the covers over my head, and close my eyes. It'd been a long time since I'd felt like I could cry, just screw up my eyes and let some tears roll down my cheeks. But now, I could have. And it took everything I had just to stay on my feet.

The steps creaked under my heels as I hauled myself up them and onto my porch, pulling open the front door and stepping into the safety of my front hallway.

I hung my head back and breathed easier.

'Nicky?' My mom called from the kitchen.

'Yeah?' I answered, my voice croaky. I was thirsty, but the last thing I wanted to do was face my parents.

'Can you come in here, please, sweetie?'

I drew a slow breath. 'I'm not feeling so great,' I answered truthfully, 'I think I need to go to bed.'

'Now, Nick.' My dad then.

My head lowered, my eyes focusing, finding the doorway to the kitchen. My dad was leaning backwards on the chair that sat around the battered old kitchen table. He had one arm over the seat back, eyes hard.

I swallowed, heart kicking up again, stomach knotting, and started forward.

By the time I reached the threshold, I knew why they were both in there, and why they wanted me. There was a woman sitting at the far end of the table. She was tall, slight, with pointed features, pale eyes, and long, wavy red hair. It fell loosely around her shoulders, over the collar of her white button-up shirt, the sleeves rolled to the elbows, exposing freckled forearms. Her hands were around a cup of tea and her expression was soft, sympathetic. She was looking at me with something as close to pity as you could get without having to use the word.

The investigator.

'Sit,' my father said.

'Nicky,' my mom said, 'are you alright? You're as white as a sheet.'

It took me a second to find the words. 'I'm sick,' I said through gritted teeth, afraid that if I parted them vomit would come spilling out.

'This won't take long,' the red-headed woman said. 'Would you mind taking a seat, Nick?'

I didn't like the way she said my name, but I figured my options were to oblige or turn and sprint from the house and never come back.

Reluctantly, I pulled the last empty chair out and sat. I was adjacent to the woman, with my mother opposite me, staring at her hands, and my father on my left, opposite the woman. His hands were in front of him, still and clasped firmly, eyes fixed on our guest.

She offered my father a brief smile, cleared her throat lightly, and then set her eyes on me. 'My name is Lillian Dempsey. I'm a senior investigator with the Washington State Police Criminal Investigations Division. It's nice to meet you, Nick. Do you prefer Nick or Nicholas?'

I sort of shrugged. 'I don't mind.' But I did mind. I hated being called Nicholas.

'Alright,' she said, 'Nick it is. Do you know why I'm here?' She lowered her head slightly to catch my eye, her voice gentle, soothing. She was obviously good at this, disarming in an easy way. But despite her kind face, her eyes were heavy, her gaze weighing on me.

I didn't know if playing dumb was the right call. 'I'm guessing you're here about Sammy Saint John,' I replied carefully.

She just nodded, as though waiting for me to go on. I elected not to.

'That's right,' she said eventually. 'I've been asked to look into his disappearance. And I suppose you also know why I'm sitting here, in *your* kitchen.'

My dad jumped in then. 'Because Thomas Saint John has a vendetta against our family.'

Dempsey smiled a little. 'Well, he probably does. But that's not the reason, is it, Nick?'

I let out a long breath, clenching my fingers under the table, willing away the building rush of blood, the pins and needles, the sudden stiffness in them. 'You're talking about the pool party,' I said slowly.

'Among other things.'

My father drew a long, imposing breath. He was aware that there'd been a run-in with Sammy Saint John. Pop had come by afterwards, explained that Thomas Saint John wasn't happy. That he wanted me arrested for that, too.

It hadn't gone that far, luckily. But it was only because my dad stood so firm, because he told Pop that he could get the four of them in a room together to talk it out if they wanted to. Things had settled after that, but I knew it would rear its head again.

'Do you want to tell me what happened at the pool, in your own words? The timeline of events is proving difficult to nail down. And you're the only person I haven't heard from, yet.'

My dad reached forward, put his hand on my elbow. 'You made a statement already,' he said, not taking his eyes from Dempsey, but speaking to me. 'She can read that if she wants to know what happened.'

'*She* is extending you a courtesy by asking you this question here, in your own home, instead of in an interview room at the station.' Dempsey's eyes stayed on mine. 'So, if you wouldn't mind, Nick?'

'When will this end?' my mother muttered.

No one replied.

I swallowed, feeling the pressure of my father's hand ease at my elbow.

'We were at the party,' I said slowly, staring right at Dempsey. I knew I'd have to be truthful here if I had any chance of getting her to believe me. But there were only two people in the world who knew what Sammy really said to me on the side of the pool, and one of them was buried under five feet of dirt and rock. 'We were just hanging out, having fun,' I said. 'And then Sammy showed up.'

'What time was this?'

'I don't know,' I said. 'Seven, eight? It was still light, warm. But it was evening.'

She nodded. 'Then what happened?'

'No one wanted him there. But he came in, with a bottle of...' I trailed off, glanced at my dad. He nodded to me. Go on. 'A bottle of liquor,' I finished. 'Whiskey, I think. I didn't recognise the label. I don't know where he got it.'

Dempsey didn't seem to care much. 'What did you do?'

'Pete pointed him out to me, so I went to try and stop him. I asked him to leave. It wasn't our house, but we knew the people who owned it. They didn't want Sammy there. No one did.'

She smiled at me a little. I'd said that twice now. I was stumbling. I needed to organise my thoughts. She let me go on.

'So, I said to him, "You need to leave." Just like that.'

'But he didn't?'

She knew that much already. 'He shoved the bottle into my chest and told me to have a drink.'

Dempsey nodded. Perhaps not deliberately, but it gave away that what I was saying lined up with the story she already had.

'He walked past me then, pulled off his shirt, and jumped into the pool with his shoes on.'

'And... how did Sammy *seem* to you?' She sat back, said the words slowly.

'I'm guessing "drunk" isn't the answer you're looking for? Because he was. He was shit-faced. And he drove there, too.'

'How was his demeanour? Did he seem happy, sad?'

'I don't know,' I said. 'He always seemed miserable. I don't think he was happy at home. But how could he be?' I watched her now as she held her stony expression. 'But you've met Thomas Saint John. And Ellison, too. You know what that whole family is like.'

She pursed her lips slightly. 'Let's get back to the pool party. What happened after Sammy jumped in the pool?'

'He made some grabs for the girls that were in there.'

'Grabs?'

I shrugged. 'By the way they all scrambled to get out of there, I assume he was trying for the parts they didn't want touched.'

My mother shook her head. My father was a sphinx.

'And then?'

'And then he started splashing around, thrashing, laughing hysterically.'

'And that seemed normal to you?'

'Nothing about Sammy Saint John is normal.' I made sure to use the present tense on that one. 'He's a troubled kid. We even felt for him at one stage. But that ended pretty quickly. And I bet you know why by now.'

Her lack of reaction told me that she did. 'Did he stay in the pool?'

'Until he threw up. Took a mouthful of water, gagged, then puked everywhere. Everyone started yelling at him to get out, to go home. Telling him he ruined everything. And then he did get out.'

'And he spoke to you again?'

'You could say that. He stormed over, demanded his bottle back. I told him to go fuck himself.'

My father cleared his throat.

I stayed with Dempsey. 'It's the truth. I'm not going to lie about it. I hate Sammy Saint John.'

Dempsey watched me closely. She wanted this in my words.

'He tried to make a snatch for it, and I held it out the way. He was smaller than me. But he was drunk, and he thought he could do whatever he wanted. So, he tried to go for it again. And that's when Emmy got in between us.'

Dempsey shifted a little in her chair, sitting more upright.

'She tried to calm Sammy down before the situation escalated any more.'

'What did she say to him?'

'She told him that he should leave before someone called the police. Before he did anything stupid. But he didn't listen.'

'Did Emmy have a... rapport with Sammy Saint John?'

'Did they have a relationship, do you mean?'

She waited.

I decided what to say. 'She had more reason to loathe that piece of shit than any one of us. What he did...' I didn't have to feign the disgust I felt. It came naturally to my voice and to my face. 'But she knew who his family was, and what would happen if Sammy got into a fight. Who would come off worse.'

'But he wouldn't leave?'

I shook my head. 'No. She pleaded with him, but he refused to go without his drink. So, he tried for it again, and barged Emmy out of the way. Hit her in the chin with his shoulder. It happened quickly after that.'

'You hit him?'

'I hit him back. After he tried to punch me.'

The words hung in the air.

'When he knocked Emmy down, I shoved him. He swung. Then I hit him. Wish I'd hit him harder.'

'And then he…'

'Fell in the pool. That's right. And now you're going to ask me to repeat what he said?'

She nodded to me, glancing at my mother.

'Fine.' I took a breath. 'He told me that I was fucked. That he was going to tell his father what I'd done. And that he would then promptly fire my father, buy our house out from under us so we'd be homeless, and that to make ends meet, my mother would have to prostitute herself for money. His exact words were that she would be "*sucking dick*" by the end of the week.'

Dempsey's eyes were fixed on me.

My mother made a strange sound. A sort of gentle, aghast moan of shock.

My father grunted his disapproval.

I wondered if Dempsey believed me. If she knew that what I'd just told her wasn't the extent of what Sammy had said. Or whether she had no clue. Did she know she just watched me lie?

I couldn't tell from her face.

'What did you do then, Nick?'

This part I couldn't lie about. 'Sammy swam to the side of the pool and I dragged him out by his arm. I shoved his face against the paving slabs, pushed his cheek into the stone.' My voice began to shake. 'I put my knee on his shoulder to pin him there, to stop him wriggling, and pressed hard enough on his head that he cried out in pain. And then I leaned in and told him that if he ever talked about my mom again that I'd kill him.'

Dempsey turned to look at my mother, to gauge her reaction. I couldn't. But out of the corner of my eye I could see her shaking, her eyes glistening.

'Okay,' Dempsey said, leaning forward. 'I know what happened from here. So, I'm going to ask you just one more question, and I want you to think carefully before you answer, okay?'

'Okay.'

'Nick, do you know where Samuel Saint John is?'

I set my jaw. 'No.'

She inspected my face. My heart had been hammering since the moment I sat down and my skin was slick with sweat anyway. I hoped she'd not be able to tell that was another lie.

'Do you know what happened to him?'

My father interjected now. 'You said one more question. He answered it. And I think we've been more than accommodating enough—'

'What I *do* know,' I cut back in, silencing my father. Dempsey leaned in further. 'Is that Sammy Saint John was deeply unhappy. That he was intensely lonely. And that he had no idea how the world worked. He grew up with everything, but the expectation he had of the world, and the one he found waiting for him were two totally different things. I don't know where Sammy Saint John is. But what I do know, is that no one wanted him here. And maybe he finally realised that and did us all a favour and went very far away.'

'Is that what you think happened? Do you think he ran away?'

'I don't think he was brave enough to do anything else.'

Dempsey readjusted her position on her seat.

'We just want to go on with our lives,' I finished. 'Sammy is gone. Can't that just be a good thing?'

Dempsey pushed to her feet slowly. 'I don't know if Thomas Saint John will ever let anyone go on with their lives. I have a feeling that things have been irrevocably changed in Savage Ridge. And I don't know if you'll ever be able to live your life without him looking over your shoulder.' She leaned in so her face was no more than twelve inches from mine. 'But you already knew that, didn't you? You thought about that before you made the choice.'

My father's chair slid back quickly and he got to his feet. 'I think it's time for you to leave.'

Dempsey nodded an apology to him and then took her jacket off the chair behind her and slipped it on. 'I'll show myself out.'

She breezed past without another word and headed for the door.

But neither my father nor I looked after her. We just stared at one another. Me, wondering whether he'd still love me if he learned the truth. And him, probably wondering if, deep down, he already knew it.

Chapter 29

Ellison Saint John

Beaumont didn't even need to speak into the intercom. The second the maids or whoever's job it was to answer the gate saw the car, they buzzed him right in.

He drove slowly up the drive. Though Ellison didn't think a big slob of a man like Beaumont could go any other speed.

Ellison stared down at his right hand, the dried blood across his knuckles. From Peter Sachs's nose, he thought. Why the hell had Beaumont been there anyway? Another minute and he would have had that confession. The guy had ruined everything.

When he pulled to a stop, Ellison just got straight out. Beaumont dragged in a wheezing breath to speak but Ellison wasn't interested in hearing anything that came out of his mouth.

He slammed the door and started up the steps towards his house. The front door opened to accept him and he entered, ready to climb the stairs and go to his room. But he didn't, he paused, all full of rage, and looked down the long, checkerboard tiled corridor towards his father's office.

He came back down off the bottom step and turned, walking towards the open door, massaging the forming bruise on his hand, feeling the roughness of dried blood. Ellison held his head high, shoulders back as he approached.

Inside, the air was cool and the room was dim. His father seemed unmoving, staring down at a piece of paper in front of him. A piece of paper that had nothing to do with Sammy.

'Hey,' Ellison said, trying to muster his voice.

His father did not look up.

Ellison came to the desk. 'Hey.' A little more assertive this time.

Once more, his father ignored him.

'Hey!' Ellison bent over the desk now, slapping his hand down onto the paper his father was reading. Dried blood flaked off onto the white surface, his fingers leaving dark red smears across the words there.

Now his father did look up. A cold, slow raise of the head that sent shivers down Ellison's spine.

He'd been all anger a moment ago, but now fear gripped him. His eyes began to well up, and the words tumbled from his mouth uncontrollably. 'You're not doing anything,' he said, feeling the first tear run hot down his cheek. 'You're not doing anything to find him!' He erupted to a roar at the end. 'You don't even love him!' The emotion burst through a dam Ellison didn't know was there, the paper under his hand crumpling into his grip. 'You don't love him. You're a terrible father!'

Thomas Saint John was on his feet so fast that Ellison didn't even realise the man was moving towards him until he'd already rounded the desk.

He tried to speak, to apologise, but before he could, his airway clamped shut. Thomas Saint John's fist closed around his son's throat and he drove him backwards, heels dragging on the hardwood floor, until his back hit one of the bookcases that lined the wall. The tomes shook and threatened to fall.

One came free and flapped to the floor with a heavy thud.

'You ungrateful little piece of shit,' Thomas Saint John snarled in Ellison's face, flecks of saliva peppering his cheeks. 'For all my hard work, you still turned into this!' He gripped harder, driving Ellison higher so that his feet came clear of the ground. He clutched at his father's wrist, fighting for breath that wouldn't come. 'You have amounted to nothing! Pathetic. Worthless.' The words were bile-filled and slicing. 'I sent you away to make a man of you, to try... but you've come back more of a snivelling boy than the one that left.'

He released his son with as much contempt as he'd grabbed him.

Ellison flopped to the ground, gasping, and Thomas Saint John looked down at his own wrist, marked by Peter Sachs' blood. He pulled a handkerchief from his pocket and wiped it off slowly. 'And this? Fighting?' he said, unable to even look at his son. 'Saint Johns don't fight. We win.' His eyes fell upon the boy at his feet. 'But I wouldn't expect you to understand. Because you'll never be a real Saint John. Not until you learn what our name means. Get up.'

He only needed to give the order once.

Ellison forced himself to his feet on shaking knees, tears streaming from his eyes, hands around his throat, massaging the darkening purple welts.

Thomas Saint John batted away his son's hands and looked at his work.

His lips curled down into a disappointed grimace, and then he balled his fist and fired it into his son's stomach so hard that he doubled up over it, a meek wheeze escaping his lips.

When Thomas Saint John removed his hand, Ellison crumpled to the floor, drool running from the corner of his lips and onto the hardwood.

And then his father stepped over him and out of the door without another word.

Chapter 30

Nicholas Pips

I didn't know whether the word, 'Shakes?' could be miscon-strued, but I was still terrified that it'd get me into trouble.

We'd pre-agreed that if we needed to talk about anything, if something was going wrong, we were worried or in trouble, then that's what we'd say. 'Milkshakes.' Innocuous. Innocent. Everyone likes milkshakes. No one – police, or state invest-igators, or anyone else – could look at a text log that said 'Milkshakes?' sent to the sender's two closest friends, and say: this is proof of murder.

Could they?

That was what was going through my head as I sent it to Emmy and Pete.

Since Dempsey had ambushed me at my house, it'd been a day spent thinking. Her last words to me: 'You thought about that before you made the choice', were clear as day. She knew it, but she couldn't prove it. So, could she even really *know*? Or did she just think? It wasn't difficult to guess what we'd done or how we'd done it, but proving any of it was going to be impossible, that much we were sure of.

And yet, going to meet my two accomplices seemed like idiocy. Though not meeting them seemed even stupider. What if Dempsey dropped in on them, too? She'd tried it with Pete's family. Which meant Emmy was likely next, if she hadn't been put on the chopping block already. She needed to be warned, either way. This needed to be discussed, but not over the phone, and not via text. In person. I couldn't be seen as being alarmed or shaken by her visit. It's what she was counting on, that I'd go running to them, frantic. And all she'd need to do was listen in.

No, I needed to remain calm. A murderer surrounded by cops. That thought had driven me to the bathroom, to my knees, to vomit into the toilet until my throat ached and my stomach hurt. And then the panic had come once more, the crushing weight on my chest, the stiffness of my hands, the humming of my heart.

I'd crawled to bed, gotten under the covers, and cried.

And then passed out from exhaustion. When I woke, I knew I had to send the text.

> Milkshakes.

Their responses were fast, they knew what it meant.

> When?

> Now?

I walked to the diner. I needed the air, needed the space, the freedom. I didn't know how much more I had left.

The day was wearing thin. The sun had sunk behind the horizon now and Savage was bathed in a warm orange glow. It was the kind of summer night where the air was heavy, the sky sharp and clear, and the bugs swirled lazily, crickets clicking, asphalt baked and exuding a palpable heat as you walked.

Bursts of sunlight lanced up from behind the western ridge, piercing the slowly darkening sky. Nothing seemed to move on days like today, the town asleep in the cradle of the earth.

The 'Open' sign buzzed above the door as I approached, the tired white exterior as timeless as the town itself. My dad had come here for shakes when he was my age, and his dad remembered it being built way back in the early Fifties. It'd been threaded through the fabric of Savage Ridge ever since. As much a part of the town as the valley sides themselves.

The concrete steps, cracked and dotted with ancient black gum, carried me up to the door. The glass and metal frame creaked on its sprung hinge, the bell above the door ringing as it opened. The stale air-conditioned interior was familiar and nauseating. I hadn't been back here since the night we... since the night that *I*... I shook my head, unable to even say it in my own mind now.

Pete was already here, Emmy wasn't.

He was facing the door, same booth we'd sat in that night. A lift of the chin, a brief smile. The corner of his mouth was bruised and swollen, his lip split from where Ellison had hit him. His right wrist was in a brace, too.

I approached, feeling as bad as he looked, and slid into the booth opposite. Neither of us managed a happy greeting. We just sat in silence.

A few other people littered the diner, a couple of truck drivers on stools sipping coffee before they hit the road again, an older couple chowing down on peach pie and cream, and a guy in the corner reading a two-day-old paper. I know it was two days old because I remembered the front headline: SEARCH FOR MISSING BOY INTENSIFIES: MORE OFFICERS JOIN THE EFFORT.

It had to be thirty, forty people out there now, day after day, combing the woods for him. Walking in a line, with sniffer dogs, flashlights, metal detectors sensitive enough to pick up a belt buckle or zipper three feet deep. Well, we buried him five feet down, and emptied his pockets for his wallet, keys, spare change. Everything. But was he wearing a belt? I don't think so, but I didn't know. That'd be just my fucking luck that Sammy Saint-fucking-John would be wearing a fucking Ralph Lauren fucking belt that cost more than my dad's car, and that's what'd get us caught.

I became aware of a presence at my shoulder suddenly and looked up, seeing Emmy standing there.

Her eyes were red like she'd been crying, and the cuffs of her hoodie were all stretched out, damp with tears, and frayed like she'd been biting on them. It looked like she hadn't showered or washed her hair, and her eyes were so deep and lifeless that it made me feel cold inside.

I slid out of the booth reflexively and she got in, shimmying across to the window. Why she wanted to sit next to me, I don't know. Pete watched me as I got up and then sat back down. He looked nervous, slightly more so than when I'd arrived. Emmy and he had run off that morning after the fight with Ellison. Had something happened? Had he said something to her, her to him? Emmy had an elbow on the window sill, chin on her hand, eyes glued to the glass.

I followed her gaze out over the roofs of the houses in town, to the green-grey wall of trees on the mountain. Shadow was on them, and we knew the woods well enough to know that darkness came hours early under the canopy. So, it was no surprise that the flashlights were so bright. They danced and strobed through the pine boughs, darting into the sky before sweeping back through the undergrowth. Half a hundred bodies all out there, scouring the entire forest for Sammy Saint John. My only solace was that they were on the wrong side. But I knew how grid searches worked. They'd move around until they found the right spot, until the sniffer dogs got a scent. And then it was just a matter of time.

I could almost hear the clamour, the barking of the hounds, the crunching of the heels in the undergrowth as the search party became incensed by the threat of victory. How much had Thomas Saint John offered as a reward for the one who found Sammy? What did he value his son's life at? Except he wasn't paying for his son's life. It was a bounty for his killer. So how much was he willing to pay to get retribution on the person who crossed the Saint Johns?

'Crying shame.'

We all turned to stare up at Darlene, the eternal waitress. She stood there, chewing gum through purple lips, eyes fixed on the distant search lights.

None of us responded.

Darlene sighed loudly, the faint, sour stench of cigarette smoke washing down over us. 'Savage used to be such a nice town. So quiet. Now… this.' She waved a long-nailed hand at the window and shook her head. 'What is this world coming to, huh, kids?' She shook her head, broke into an unsettling, toothy grin, and pulled her pad to attention. 'So, what'll it be? The usual? Shakes all around?'

'Th-thanks,' I mustered, nodding. 'That'd be great.'

'You okay there, Nicky?' she asked. 'Looking a little peaky. Let me get you some water, hey, hon?' She reached out then, touched my shoulder. 'And don't you worry a lick, all this business with the Saint Johns, their missing boy, it's nothing for you to pay any mind to.' She looked at Emmy and Pete. 'There are more cops here than I've ever seen. We never made so much coffee! I don't think Savage Ridge has ever been safer. They'll find that boy, for better or worse, and then the person who did it to him. I promise you that.' She grinned at us again, as if it were the thing we wanted to hear, and then turned on her heel and left.

Emmy made a whimpering sound, threw her hand against her mouth, and then clawed her way across the bench, shoving me out of the way.

I got to my feet and she ran past, making a beeline for the bathroom. To throw up.

I knew because I was on the verge of doing the same.

Pete reached out across the table and grabbed my arm, pulled me back down into the booth.

Even when I sat, he didn't let me go. 'We've got a problem,' he said, leaning over, voice low.

I glanced around, made sure no one was within earshot. The milkshake machine began whirring behind the counter, drowning out everything else.

'Emmy was talking about coming clean, Nick.'

My heart kicked up.

'Earlier, on the way home, saying she didn't think she could do this anymore, couldn't hold it in any longer. We need to do something.'

'What can we do?' My voice was choked.

He shook his head. 'We've got to move things up. We can't wait.'

'It's just a few weeks,' I said, trying to reassure myself as much as him. 'It's all arranged. You're going to San Jose, I'm going to Portland U. And Emmy is going to Arizona State. We got our admission letters. It's done.

'It's not a few weeks, it's *three*. And I'm not sure Emmy's going to last three days. Especially not with everything going on here.'

Jesus, I hadn't even got to the part where Dempsey had come to my house and told me she knew. If I said that now, hell, Emmy would probably explode by the sound of it, and Pete, God, I didn't even know. I didn't even feel like I knew who he was anymore. I didn't even feel like I knew who *I* was anymore, either.

But it didn't matter, because we'd all agreed to this, then, with sound minds. And we knew it wasn't going to be easy. 'Alright,' I said quietly.

'Alright?'

'Alright, we get Emmy out of here.'

Pete swallowed. 'How?'

'Emmy's got an aunt in Arizona, right? That's why she picked it. We just… we talk to her mom, we explain the situation, say that it's just too much for Emmy, being here, with Sammy, and the pressure from the police. Yeah. We tell her that Emmy's coming apart – she'll see that much herself. And we'll say… we'll say we think it's best if she leaves. She already turned over her phone to Pop, she's got nothing to hide. We buy her ticket if we have to, then we put her on a bus, and—'

'Send her away.' The words sounded grave coming from him.

'I don't like it, either. But if it's that, or the alternative…'

'You'd do that to Emmy?'

'Do we have a choice?'

His head began to shake slowly as he searched for one.

'Her aunt can put her up until she gets to orientation. She'll be fine.'

'Will she?'

'I don't know, but being there, maybe she'll get some space, some time to think, to realise that staying quiet is the right thing. That it's not just her life, it's ours, too.'

'And if she talks?' Pete had paled a little.

'Then what's the fucking difference? If she comes clean there, or here, we're screwed either way. At least… at least if she's there—'

'If she's there,' Pete said, 'then we won't be able to look out for her.'

I bit down on my tongue, willing myself the strength, or the cowardice, to say the words at the front of my mind. 'We need to look out for ourselves,' I muttered bitterly. 'Dempsey came to my house, too. She knows, Pete.'

'She knows?' The words were thin and weak.

'She can't prove it, but she knows. So, I think we need to consider what happens if this all comes out. If they find Sammy. If they somehow tie this to— Hey, Emmy,' I said, seeing her coming around the corner of the bar, wiping her mouth off on her cuff.

Pete stiffened and I stood. Emmy slid in and put her hands on the table, staring down at them.

We sat there in silence, Pete looking at me, and me looking back at him. I could feel Emmy shaking next to me.

The sky continued to darken beyond the glass.

The clicking of Darlene's heels as she approached with our shakes was deafening.

Her words were garbled and distant as she began unloading the tray.

For as long as I could remember, I'd loved nothing more than slurping down a chocolate shake right here in this diner.

But in that moment, as I stared down into the silky, decadent, sweet, cold liquid, I felt repulsed. I never wanted to see a milkshake again.

The realisation came quickly. I never wanted to see any of it again.

If we put Emmy on a bus the following day, I'd feel jealous more than guilty. Because I'd have to endure another three weeks in Savage. Another three weeks of hell in this place.

We'd wrecked our lives here. We'd killed someone. And now, every second spent in this place was like a twisting of the knife lodged between my ribs.

I had decided.

I was leaving Savage Ridge.

And I was never coming back.

Chapter 31

Lillian Dempsey

Dempsey held her phone up in front of her, willing it to reconnect to the internet. She'd been tracking up a forest service road for the best part of fifteen minutes now, following her GPS to the location Pop had set for the start of this morning's search.

They'd combed almost half the valley, and Thomas Saint John was calling in more and more state troopers every day. His pockets ran deep, and he wanted his son found. But if it was sniffer dogs and forest combing, did he have *any* hope that Sammy was still alive?

'Screw it,' Dempsey muttered, dropping her phone onto the passenger seat and speeding up a little. She'd always thought that having a pickup truck or SUV was pointless. But then again, she'd never spent much time jostling up forest service roads. Now, she saw the appeal.

It felt like her spine was rattled to gravel by the time she rounded the corner and came upon a turn-out. A metal gate barred the way ahead, but there were a few cars parked in front of it. Two state patrol vehicles, and Pop's Chevy Tahoe.

Dempsey eased to a stop behind it and killed the engine.

Pop was already out of his truck, pointing to an ordnance survey map spread out across the hood of the patrol car at the front.

He glanced up, lifted a hand, then went back to the task at hand, gesturing and circling with his finger, giving instructions to the six guys around him. This was just part of the search party;

there were so many logging tracks crisscrossing the landscape that starting everyone in the same place was pointless. So much of the terrain was near vertical, impossible to climb or walk. So, they were starting in groups, fanning out, working grids and blocks, crossing off the valley one section at a time.

Dempsey got out of the car, feeling the heat of the sun on her face already. She'd slathered herself with sunscreen, but she knew she'd still get burnt anyway. She was just that fair.

'Found it okay, then?' Pop asked, smiling a little.

'Yeah, not that there's any damn cell service out here,' Dempsey grumbled, readjusting her holster on her hip and approaching the group.

'Well, if you get lost, just head downhill,' Pop said, pointing into the trees off to the side of the track. 'All roads lead to home.'

'Noted,' Dempsey replied. 'What's the plan for this morning?'

Pop sighed, pointed to the map. 'We comb this area here, D3 through D5. It's about six square miles, steep terrain, thick brush. Easy to get sloughed out. If Sammy came through here—'

'Sloughed out?' Dempsey interrupted.

'Yeah, it's, uh, when the ground gives out under you on a steep slope. When it's dry like this, with the loamy soil up here, if you don't watch your footing, you can create a little cascade. A mini-landslide. Can sweep you off your feet, take you down. And these slopes can be three, six, seven hundred feet in places. That happens, you don't got much hope of slowing down.'

'And you think Sammy was out here walking around, and then got… "sloughed out"?'

Pop looked back at her apologetically. 'I don't know. But…' He dropped his voice, stepped away from the troopers acquainting themselves with the map from under their wide brimmed hats, and came closer. 'But Thomas Saint John is so far up my ass I can taste the brass of his class ring.'

'Nice image, Sheriff.'

'I'm just trying to do… something.' He ran his hand over his head, beads of sweat already glistening in his short hair. 'We got all these guys here for the search. And Thomas Saint John's not going to be happy until we've scoured this whole valley five times over.'

She looked at him, the beaten down look, the bags under his eyes. She thought he'd even lost weight. He was working like a dog, and she thought that Thomas Saint John wasn't liable to let up on him any time.

So instead of berating him, she nodded instead. 'Alright, Poplar,' she said. 'Just tell me where to go, and I'll be glad to help.' She didn't think that they were going to find Sammy out here either, but honestly, she wasn't sure where else to turn. Her investigations had turned up nothing. Sure, she had her suspicions. And Nicholas Pips did fit in the frame. He had motive – bucketloads of it. And he threatened the victim personally. There wasn't a person in Savage Ridge that would have wanted to see Sammy Saint John gone more than him. But the fact remained that Nicholas Pips couldn't be in two places at once and that his alibi was solid. And even if it could be disputed, he had no way of getting from the theatre to the Saint John house and back all inside two hours. It was five miles from point A to point B. And even if he could, what the hell would he do with Sammy Saint John?

Dempsey had questions, but no answers. And for the first time in her career, she wasn't sure she even wanted them. The deeper she dug, the worse it seemed to get. But she was trapped in Savage Ridge until the investigation fizzled – unable to find Sammy Saint John, and unable to use what she knew to do it. Thomas Saint John had threatened to end her career if she went anywhere near the truth that she thought was the key to all this. How he expected her to find Sammy when she was being hamstrung, she didn't know. So all she could do was run out the clock. Join the search she knew would yield no results.

She'd never disliked her job. Not until now.

Every current and retired Savage Ridge cop, fifty state troopers, and a handful of townspeople had all turned out to comb the woods. She'd honestly expected more of a show of public support for the effort. Though on reflection, it wasn't surprising. Either people didn't think he was going to be found in the forest, or they simply didn't care.

Perhaps this was just Sammy Saint John's ultimate revenge against his father. Perhaps he'd escaped this town and was going to start a new life somewhere else. And his final screw-you was wasting as much of his father's money as was humanly possible.

She didn't know if she took comfort in that idea, that he was still alive out there; or if she was disappointed that another rich kid had gotten away with something terrible and then gone on to live a guilt-free, gilded life. That he'd hurt an innocent girl and gotten away with it. Did she have a right to be disappointed? To be pissed off at the world?

Her duty was to justice.

But that didn't seem to exist in a place like this. Savage Ridge was beyond the reach of the civilised world. This was a place where money ruled, and the only law that existed was the law of the Saint Johns. Thomas Saint John had told her as much. So, whatever had happened to Sammy Saint John, she was happy to watch the old man bleed gold.

'Ready?' Pop asked, round-shouldered and exhausted.

Dempsey just nodded, walking unhurriedly after him as he went back to the hood of the car and rolled up the map.

Lunch came and went.

They walked the ground slowly, the crickets buzzing and clicking as they picked through the bed of pine needles, looking for any hint of disturbance or anything suspicious.

Pop had been right; the ground was liable to slough out. A few times Dempsey had caused a little cascade and watched a river of dried brush and loose earth make its way to the bottom of the slope, winding around trees coated in silver sap, dripping off round, smooth boulders and getting hung up on soft blankets of moss.

As another afternoon wore on, they headed back to their cars, ready to circle down to the next meeting point nearer the bottom of the valley.

As they reached the gate, sweaty and hungry, Pop called out.

'Hey,' he said, ducking under the metal bar and jogging the last few metres to catch up with Dempsey.

She turned to greet him.

'I just wanted to say that I'm sorry.'

'Sorry for what?'

'Sorry you got dragged into all this.'

She sighed. 'If it wasn't me, it would have been someone else.'

'No, I know,' Pop said, laughing a little. 'Thomas Saint John was never going to leave a case like this in *my* hands.'

She found that a little sad, but held her smile anyway.

'I just meant... I know he's not exactly the most personable man.'

'That's putting it mildly. *Very* mildly.'

'And I know how he talks to me. So, if you got the same treatment, I just... I'm sorry, alright? Savage Ridge is a nice place, and there are good people here. And it's really quite beautiful, if you give it a chance.' He turned to look out over the valley, hazed by the sun, languid in the summer heat.

She had to admit that he was right. Dempsey extended a hand slowly. 'You're a good man, Poplar. But I don't envy your position, beautiful scenery or not.'

He took it, shook firmly. 'I'm just trying to do what's right, whether Thomas Saint John lets me or not.'

She laughed a little now, allowing the handshake to fall. 'That's an uphill battle.'

'The only kind I know.'

Pop turned his SUV around and trundled down off the valley wall, leading them on a tour of the gravel tracks circling the town until the pulled into a big parking lot. There were more than two dozen cars there. A mix of local and state patrol cruisers, and a few civilian vehicles.

Dempsey pulled into a space and got out, spotting a sign at the far end that said 'Pend Oreille State Park'. Pictures of birds and a little trail map showed the various hiking loops that could be taken.

Dempsey cast her eyes around the bodies there, seeing both familiar and unfamiliar faces. But no sign of the people who had the most interest in finding Sammy. No Ellison and no Thomas Saint John. No Dickie Beaumont, either.

Her search of the crowd stopped when her eyes fell upon the three people she definitely didn't expect to see.

Nicholas Pips, Peter Sachs, and Emmy Nailer.

They stood at the far end, near to Pips' father's car. Dempsey knew the model and licence plate. They were just standing there, not really talking, or doing anything.

But why the hell would they be out here? They didn't have a vested interest in Sammy Saint John being found, surely? Or maybe they were out here solely because they knew he *wouldn't* be found.

Pop's heels crunched on the stones as he walked into the middle of the space and held his hands up. 'Everyone? Everyone?'

Dempsey turned her attention to the man in khaki. Polished black boots dusted with summer, his overly tight belt straining at his hips.

'I know it's been a long few weeks,' he announced as people began to file in. 'And I thank you all for your service. The initiative you've all shown and the time you've all taken away from your families hasn't gone unnoticed.'

Dempsey felt a pang. She'd not seen Simon in two weeks now, and he hadn't returned her phone calls in days. This case was taking a toll on everyone.

'But we're hopeful,' Pop went on. 'We've covered more than eighty per cent of the marked-out search area already. So, if there's anything to be found out here, we're close to finding it.' He clapped his hands together and wrung them like he'd just won an Olympic footrace. 'I'm sure you're all familiar with your maps by now. So, for this afternoon, we're going to push through zones F and G nine through eleven.' He glanced around the crowd. 'Metal detectors all charged? Dogs all fed? Everyone eaten lunch, got water? It's hot today, and I don't want to have to send out a second search party to find the guy who collapsed from the first search party, alright?'

A few chuckles rolled through the tired officers in front of him.

She had to admit, Pop had a certain way about him. People liked him, respected him, whether Thomas Saint John did or not. Dempsey didn't think the town could have been luckier with a sheriff.

When he'd finished, everyone slowly geared up and then headed out into the wilderness.

They pushed through the initial wall of trees and then fanned out into a wide line, stepping carefully through the under-growth. People probed with long rods, others swung metal detectors around, and the chains and tags around the necks of the dogs jangled and tinkled in the still air.

Dempsey held a position between two troopers, scanning for anything amiss on the ground in front of her. But there was nothing. Just the rustling of everyone else's footsteps, and the beads of sweat running from her armpits and down her ribs.

She'd left her jacket in the car, wearing just a shirt, a pair of jeans, and her walking boots. But still, she was hot and her mouth was dry.

They'd been walking almost an hour already, and though she didn't know how far they'd gone, she figured there was still a long way to go.

She slowed, paused, and leaned on a tree to catch her breath.

A trooper noticed and came over, offering his water bottle. The sun was bearing down through the canopy in bright shards, forcing her to squint at the guy. He was maybe six feet, young, with a square, stubbled jaw and moustache. He smiled at her, handsome and bright eyed, and she stared back, taking the water bottle. His shirt was rolled to the elbows, showing off tanned, muscular arms. As she pulled the lid off and drank, her eyes lingered there. She felt a pang of guilt, thinking of Simon. She'd been away for too long, had missed too much.

'Hot as hell, huh?' the trooper asked.

Dempsey lowered the bottle, nodded, and wiped off her chin with the back of her hand. 'You said it.'

'You think we're gonna find anything?' he asked, before taking a drink himself, pushing the rim of his hat up with his index finger as he raised the bottle.

Dempsey didn't know how to respond. 'Hard to say,' she said. 'All depends on what happened to him. We might be combing the forest for nothing. Honestly...' Her eyes found his in the shade of the tree. 'I think this is a wild goose chase. If there's one thing I'd put money on, it's that no one will ever find—'

A whistle cut the air. Dogs barked.

The troopers in the line paused, turned, and then began converging.

Someone yelled, 'They got a scent!'

The trooper righted his hat and took off and Dempsey turned, running after him.

They churned through the bed of pine needles until they reached the wall of brown shirts. Sweat stains outlined curved spines as everyone bent forward, panting and breathless.

People murmured, talking excitedly. The dogs chuffed and barked.

Dempsey stopped short of the clamour, catching her breath.

'What is it?' someone asked.

And then it appeared, raised into the air above the heads of the search party.

A shoe.

Dirtied, the laces loose, gummed up with leaves and other debris. But a shoe all the same. One that the dogs had led them to.

Sammy Saint John's shoe.

Pop held it aloft for everyone to see and then started barking orders. *Everyone watch their footing, form a circle, keep it right, fan out from here. One hundred paces, then report back if you find anything. If you do, don't trample it, don't—* she tuned him out, his voice fading to a distant din. Her attention was elsewhere as she searched the forest for her own prize.

Where were they...?

And then she spotted them. Nicholas Pips. Emmy Nailer. Peter Sachs.

They were standing off to the side, about thirty feet away, watching the search party, spirits renewed, formed up under Pop's command.

They watched carefully, wordlessly. Dempsey inspected their faces, their expressions. Nervous, but not the nerves of a group of kids about to get pegged for murder.

Whether he noticed her looking or he could just feel her eyes on him Dempsey didn't know, but slowly, Nicholas Pips turned to meet her gaze.

He did nothing. Said nothing. Just looked.

And in that moment, Dempsey knew. She was sure now of two things. More sure than she'd ever been of anything before in her life.

First: they'd never find Sammy Saint John's body.

And second: tomorrow morning, she was going home.

Night was closing around Savage Ridge like the wings of some great beast. It came quickly here. The sun sank behind the western mountains, bathing the town in twilight. That hung in the air for an hour or so, and then darkness just flooded through the town seemingly all at once.

The streetlights flickered to life as Dempsey drove through the last stretch of Main and out onto the highway that led to the Saint John estate. She had been mulling over how to deal with Thomas Saint John, figuring out the right words to say, knowing that the wrong ones would likely crush her career. But before she'd settled on the solution, Dickie Beaumont called her and ordered her to the Saint John house. Said that Thomas Saint John wanted a progress update. And no, it couldn't wait until morning. Non-negotiable. *Get your ass in the car.*

She figured they were watching on the cameras as she approached because the wrought iron gates emblazoned with the Saint Johns' initials opened to accept her as she neared, no buzzer needed.

Dempsey crunched up the driveway and pulled in behind Beaumont's patrol car, killing the engine. The man himself opened the front door, pudgy and sour-faced.

'Beaumont,' Dempsey said, walking up the steps tiredly. Her legs were aching from a long day of trudging around the woods. And since they found that shoe, the effort had been almost too much. Especially because she knew they were running a fool's errand.

'He wants to see you,' Beaumont replied, pressing himself against the frame to let her pass.

Despite the door's grand size, she still felt like she needed to squeeze past him to get inside. 'I got that from your phone call,' she muttered, entering and stretching her back.

Beaumont closed the door and led the way to the study without another word.

Dempsey felt strangely nervous following the sidling man in front of her. Beaumont's laboured breathing cut the silence of the hallway while cautious eyes watched from doorways of polished wood. House staff, looking on as Dempsey headed towards her fate. She couldn't help but feel like someone being led to the gallows. She just wondered if it would be the noose or guillotine. She preferred the quick and painless option, but none of her interactions with Thomas Saint John had been close to that so far, so she thought she'd likely just hang instead.

When Beaumont knocked and entered, Thomas Saint John was sitting behind his sprawling desk, leaning backwards in his leather armchair, hands laced across his stomach, thumbs gently batting against each other, bottom lip out, eyes fixed on the muddied Converse sneaker on the surface in front of him.

Dempsey stopped in front of him and waited.

'What the hell is this?' he asked, voice low, acerbic.

Dempsey felt her body tense a little. 'It looks to be a shoe.'

His eyes flashed upwards, setting her skin alight with goose-flesh. 'Don't be insolent with me,' he growled.

She swallowed, steeling herself.

'Where the hell is my son?'

'I don't know,' she answered plainly.

'Two weeks you've been here, and the only thing you have to show for it is a shoe? A fucking *shoe*?' He leaned forward suddenly, snatching it off the desk and hurling it at her.

She ducked quickly, the shoe bouncing off the wall behind her. A few glass ornaments on the bookshelf next to it rattled slightly, but she didn't turn around to look.

Feeling her heart thrum in her neck she took a breath, straightened, brushed flecks of dirt from her jacket.

Thomas Saint John was propped up awkwardly on his desk, weight on one arm, like a man trying to drag himself out of a grave. 'He's dead,' he breathed. 'You think I don't know that?'

Dempsey stayed quiet.

'Nicholas Pips. Arrest him. Tonight. Charge him with murder. And I'm not asking.'

She thought if she spoke right away, her voice would crack. She took a moment. 'I can't.'

'Why not?'

She met Thomas Saint John's eyes now. 'Because… because there are pieces of the puzzle still missing.'

'Puzzle? You think this is a fucking game?'

223

'No, I don't. But Nicholas Pips has an alibi, and if you want me to arrest him then things will come out that I know you want to stay buried.'

'Is that a threat?'

'I expect a man like you knows when he's being threatened.' Dempsey stepped forward so she was looking down at Thomas Saint John. 'I'm simply stating the truth. If you want Pips arrested and charged without question, ask your lapdog here.' She didn't need to gesture to Beaumont for Thomas Saint John to know who she meant. 'But if you want it done right, and you want it to stick, then the whole story needs to come out. It gives Pips motive. The motive you need to get a conviction.'

'And what is the *whole* story?' He sat upright, watching her closely.

'The whole story is the girl.'

Thomas Saint John's mouth contorted and then tightened. 'Out of the question. That mess is done with. Finished. Find another way.'

'I can't,' Dempsey answered firmly. 'You want me to pull on this thread, then the whole thing unravels. And if we even made it to trial without it coming out, and they put Pips on the stand, you think he's not going to spill the truth? The truth of what Sammy did? And how is that going to look in front of a jury? You think they'll side with Sammy then? You think they'll rule guilty when they know the truth? No, the only chance you have is to let me do my job, and lay it all out there. If you want Pips arrested, that's how it has to be. There's no other way.'

Thomas Saint John's jaw quivered.

'I'll make it simple for you: if you don't out what Sammy did, then Pips walks for Sammy's murder. It's his motive, and it's enough to make an arrest stick. Without it there's no chance, and I won't be the one to try. I don't look the other way. I won't. Not on something like this.'

'It can't.' Thomas Saint John looked away, shook his head. 'If people found out, then—'

'Then you need to decide,' Dempsey said, not a hint of pity in her as she finally saw the decision that Thomas Saint John was reckoning with. 'What's more important? The Saint John name, or putting the kid who murdered your son behind bars?'

His silence was all the answer she needed.

NOW

Chapter 32

Nicholas Pips

When I woke up, Pete was staring at me.

I sat up on the couch in his basement and rubbed my eyes. The number of nights I'd spent on this thing as a kid. Hell, it even smelled the same.

We had gotten back late last night after the incident at Sammy's grave, dropped Emmy off and sat outside her house for an hour to make sure she was asleep. Then we'd come back here. I hadn't wanted to wake my parents, so I crashed at Pete's. I practically lived here my teenage years anyway, it was no big deal. He'd sat in the chair across the old rug and we'd talked about nothing. Definitely not about what had happened. I guess I must have drifted off, because now it was light. Pete had changed clothes, and I expected he'd gone up to bed at some point as he looked fresher than I felt. I didn't know what time I'd fallen asleep, or how much sleep I'd got. Not much by the way my head was feeling.

'Get up,' he said.

'What, no coffee and eggs?' I asked, pulling myself upright with a groan.

Pete reached out and swung my legs off the couch, spinning me into a sitting position. He stayed leaned forward, elbows on his knees, looking into space.

'What time is it?' My mouth was dry, my stomach aching.

'Early,' was all he offered.

By the angle of the sun coming in through the window, I didn't disbelieve him. The air down there was close, the basement half storage room and half den. There was an old couch, two recliner armchairs, a TV from the Nineties we used to play Nintendo on, a coffee table that we used to play boardgames on, a rug we used to sit on without a care in the world. I wondered now if the stains all over it were us or if they were always there. I never noticed before.

'We have to do something,' Pete said then.

'Well, that's not ominous at all,' I muttered, sighing and rubbing the back of my neck, trying to crack it.

'I'm serious, Nick,' he said, eyes wild and cold. He turned them on me and I all but shuddered.

'Jesus, okay,' I said, taking more notice all of a sudden. 'What are we talking about here, Pete? I know last night was—'

'Last night was enough to tell me we have a serious problem. With Emmy.'

I didn't like where this was going. 'Okay, so she freaked out – not surprising considering what happened, right? What we did? But hell, Pete, we just shove her on a plane out, and then we're good.'

'No, we're not, Nick,' he said, shaking his head. 'Sloane Yo – I looked her up.'

'When?'

'Last night.'

'Didn't you sleep?'

'How could I?' Those eyes again.

'Okay, let's talk about this, think it through.'

'Sloane Yo used to be Detroit PD, a detective there. A few years ago, she got booted off the force. She got into an accident, with her kid in the car.'

'Shit,' I muttered, finally getting my neck to crack. It didn't help.

'Driving under the influence – there was a piece in the paper about it. They said she'd been working an undercover case, got addicted to drugs, then this happened.'

'Fuck,' I said, mostly to myself, recalling how she'd been in the liquor store.

'And now she's here, working as a PI,' Pete went on. 'And you know what all that tells me?' I just shook my head. 'It tells me she's got nothing to lose. Her kid's not with her, right? Which means she doesn't have custody.'

'We don't know she doesn't have her kid with her.'

'You think she dragged her daughter out here to Savage?'

I stayed quiet.

'And we know she's been messing with us, did some shady shit to get us here, right? So, she's not afraid of breaking some laws.' He exhaled, started bouncing his knees. 'While Emmy's here, at least we can play defence, be a buffer between them. But if we put Emmy on a plane, Yo will just track her down, get at her without us there. Us shipping her off will be all the confirmation Yo needs to drop the hammer on her. And if that happens, we're all screwed.' He looked up at me, knees falling still.

Now I really didn't like where this was going. 'You wanna grab some breakfast?' I asked, reaching forward and slapping him on the shoulder. 'Come on, I'll treat you. Diner must be open now and I could do with some coffee—'

'Sit down, Nick,' he said, grabbing my arm. He didn't pull but his grip was tight.

I sank back onto the couch, watched him carefully. 'You're going to have to say exactly what you mean here, Pete, because I *really* hope you're not saying what I think you are.'

His eyes glazed over, the words coming slowly. 'We need to… *take care* of Emmy.'

I swallowed, trying to work out if he'd really said that or if my brain was just stuttering.

'We could do it,' he said then, looking at me. 'We did it before.'

'No, Pete,' I said, lowering my voice, speaking slowly, 'we got rid of a kid who didn't deserve to be here anymore. We all agreed on that. Sammy had to go. But this is… this is *Emmy* we're talking about. Our Emmy.' I couldn't believe we were even having his conversation.

'I know, I know, Nick,' he said, shaking his head. 'But I've gone over this and over this. We don't have another choice.'

'We do, Pete – and it's *not* killing our best friend.'

'Best friend?' he scoffed. 'We haven't spoken to her in ten fucking years!'

'We haven't spoken to each other in ten years, Pete. You gonna kill me too?'

He stared at me and I was instantly sorry I asked.

'No,' he said then, 'I'd never do that to you. But then I wouldn't have to. Because we can trust each other, can't we, Nick? You remember what we said, don't you – that we take this to our graves?'

The look in his eye was making my spine feel stiff, my heart beat harder than usual.

'We just never said,' he went on, shrugging, 'when that would be.'

'And then what, huh? You want to kill the investigator too?'

'If we have to.'

I shook my head. 'We're not having this conversation, Pete, alright? We're not killing anyone.'

'We may not have a choice, Nick. What if Emmy decides to come clean? What if Sloane Yo had picked her up last night instead of us? What if Emmy opens her mouth, tells the truth?' He was on his feet now.

I set my jaw. 'Then we deal with it. It's her word against ours.'

'And if she tells them where the body is?' Pete turned to face me.

'Then… then they'll have no DNA, and our alibis are still airtight.'

'Not if Emmy tells them what really happened. Where we really were.'

I felt my jaw begin to throb under the pressure. 'Jesus, Pete. Fuck! Fuck you!' I got up, walked in a circle, racking my brains. 'Let me talk to Emmy first, okay? See what she's thinking, where her head is at. We still have time. It's not too late. We can fix this.'

'Not too late? After last night? You think she's going to want to speak to either of us? No, if she's going to talk to anyone, it'll be the police. Or that investigator. And if she does, we're fucked. You get that? Fucked. Not like we'll be in trouble, like *fucked* fucked. Like go to prison for murder, and get fucking stabbed with a toothbrush and raped in the showers for the next twenty years. Is that what you want?'

There was silence between us.

'I won't let that happen, Nick. I won't. And if I'm going to do this, you're going to help me.'

My head was shaking but I had no words.

'It'll be easy,' he said then. 'Emmy's not okay, right? She's screwed up. So, all we gotta do is get her drunk, then give her a little nudge.'

'A nudge? What are you talking about, Pete?'

'She wants to go out to the woods, across the river on the old bridge… It's dark, that thing is ancient now – slippery boards, rusted rails… Hell, if it doesn't give out under her, maybe she slips. Maybe she jumps. Who can say for sure? When her body washes up ten miles downstream, blood more booze than anything else, what are people going to think?'

'Probably that we fucking killed her,' I spat. 'Just shut up, Pete. Just shut up, okay? Please. I don't want to have this conversation anymore. We're okay. Let me just talk to Emmy. I'll keep her safe, won't let her out of my sight. I promise. Sloane Yo won't get anywhere near her.'

'And if she comes for you instead?' Pete's hands had closed into fists at his sides.

'Then I'll deal with that when it happens. But she won't. She won't find us. We know Savage like the back of our hands

233

– we'll just run out the clock. Eventually, she'll get bored, the Saint Johns will lose faith in her, or they'll stop the investigation when she starts looking at them, which, if she's as good as you think she is, she will. And you know what she'll find. And then all this will be over.'

He lifted his chin slowly. 'You don't really believe that.'

'I have to, Pete,' I said. 'Because the alternative isn't worth considering.' I made for the stairs then.

'Nick,' Pete said.

I paused, closed my eyes, then looked over my shoulder at him.

'I know you don't want to accept it.' He sat again, faced the other way, knees starting to bounce, hands clasped and kneading in front of him. 'But this is the reality of things now. I'm not going to prison for killing Sammy Saint John.'

'So, you'll kill again to stop that from happening. You don't see the irony in that?'

'I'm not looking for irony,' he said, voice as strange to me as someone I'd never known, 'I'm looking to get out alive.' He turned his head, looked at me. My knees nearly gave out. 'And if you want to do the same,' he said, 'you'd better accept that as the only truth there is. Nothing else matters now, Nick. Nothing. It's either you and me… or it's just me.'

I went straight to Emmy's from Pete's house. Pretty much ran the whole way.

When I turned onto her street, the reality of things dawned on me. Had Pete really just told me he was going to kill Emmy? And Sloane Yo? And… me, if I didn't help him? *No, no, that's stupid. Come on, this is Pete*, I told myself. Little Peter Sachs, the kid who used to cry in gym when he couldn't climb the rope. The kid who'd sit at the front of the class so he could hear the teacher better. And now he was, what, talking about a double murder? Triple murder?

I shook it off and climbed Emmy's steps, knocked on her door.

Mrs Nailer answered, smiled weakly. 'Nicky,' she said, sighing as she did. 'I'm so glad you're here.'

'Why? Is everything alright?'

She rolled her lips into a line, shook her head. 'It's Emmy.'

'What's wrong, is she okay?'

'She came in late last night, curled up on the sofa, hasn't said a word since. She's just lying there, staring into space, won't speak, won't eat. I was just about to call the doctor and—'

'No!' I practically yelled. 'I mean, you don't have to do that. We were with her last night, Pete and me – I... I know what's eating her. Lemme see if I can't get her talking, alright?'

She watched me for a second, then nodded. 'Okay,' she said. 'Come on in. Can I fix you some breakfast?'

'I'd never say no,' I offered sheepishly. I was actually starving and the last thing I'd had in my stomach was beer and that was going on twelve hours ago now.

I stepped inside the same tired living room I'd stood in the day before, and clocked Emmy right away. She was lying on the sofa on her side, holding a cushion to her stomach, clutching it with both elbows and both knees, eyes wide and vacant. Checked out.

I approached slowly, boots rustling on the Aztec-style rug. All reds and oranges and yellows. It clashed horribly with the sage-green velveteen couch, complete with tassels and buttons.

I knelt, tried to catch Emmy's eye, but she wouldn't look up.

'Hey,' I said softly, getting down onto my hip on the floor and then sitting properly. 'Em?'

She looked right through me.

'Look, I know last night was messed up,' I whispered, keeping an ear on the clanging pans in the kitchen. 'But... Okay, Pete's *not* right. I'm not saying that, I'm not. But when you disappeared?' She looked at me. I shivered. There was nothingness in her eyes. A vast, yawning chasm of cold. 'We thought it was over. We thought that investigator had gotten to you, and—'

'And what?' she muttered, eyes searching my face.

'And I thought we were all going down for Sammy Saint John.' I sighed. 'You can't tell me you think it's worth it? That *he's* worth it? After what he did? I know you're feeling guilty...'

'It's not guilt,' she said then, closing her eyes. 'I don't know what it is. But it's not guilt. He deserved to die. And I'm glad he is. I'm sorry I'm not the one who hit him with that fucking shovel. I'm sorry I'm not the one who caved his skull in. I wish I had been.' Her eyes opened, full with tears.

I didn't. I'd never wish that on anyone.

'What's tearing me up is that no one knows the truth. No one knows why. That his death wasn't *justice*. That there are people out there trying to prove that we're the bad guys in this. That we didn't do the world a huge goddamn favour getting rid of that rat. That there's a chance we could go to jail for it, while he's remembered as a *victim*.'

I didn't think I'd heard anyone say a word with so much venom in all my life.

I looked down then and realised my hand was on hers, that I was clutching it, that she was squeezing back. 'Em, I need to know.'

'Know what, Nicky?'

'I need to know if you're going to say anything to that private investigator, or to anyone. Pete's worried.'

'Are you?'

I didn't answer.

She scoffed a little. 'I don't want to tell the truth because I can't live with it. I want to tell the truth so that everyone knows exactly what happened. I can't forget it. Any of it. And coming back here, it's all just too—'

'Breakfast!' Cynthia Nailer walked into the living room with two plates of eggs, bacon, and toast.

Steam trailed from the food and my stomach twinged.

I stood up and accepted both plates, then offered one to Emmy, high enough that she'd have to at least sit up before she could take it. She seemed to consider it for a while but then she did, and gave me a little nod.

I sat next to her so she couldn't lie down again, and we both began to eat in silence. It felt wrong to say anything in anyone else's presence.

'Well,' Mrs Nailer said awkwardly after a few seconds, 'I'll leave you two to, uh, catch up.' She clasped her hands. 'Say bye before you go Nicky, just in case I don't see you for another ten years.'

I smiled, mouth full of bacon, and nodded. If all this went sideways, it'd probably be more like twenty-five to life.

She left.

'You know,' Emmy said slowly, eating even slower, 'there's no statute of limitations for killing someone.' She crunched some blackened toast.

'No,' I said, grinning. 'There isn't.'

'What's so funny?'

I shrugged. 'I looked into it, too.' I met her eye. 'You think I want to carry this around forever?' I shook my head. 'I don't, but I still want to live my life. If we got caught, if one of us came clean, I wouldn't stick around for it.' She stared at the side of my face. 'I was thinking about it last night – what I'd do, you know? If that investigator had gotten to you.'

'You have a plan?'

'You don't?' I stared at her, our faces no more than a foot from each other. She'd been so beautiful when she was younger – hell, she wasn't even thirty yet. But she'd been punishing herself. Mentally, emotionally, physically. She looked older than her years.

'I just want to hear yours.'

I chuckled a little. 'So long as you don't steal it.'

'Cross my heart,' she said, drawing her finger in an X across the faded sweater she was wearing.

I stared down at the food on my lap. 'A neighbour back home – in Oregon – he's got a storage unit on the 84. Big thing, just off the highway. He gets out to Flathead, Kootenai Forest – hunts, camps, that kind of thing. He's got a truck in there prepped for over-landing, a sled too, fishing gear, rifles, tents, all that kind of shit. It's too big to use around Portland, so he drives out there every week or two, takes the thing out for the weekend. Been with him a few times. Not really my scene, but I thought it'd be good to know how to fish, hunt, survive, I guess. The thing is locked up, of course, but it's a combo and I know the code.'

She watched me as I spoke.

'I rented a unit in the same place – a smaller one. It's stocked with food, water, clothes, gas, some cash I scraped together.' I shrugged. 'If I thought things were going to shit, I'd head out there, take his truck, load it up with everything from my unit, and...' I made a rocket motion with my hand. 'Straight up the 84 to Hermiston, jump on the 82 to Kennewick, take the 395 to Ritzville, hit the 90. At Spokane, you got two choices, either the 2, the 211, the 20, then the 31 all the way to Nelway. Or you take the 395 through Chewelah, cross the Columbia, and then head for Laurier. That'd be quicker, but if there's a nationwide APB out, there's more chance they'd be patrolling it. Laurier's also a bigger border crossing. More border officers.

'Nelway's quieter, wilder country out there, tougher terrain – you could get lost for a few days, probably even sneak across the border on a forest service road if you had to. Doubt they'd have much luck tracking you. Then, just find a road, and head north. There're a few ways, a couple highways, lots of back roads and logging tracks. It'd be impossible for them to catch me – especially in that truck.' I laughed a little. 'Once you get north of Banff Park, up towards Jasper you can take the 16 east or west. Head for Prince George or Edmonton. Then the world is yours. British Colombia, Alberta, on to the Northwest Territories, the Yukon, Alaska. Hell, if things are real bad, it's a big world, lots of places to get lost for good.'

She swallowed, cleared her throat a little. 'That's, uh… you sound like you've got it all worked out.'

'Something like that.' I shook my head, looked down at my food, didn't feel hungry all of a sudden. 'I just, I dunno. The first few years, I was scared, but I felt like planning anything was tempting fate. Now I just think it's smart. You never know, you know?'

She nodded, didn't speak.

'I figure, if that ever happened, I'd find a little cabin or something in the middle of nowhere, work locally for cash, rent for cash, use a different name, keep my head down, hope no one comes looking.'

'And that's a life?' she asked, voice subdued and quiet. She was pushing her eggs around her plate.

'Better than prison.'

'Just sounds like a different kind.'

'And you got a better plan?'

She shrugged now. 'Hop a bus south, hope to cross the border into Mexico before they know I'm even gone.'

'You know anyone down there?'

She shook her head.

'Any cash saved up?'

Another shake.

'Anywhere lined up to stay, to work?'

She didn't bother shaking her head this time but it wasn't a yes either.

I sighed, leaned in, nudged her with my shoulder. 'Good thing the truck has a passenger seat then.'

She looked up, eyes questioning.

'Come on, it'd be an adventure. I know I'd rather not do it alone. The Yukon is cold as hell, I hear.'

She laughed a little. 'Shut up.'

'I'm serious,' I said. 'If it all went to shit and that's all there was, I'd want you with me.'

Her lip quivered a little.

239

'Of course, you'd have to come to me. Arizona is a bit out of the way to just swing by and pick you up, you know?' I gave her a smile. She tried to give one back.

'You're serious?'

I nodded.

'You don't even know me – not anymore.'

'Em,' I said, nudging her again. 'I know I haven't changed in ten years, and looking around here, talking like this—' I gestured around with my fork '—feels just like old times. So, I think we'll be okay. We used to get on, didn't we?'

She thought about that, then nodded once.

'Right, so as long as you don't mind taking the bottom bunk, I think we're good.'

'You're envisioning bunk beds?' She raised an eyebrow, laughed a little more. It felt good to hear.

'Honestly, I'm envisioning a tent in the woods, with us huddled in a sleeping bag freezing our nuts off, hoping a bear doesn't come and eat us.'

'I think I'll stick with Mexico.'

'Whatever you say, Em,' I chuckled, throwing back a little more food. My throat didn't seem to want to work.

She kept watching me, then asked, 'Why wait?'

I paused chewing, looked at her.

'Why wait?' she said again. 'This fucking place, this town… why don't we just head down, take the truck, everything… go now? Just… escape. While we can.'

'To the Yukon?'

'To wherever!' she said, voice growing again. 'Why wait for it to all go to shit while we can run away now? Let's just go, Nick – let's go. The two of us. While we can.'

'You're serious?'

She nodded, searching my face.

'Em…' I said, looking down. 'We can't just—'

'Why not?'

'Because… because we've done nothing wrong.' I met her eye now. 'We're innocent, remember? We were at the movies, and that's it. We've got no need to run. And if we do, we'll just be truck thieves in the Yukon with frostbitten toes.'

'But we'd be free.'

'We're free now,' I said, reaching for her hand again.

She pulled it away. 'Do you feel free, Nick? Because I don't. And I can't remember a time when I did. When I heard sirens in the distance and didn't run to the window and peek through the blinds. When I didn't see a cop and turn my head away. When I didn't get a phone call and think: Shit, is this it? Is this finally it? Has it finally caught up with me?'

'And you think you wouldn't feel that if we ran away?'

'At least we'd have each other.'

'I'm right here,' I said, going for her hand again. She let me take it, but didn't squeeze back. 'We have each other.'

She turned her head slowly, the vacancy returning to her eyes. 'Yeah, and where were you the last ten years, Nick?' Then she pulled her hand back, stood up, and walked into the kitchen.

The plate clattered into the sink.

She didn't come back.

And I just sat there, pushing the last of my eggs in slow circles, thinking about it.

Six, seven, four, three.

Four numbers that would unlock that unit, that would set us free and seal our fate forever.

But if we ran, would anyone chase us?

Would Sloane Yo track us down? Would Ellison Saint John?

I remember the words clearly: innocent people don't run.

And that's what we were, right?

Innocent.

I swallowed, felt like hurling the plate into the wall.

Innocent.

I fucking hated that word.

Chapter 33

Sloane Yo

Sloane would give it until two in the afternoon, then head back to see Beaumont.

She'd been sleeping like shit, eating like shit, and she needed to get her mind right. For herself, and for her daughter.

As such, after she saw Beaumont that morning and he'd told her to come back later, she had headed back to the motel, thrown on her gear and squeezed in a quick run. It always gave her time and space to think.

Sloane had taken a trail out of town that climbed up into the hills, and when she'd reached the top, exhausted and drenched in sweat, she'd stopped and tried to reach her mother.

She called four times before her mom picked up. 'What, Sloane?' she asked flatly.

'Hey, I was just checking in…'

'Checking in?' Her mom scoffed a little. 'Jesus, Sloane, is that what you think this is all about? You need to be here.'

'I'm working,' was all she could say.

'You were working when you started using heroin. You were working when you started taking vodka in your morning coffee. You were working when you wrapped your car around that—'

'I gotta go,' Sloane said suddenly. 'Something came up, I'll call back later.'

She hung up before her mom could twist the knife even further, and then let her phone slip from her grasp into the dried grass between her feet.

Sloane stared down at Savage Ridge from the overlook. The town seemed almost asleep, bathed in the summer haze, the still air lying heavily on top of it. Her mouth was salivating so hard that drool began to drip from her lips. Usually she swallowed it, but letting it fall felt disgusting. And she was disgusting. She wanted to remind herself of that. She was an addict, and an alcoholic, and one tough phone call was enough to make her skin itch, and for strings of saliva to pour from her lips in anticipation of a fix.

She hung her tongue out, watching the translucent liquid bead and fall to the ground, forming a dark spot on the earth beneath her.

Her fists closed, then flexed, and she threw her head back, letting out a guttural scream that sprayed flecks into the air and down off the cliff in front of her. She gripped at her hair, taking handfuls and pulling until her scalp hurt.

When her lungs had emptied and closed up, aching and folded, the noise died. But her silent scream sustained until the blood rushed in her ears and the lack of oxygen getting to her brain made her snap back to reality.

Sloane collapsed forward onto her knees, panting, her eyes wet with tears. Jesus, she hadn't done that in so long.

She took a breath, then clapped her ears with her knees, banging the sides of her patellas against the crown of her head.

Again.

Again. You piece of shit.

Again!

The pain blinded her, centred her, focused her.

Breathe slow. Think slow.

Sloane closed her lips, moved the spittle around until it pooled on her tongue, and then spat it onto the ground and pushed herself to a shaky stance.

Savage Ridge waited below. And once this case was done, she was going to see her daughter. Regardless of how much she hated her mother, she'd be there for Zoe. That much she promised herself.

As she started back down the hill, slick with sweat and shame, her mind drifted and eventually came back to the case, to Beaumont.

What did she know so far? That Sammy Saint John had been causing his father some serious issues – legal issues, by the sounds of it. That something big had happened that needed to be swept under the rug. That needed to be handled.

Did that involve Emmy Nailer? She needed to speak to Emmy. Alone. But that didn't seem to be happening any time soon. Not the way Pips and Sachs were cloistered around her.

After Sloane got back to the motel, she cleaned up, and then cruised by Emmy's. Peter Sachs was parked up the street in his Mercedes. Keeping watch, perhaps. She had no doubt that if she got out and made for the front door, he'd intercept her. And he, by now, had no doubt worked out that she'd used a little bit of gentle manipulation to get the three of them back in town. And Pete had the most to lose if her investigation came to anything.

She didn't want to push him, make them close ranks any harder.

Sloane had parked a block over, walked back with her monocular, checked out the Nailer house from the corner. Nicholas Pips was inside. They were talking a bit. She didn't know what about. But it struck her as odd that Pete was outside and Nick was inside. Maybe they'd divided their efforts to make sure Sloane couldn't get at Emmy.

She lowered the monocular and thought on that.

If they were protecting Emmy, that meant that they thought she might talk. And why would they need to stop her from talking if she didn't have something to say that would impact the investigation?

Sloane drew a slow breath, resisted the urge to march across the road and ask her point blank. What did Sammy Saint John do to you? But she had to bide her time. If Beaumont had spoken to his lawyer, she hoped he'd come clean, tell her the missing parts of the story she was trying to piece together. Then, once she knew what Sammy had done, she could look Emmy square in the eye and lay it all out. All she would need then would be a simple nod of the head.

And that would be enough.

Sloane left them for now, backtracked to the truck, and then headed for Beaumont's.

She pulled the Ford to a stop outside his house on Pinewood Drive and disembarked, stepping down onto the quiet street.

Nothing moved.

Sloane walked up. Car still on the drive. That was a good sign. He hadn't blown out of town in a cloud of tyre smoke then, and she thought that was something.

Sloane knocked loudly, didn't bother waiting before she called through the wood. 'Mr Beaumont, it's Sloane Yo, the investigator looking into the Sammy Saint John case. You told me to come back – I hope this is a good time.'

No answer.

She knocked again. 'Mr Beaumont?' Louder this time.

Sloane sighed, stepped back, peered through the window to the side of the door. Blinds drawn.

She opened the fly stopper and tried the handle. Locked. Shit.

This wasn't good.

Sloane jumped down off the porch and circled the house, hopping the low gate and moving down the side path in the hopes that Beaumont was just at the back of the house.

She approached the back door, the kitchen visible through the window, set up in a lean-to style extension off the main house. She knocked again. No response.

'Mr Beaumont?'

Sloane cupped her hands on the glass panel in the middle of the door and stared into the darkened interior, trying to pick out some details.

The kitchen door was closed to the rest of the house. She couldn't see shit.

How sure was she he was inside? Fifty-fifty?

Sloane looked up then, saw that one of the upper floor windows was open. The second floor appeared to be in the truss of the roof, with a single window under the apex looking out over the backyard. It was ajar, an old wooden sash window she could slide up.

Could she get up onto the roof?

She bit her lip, then decided. If he was inside, she'd find him and get some answers out of him – like why the hell he wasn't opening the door, and what Thomas Saint John had covered up. If he wasn't, then she'd poke around a little, see what she could find.

Sloane checked the neighbouring houses for signs of life, found none, and then went back to the side passage.

Next door had a chain-link fence with a metal rod at the top. It was five feet high, but close enough to their house to steady herself she hoped. From there, she might be able to jump to the roof, pull herself up.

She didn't really have any other options and she wasn't about to let this lead expire. Beaumont knew something and she was going to find out what. Hiding in his house wasn't going to help him. Not today.

Sloane took the fence in her hand, pulled herself up so she was supporting her weight on her hands, and then swung her leg up. She pushed to a stance, wobbled, and then reached out, touching the eave on the next house. She had her fingers outstretched to keep herself above the fence, and then turned carefully. She lined the jump up, let go of the neighbouring house, and sprung forward.

The fence waned as she leapt and she came up short, her elbows connecting with the rough shingles. Sloane grunted, legs swinging. Her toes hit the wooden panelling on the side of the kitchen and she scrambled for purchase, hauling herself up, the moss that had built up on the roof coming away under her grip.

She managed to swing her leg over and then rolled onto her back, dirty and panting. 'Jesus,' she muttered, putting her hands on her stomach and catching her breath.

She stared into the pine canopy that surrounded the house, watched the clouds move above them, and then became distinctly aware of the quiet that seemed to have a stranglehold on the street.

Sloane sat up, suddenly uneasy, and then, without wasting any more time, she made for the window, slid it up, and climbed into Dickie Beaumont's bedroom.

Chapter 34

Nicholas Pips

I stepped down from Emmy's porch feeling both reassured and terrified. A part of me wanted to do it, to agree, to get out of there. To run. But I was right, we had nothing to run from. We were innocent in the eyes of the law. And to drop off the face of the earth now would be crazy. Never see our families again, and for what? To freeze in the northern reaches of Canada? To kick back on a Mexican beach, live in a little cabin, sip beers and watch the sunset, and… shit, that did sound pretty good, actually.

'Nick.'

I picked my head up, saw Pete coming towards me, the bags under his eyes chiselled deeply into his cheeks.

I felt guilty suddenly. 'Hey, Pete,' I said. 'I was just—'

'Shut up,' he growled, taking my arm and leading me back up the street towards his car.

I cast a glance back at Emmy's house, thought that whatever he was about to say was probably best done out of earshot of her.

He stopped short of his bumper. I wasn't sure if he'd followed me to Emmy's or just came here to intercept Sloane Yo if she decided to appear. But either way, he'd staked the place out just far enough up not to be seen from the window. But close enough not to miss a thing.

He didn't seem angry though, not anymore. He seemed wired.

'Tonight,' he announced, nodding. His voice was hushed, but forceful.

'Tonight?' I was afraid to ask.

'Yeah,' he said, his nodding become more frantic. 'First, we deal with Emmy. Then the PI.'

'You can't be serious.' I blinked at him.

But he wasn't stopping. 'I'll pick you up, we'll pick Emmy up, we'll go to Rock's and get drunk, make sure everyone sees us, and then—'

'No, Pete,' I said, strangely breathless. 'We're not doing this. It's Emmy. *Emmy!*'

'I know, Nicky, but it has to be—'

'The fuck it does!'

'Keep your voice down.' His words were ice.

I took a breath. 'This is Emmy. We grew up together, spent a million hours at her house. She was your first kiss. She was... she *is*... we both had a crush on her, remember? But we made a pact, you and me, said neither of us would ask her out.' I reached out and squeezed his shoulder. 'So we wouldn't ruin our friendship. Do you remember that?'

'It's been ten years, Nicky,' he said coldly. 'We're not friends anymore. Not for a long time.' He shrugged my hand off. 'Eight o'clock. Be ready.' He turned towards the car.

I clenched my jaw, mind racing. 'Do this...' I started, the words coming on their own. 'Do this and...'

He paused, looked back. 'And what, Nicky?'

'And...' My voice was quaking, hands in fists at my sides. 'And I'll go to the cops.'

He was perfectly still.

'I will.' I tried to sound firmer, not sure if I got there. 'I'll tell them everything.'

'You'd send us all to prison for Sammy Saint John?'

'I would for Emmy.'

He set his jaw, eyes fixed on me. 'Think she'd do the same for you?'

I swallowed. 'It doesn't matter.'

He seemed to linger then, as though unsure whether to speak or leave. And then all at once he was sweeping towards me. I took a step back, but he didn't stop until his face was close enough to mine that I could see the inflamed veins bulging red around his irises. 'You're weak,' he whispered. 'You've always been weak.'

I was paralysed.

He looked me up and down, his face contorting in anger, then in sadness, so intense it looked like he was going to cry. Then, something like disgust rooted itself there. 'I wish it was me.'

'You wish *what* was you?' I squeezed out.

'I wish I was the one that grabbed that shovel.'

There was a pang of pain in my throat. As much as I hated the man standing in front of me at that moment, that's not something I'd wish on anyone. 'No, you don't.'

'I do,' he said again. 'I do. Because you're weak, Nick. And all these years, all these years you made me feel weak, too, for not doing it. You made me feel pathetic because you had to be the brave one. But you're not brave. You never were. You needed me to feel like nothing so you could be *something*. And you've been riding on that the last ten fucking years, making nothing of yourself.' His lips quivered. 'You swung that shovel because you needed an out and you knew deep down that that was all your life was ever going to be. Everything you ever did that mattered happened on that day. And even now, you're hiding behind it. Don't you see that, Nick?'

'Pete...' was all I managed.

'But it doesn't have to be, Nick. You can still do something with your life. It doesn't have to define you. But you can't do that if we get caught. And we can't get caught. We can't. So, do this with me. Do this with me, Nick. Be brave again.'

I searched his face for any hint that he was joking. Just making some sick joke. But I didn't see any. And then the rage came, like a river bursting a dam and raging down. 'You've got no fucking clue.' I stepped forward now, regaining my balance, my voice. 'You've got no fucking clue what it's like to kill someone.'

His face was stone.

'You think I'm using it as an excuse? You've got it backwards. That's you. You were so fucking scared that day. The only reason I picked up that shovel was the look in *your* fucking eyes. One more second and I knew you'd go running straight to Pop. So don't tell me that *you* had the guts, that you wanted it then and you want it now. Because you don't know what it's like, and, fuck, Pete, I hope you never do. You can't take it back. Ever. You can't. No matter what.' My voice was shaking now. 'And don't be naïve enough to think you can. Please. Don't.'

He remained perfectly still for what seemed like a long time. And then he looked down, a thin smile breaking across his lips. He lifted a hand slowly and I flinched. He rested it on my shoulder and squeezed, seemingly unable to meet my eye.

And then he let it fall, turning and moving towards his car. The first step was hesitant, and then he moved quickly, pulling the door open and sliding into the driver's seat without looking at me.

By the time he turned the engine on, his smile was gone, his eyes fixed on the end of the street.

He pulled away from the curb at speed, the engine noise echoing through the quiet air. He didn't brake at the end of the road, just swung around the stop sign and disappeared, leaving me standing there at the curb, wondering what had just happened. And even more frighteningly, what he was going to do next.

Chapter 35

Sloane Yo

Dickie Beaumont's bedroom was dark and musty. Sloane cast her eyes around, the bed a mess of tangled, unwashed sheets stained yellow with sweat. There were clothes on the floor, plates of half-eaten food balanced on different surfaces, cans of beer gathering dust in every free space.

She touched nothing, hyper aware that one of two things was happening. Either Dickie Beaumont wasn't here, and she'd just broken into his house for no reason. In which case she'd be leaving swiftly. Or, he was here, and simply declined to answer the door. In which case she'd broken in and was about to confront a former police officer in his living room.

Or, thirdly, the idea struck her, was… No. She didn't want to think about the third option. Didn't want to tempt fate.

She pulled the bedroom door open with her foot and stepped onto the thickly carpeted landing. The house was silent, which wasn't a good sign. The way he'd been wheezing earlier, Sloane thought that she'd most certainly have heard him by now if he was home.

Still, she moved cautiously, pausing at the guest room and bathroom to listen. There was nothing. Sloane let out a slow breath, steadied herself, and descended the creaking stairs. The shag pile dulled her footsteps, but the wood still gave her away. Though she didn't think Beaumont was here. Once quick sweep of the downstairs, and then she could— shit.

Sloane paused on the fourth step from the bottom, her nose detecting the distinct metallic tang in the air first, her eyes homing in on the source a second later.

Dickie Beaumont was slumped on his side in front of his couch, a wide pool of blood around him. It looked black in the gloom, the sunlight bleeding in through the blinds, enough to give her a sense of what had happened immediately.

The shotgun.

The pillow, its stuffing blasted around the room.

The entire front of Beaumont's face missing.

He'd sat on the couch, put the shotgun's stock on the floor, balanced a pillow on the muzzle and pinned it there with his chin.

Then he'd pulled the trigger.

The pillow culled the noise, but not the power.

Her eyes only flitted over the wall, the splattering of scarlet all around the room.

Sloane sucked her teeth for a second, then closed her eyes, let out a long exhale, blocking out the smell, the scene. She went back upstairs without a second look, pushed Beaumont's bedroom door closed with her heel, and then climbed out onto the window sill.

The sloping roof let down towards the lawn below her. Sloane checked the other gardens, the neighbouring houses. Nothing moved. No one was around, and she hoped no one had seen her.

She got onto her hip quickly, shimmied down the roof, and then dropped lithely onto the lawn, her ankles complaining as she landed.

A second later she was over the side gate and down the driveway.

She got into her truck, watching her flanks, careful not to slam the door to draw any attention. She let the handbrake off, put it in neutral, and let the truck roll back silently, guiding it into the street. When she was a few hundred yards down, she swung it around and put the clutch in. The hill took the car in silence and she slotted it into second, turned the key, and then bump-started it, the engine kicking to life quietly.

Then she drove.

Like hell.

Less than ten minutes later, she was jabbing the call button at Ellison Saint John's front gate.

The house staff didn't bother talking this time. They knew her car, knew they'd get a snide answer if they asked. So, they just opened the gate instead.

Sloane roared up the gravel drive, the brakes squealing as she stood on them, the tyres crunching. The truck hadn't even stopped before she was out of the cab and marching up the steps.

One of the maids opened the door before she got there. 'Mr Saint John is—'

'Move,' Sloane said, shoving past her and into the vaulted reception. 'Ellison!' she bellowed, voice ringing through the stone and wood halls.

He appeared quickly at the top of the stairs. 'Sloane?' he asked, the look of confusion on his face exaggerated enough to either be completely genuine or utter bullshit. She didn't know which.

'Dickie Beaumont,' she called back.

The maid still lingered at the door.

'What about him?' Ellison asked, taking a few steps down, his royal blue polo shirt straining at the arms, the chest, and everywhere else.

Sloane tempered herself, barely.

He read the look on her face, then lifted his chin to the maid, reaching the middle landing. 'That'll be all, Linda.'

She smiled, closed the still-open front door, and then disappeared into the maze of rooms and hallways.

When Sloane was sure she was out of earshot, she started up the stairs. Ellison stayed where he was, towering above her.

'Dickie Beaumont,' she said again.

Ellison just raised an eyebrow.

'You kill him?'

Ellison scoffed, leaned on the bannister. 'Kill him? God no,' he said, shaking his head. 'Honestly, I thought he was dead already.' He watched Sloane for a second, his face dropping. 'Wait, he's actually dead?' The shock was apparent. 'Someone *killed* him?'

Sloane nodded. 'He was slumped on his living room floor with a bloody shotgun in his mouth.'

'Jesus.'

She couldn't see any falsehood in his reaction. 'It'll be ruled a suicide. But I suppose that's the point.'

His brow crumpled in thought. 'Am I missing something here? Why *isn't* it possible that it's a suicide, and what does it have to do with me?'

Sloane was done playing games. 'I went up to his house this morning and spoke to him. He told me that there was a cover-up, with Sammy. Ten years ago. A legal cover-up. Something Sammy did. But he wouldn't say what.'

'A cover-up?'

'It's been a shitty few days, I'd really appreciate it if you didn't repeat everything I say.' Sloane sighed. 'He told me he needed to make a phone call, that I should come back later. He obviously played a part in the cover-up, so I assumed he was calling you or your father to talk about it.'

Ellison shook his head. 'My father's bedridden,' he said, a fair amount of contempt in his voice. 'And it's the first I'm hearing about any of this.'

Sloane stared up at him, but she didn't know what else to say. 'Shit,' she said then, turning and sitting on the stairs. She hung her head, sighed.

Ellison sat next to her, put his hand on her back.

She stood quickly. 'What the hell are you doing?'

'I just…' he said, lifting his hands innocently. 'I just thought…'

Sloane took a few steps down. 'I want to know who he called, and why.' She was as much saying it to herself as to him. 'If it wasn't you or your father, then it must have been someone else who was involved back then. Your father is well connected – lawyers, police… he must know someone who can take care of people.'

'Take care of them?'

'Kill people, Ellison,' she said coldly. 'Don't play dumb. You think the Saint Johns won everything they had in a friendly card game? This whole damn palace is built on a foundation of bones.' She headed for the front door.

Ellison watched her go in silence.

She opened it, stepped into the afternoon sun, and then pulled it shut, reaching for her phone as she neared her car.

It was already dialling by the time she started the engine.

'Hello, Savage Ridge Police Department?' came the voice of the clerk who worked the weekdays.

'I was just driving along Pinewood Drive and heard a gunshot,' Sloane said in a high, nasally voice.

'A gunshot?' The woman sounded surprised.

'Yeah, it sounded like it came from 122.'

'Okay, ma'am, please hold on. Are you driving? Is it safe to pull over? I need your name, and—'

Sloane hung up, pushed the truck into first gear, and then peeled out of the driveway in a cloud of exhaust smoke.

Chapter 36

Ellison Saint John

Murder? Jesus. Dickie Beaumont. Ellison hadn't heard that name in years.

He remembered Beaumont from his teen years. He'd been around the house some, brought Sammy home that one time when his father had struck him. And, of course, there was the time that he interceded when Ellison was trying to get a confession out of Peter Sachs and Nick Pips. Another minute and they would have talked. Ellison always hated the man for that. But despite his short-sightedness, Ellison thought he'd been a decent enough guy. Why would anyone want to kill him?

Ellison watched the black smoke from Sloane's tail pipe rise in front of the house through the glass above the door.

The question changed in his mind then. The cover-up. What had Sammy done that was so bad? And what did that have to do with his death?

He turned his eyes towards his father's study. He'd been saying the same lines over and over to Sloane. That he was working on getting Sammy's phone records and the other information for her. But he wasn't. He was just echoing his father, who'd said all that to the other PIs, too.

He continued to stare at the dark, wood-panelled door.

Local police. State police. They'd all been through here, all worked the case, all failed. What could a PI possibly hope to achieve, and with the same information, too?

Ellison swallowed, making the decision. The decision to finally open his eyes to the truth. Whatever that may be. And damn the consequences. He wanted to know. It was his right to know.

He let himself in through the door, the room dark despite the hour being early. It wasn't even mid-afternoon yet.

His father lay quiet in his bed, the respirator whispering away.

Ellison moved softly, knowing where he was going. Behind the desk, underneath the bookcase. The locked sliding cupboard there accessed by the key stashed on the concealed shelf under the second drawer of the desk.

The mechanism turned smoothly, the wood shuffling in silence, revealing the safe.

It was one of four in the house, this one reserved solely for documents.

There was another in his father's bedroom, containing his most expensive watches. Half a million's worth, easily. The third was in the security room. It contained two pump-action shotguns, two automatic rifles, two ballistic vests, two pistols. The security that worked the house – one watched the cameras, the other patrolled the corridors, but never more than ten seconds from his father's side – needed to be ready for anything. The fourth was in his father's panic room, hidden in the back of his closet. It contained a revolver, about a quarter of a million in cash, another bulletproof vest, as well as two smoke grenades, and a mask that was both an air filter and night vision.

Ellison and Sammy's rooms were on the other side of the house from his father's. Which meant that the panic room was where Ellison's father would run to in order to ready himself to escape, that the cash was probably for on-the-spot ransoms if the kids got taken, or to buy his freedom. And if it happened not to be enough to cover both, Ellison thought he knew which his father would choose. The revolver was for self-protection, the vest, too. The mask and smoke grenades were to make that escape that much easier. His father was cautious, meticulous. Heartless.

It's why the combination to this safe wasn't his or Sammy's birthdays. It wasn't a sentimental date or anything like that. It was six random numbers that had no link to anything.

And Ellison knew them. But not because his father had told him. But because his father's lawyer had sat him down when his father had been placed on the ventilator, and walked him through his father's end-of-life procedures.

The management of the several large businesses that his father owned had been transferred to their respective boards. His father had officially stepped down as the CEO, or director, or whatever position he held. Ellison was not awarded any of those seats, though his father's council had told him that he had an entry level position waiting at any of them if he wished. That if he was destined to run any of them, he'd work his way up.

All of his inheritances – the properties, the money, the shares, the assets – they would all be placed into a trust to be released to Ellison on his forty-fifth birthday. Until then he would be a live-in, non-rent-paying tenant. All bills and upkeep costs would be paid for via this trust, assessed by his father's retained post-death council – also paid for out of the trust.

And should he be deemed by that council to be a liability to the empire, the assets, or any of the holdings, they reserved the right to withhold it. Indefinitely. At their discretion. Meaning that some heartless legal firm held all the cards, and had total ongoing control of the Saint John fortune.

All of which meant that Ellison was the most penniless multi-millionaire in the country. That there was a good chance, even when he turned forty-five, that the money would not come to him. That he, his children, and his children's children, would never see a single dime of the family money.

But if he could find Sammy's killer, maybe, just maybe, that would be enough.

Ellison wiped his cheeks thinking about it and then punched in the numbers.

His father's council had also gone over some paperwork in the event of Thomas Saint John's sudden death. Who he should call, what he should say. What documents needed to be signed, what steps needed to be taken. How to get said documents, too. The funeral arrangements were all in hand, as were the business matters. All Ellison had to do was sign away his rights to the Saint John name and the empire that came with it.

The safe opened in front of him and he stared into the interior, seeing a single stack of manilla folders.

He withdrew them carefully, removing one from the stack at a time, opening the front cover, reading, discounting it. When he reached the very bottom, there was one stamped 'Property of Savage Ridge Police Dept. Do not remove. Do not copy.'

His hands quivered, and then he lifted it, turned to his father's desk, and sat.

The heart monitor beeped monotonously, but Ellison could have sworn it quickened slightly.

Ellison flicked on the reading lamp, opened the file, and began to read the parts of the investigation into his brother's disappearance that his father never wanted anyone to know.

Much of it was familiar – the pool party, the fight, the threats. There was an accident report from the side of the highway, his father's S-Class rolled into a ditch, totalled. The same date as the party.

Ellison thought back to the night that Dickie Beaumont had brought Sammy home. The night his father had struck him. Ellison looked up at his father's withered body. He'd always been so indomitable. So fierce. And Beaumont… Beaumont must have known so much. About Sammy and about his family. Was this the legal cover-up? Destroying the car? Driving drunk? Is this what Beaumont had made the call about? To his father's lawyers? Had they gone there, like Sloane said, and made sure he couldn't say another word?

Beaumont was on his father's payroll. Ellison recalled that his father had paid for Beaumont's medical bills in return for his loyalty. Was Beaumont trying to leverage more money? He was old, maybe he finally wanted out of Savage Ridge, thought that he might be able to threaten the Saint John family now that his father was incapacitated, thought maybe he'd get one last payout for all his hard work.

Ellison swallowed, went back to the file.

He leafed through the pages until he reached Sammy's phone records. Incoming and outgoing calls, text logs.

Incoming calls, none. Outgoing, lots. To different numbers. In batches. He'd call one for a few weeks, repeatedly, then move on to another. Same thing. Ellison ran his finger down the times of the calls. Evenings, late nights. Then he moved onto the durations. 00:00:00; 00:00:03; 00:00:01. They were all like that. He had to double check that he was seeing this right. Every phone call was less than a few seconds. Often less than one second. What did it mean? The calls were ringing out, going to voicemail, then Sammy was hanging up? Who were they to, and why?

He turned to the text logs now, and then he saw.

Hi.

Hey.

How's it going?

Hello?

This is Sammy, hope you don't mind me texting.

261

> I found your number, hope it's okay to text like this.

> I think you're really cute.

> Hi, I know this is weird but...

> Hi, this is Sammy Saint John...

> Hey...

> Hey...

All the same. Outgoing texts to the same numbers he was calling. All the same thing. Just him saying hi, hello, hey...

Ellison's mouth was dry, ears ringing as he kept moving down. He clamped his teeth together to stop his jaw from shaking.

> Why won't you answer?

> Answer me.

> Please.

I just want to talk.

Come on, we could have fun...

I'll take you to dinner...

I'll buy you things...

Don't be like this...

Ellison's hands grew sweaty, his heart beating shallow and fast.

Fine then.

Have it your way.

Fuck you.

You're a slut.

Don't want to talk to you anyway.

Your loss.

Fucking bitch.

Whore.

It kept going. It kept getting worse.

Ellison screwed his eyes shut, slapped the folder closed, unable to read any further. This was over the course of months. Years, probably. No one called him, no one texted him. But he'd been incessant. And alone. And where the hell had Ellison been? This was his fault. If he had been here, if he'd have known…

He opened his eyes, saw the manilla folder spattered with wet marks from where the tears had fallen.

He was on his feet then, folder in hand.

Ellison stormed to the window, standing at his father's side.

He brandished the folder in his face so he could see. So he couldn't *not* see.

'What the hell is this?' Ellison demanded, knowing his father couldn't answer.

The folder shook with his rage.

His father's eyes moved across the cover, then slowly drifted to his son's. And then Thomas Saint John did something he'd never done before. He lifted his hand, pulse monitor around his index finger, eyes shimmering in the afternoon light coming in through the blinds, and held it up.

It took Ellison a few seconds to realise what he was doing, but then he understood.

His father nodded, and Ellison let the folder fall onto his father's chest.

He put his hand inside the old man's and felt his grasp tighten.

And then his knees gave out, and Ellison Saint John sank to the floor, laid his forehead on his father's knuckles, and wept.

Chapter 37

Sloane Yo

Sloane approached 122 Pinewood Drive for the third time that day, and slowed beside a police cruiser parked sideways on the road.

The deputy there lifted his right hand, his eyes shaded by black sunglasses. 'Road's closed, ma'am,' he said. 'What's your business?'

'What happened?' she asked, playing her part.

'Can't say anything at this time,' he replied diligently. 'Unless you live here, you need to turn this vehicle around.'

Sloane's patience had already worn thin. 'Poplar up there?' She lifted her chin ahead.

The guy hesitated.

She leafed her badge over the sill of the open window and he looked at it. 'Private investigator?'

She nodded. 'I'm here to see Dickie Beaumont,' she said. 'He told me to come back this afternoon. It's about a case I'm working, for Thomas Saint John.' She figured Thomas' name would carry more weight than Ellison's.

The deputy, a mid-thirties guy with tousled hair and close-set eyes that made him look like a child, fell quiet then stepped back. 'Uh, hang on a sec,' he said.

He turned away, reached to his shoulder, to the radio there, and muttered something into it. He waited for a response, then waved Sloane through.

She trundled up the hill towards Pop's waiting Chevy Tahoe. No lights flashed, no sirens wailed. She noticed the door to 122 was open, but there was no one else here. Yet. She figured a town as small as Savage Ridge probably didn't have its own coroner's office or CSIs. She didn't even know whether they'd be called. If a coroner ruled suicide, then this wouldn't be a crime scene, and everyone would just go on living.

Nice and neat, Sloane thought bitterly.

Pop, hands on his belt, pointed her in to the side of the road and she got out.

'What're you doing here?' he asked.

She played dumb, looked up at 122. 'What happened?'

He measured her for a few seconds. 'Beaumont is dead,' he said plainly. 'Choked on the barrel of his Model 12.'

Sloane blinked for effect. 'I was just here a few hours ago,' she said, knowing full well it was Pop who'd sent her up here.

'And I suppose he was alive when you were?'

'Barely,' she said truthfully, shrugging. 'Cagey, though. Wouldn't talk. Said he had to make a phone call, that I should come back.'

Pop pursed his lips. 'Wasn't you who did this, was it? Gotta ask. You're probably the last person to see him alive.'

'And kill my best chance of breaking this case and making a payday?' She scoffed. 'No, I didn't. And if I did, you think I'd just roll up here and talk to you about it?'

He stuck out his bottom lip. 'We got an anonymous tip. About thirty minutes ago. Someone said they heard a gunshot.' He eyed her. 'Wouldn't know anything about that, would you?'

'I was just at the Saint Johns. They'll corroborate that.'

He nodded slowly, then sighed, knowing that Sloane was well versed in the law, and better experienced at skirting it than he was at catching people out. He kicked a pinecone into the gutter, looked at his feet, then rocked on his heels. 'Don't suppose he said who he was calling?'

Sloane shook her head.

'Wanna take a guess? I struggle to believe that he'd ask you to come back if he planned on doing this.'

'I'm inclined to agree,' Sloane said, looking up at 122.

'If we got no leads, good chance the coroner will rule this a suicide.'

'Suppose that's the point.'

He nodded, kicked another pinecone. 'So, if you had to guess?' He squinted at her in the sunlight coming through the branches above.

'If I had to… maybe Thomas Saint John's lawyer? Or at least someone they paid.'

He was silent for a second. 'That's a big claim,' Pop said, keeping his voice low. 'Why do you say that?'

Sloane leaned against her truck, folded her arms. 'Beaumont said there was a cover-up, ten years ago. Something to do with Sammy and Emmy Nailer.'

Pop stiffened a little, over-tight leather belt groaning.

'Beaumont was knee-deep in it at the time. I figured he was maybe trying to use me as leverage to score himself a sweetener. Maybe get some decent healthcare. Maybe so he didn't have to die here.' She lifted her chin at the house again, the open door dark and sad.

Pop considered that. 'So, he called Thomas Saint John's lawyer – the one who orchestrated this cover-up. Says a PI is sniffing around, that he's thinking about coming clean unless he can be persuaded…'

Sloane shrugged. 'Is something like this beyond the Saint Johns' reach? Beyond their capabilities?'

'The old man's laid up on a respirator last I heard,' Pop replied. 'So I doubt the order came from him.'

Sloane didn't think he was perceptive enough to read her mind or expression. So, what he said next was probably coincidence.

'And I don't think Ellison has the spine – or the connections, or know-how – to make something like this happen.' He put his hands on his hips now, moved his head side to side. 'But I don't doubt that the old man's lawyers wouldn't have to think too hard about solving this issue. Whatever Beaumont was asking for must have been more than this cost.' He glanced up at the house, then checked his watch. 'Even with rush service.'

Sloane cursed silently, wishing she'd pushed Beaumont harder the first time. 'This cover-up,' she said, not about to make the same mistake twice. 'You know about it?'

'A cover-up involving Sammy Saint John and Emmy Nailer?'

Sloane nodded, not confident in the vacant look on Pop's face.

'Nothing comes to mind,' he said. 'Far as I knew, they were strangers. That's what it read like in her interview. But that might only be half the story.' He shrugged. 'Though, like I said before, things that the Saint Johns used Beaumont for weren't things they generally wanted me to know. I give the Saint Johns a certain grace, but if something's serious, we can't *not* write it up. That's me, anyway. But I guess they had Beaumont by the shorthairs. Could apply a little extra pressure. If Sammy did something bad, then told his father before it got to me… I guess Beaumont could have kept a lid on it long enough for his lawyers to sweep up.'

Sloane wasn't thrilled with that idea.

'I don't like the idea there's shit going on in my town I don't know about either, alright? But,' Pop said, 'there probably still is someone who might know what happened between Sammy Saint John and Emmy Nailer.'

Sloane looked at him. Thomas Saint John was barely breathing, Beaumont wasn't anymore, Sammy Saint John had been gone for ten years, which only left one person: 'Emmy Nailer.'

'They do train you big city cops well, don't they.'

'Screw you, Poplar,' Sloane grunted, opening her car door and climbing up into the cab.

'Good to see you too. Call me if you need anything. I'll be here for the next while.' He stepped away, lifted a hand.

She nodded, turned, and then peeled out of Pinewood Drive, leaving the swaying trees and the splintered sunlight behind.

Pop shrank in her rear-view, hand still raised, and then turned back to Beaumont's house. And the secrets that died within.

Sloane drove quickly, passing Emmy Nailer's street. She slowed enough to get a good look, and stopped just past the corner, sighting Peter Sachs' car parked a few houses up from Emmy's. It'd moved from its spot that morning, but the fact remained: he wasn't letting anyone near her.

Sloane sighed, thumped her fist against the wheel, then drove on. It throbbed all the way to Nicholas Pips' street, where she swung in and parked right in front of his house.

She got out, marched up the front steps, and banged on the door with her left hand, her right still smarting.

It was a minute before Nicholas Pips' father, Gene, answered the door. 'Yes?' he asked, looking at Sloane with her bruised face with some confusion.

'Is Nicholas here?' she asked plainly.

He stared at her for a second, then shook himself out of his shock and stepped back. 'Yeah, I'll, uh, get him for you.' He stepped back, went to the bottom of the stairs, and leaned on the bannister. 'Nicky?' he called out, 'there's, an, uh…' He looked back at Sloane, not sure how to describe her. 'There's a woman here for you.'

'A woman?' The reply was muted, tentative.

'Yeah, uh…' His father looked at Sloane for a third time. 'You want to just come down?'

There was no reply this time.

Nick's dad came back. 'He'll be right down. Fix you some coffee, or—'

'I won't be staying.'

'Right.' He lingered.

'You can go. I don't care,' Sloane said.

He just sort of smiled. The words were impolite, but he was glad she gave him a ticket out. Gene Pips disappeared into the living room without another word.

His son came down the stairs a moment later, cautious.

He watched Sloane all the way to the bottom step, where he stayed. 'What do you want?' he asked from the shadow of the hallway.

'Why was there a legal cover-up involving Emmy Nailer and Sammy Saint John?'

Nick stepped down onto the carpeted floor of the hallway now. 'Emmy?' he asked, seemingly thrown by the question. Guess he didn't expect her to have dug this hard. Or this far.

'I know something happened. That there was a cover-up. That Sammy did something. That Beaumont helped keep it hushed.' She risked a step forward now, onto the threshold. She knew how trespassing laws worked, so she didn't push it. But she wanted to get closer, to get a better read on him.

Nick swallowed, looked at the ceiling, and then sat back on the bottom step, pinched the bridge of his nose. 'Jesus.'

'It's okay, Nick. Tell me the truth. I'll find out sooner or later.'

'Why?'

'Why what?' She placed her hands on the doorframe, hems of her leather jacket opening like wings around her.

'Why does it even matter so much? What happened?' He shook his head. 'Sammy Saint John was a piece of shit, and it's better for everyone that he's not here anymore.'

She noted that he didn't say dead. Nicky Pips wasn't dumb. 'It matters because it matters. People don't just get to disappear without anyone knowing what happened to them.'

'You mean *rich* people.'

Sloane took a breath. 'I'm getting paid to investigate this, yeah,' she said. 'It's my job. But if I was in Sheriff Poplar's shoes, I'd be doing the same thing for my state salary.'

Nick snorted a little. 'You found out enough about Sammy Saint John to know what kind of kid he was?'

'I've got a picture forming.'

'So why not just do everyone a favour and give up, huh? Even if you keep going, you're not going to find anything that'll make you think Sammy deserves to be here.'

'Or you could just tell me the truth and save me the trouble.'

Nicky Pips stood then, walked at Sloane. 'Look at you,' he said coldly. His eyes roved her face, the bruise, the bags under her eyes, then fell to her hands, the chewed nails and bloodied cuticles from where she'd scratched and picked raw. 'You're a mess,' he said.

Sloane stepped back, felt anger bubble in her chest.

'You're out here, trying to dig up old secrets when you could be home. With your daughter.'

Her eyes widened, her hand leaping to the small of her back, ripping the compact pistol free.

She held it with both hands, standing on Nicky Pips' porch, the muzzle no more than six inches from his heart.

He drew a sharp breath, and for a second, she thought he was going to cower, beg, put his hands up. But he didn't.

He hadn't threatened her, or her daughter. Christ, what was she doing?

'You want to kill me?' he asked coolly. 'Go ahead. Put a bullet in me over Sammy Saint John.' He spat the name, stared at her for a moment, then stepped back, and shut the door.

Sloane let the gun drop, and breathed heavily. 'Fuck,' she hissed, shaking her head in anger. *Stupid, Sloane. Fucking stupid.* She holstered her pistol and headed for her truck, the image of Nick's eyes burning in her mind. There was no fear there – well, maybe for an instant, just a glimpse of it. And then it was gone. And all there was… was acceptance.

He'd have died just then. Was prepared to.

Why? Guilt?

Sloane got into her truck, stared up at the Pips' house for a few seconds more. Then she started the engine and swung around, gunned it towards the end of the street and the reddening sky above the ridge.

Chapter 38

Ellison Saint John

He picked himself up slowly, looked his father in the eye.

The old man mustered what little strength he had left, and lifted a shaking hand to his mouth, pushed the tube that was fixed into his trachea tighter into his neck, and spoke. 'Sammy,' he said the word barely audible, the tube stamping out the words before they even reached his tongue. 'Was…' he croaked, wincing, each word agony. 'Family.'

His hand dropped, the ventilator forcing oxygen down into his father's lungs. Tears rolled down his cheeks, his eyes not leaving Ellison's.

Thomas Saint John took his son's hand again and squeezed, then nodded, with the ferocity of a dying lion. As though if he'd had the strength to get out of that bed and avenge the death of his son, he would have in a heartbeat. There was fire in his gaze and it burned into Ellison's skin. Whatever Sammy was, whatever was in that file… it didn't matter. It didn't fucking matter.

Sammy was a Saint John. He was family. And nothing changed that.

Someone had come for him, had taken him away, had killed him.

And then they'd gotten away with it.

And it would be stood for no longer.

Ellison felt tears roll hot down his own cheeks, his knuckles white in his father's hand.

He looked through the half-drawn blinds at the setting sun, clamped his teeth together, and swallowed the bile rising in his throat.

Ellison steadied himself for what was to come, and then went to his father's liquor shelf, took the first bottle he saw, and made for the door.

He paused at the threshold and looked back at the old man, an after-image of the monolith he once was.

Ellison felt disgust. He closed his eyes, uncorked the bottle, took a long, sour mouthful, and then set off into the night with hatred in his heart.

Chapter 39

Sloane Yo

Night was on her by the time Sloane pulled off the highway and into a motel called the Rushing River Inn. She'd been sleeping there since she arrived in Savage. It was about three miles out of town and straddled the border between two stars and three. It wasn't a palace, but she was barely there and the sheets were clean. Honestly, did much else matter?

Sloane pulled up outside room eight and killed the engine, letting the headlights die against the paint-peeling red door. She sighed, took her hands from the wheel, and let them rest on her knees for a second or two.

She was still cursing herself for pulling that gun on Pips. He wouldn't go to the cops or anything, he had no reason to. But it was still bad. One mention of her daughter and she was pulling guns on people? She felt rage, then sickness. Then *the* sickness. Her mouth salivated, her brain pulling itself apart, searching for memories of the taste, the smell, the feeling of a fix. Of a drink or a line or a key or a pill or a bag and a spoon and a syringe. On the spoon, on the flame. The bubble, the smell. Belt around the arm, tap the veins.

She screamed and threw herself back against the seat and punched the ceiling of the truck hard enough that her fist rang off the metal, right through the headliner.

Sloane clutched her hand, screamed even louder, until her throat ached. Tears streamed down her face, hand throbbing. Broken knuckle? She hoped so. *Stupid bitch. Stupid fucking cunt!*

Sloane opened her eyes, the world bleary, and stared out the windscreen.

She swallowed the bile in her throat and reached for the door. It opened into the cool night air, the rest of the lot empty around her, and hung her leg out. She saw it in the gap between the door and the frame, thought about slamming the door closed on it. She'd break it probably. Shatter her goddamn tibia.

How far was the nearest hospital? Not in town, she bet. And she couldn't drive with a broken tibia. The pain didn't scare her, though being laid up with nothing to do wasn't going to be a picnic. Especially not when they'd prescribe her Oxy or Vicodin. Maybe Percoset. And that wouldn't be good for the whole staying clean thing. Especially not when pain was the whole fucking idea.

And she wasn't about to shell out a couple grand to be driven halfway across the state to the nearest ER, either. Sloane's mind began to settle, her breath returning, her logical brain taking over again.

She swallowed the wetness in her mouth, pushed her foot down to the ground and braced her weight. There we go. Inhale, exhale. Inside now, take a bath, then go to bed. If you can't sleep, go for a run. Then shower, then bed. If that doesn't work, rinse and fucking repeat.

Sloane was outside now. She reached for her keys, shut the door to the pickup, and paused.

She lifted her head, key in hand, and saw a man in the reflection of her motel room window half an instant before he shoved a bag down over her head.

She didn't make him out, he came up quick. His knuckles hit her shoulders as they ripped it down tight and then she was dragged off her feet as he wrenched it backwards, the collar of the bag strangling the yell before it even escaped her throat.

He pinned it tight around the nape of her neck, choking as well as dragging her.

She clawed at it, heels scrabbling at the tarmac as she was manhandled backwards.

He grabbed her coat then, swung her around, blind, suffocating, and threw her.

Pain in her thigh.

She was tumbling.

Her face hit something hard, arms folding awkwardly under her.

Sloane grunted, gasped, felt the guy grab her legs, try to wrestle them.

She kicked out, hit nothing, tried to roll over.

But before she could, he hit her. A single, hard blow to the side of the head. Stunned her.

She quietened, the thoughts in her brain extinguished.

The guy took her feet again, crammed them into what she vaguely guessed had to be a trunk by the feel and smell.

His hands roughly searched her thighs, midriff, took the pistol from the holster in the small of her back.

Then the trunk slammed shut and she was in darkness, drowning in the stench of rust and mould.

Footsteps, car door open, close. Seat squeak. Ignition. Engine noise. Throaty, lumpy. V8. Small block, mid-sized displacement. She tore the bag from her head, gasping for air, her brain began to work slowly. She knew about cars. About engines. Had fixed up her truck herself. '74 F250. It had a 360 cubic inch V8. The FE engine. Restored original. This didn't sound far off. A GM motor she guessed. She was Detroit born and raised, breathing exhaust fumes before she left the hospital. Maybe a 350? But what the hell did that help? If she knew the car, she could track it down, find the owner, find out who the hell was about to… shit. Kill her. They'd snatched her, and she was about to be executed. She knew this routine. Go somewhere quiet, pop the trunk, put three bullets in you before you can do anything, then roll you into a shallow grave, power-wash the trunk, get on with your day.

Fuck. Fuck. Fuck.

They wouldn't drive far, didn't need to. Savage was quiet, and the further you drove, the longer the person had to find their way out.

Sloane's mind raced, her cognition returning swiftly.

She shimmied around, felt around in the dark, ran her hands over the rough, rusted out floor panel.

The locking mechanism. Her fingers groped at it, found the spring, the hook. No trunk liner meant it was exposed. That was good.

Rusted to hell. Seized.

That was bad.

Fuck. Fuck. Fuck!

She turned, twisted herself up, then kicked it with the heel of her boot.

The spring was barely clinging on. She was surprised it even managed to latch.

Sloane's hand was throbbing violently. She seriously might have broken a knuckle. But there was no time to think on that now. *Just kick the mechanism, break something, get out, live.*

She kicked again, felt it move, heard the crunch of tearing metal.

The engine revved harder, the car juddering, struggling to accelerate. The noise she was making was audible. He should have hit her harder. He was driving faster, more concerned with getting there now than keeping a low profile.

She kicked harder, knowing this was it, that life and death was being decided in the next few minutes.

Sloane gritted her teeth, sucked in a lungful of stale air, aimed as best she could in the dark, and then kicked.

The metal crunched, the mechanism breaking.

The trunk lid moved an inch, rattled, kept closed under its own weight.

Sloane grinned, joyous, clambered around, shoved her shoulder against it and levered upwards.

The ancient actuator sighed and the trunk lid rose, the orange of the passing streetlight burning her eyes suddenly.

The road rushed away underneath her, a single-lane highway she didn't recognise. Could be anywhere. Closer to a shallow grave than to her motel, she thought.

Sloane took a deep breath, didn't waste any time.

She threw herself from the trunk, tensed, folding her arms across her chest, lining herself up perpendicular with the road, and landed hard on the cracked yellow divider.

She bounced, grunted, rolled, flipped, rolled, and then came to rest on her front, panting hard.

It took her a second to get her bearings, realise she wasn't dead or mangled, and then braced herself slowly on her hands, pushing herself up a little. Everything hurt.

The tail lights flared ahead as the car braked, now one passenger lighter. She couldn't make out anyone through the back windshield, the interior obscured by the open trunk lid.

She narrowed her eyes, trying to make out the details of the make in the shadow between the streetlights.

She knew the guy driving, the one who'd taken her, hit her, was watching in the wing mirror. Deciding whether he should get out and chase her down, whether he could back up over her instead.

Sloane caught her breath, stayed right where she was, recognizing the car finally.

Chevy. Impala. '69 or '70 she guessed. White. Rusted out. Coupe or a saloon, she couldn't tell from here. No plate.

She swallowed.

The brake lights faded, the old small block V8 chugging and sputtering as the car took off again, accelerating as hard as the ancient engine would let it.

The Impala shrank into the distance, disappearing into the night, trunk lid flopping.

They didn't have the stomach, or the balls, to try when she knew they were coming.

Sloane got to her knees, winded and sore, and cradled her hand, head pounding.

She looked around, saw nothing but silent pines lining the road, the sky starless overhead. For a moment, she considered what to do, what she would do if they came back. Either way, it didn't matter, because she couldn't stay out here. So, she got to her feet, dusted herself off, turned around, and started walking.

Chapter 40

Nicholas Pips

It was dark when I came to.

I was staring at my bedroom ceiling and the moonlight coming in through the window made everything a strange translucent blue. I knew it wasn't morning, or even close, but I was suddenly alert, wide awake.

The smell was odd at first, unnoticeable, like when you've been sick but can't smell it until you re-enter the room after leaving. It took me a few seconds to realise, to recognise, to react.

And then it clicked.

I sat bolt upright in bed, the stench of smoke now clear in my nostrils and in my mind.

There was a slight haze in the air, the unmistakable presence of fire somewhere nearby. Every neuron was firing, every ounce of adrenaline my body could muster now coursing through my system. Images of my mom and dad flashed in my mind and I was out of bed before I knew what the hell I was doing.

I grabbed my jacket from the back of the chair, throwing it around my shoulders, snatched my boots from the rug and pulled them on hastily, hopping towards the door as I did. I tried to fill my lungs to scream my dad's name, but choked on the smoke and coughed.

Without thinking I grabbed the doorknob, forgetting to check how hot it was. It felt warm to the touch but before that even registered, I'd ripped the door open.

Smoke billowed inwards, already coating the ceiling in an eight-inch blanket.

The hallway was bright, yellow flames reflecting off the wall, coming from downstairs, the fire spreading, but I didn't know how far or where from.

My parents' room was down the hall and I rushed to it, threw my shoulder into the wood, hand on the knob. It flew open and my eyes fell upon my parents' bed, my father already up, trying to wrestle my mother from the covers. She was fighting him off, screaming, 'No, no!'

She was confused, frightened, her eyes wide with terror.

Her hand caught my father's face and he stumbled, swore. He turned to me, wearing the same blue pyjama bottoms and white vest I pictured him in when I thought of Christmas morning as a six-year-old. But in that moment, he wasn't the indomitable giant I knew, he was a scared old man in a burning house.

'Nicky,' he said, breathless. 'Your mother.'

I nodded, knowing what to do and what he meant.

He stripped the covers from her, dragging them from her grasp, and I ran around the bed and scooped her up, wriggling like an eel.

She clawed at me, but I was blind to the pain.

I felt my father at my shoulder, smoothing her hair, catching her hands as we moved through the doorway and towards the stairs.

The flames were taller now, the reflection brighter. The air was hot and acrid, the smoke black.

My dad went first, hitting the stairs two at a time, his bad knees, sore hips, stiff back all screaming at him no doubt. But he still moved quick, descending into the blaze.

By the time I got halfway down, Mom gripping at the bannister posts, shrieking in my ear, he was already at the front door, the fire at his back. It was in the living room, and as I looked in, I saw our couches, our carpet, all aflame. The drapes were rippling white, the pictures above the mantle and on the wall all like mirrors showing nothing but fire.

I stopped, knees nearly buckling, felt my father's hand on my shoulder.

I turned, looked at him, his watery blue eyes as sad as any I'd ever known.

He nodded once, and I moved, tipping forward through the door and out onto the porch, down the front steps and onto the lawn.

The air was all at once cold, my skin coated in ash.

We collapsed into a pile on the lawn and I went to my hands, hacking violently.

As though she was on fire, too, my father dived on my mother, covered her with an old parka coat, swaddled her, fought her, subdued her. But she kept screaming, as though he was killing her, not saving her.

He hushed her, said her name, but she writhed like she was in agony, screeched with such volume and pitch it made me want to vomit.

All the lights in the street were on, people already gathered on the asphalt to watch. Every neighbour.

Sirens rose in the distance.

I looked around, searching for Pete, but couldn't find him. Even his car was gone. He was out. Where, I didn't know. I didn't even know what time it was.

My eyes went back, seeing the faces of each of my neighbours, now older, lined, scared, as my house crackled and roared behind me, the flames taking the upstairs, bursting the windows.

And then I saw him.

Ellison Saint John.

Standing among the others, the families clutching one another, their children. The ones looking on at the house in horror.

But he was looking at me, standing right there on the curb, grinning, glassy eyed, a bottle of liquor in his hand. He was swaying slightly, posture hunched. And in that moment, I knew.

I knew what he'd done, why he was here. There wasn't a doubt in my mind.

I launched at him.

I don't even remember stepping, just flying at him like a rabid dog, hands raised, teeth bared, ready to rip his goddamn throat out.

His fist came up quick. He was expecting it, waiting for it.

The blow stunned me, a hard punch to the cheek that sent me reeling.

He let go of the bottle and it smashed on the walk, spilled its contents into the gutter as he bore down on me.

I barely made it to my knees before he hit me again, flooring me.

I don't know if I blacked out or not, but by the time I breathed again, his hands were on my throat and I was flat on my back. I could taste blood, see the whites of his eyes reflected in the light of the fire. My windpipe closed, my head throbbing. A ringing spun up in my ears and my father's voice, his words, 'Stop! Stop! Nicky!' faded to nothing.

I stared up at Ellison Saint John, my hands on his wrists, his weight pinning me, the flecks of hot saliva spilling through his gritted teeth landing on my face. And in that moment, there wasn't a doubt in my mind that he was going to kill me. Right there, in front of everyone. He was going to strangle me.

And there was nothing I could do about it.

I felt myself weaken, my eyes fall closed, my hands loosen on his wrists. All I heard was my heart, fast and distant. I could feel it thudding behind my eyes. The ringing became a roaring in my head and the pain began to recede from my neck.

All I felt then was cold. Thoughts became incoherent, the faces of my father, my mother, my friends, all grew blurry in my mind. Sammy's was the last to go, the last to fade. It had been seared there for as long as I could recall now, vivid, engraved on the inside of my skull. And even he was fading... sinking into the darkness.

It grew like a flower in bloom, rolling outwards from the centre of my waning consciousness, engulfing everything.

My hands became someone else's, fell from Ellison's wrists.

And then, for the first time in ten years, I felt nothing. No pain. No guilt. Just... nothing.

Peace.

And I accepted it.

And then it all came hurtling back.

My eyes opened and the darkness receded from the corners of my vision. I thought I was dead, but then my chest expanded suddenly, my lungs filling with air, throat burning and aching as I sucked in great breaths, gasping away the pain built up behind my ears.

I sat up, clutching my neck, watching as Ellison Saint John receded from me. He was kicking, yelling, head whipping back and forth wildly. I didn't understand what was happening at first, but then I saw the arms around his, pinning them behind his back. I could see the khaki trousers and shined boots, in the background the flashing blue lights. Sheriff Poplar was dragging him off me.

I wheezed, keeling over onto my side.

My father was looking at me, tears in his eyes, still clutching my mother whose screams had now become long, mewling sobs. Like those of a dying dog. Tears ran down her cheeks, glistening in the firelight.

Poplar got Ellison to his car, the back door waiting, and shoved him in, slamming it closed. He turned to the burning house, looked up at it for a moment, and then glanced at me. I clutched at my chest, still unable to catch my breath, and saw the sorrow in his expression. Then he turned away, got in the car, and peeled out of the street, saving Ellison Saint John from doing something stupid.

From killing me.

As he reached the end of the street, a fire engine roared in, sirens blaring, and then he was gone.

I could feel the fire hot on my side, and the anger hot in my gut, my hatred for the Saint Johns burning brighter than ever before.

Chapter 41

Sloane Yo

Sloane woke with the sun, the windscreen in her truck doing little to dull the light.

She was parked in the Savage Ridge High School parking lot, in one of the teacher's bays that was hemmed in on three sides, in a little inlet formed by the main building.

Sloane opened one eye and sat up on the fold-down bench back seat. It was a one and a half cab, so the back wasn't roomy. But then again, Sloane wasn't that big.

She swung her legs forward and rubbed her head. It was throbbing like hell and her memory of how she got there was a little fuzzy. Concussion, low grade probably.

She grimaced, felt sick, bent the passenger seat forward and climbed out. Stiff back, sore legs, arms, shoulders, sore everything. Throwing yourself from a moving car would do that to you.

Sloane checked her watch, squinted into the brightening sky, and then locked her truck. She'd made it back to the motel late last night, grabbed her bag, and then jumped in the car. She wasn't sticking around there waiting for whoever snatched her to grow a pair of balls and come back. She doubted they'd try the same thing again, but she didn't really like the idea of getting ambushed sometime during the night.

What she was doing at the school though, was easily explained. It was going to be her first stop this morning regardless. She just guessed now she was getting a jump on it.

The diner would open soon enough and she could get some coffee, some food, then walk back over. She was without her weapon now, but she hoped in daylight she would be safe enough.

When she arrived, it was already open. It was still before seven, but she figured the only diner in town was probably a family affair, with Pop's 'Darl' being either the owner, wife of, or long-time manager. She'd been there both times Sloane had, and she was there now, purple eyeliner and all.

Sloane entered. The bell above the door rang.

She took a booth that faced back down Main towards the school and welcomed the cup of coffee Darl brought over without asking.

'Thanks,' Sloane said, wrapping her hands around it.

'Anyone comes in a lick past six looking like that don't need to ask to get coffee.' She grinned at Sloane as though it was some kind of joke, or otherwise just idle conversation.

Sloane thought it was pretty fucking rude. 'Still gotta ask for cream though.'

Darl's yellowed smile faded and she stomped off to oblige.

Sloane had some time to kill now, and it occurred to her that a permanent town fixture like Darl would probably know a good amount about what happened in Savage Ridge.

When she came back, Sloane asked, pushing the dark hair out of her eyes and back over her head. 'Do you know much about the Sammy Saint John disappearance?'

Darl put the cream down hard enough that some of it spilled over the table. 'Much as anyone,' she said flatly.

Sloane read the woman's face, the disinterest, and pulled her wallet from her inside pocket. She leafed a twenty onto the table, looked up at Darl. 'I know the three kids who were accused of it came in here that night.' She leafed another twenty out. 'Remember much about that?'

'Memory's a little foggy these days,' Darl said, her grin returning.

Sloane leafed out another twenty. Damn, if she'd just taken the insult on the chin, she'd probably have paid five bucks for this coffee instead of sixty-five.

Darl reached down, pulled the notes towards her and folded them, stuffing them into her top pocket before clearing her throat. 'I think everyone in town recalls that night. The police were up and down Main like clockwork. Seemed like every flashing light in a hundred miles descended on Savage Ridge in the following days.'

The Saint Johns and their reach, Sloane thought. 'What about the kids? Nicholas Pips, Peter Sachs, Emmy Nailer. Do you know them?'

'Hon, you do this as long as I have, you know *everyone*.' She cut her hands through the air in opposite directions to illustrate.

'They came in that night, right?'

'I guess so, yuh,' she said, nodding and chewing on her cheek. 'They came in, maybe seven-ish, sat in a booth, stayed until late. Kicked them out around closing.'

'Was that odd?'

'Not many other places for kids to go around here. Back in those days we still did a ten-buck deal: burger, fries, shake. Popular with the kids. These days it's eighteen. Inflation, you know?'

Sloane nodded. 'Did they seem odd to you?'

'Odd?'

'Quiet, distracted? Did anything out of the ordinary happen?'

She seemed to think on that. 'It was busy in here, don't think I really took much notice. They drank some shakes, normal, I guess? It was ten years ago.'

Sloane sighed, rubbed her head. 'Okay, thanks.'

'Why do you ask? They were cleared of it, right? At the movies, then here. That's what Pop said, they couldn't have done it.'

'Right, right.' Sloane forced a smile, reached for the cream.

'Not unless people can be in two places at once, huh?' She knocked on the table with her knuckles. 'Just let me know if I can freshen your coffee. And thanks for the tip. Appreciate it.'

Fat lot of good it did, Sloane thought but didn't say.

Instead, she just slurped her coffee, counted down the minutes and thought on what Darlene said.

Not unless people can be in two places at once…

By eight, the high school parking lot began seeing its first arrivals.

Sloane strode through it, passing a few odd teachers and kids. It was still summer, but it looked like a few students were either catching up or getting a jump on next semester. Though no one seemed to take any notice of her and she strolled right in. There were no security guards here, no lines and metal detectors and scanners. A lot different from a Detroit high school, that was for sure.

The Pacific Northwest. Safe, quiet, and boring as shit. Sloane grimaced and slid through the students who were milling around, heading for the principal's office.

On the way, she slowed. This was the route the boosters would take – the parents who the school hoped would donate. And as such, the walls were lined with photographs, trophy cases, ribbons and other accolades the school had earned. $10,000 raised for spina bifida in 2007. First place in the Worthington Cup for lacrosse, whatever the hell that was, in 2011. Second place PNW De-Mathalon 2013. Jerry Davis 2015 third place at the national chess championships, under-16 division. Sloane looked across the trophies, then came to the photos. Class of 2002, 2003… She kept walking. 2007… 2008… She quickened her pace, looking for 2012.

She found it soon enough. Though it wasn't so easy locating specific faces. She mouthed Sammy's name under her breath, looking for his face, but didn't find it. There was an entire section dedicated to the class year, maybe a hundred, hundred and fifty photos. But no Sammy Saint John.

Sloane furrowed her brow, thought about the others. Nick, Pete, Emmy.

She searched methodically, across the top row, down one, then back, left and right, left and right until she found one of them.

Emmy Nailer, arms around another girl. They had their cheeks pressed together, both grinning, both young, rosy faced, happy. The girl had dark hair, bright eyes.

Sloane kept going, found one of Nick and Pete arm in arm at what looked like a school rally.

Then there was one of Pete and Emmy, and the girl with dark hair again.

Then one of Nick and Pete… and the girl with dark hair.

Then Emmy and her again. Emmy and Nick and her. Pete and her and Emmy.

Then the four of them, all cheering together at a school football match. Then another of the four of them, at what looked like a school dance. Then another…

'Ms Yo?'

Sloane looked up, saw the woman she guessed was the principal looking back at her. The woman was mid-forties, with curled brown hair, thick-rimmed glasses, and a bright blue blazer rolled to the elbows over a white blouse.

'Mrs Hannigan,' Sloane said, standing up from the photos and extending a hand. 'Thank you for meeting me.'

She laughed a little. 'Telling me you'll be outside my office at 8:30 a.m. didn't really give me too much choice.'

Sort of the point. 'I appreciate it all the same.'

The woman clasped her hands in front of her. 'What can I help you with?' Her eyes roved across Sloane's bruised face, but she said nothing, holding onto her smile. 'You said it was regarding Samuel Saint John, but I'm not sure what I can tell you that's not already in the police files.' She checked her watch obviously. 'Morning announcements are in twelve minutes, will this take long?'

Sloane gave a brief, unenthusiastic smile. 'It shouldn't. I've been told that the summer Samuel Saint John disappeared there was some sort of legal issue with his family and another in town. Does that sound familiar?' Sloane asked, fishing a little.

Her brow furrowed. 'I've been principal here for fourteen years.' She sighed. 'I don't remember any legal troubles they had. Though the Saint John family was always very private. Never cared much for involving the school in anything.'

The bite in her tone told Sloane that the Saint Johns weren't big supporters of Savage Ridge High. Monetarily or otherwise.

Sloane just nodded. It seemed like the woman didn't really care much for the Saint Johns, and if she knew anything about Sammy's disappearance, she'd have no reason not to be forthcoming about it. With the time constraints, Sloane thought it best to move on. 'There was a lot of talk surrounding a few of the other students here and their relationship with Sammy Saint John.'

Mrs Hannigan stayed stoic.

'Nicholas Pips, Peter Sachs, Emmy Nailer.'

'Ah.'

'You knew them?'

'Of course. Savage Ridge is a small town, and the Saint Johns weren't bashful about voicing their thoughts about them after Sammy disappeared.'

'And what are your thoughts?' Sloane asked.

'About whether they killed Sammy Saint John?' She practically snorted, then shook her head. 'The sweetest kids I knew.' She smiled wistfully. 'Nicholas Pips, ah... relatively popular, funny. Less funny than he thought he was. But always looking to get a laugh all the same. Usually at his own expense. A rare quality in someone so young. Most kids can be cruel, but he never was.'

Sloane listened intently, thinking how strange that description sounded. He was anything but funny now.

'Then there was Emmy Nailer. A pretty girl. Matured quickly. Always had lots of attention from the boys, but was never interested. She had ambitions, dreams. Wanted to go to college, do big things, leave Savage Ridge in the rear view.'

And she amounted to exactly nothing, Sloane thought. Two failed marriages, a few DUIs. Hardly the overachiever Mrs Hannigan was describing.

'Peter Sachs was quiet, shy. A bookworm. Smartest boy in the room but always afraid to speak up. Wouldn't say boo to a ghost, that kid. I always hoped he'd come out of his shell. I sometimes wonder whether he did.'

You could say that, Sloane thought, thinking of the confrontational, confident man she'd butted heads with. She was about ready to close out the conversation, having learned exactly nothing.

'And Bethany was just the sweetest.'

'Bethany?' Sloane asked, looking up quickly.

The principal nodded. 'Bethany Winlaw. Nicest girl I think I ever met. She was a school volunteer, helped organise the food drives, the Help for Homeless walks, she was on the dance committee, if other people needed help, you could bet Bethany was there.'

Sloane took a step back, looked at the photos.

Mrs Hannigan came forward, put her finger on the photo of Emmy and the girl with dark hair. The one with their faces pressed together. 'There she is.' She shook her head. 'Best friends, her and Emmy. The four of them, in fact, inseparable. If you saw one of them, the others weren't far behind. You could bet on that much.'

Sloane stared at the photo of the four of them, feeling utterly stupid. And furious.

'It was such a shame to hear the news,' Mrs Hannigan said, bunching her lips sadly and leaning in to look at the photos more closely. 'When we heard that she'd died, it was... it was just such a shock. To everyone. All the kids came together to remember her. There was a memorial outside the school for weeks. Everyone was shaken. Emmy, Nick, and Pete especially,' she went on, drawing a slow breath. 'To lose a friend like that so suddenly. So unexpectedly. And not long after her family moved, too. Though it was all overshadowed when Sammy went missing, of course. The town's attention turned to the search, and…' Mrs Hannigan lifted her head to look at Sloane, but by the time she did, Sloane was already twenty feet away and breaking into a run, heading straight for the door, and Ellison Saint John's house.

Chapter 42

Ellison Saint John

The pain came first. Before his eyes even opened it lanced through his skull and then festered somewhere at the back.

His lips were dry, throat aching. He could taste vomit, feel the furriness on his teeth.

Ellison Saint John groaned and then rolled onto his side, felt the wetness on his cheek. He forced his eyes open, saw the dark patch on the bed from where he'd thrown up.

'Shit,' he grumbled, trying to force himself upright. A wave of nausea came quickly and he flopped from the bed to the floor and reached out for the waste basket under his desk. He almost grabbed it in time, emptying bile over his knuckles and the rim instead. It splattered on the hardwood floor and he keeled over, breathing hard, the world spinning.

It took him a few minutes to get himself together and get to his feet. He made for the bathroom, but paused at his desk, leaned his weight on the back of the chair there, squinting down at the open file in front of him.

Sammy's phone records, opened to a page that showed 129 outgoing calls to the same number.

Ninety-seven unanswered texts.

A name was written next to the number.

Bethany Winlaw.

All of them the same. Apologies. Profuse apologies. Grovelling apologies.

The texts finally stopped when a single reply came through.

This is Bethany's father. Your lawyers agreed on zero contact. Please do not call again. Don't text. Just leave Bethany alone. Please.

Ellison felt sick again suddenly, rushed to the bathroom and threw up some more.

He was splashing water on his face when he heard his phone ring on the nightstand. He stumbled out there, walking around the puddle of vomit on the floor – the maids would clean it up – and picked up his phone. Sheriff Poplar.

'Yeah?' he croaked, squinting in the glow coming in through the blinds. What time was it? He held the phone away from his face. Early. Too early to be up with this bad a hangover. Ellison sighed.

'You dumb fuck,' Pop grunted.

'Good morning to you too.'

'Good morning?' He scoffed. 'You remember *anything* from last night?'

Ellison cast his mind back, tried to remember. He recalled the safe in his father's study, the phone records, speaking to his father in bed, grabbing the bottle, coming up here. He looked at the desk, the file. His skin prickled, blood running a little cold. He drank... he drove to Pips' house. 'Oh, Christ...' he muttered, throat closing, heart suddenly pounding in his chest.

'I'm on the way,' Pop said quickly. 'Ten minutes. Be ready. We have to move quickly here, get all this straightened out before things get out of hand.'

Ellison couldn't speak.

'Ellison,' Pop said bluntly, 'speak.'

'Uh... yeah, yeah.' The phone shook violently in his hand.

'Ten minutes, okay? And listen to me—' Pop took a breath, calmed his voice '—everything's gonna be alright. Trust me.'

Ellison nodded but couldn't speak.

Pop hung up, Ellison dropped his phone, and then ran to the bathroom and threw up again.

Chapter 43

Sloane Yo

Sloane tried Ellison's phone three times but he didn't answer.

She drove quickly through Savage Ridge, saw smoke rising over the tops of houses. She thought little of it, her mind only in one place: Savage Ridge, ten years ago. Everything was finally coming into focus. Nicholas Pips, Emmy Nailer, Peter Sachs, Sammy Saint John… and the final piece of the puzzle, Bethany Winlaw.

Traffic was moving slow down Main, so Sloane swung out towards the highway where she could get the pedal down.

The houses began to thin, the pines taking over. Sloane's eyes roved as she passed out of the town and into the outskirts of Savage. Billboards and signs began to line the road, advertising car garages, lumber mills, wreckers' yards.

She took it all in, the town in a time warp. And then she saw it.

Sloane stamped on the brake and wrestled the truck off the road and down onto the verge, the bumper stopping a few feet short of the chain-link face. She looked up, the engine hot and gasping.

Through the fence she could see stacked up cars, all flattened and rusted out. There were mountains of old kitchen appliances, piles of girders and scaffolding pipes. Cubes of crushed metal arranged in pyramids. Her mind flashed to the Saint Johns' Mercedes, the one Sammy had rolled off the highway.

But that wasn't what had caught her interest and pulled her off the road.

Sitting there in the middle of the yard was a 1970 Chevy Impala saloon. Rusted out, no plate, just sitting, the trunk lid hanging ajar. Because the latch was broken. Because Sloane had broken it the night before, kicking her way free.

This was the car, the one that she'd been tossed in when she was taken.

She swallowed, looked around, then shoved the truck into first and spun her wheels back up onto the road. Sloane circled the yard quickly and found the entrance. She stopped in front of the gate and got out.

The grasshoppers chirped in the dried grass at the side of the road and the sky overhead was a cloudless blue. The smell of the pines was thick here, but none of it registered with Sloane.

'Hello?' she called, coming up to the fence. No response. She sighed. There was no time for this. She went back to her truck, opened the door, and laid on the horn.

The noise cut the silence and a minute later a guy in his forties walked out from behind a great iron machine Sloane suspected was used to crush the cars. He had a dirty overall on, tied off at the waist, a white vest above. His arms were already dirty with oil and his grease-stained hat shaded his face.

'Yeah?' he called, stopping twenty feet short of the gate.

Sloane came to the wire, held her PI licence up. 'I want to know about that Impala,' she said, lifting her chin towards the back of the yard and the white car she could see in the distance.

He seemed thrown by the question but approached anyway, inspected the badge. 'Private investigator?' he read aloud, then looked Sloane up and down. 'Whatcha investigating?'

'A murder,' she replied coolly.

'An' what's that got to do with our runaround?'

'Your what?' Sloane asked.

He scratched the back of his neck, then ran his tongue over his teeth. He had a scruffy beard, wide-set eyes. 'Our runaround. The yard's near forty acres – mostly car parts and appliance bits – we use the Impala when we need to pick something up, saves us walking. Thing's a junker. Runs good though.' He shrugged.

'Can I see it?'

'Not really sure there's much to see,' the guy replied.

'Humour me.'

He read the determination in her face, or maybe he just wasn't paid enough to argue. Either way he grabbed the gate and pulled it across. It didn't seem to be locked.

Sloane watched it go. 'You lock this at night?' she asked.

He shrugged. 'No point, really.'

'Why not?' She stepped inside and they started walking.

'Easier. We used to chain it, but people just kept cutting 'em, pulling the gate down with a tow rope, or just slicing through the fence wherever they wanted.' He flicked a wrist in the general direction of the far side of the yard.

'People steal from here a lot?' Sloane asked, eyes fixed on the Impala.

'Not a lot. Though not much way to tell, really.' He let out a lengthy sigh, then hawked and spat in the dirt. 'So much shit out here, people sneak in all the time and take stuff. Parts for cars, whatever. We have an honesty bucket, often enough find tens and twenties in there. The old man don't care much for the phones or the online thing, has owned this place forever. Don't much care about money neither.'

'And how long have you worked here?'

'I dunno, maybe eight, nine years?'

'And the Impala,' Sloane asked as they closed in on it. 'Been here all that time.'

'Yuuurp.'

'Anyone ever take it out of here?'

He looked at her quizzically, though she doubted he could spell the word. 'You ask a lot of questions.'

'Kind of comes with the territory.'

He laughed, nearing the car. 'Right, right. Well, all I can tell you is that I come in by nine and I leave at five, Monday to Saturday, and what happens before or after or on Sundays, I don't much know about. People come over the fences, they come in through the front gate. If they know what they want or they can be bothered to look, then they'll take something. And if it's in their means, they'll leave a few bucks. Most of our bills get covered by the towing and crushing.' He turned towards the great iron machine. 'Everything else is just…'

'Junk,' Sloane finished for him.

'Junkyard.' He chuckled, stopped, then kicked the bumper of the Impala to illustrate that they had arrived. 'Seen what ya need to?'

Sloane stared down at the car, then did a slow lap. The inside was spartan, the lining almost completely gone, showing off the bare, rusted metal. There was a muffler in the back seat, a set of hubcaps in the passenger. The steering column was missing its plastic shell, the metal exposed. A screwdriver handle was sticking out of the ignition. She guessed a quick twist would fire the thing up. She reached the back, lifted the trunk lid. 'You know this was broken?'

The guy shrugged again.

Sloane let it fall and it bounced gently above the latch. 'Do you have cameras here?' she asked, knowing the answer.

He shook his head. 'I gotta get back. You take all the time you need,' he called, and then turned away.

Sloane lingered, looking over at the fence she'd parked at, at the bent cross-poles from where people had climbed over. She scanned the other sections, saw a few holes patched with wire ties. Someone could have just strolled in here last night, taken the car, then brought it right back. She let out a long breath and started walking back towards the gate, wondering to herself how long it would take to walk over here from the theatre on main.

Sammy Saint John disappeared on a Sunday.

And Sloane thought she just about had all this figured out.

As she reached her truck, she pulled out her phone again. She didn't need to see Ellison anymore. But she did need to confirm something. And for that, she'd need to reach out to someone that she now figured was probably dodging her calls. No, she was definitely dodging her calls.

Sloane reached into the passenger footwell and pulled her work satchel onto the seat. Inside, she found the file she was building on the case, and leafed to the first page. A list of contacts. At the top of that list, the name Lillian Dempsey. The lead investigator on the original Sammy Saint John missing persons case. She'd been in Savage two weeks, had turned up nothing it seemed, and then left abruptly, her name taken off subsequent paperwork. Sloane's call to the records department at the Washington State Police HQ yielded that Dempsey had taken a sabbatical after the case, returned briefly to the department riding a desk, and then had been put on paid sick leave for a year before being given early retirement. In her forties.

The department wouldn't reveal any more information, and Sloane had always figured that it smelled a little funny, but she'd not had that much time to look into it. Now felt like a good time. If Thomas Saint John was covering something up, then Dempsey's sudden departure from town followed by early retirement was looking less and less like coincidence.

There was a red circle around her name, along with three dates and times. Sloane's notes for when she'd called the number she had for Dempsey and left a message.

She tried dialling again but it rang out to voicemail. She didn't bother leaving another one.

Sloane let out a long exhale, checked the time on her phone, looked down at the last known address printed under Dempsey's name, and made the decision. 'Screw it,' she muttered, throwing her satchel onto the passenger seat and climbing into the cab.

She fired the engine, locked the wheel to the left, and then peeled off the verge and onto the tarmac in a cloud of dust. By the time it drifted over the adjacent field, Sloane was gone, the sound of a V8 hitting the rev limiter already echoing in the distance.

A few hours later, Sloane pulled off the 90 for Roslyn and followed the road until her phone lost signal and the little arrow moving along the white line of the road on her screen started looking right and then left as though trying to find the way.

She locked her phone instead and pulled the paper from the file onto the wheel, pinning it under her right hand as she looked for house numbers. She slowed, the road quiet, the vista familiar. Pine trees, a million of them. Dempsey's last known address was up here, number 874 Heron Road.

Sloane picked up the pace a little, the numbers climbing. When she reached 860, she slowed, creeping along until a worn old sign bearing the right number loomed out of the scrub.

She didn't really like the idea of scratching up her paint squeezing down through the overhanging branches, but the ditch at the side of the road didn't look all too inviting and if she left it parked here, someone would likely side-swipe her coming down the way. And wing mirrors for '74 F250s weren't all that easy to come by.

She sighed, then pulled off the road and crept down the stony track towards a house peeking out of the trees ahead. The boughs screeched along her paintwork and she swore under her breath as the truck made it into a wider opening, following the tyre marks and swinging in a wide circle in front of the home.

The paintwork was peeling, the front yard overgrown. What would have once been a lawn was now just scrubby grass, and the old Volvo station wagon parked out front was heavy with summer dust.

Sloane stared up at the place for a minute, wondering if it was inhabited, let alone whether Dempsey was here or not.

She cut the engine anyway and stepped out, freezing at the sound of a shotgun being cocked.

Sloane looked up, watching a woman coming onto the covered wooden porch, looming from the darkness of the front door, pump-action shotgun in hand.

'Get off my property,' Lillian Dempsey said. She was tall, that was the first thing Sloane noticed. She'd been a redhead, but now, in her late fifties, her hair had greyed. Her skin was pale, eyes lined, lips turned downwards into a mean line.

'My name is Sloane Yo,' Sloane announced, raising her hands. 'I just want to—'

'I know what you want,' Dempsey cut in. 'But when someone doesn't call you back, it means they don't want to talk.'

'I'm working in Savage Ridge, for the Saint Johns, looking into Sammy Saint John's disappearance. I need your help.'

Dempsey scoffed a little. 'No, you don't. Now get in your truck and go.'

'Please,' Sloane said. 'I need to know—'

'Are you deaf?' Dempsey called. 'I don't want to shoot you, but I will.'

'They forced you out of a job, didn't they? Was it because you wouldn't let it go? What happened in Savage Ridge?'

'Jesus Christ,' Dempsey muttered, lowering the shotgun. 'You're not going to quit, are you?'

'It's not in my nature.'

She sighed. 'You best come inside. Though I doubt you'll like the truth about this case.'

'I don't like anything about this case,' Sloane replied, stepping up onto the porch.

'And what do you make of Savage Ridge?'

'I hate the place.'

Dempsey chuckled. 'Well, at least you've got *some* sense then.'

Inside, the interior was gloomy and tired. Dempsey laid the shotgun against the hallway wall and walked towards the kitchen.

Sloane paused, looking into the living room. There was an old TV, a couch covered in a knitted blanket, and a silver urn on the mantel, the name DUKE inscribed on it.

'My dog,' Dempsey said, appearing next to Sloane.

303

'You live alone?'

'Yep. Just me and Duke there.' She nodded to the ashes, then headed for the kitchen again.

By the time Sloane caught up to her, Dempsey had already disappeared into another room and returned with a binder in her hands. It was brimming with papers, and through the closing door behind her, Sloane saw an office littered with notes, a big board with photographs attached to it. She didn't make out what was on it before it closed.

'Here,' Dempsey said, dropping the folder on the kitchen table with a loud bang.

The whole thing jumped an inch under the weight.

'What's that?'

'Everything I scraped together on Thomas Saint John before I got the axe.'

'The axe?' Sloane asked, surprised. Though early retirement was just another word for being fired without having to do the paperwork.

Dempsey sagged into a chair. 'I got taken off the Sammy Saint John case the second I left Savage Ridge.'

'Why?'

'Because I learned the truth of what happened to Sammy and Thomas Saint John didn't want to lose.'

Sloane sat now, too, the folder, string-bound, between them.

'I gave him an ultimatum – I'd arrest Nicholas Pips for Sammy's murder, but he had to come clean about the reason why.'

'And he wouldn't?'

She tsked, shook her head. 'The guy wasn't interested in anything except what he wanted, and I refused to give it to him.'

'So, the state police fired you?'

'No, they fired me because after I got back, I cashed in the time off I'd saved up, and built a case against Thomas Saint John. Once I started digging, it wasn't long before I hit blood. Legal cover-ups, shady business dealings, disappearances and apparent suicides that seemed to mysteriously benefit the Saint Johns… it ran deep.'

Apparent suicides… Dickie Beaumont's body flashed in Sloane's mind, his brains decorating the wall above his couch.

'Once I had enough to go after them – or what I thought was enough – I presented it to my boss, and—'

'They wouldn't go for it?'

'They seemed receptive at first, but while they looked it over, they made me work a desk, so they could do their due diligence. And then, all of a sudden… Phone call. Don't come to work today, sorting some things out. Yada yada, and then the letter in the mail. Restructuring the department. They offered early retirement with a severance bonus, full benefits and pension equal to what I'd have gotten if I paid into it until I was seventy, the works. My husband, Simon, he pushed for it, said it was a blessing in disguise. That if the department was willing to offer this to keep me off Thomas Saint John's back, then it was for the best. That he probably knew that there was a case against him – that it probably wasn't the first. That going after it would only make things worse, would put a target on our backs. And that I already knew what kind of man he was, what he was willing to do to keep his house in order. I couldn't disagree with him. So, I went for it. I accepted. I took Thomas Saint John's blood money, like everyone else.

'Things were fine for a while. Simon and I, we were happy enough. We travelled, did some work to the house, enjoyed our lives as best we could. But…'

'You couldn't let it go.'

'Could you?'

Sloane shook her head. 'Doubt it.'

'So, I kept working, kept digging, reaching out quietly. I thought if I could gather enough evidence, build a strong enough case, I could go higher – FBI, IRS, SEC, whoever would listen.'

'Did you get there?'

'What do you think?' Dempsey stared at Sloane across the table. 'I made phone calls, pleaded my case, got the same answer. "We'll look into it, we'll look into it, keep gathering more information." But it was never enough, and by the time I came up for air… Simon was gone, and all I had was that fucking folder.' She slapped her hand onto it, and then shoved it across to Sloane. 'It's your problem now.'

'Why wouldn't you help me before?' Sloane asked, staring down at it.

She let out a long sigh. 'Honestly? I wanted to save you from it. From this.' She gestured around. 'It's not a path you want to start down. It doesn't lead anywhere. Trust me.'

Sloane considered that, then pushed back from the table and stood. 'Thank you,' she said, gathering up the folder. 'Before I go, do you know the name Bethany Winlaw?'

'Bethany Winlaw,' Dempsey repeated back. 'I haven't heard that name in so long.'

'So, you know what happened to her?'

'I do,' Dempsey said sadly. 'But you want to know the worst part?'

'What?'

'That poor girl is just the tip of the iceberg – it's all in the file. The whole thing. Thomas Saint John has done what he likes since he was old enough to sign a check. It was no surprise that Sammy grew up the same. All I can say is that it's no great tragedy to have one less Saint John in the world. Tell me, is the old man still as much of a cantankerous fuck as he was ten years ago?'

Sloane's grip tightened on the folder. 'Thomas Saint John is dying. Cancer. He's laid up on a ventilator. A stiff breeze would finish him now.'

Dempsey sat in silence for a few seconds, and then her mouth began to twist into a smile.

Before she could say anything, Sloane headed for the door, already unwinding the string around the button, knowing what she was about to find, but still dreading it all the same.

Chapter 44

Nicholas Pips

Hospitals all smelled the same. Like bleach and piss and day-old food.

My father was asleep in a chair opposite, head lolled to the side, breathing shallow.

I'd not slept at all since last night.

The fire trucks had arrived, then the ambulance. The house was still in flames by the time they strapped my mom to a stretcher and pushed her into the back. They dosed her with a sedative and she got quiet, face still contorted in pain.

We rode in silence, my father and I crammed in against the doors, knees touching, eyes fixed on the floor. We didn't speak, didn't know what to say or how to say it. I don't think he knew I killed Sammy. I don't know if he even thought me capable of something like that. More than anything, I think he was just heartbroken. Mom, me, the house… it was all too much for him.

When we arrived, they took Mom in, let Dad go with her. I was told to sit in the waiting room and that they'd fetch me some clothes. I was still in just my jacket, underwear, and boots.

An hour later an orderly brought me a laundry bag and told me the clothes inside should fit. I pulled out a pair of sweatpants two sizes too big that I guessed must have been left behind when someone died. But they were clean so I pulled the drawstring tight and tied it off. There was a T-shirt, too, baggy and stretched out of shape. But it worked.

I got called on by a nurse at about 4:00 a.m. and checked over for signs of smoke inhalation. Minor, no need for treatment. Bruising from where Ellison strangled me.

I cleaned myself up in the bathroom, and by the time I got back to the waiting room, my dad was there, elbows on his knees, head in his hands. He wept softly until dawn, and then fell asleep.

I didn't manage to, and watched the sun come up through the blinds, the pines on the ridge cutting out jagged shapes in the early morning mist, like teeth of a saw hacking at the sky.

My mind went in circles for hours. I didn't know if I was awake or not.

Something began vibrating on my leg and I looked down, realised I had my phone in my hand. It had been in my jacket pocket. The screen was lit up, a call coming in. I didn't recognise the number.

'Hello?' I said, my voice catching in my throat. I shivered, then felt like I was about to burst into tears.

'Don't hang up,' the woman said. 'This is Sloane Yo, we spoke briefly in the bar. And at your house.'

I began shaking my head, tears coming. 'I… I can't talk right now, I have to—'

'Bethany Winlaw,' she said then, before I could hang up.

I was silent, my breathing quickened.

'I know what happened,' Sloane said. 'I know everything.'

I didn't answer.

'Come downstairs, we need to talk.'

'I'm not at home,' I managed to muster.

'I know, I'm at the hospital. I'll be waiting by the entrance. And Nick?'

'Yeah?' I asked tentatively.

'Don't make me come up there.'

I left my father asleep and descended cautiously, trying to figure out what I was going to say, what I was going to do here.

Knowing wasn't the same as proving. I kept reminding myself that. She didn't have any proof. She couldn't.

I reached the ground floor and stepped into the mid-morning sun. Sloane Yo was parked in a spot about twenty yards away and was leaning on the front of her pickup with her arms folded.

She pushed off as I approached, but didn't walk out to meet me.

'I heard about your house,' she said first. 'I'm sorry.' Her face was straight, her expression not exactly one of remorse or compassion.

'You hear who did it?'

She didn't answer, just sort of bunched her lips. Whether she knew or not, she probably had a fair idea. Especially if she was as good as she was making out to be. 'How's your mother?' she asked instead.

I tried to clear the lump in my throat, but couldn't. I looked down so she wouldn't see the tears forming in my eyes. 'Not good. The stress of last night... she had a pretty bad episode. They don't know if she's going to come around. The doctor told us to start thinking about palliative care.' The words were small and squeezed out. I stared at my boots the entire time.

'I'm sorry to hear that.'

'I bet,' I muttered. 'What do you want?' I looked up now and her face twitched just a fraction, the mask slipping for just an instant.

'I know about Bethany Winlaw,' she said then. 'I know what Sammy Saint John did to her. I know he raped her... and I know that's why you killed him.'

She watched me closely.

I clenched my jaw. 'You don't know shit.'

'I know you four were inseparable. You, Pete, Emmy, Bethany. I know that she was the kindest girl in school, probably the only one to give Sammy Saint John the time of day.'

I had no words. But Sloane kept talking.

'I know what he did to her. And I know that he ran back to his father afterwards and that they sorted it all out. That officer Dickie Beaumont helped keep it under wraps long enough for Thomas Saint John's lawyers to get their claws in. I know the Winlaws took a big payoff, signed an NDA. I know Thomas Saint John bought them a house in California, on the beach, agreed to pay for Bethany's college tuition.'

My jaw quivered.

'And I know that Bethany Winlaw took a handful of pills and walked into the ocean seven weeks later.'

'Did you know her body was found eighty miles up the coast four days after?' I spat, my hands clenched so hard they hurt.

She didn't answer, so I took her silence as confirmation that she did. Sloane let out a long breath. 'I know that Emmy jumped the Saint Johns' back wall – nine feet – with your and Pete's help. I know she crept up the lawn next to the pool, tossed stone chips at his window until he answered. I know she asked Sammy to meet her on a Sunday afternoon at 5:30 p.m., right in the middle of the movie showing. I know you chose that movie because it was long enough to slip out the fire escape and run over to the junkyard on the highway, through the woods. I know you chose a Sunday because the junkyard was closed and you could sneak in and take the white '70 Impala without anyone noticing. I know that Emmy drove up to the Saint John house and picked Sammy up. And I know that she drove him to meet you, and that you killed him.'

She met my eyes and I saw no anger, no hatred in hers. I saw nothing.

'What I don't know,' she went on, 'is how you did it, where you did it, or where you buried him. But I know he's out there somewhere.' She turned her head, lifted her eyes towards the pine-laden mountains that cast a shadow over the town. 'I know that Peter Sachs also stole that same Impala last night and tried to do the same thing with me.'

I blinked in surprise. 'What? Pete did what?'

'I can't prove it, I never saw his face,' she said casually, shrugging. 'But someone abducted me, threw me in the trunk. Was taking me out of town. To kill me.' She shook her head, scoffed a little. 'I spoke to Mrs Hannigan, your old principal. She said Peter Sachs used to be the shyest kid in school.' She smiled strangely. 'Guess everyone has to grow up some time.'

I swallowed the vomit rising in my throat. Pete said he was going to take care of her, but I didn't think he actually would. Jesus, did that mean Emmy was already... I felt cold then. 'Do you...' I started.

'Have any proof?' She answered the question I didn't even ask. 'No. Not for any of it. But you and I both know that's what happened. Don't we, Nick?'

I cleared my throat, looked up at her, and shrugged. 'I don't know what you're talking about.'

She laughed through closed lips.

'What I do know,' I said slowly, choosing my words, 'is that the world is better off without Sammy Saint John, wherever he ran away to.'

'Ran away. Tight,' she muttered, still smiling.

'And that the Saint Johns are a fucking plague. That they move through life using and abusing people, paying them off and leaving a wake of destroyed lives everywhere they go. I know that they do whatever they like without consequence. That they get drunk, and burn down people's houses with them still inside. The houses of people who are dying because they can't afford decent healthcare. The houses of the people they feel are *less* than them. And I know that it takes a special kind of heartless *cunt* to work for people like that and do their bidding.' I never used that word. I hated it. But it was the only thing – the *only* thing vile enough to describe the Saint Johns and the people that chose to do business with them.

Sloane just stared at me.

'All you have proof of, Ms Yo, is that Sammy Saint John raped the only girl who was ever nice to him, and that his father

312

threw so much money at her parents that they let that piece of shit get away with it. And that their daughter, her life stolen and reduced to a fucking *number*, couldn't live with that knowledge, that her parents could sell her like a piece of meat, so she killed herself. And they felt so guilty about it that they broke up and moved to different sides of the country. That her father is an alcoholic, homeless, probably dead himself by now—'

'He's not,' she whispered.

'And her mother—'

'Works at a youth rehabilitation and homeless shelter in Florida which cares for abused teens, helps them fight for justice, trying to make up for it. I know.'

I sneered at her. 'And you still accept money from these people?'

'I didn't know then.'

'Well, now you do.'

She swallowed, looked into the sky, her own eyes glistening. 'And now I do.' Sloane let out a long breath, but didn't seem to be able to look at me. 'No one knows what happened to Sammy Saint John. No one except you and Emmy and Peter. So, without a confession there'll never be any way to prosecute. And I'll make sure that anyone else who comes sniffing around Savage Ridge on the Saint John dime will come into this with their eyes open. Will know who Sammy Saint John was. Who he *really* was.'

I didn't respond.

'I'm leaving Savage Ridge.'

'Just like that?'

She shrugged. 'The case is cold. No more leads.'

I shook my head. 'Must be nice to pick and choose.'

'I don't think they'll drop it, Nick. I don't think it'll stop.'

'It'll stop,' I said, folding my arms, determination rising in me. 'Ellison will go down for what he did last night.'

She smiled like she was humouring me. 'I hope so.'

'He will. I don't care about money. I won't take a payoff. And I won't be satisfied until he's in prison getting gang-fucked in the shower. It's about time the Saint Johns felt what it was like.'

She raised her eyebrows slightly. 'I won't stand in your way.'

There was silence then, neither of us speaking. Sloane Yo watched me for another minute, then opened her mouth to say something else. But before she could, my phone rang.

It might have been my father, something about my mother. I tore it from my pocket and answered quickly without looking at the name. 'Hello?'

'Nick?'

It took me a moment to register the voice. 'Emmy?' I said, surprised. 'What's wrong?' I asked, reading the alarm in her voice.

'Nick, I need you,' she said. 'Right now. You have to come right now.'

'Hey, slow down,' I said, 'tell me what's wrong.'

'I can't, Nick, there's no time. Please just come. Right now. I need you. Please!'

'Okay, okay,' I said, looking around wildly, putting my hand to my head. 'Jesus, where are you?'

'I'm…' She cut off, sobbed. 'You know where. Please. Hurry.'

She hung up and I lowered the phone, heart pounding.

Sloane narrowed her eyes, a little. 'Need a ride?' she asked lightly.

I swallowed, stared at her. I had no car. My father and I had both ridden in the ambulance. And who knew what the hell was going on. Pete? Had Pete finally got to her? Was he about to kill her? Jesus Christ.

'I'm off the clock,' Sloane said, reading the panic in my face. 'Case closed.' She held out her hand. 'You have my word.'

'What's that worth?' I asked, shaking my head, breathless.

She kept her hand there, her gaze as hard as steel. 'Everything.'

Chapter 45

Ellison Saint John

Ellison Saint John could barely stand straight when Pop showed up. So, he sat on his front steps instead.

Pop drove quickly up the long drive, and by the time Ellison looked up he was skidding to a halt in front him. He left four deep welts in the gravel behind the tyres and the engine was idling hot, the intercooler gasping. Pop had driven hard.

The window was already down and he was leaning over the centre console, small in the hulking Chevy Tahoe; a hair short of eighteen feet long. Pop was wearing mirrored aviators, shirt buttons straining to the point of bursting. 'Get in,' he ordered.

Ellison stood, held his knuckles to his mouth like he was about to throw up, then stumbled down the steps and opened the car door.

'Jesus Christ,' Pop muttered, 'you stink.'

Ellison just swallowed, looked out the window. He kept telling himself that Saint Johns didn't feel guilty. Not for doing what they needed to. That's what his father would have said. He'd never felt guilty a day in his life. Saint Johns don't fight. They win. And this was winning. Wasn't it?

Pop didn't give Ellison a chance to buckle up before he drove out of the grounds. The gate was still open and he swung through quickly, almost clipping the wing mirror, before understeering into the road and hammering it back towards town.

Ellison stifled a gag, the water in his stomach threatening to make a second appearance. He wanted to ask where they were going, what was so important that Pop had to pick him up right then. He was fully aware by now that he'd gotten drunk last night, driven to Nicholas Pips' house, and… He grimaced, and then did gag this time. He'd burned it down. And it wasn't even a spur of the moment thing. He'd gone out to the groundskeeper's shed and taken a gas can. He'd taken the matches that the gardener used when he lit fires to stave off the knotweed and Himalayan Balsam from the rose beds. And then he'd driven out there, walked right up to the front window, and sloshed gas on it. Then he'd lit a match, watching as the fuel dripped down the cedar cladding, and held the flaming end against it slowly. Without hesitation. He'd waited for the flare of the match to subside, stared into the ember for a full five seconds, and then touched it to the wood.

It caught, licking upwards at speed. Ellison stood there, no remorse, feeling the heat on his skin with glee. And then only retreated to his car when his throat ached for another drink. He went slowly, listening as the wood crackled, and then as the yells and shouts began to echo from inside. Only letting a smile play across his lips after. He'd wanted them to burn to death. The whole family, for what they did.

'Hey,' Pop said suddenly, snapping his fingers in front of Ellison's face.

Ellison looked around.

'You listening to me?' he asked, and Ellison thought it probably wasn't the first thing he'd said.

'No, sorry,' he replied. 'What did you say?'

Pop sighed. 'We gotta get this sorted out,' he muttered, shaking his head. 'I've already had your car towed from the Pips' house, got the fire chief to give me a little time before he puts in his report.'

'Does he know?' Ellison asked, watching the side of Pop's face.

'That Ellison Saint John burned down someone's house, tried to murder three people?'

Ellison swallowed.

'I'll take care of it.' He shook his head then, chuckled a little. 'Jesus Christ, if I had a nickel for every time I've done your family a fucking favour.' The bite in his voice was apparent. 'You owe me big for this one, Saint John,' he said, turning to face Ellison now. 'You know that, don't you?'

Ellison drew a slow breath, wondering how this was going to stack against him, and if Pop needed paying, where he'd get the money. And then, as if reading his mind, Pop said the thing that Ellison had been waiting ten years to hear.

'There's something else. Something I've been working on for a while. But after last night... I know this needs to end. Once and for all. Especially since your investigator hasn't come up with shit.'

Ellison breathed slow, heart beating hard.

He seemed to labour over the words. 'I got her to flip,' he said quietly.

'Who?' Ellison asked, voice strained.

'Emmy Nailer.'

Ellison wanted to say a lot, but didn't seem able to say anything.

'I picked her up early this morning,' he went on, 'talked to her one on one. Got her to admit it.'

'H-how?' Ellison asked, words catching.

Pop bit his lip. 'I spoke to her. *One on one.*' The intonation in his words was enough to let Ellison know that more than words had passed between them.

'Wha— what happened?' He steadied his voice, lowered the timbre. 'What did they do to him?'

Pop drove on, thinking about it before he spoke. 'They picked him up, drove him out of town. Then they killed him. Buried him.'

Ellison's throat had closed to a pinhole. 'How? How did they kill him?'

'They beat him to death. With a shovel.'

A wave of nausea rolled through Ellison Saint John and he closed his eyes, the intense fury he'd felt the night before roiling in him once more. The flames of the Pips' house burned bright behind his eyes and he let their heat warm him, turn his hands to fists. A tear rolled down his cheek and he felt the thunder of the road under him, his entire body vibrating, all fuzziness gone, all unease expelled. Now, there was only anger. And the satisfaction that would come after. 'Is that where we're going now?' Ellison asked, watching the road stretch out ahead. They weren't headed to town.

Pop nodded gravely. 'They're all there. Nailer, Sachs, Pips. Waiting for us.'

Ellison let out a shaking exhale. 'What are you going to do?'

'I'm going to do what I've always done for the Saint Johns,' he said, reaching to his hip and unfastening the safety latch on his holster. He tugged the Glock 17 free, and pushed it into Ellison's waiting hands. 'I'm going to look the other way.'

Chapter 46

Nicholas Pips

Sloane drove fast. Not recklessly, but fast. With the kind of precise control that told me that she was in total command. That she knew what this truck could do and what it couldn't, and that there was no risk of anything going wrong.

Still, when she swung off the road and onto the dirt logging track, the whole truck sliding sideways like a river barge, I still hissed and grabbed onto the dashboard like it'd save me if we T-boned on a tree.

But then Sloane got us straight again, shifted down and spun all four wheels, and sent us flying along the side of the river.

'How far?' she asked.

'Not far,' I said, knowing that sooner or later I'd have to loop her in on where we were headed. I figured she'd already guessed, but eventually, the words would have to come out of my mouth, whether I dreaded it or not.

'Where are we going, Nick?' she asked, accelerating even harder. The wheels rumbled terribly over the stones, the whooshing of the passing trees enough to turn my stomach sick.

'We're going…' I had to say it. 'To…'

She stole a glance at me.

'To where we buried Sammy Saint John.'

She didn't answer, didn't slow down. Didn't even flinch. 'Tell me when to stop,' was all she said.

I knew then that it wasn't a case of hearing it so she'd finally have the confession, or for anything other than just that show of implicit trust. Her word meant everything, she'd said. We'd have to see about that. I hoped to God that she was on my side, but there was no way to tell.

And there was no way to tell what awaited us at the side of that river, either. Why Emmy was there and who was with her. Whether it'd be Pete with a gun to her head, or whether, by the time we arrived, she'd already be dead. And if she was, what would we do?

I looked at Sloane Yo, tired, thin, bruise on her forehead from who knows where, grazes on her cheek from the abduction. Her hands were raw, knuckles bloodied and scratched. Her right hand was bandaged tightly, and the fingernails showing from under the gauze were chewed down so low the flesh around was bright red and swollen. The skin was in ribbons around her cuticles, and the veins in the corners of her eyes bulged scarlet, lancing towards her dark irises. I don't know that I'd ever met anyone like her, or that there was anyone else like her out there.

Who was Sloane Yo? Ex-cop, ex-junkie... mother... just another broken human being.

We rounded the last corner, my hands growing sweaty, and Sloane stamped on the brake.

All four wheels locked up and the car slid to a stop behind Pop's black and white Chevy Tahoe.

For a second, I had no idea what was going on. My first thought was that Pop had responded to the sound of a gunshot. Pete and Emmy. But there were no lights flashing, no sirens blaring.

The cruiser was parked sideways, blocking the view of what was beyond.

Sloane and I looked at each other for a second, then got out.

My heart hammered as I swung around the nose of her truck, stumbling to a halt as I saw the scene in front of me.

Sloane caught up, slowing as she got to my side.

We both froze, wordless.

Pete's Mercedes was parked ahead, side on, forming a space about twenty feet square. The steep bank fell away to our right, down to the rushing river, deep green and freezing cold even at this time of the year. It flowed down from the high mountains, rapid and wild.

On the other was a steep bank layered with pine needles and towering, swaying pines, sharp and dark, their trunks rough and gnarled.

My eyes moved across the stony ground in front of us, from Pete and Emmy on their knees in front of Pete's car, eyes wide with terror, hands laced behind their heads, to Ellison Saint John, pistol in his hand, pointed right at them, to Sheriff Barry Poplar, with his own pistol, aimed directly at Sloane and me.

I stared at Pop dumbfounded. To my right, Sloane raised her hands slowly. I caught it in my periphery and followed suit, lifting them to the sides of my shoulders.

'Pop…' I started.

'Shut it, Nicky,' he grunted, then dipped his head sideways. 'Over there, with the others.'

I blinked in shock, then followed the order, stepping slowly towards Pete and Emmy. Pete had his eyes on the ground, breathing fast. Emmy was shaking, eyes closed, lips moving in silent prayer.

'Knees, Nicky,' Pop called.

I got down awkwardly, put my hands behind my head, looked across at Emmy and Pete, swallowed, said my own prayer, and then turned my eyes towards Ellison Saint John.

He was ten feet away. And even with the way his hand was shaking, I doubt he could miss a shot from there. There wasn't a doubt in my mind this was an execution.

I wasn't scared, though. If anything, there was a strange sense of relief washing over me. I met Ellison Saint John's eyes, saw the thin veneer of courage laid over fear. He didn't know what the hell he was doing. But he was still going to do it anyway. Spitting distance from his brother's unmarked grave. I wondered if he knew. If he knew everything. Or if this was just one more twist in the noose that seemed forever fastened around this town's neck.

'I've waited so long for this,' Ellison muttered then, taking a step forward.

'No. Not yet,' Pop commanded him, eyes not leaving Sloane.

'Why not?' Ellison's eyes flashed as he looked at us. He wanted this. He wanted to kill us.

'You want to hear it first, don't you? Want to hear them say it?'

Ellison nodded. Vigorously. 'Yes. Yes.' He jabbed the gun at us. Emmy sobbed a little. 'Say it,' Ellison demanded. 'Tell me what you did.'

Pete looked at me then, his expression asking what the fuck was going on. What could we do?

Pop was a statue, Sloane still in his sights.

I let out a slow breath. 'It was me,' I said then, the weight that had pressed on me for so long finally lifting. 'I killed Sammy.'

Ellison's lips quivered. 'Why?'

'Because he deserved it.'

Ellison lifted his chin slowly, fingers flexing on the pistol. 'Close your eyes,' he ordered.

I shook my head. 'No. You want to pull the trigger, you're going to have to do it while I'm looking at you. Like Sammy looked at me. Except I'm not going to beg. Not for a Saint John.'

His temples were slick with sweat, the forest holding its breath around us as Ellison searched himself for the strength to do what he'd always promised himself he would. 'This is your one chance,' Pop said then, anticipating the shot. 'Get in your truck, leave Savage Ridge, forget everything. And don't come back.'

Ellison's brow crumpled in confusion and he risked a glance at Pop. But didn't say anything.

Sloane drew a slow breath, then let it out, flexed her fingers next to her head. 'I can't do that.'

'I'm not gonna ask again.'

'I can't let this happen,' she said. 'I can't just walk away.'

'You don't really have a choice,' Pop replied, tightening his grip on the pistol.

Ellison spoke then, turned towards Pop a little, gun still waving in our direction. 'What are you doing?' he hissed. 'Shoot her!'

Pop glanced at him. 'You fucking shoot her. You hired her.'

Ellison made a sort of frustrated growling noise. 'No, *you* shoot her. That's what you're here for! That's what we *pay* you for. To protect the Saint Johns.'

Pop clenched his jaw, narrowed his eyes slightly at Sloane. 'You're right,' he said, voice barely a whisper.

Pop looked at me then.

A single, knowing look.

And then he swung the pistol around, and put three bullets into Ellison Saint John's chest.

The shots echoed through the valley as Ellison convulsed, staggered backwards, and then fell, heels coming clear of the ground as he landed in a plume of dust, gasping for air that wouldn't come.

Sloane moved instantly, diving forward for the spilled Glock 17.

Pop fired again, chasing her with bullets.

She made a grab for it, rolled, and then got back to her feet.

Pop kept shooting.

Bullets pinged off the trunk of Pete's Mercedes and we threw ourselves forwards, protecting our heads. Emmy screamed.

Sloane got to her feet, doubled back, tried to fire blindly over her shoulder, making a run for cover behind the bumper of Pop's SUV.

The gun clicked uselessly in her hand, the chamber empty.

I looked up just in time to see one of Pop's shots clip her.

323

She yelled out, the bullet striking her ribs, and she spun, off balance.

Pop moved forward, stepping powerfully, trigger rebounding off the grip, muzzle flash dancing in my eyes.

He put two more into her, centre mass, and she stumbled back, lost her footing, and went over the edge.

Her dark eyes met mine. Her face, flecked with blood, full of fear, full of confusion, hung there for an instant… and then she was gone.

Sloane plunged down the bank in a cascade of stones and hit the water with a heavy splash.

I scrambled towards the edge just in time to see the ripples swallowed by the white water. After a few seconds, it was like she was never there at all.

Pop's boots crunched in the stone next to my head and I froze, looked up slowly. The muzzle of his pistol was aimed at my head.

He stared down at me over the top of his over-tight belt and strained shirt buttons.

And then he sighed, and offered me his hand.

THEN

Chapter 47

Barry Poplar

Sheriff Barry Poplar hunched over the desk in his office, hearing the words but struggling to process them.

'Is there anything else I can do for you, Sheriff?'

'No, no,' he said slowly, swallowing, feeling his throat burn and ache. 'Thank you. I appreciate the call.'

'Sorry to be the bearer of bad news.'

'Yeah,' Pop said, putting the phone down and laying his head in his hands.

There was a knock at his open door and he looked up from his desk, seeing Beaumont's big frame filling his doorway, knuckles poised at the jamb. He was eating a bear claw, his shirt sprinkled with pastry crumbs.

'Who was that?' Beaumont asked through a mouthful of powdered sugar.

Pop did his best to hide his disgust. 'That was the sheriff of the Cambria Police Department.'

Beaumont just kept chewing. 'What'd he want?'

Pop narrowed his eyes. 'They found Bethany Winlaw,' he said, trying to keep his voice even. When the Winlaws had moved to Cambria, Pop had gotten in touch with the sheriff there, asked to be kept updated if anything happened with the family. He wanted to know. Four days before, he'd had a call to say that Bethany's parents had reported her missing. They'd woken up one morning and she was gone, the door that led onto their deck and down to the beach wide open.

'Oh?' He took another bite.

'She's dead. They found her body on the beach eighty miles up the coast. They think she killed herself.'

Beaumont chewed slowly. 'Mm.'

'Mm?' Pop felt his skin prickle, his hands scratching up into fists on the desk.

Beaumont shrugged then. 'Not surprising. She had problems.'

'Problems?' Pop's teeth were clamped together so hard they hurt.

Beaumont sighed, brushed crumbs off his chest and onto the floor. 'What can you do, huh? The world at her fingertips, and then she goes and does a stupid thing like that.' He finished off the bear claw, gave Pop a nod, and then walked back towards the bullpen.

Pop watched him go, hatred bubbling away inside him. *The world at her fingertips?* Was he that ignorant, that stupid, or just that goddamn heartless? Pop didn't know. But he swore then that Dickie Beaumont would get what was coming to him. No matter how long it took.

But before that, there was something else that needed to be done.

The Saint Johns needed to pay for this. To really pay for this.

And an idea was already forming in Pop's mind as to how he could make that happen.

NOW

Chapter 48

Nicholas Pips

'It's time to get up, Nicky,' Pop said, hand still hovering.

I gathered myself and took it, felt him pull me upright. My knees wobbled a little, almost gave out when he clapped his hand onto my shoulder, took a fistful of my shirt, and then shoved me back towards Pete and Emmy. Right past Ellison Saint John. He was lying still, eyes staring into the swirling grey sky above.

I didn't know if he was dead yet, but he wasn't moving, wasn't breathing. I felt nothing as I looked down at him. No urge to save him. No urge to do anything except watch the light go out.

'You two,' Pop called, pulling a rag from his pocket and cleaning off the gun in his hand. 'On your feet, now.'

Pete pushed himself up, face twisted up in anger. Emmy didn't. She just whimpered into the dirt, hyperventilating.

'Pips, get her up,' Pop ordered, wiping the last of his prints from the weapon.

I reached for her hand, tried to do it, but she was limp and heavy.

Pete helped, took her other arm, and we pulled her to her knees, where she stayed mewling and trying to catch her breath, tears streaming down her face, painting dark lines of smeared mascara onto her tanned skin.

Pop walked to Ellison's body and stooped, pushing the pistol he was holding into Ellison's grip. 'Christ,' he muttered, curling Ellison's fingers around it to get his prints.

I watched, thinking how small the gun looked in his hand. Thinking how familiar it looked, too. I'd seen it before, recently. But not in Pop's possession.

It had been pointed at me just the day before. By Sloane. It was her gun. But how did he get it?

'You should have never come back,' he grunted, standing up straight and turning to us.

We didn't say anything.

'I told you, didn't I? The one thing I said before you left, before we did any of this—' his hands waved in the air, towards Sammy's grave '—that there was just one rule. One rule.' He stuck his finger up to illustrate. 'Don't come back to Savage Ridge. Ever.' He cut the air with his hands. 'We got away with it. Clean. Like I said. Like I planned. And all you had to do was stay away. That was it. And you couldn't even do that!'

'The investigator—' Pete started.

He didn't get to finish. 'I was handling it,' Pop said. 'Like I promised I would. She was getting nowhere. The only lead she had was Dickie Beaumont. But like he was supposed to, if anyone came sniffing around, he called me. And I fixed it.'

'You killed him,' Pete answered coldly.

Pop came forward, stepping over Ellison's corpse. 'I did what I had to.'

'You didn't need to kill Sloane,' I found myself saying, remembering what she'd said about last night. That Pete had abducted her... but it was Pop who had her gun. He was the one who'd taken her. And she knew it. The second he'd pointed her own weapon at her.

'The investigator?' Pop snapped. 'I just did you a fucking favour!'

'She knew,' I said then. It was all I could. 'She knew everything, and she was leaving it alone. She was letting it go!'

'Bullshit,' Pop said, shaking his head. 'She wasn't letting anything go. And if you think that, then you're even dumber than I gave you credit for.'

I clenched my jaw, knowing that the second Sloane arrived, her fate was sealed. Pop was going to kill her if she stayed in Savage Ridge. He'd already tried once, and failed. He hadn't expected her to be there, but the result was ultimately the same.

It all played out in my head, the alternate version that Pop had expected. Give his gun to Ellison, empty. Tell him to execute us. Then, shoot him in the back with Sloane's pistol.

And now her death was on me.

'I gave her an out, she didn't take it,' Pop lied, poking at his temple with his finger. 'But the stupid bitch didn't know when to leave things alone.' He sank into a crouch then, between us and Ellison Saint John, laid his elbows on his knees and massaged his mouth, head turned towards the place Sloane had gone over.

He let his eyes slowly drift to the spot we buried Sammy.

I remembered that night. The way that Pop came by as we were filling the hole in, to check that it looked good. The way he left his cruiser at the end of the track, drove the Impala back to town, dropped us at the fire escape of the theatre before taking it back to the junkyard. It was his plan from the start, the whole thing.

He'd known it all: what had happened to Bethany. Thomas Saint John had kept him out of it, had Dickie Beaumont do the dirty work, threaten the Winlaws to keep quiet until Thomas Saint John's lawyers could rally.

He'd told Pop to stay out of it, keep his hands clean of the whole thing. The less he knew, the better. He'd tried to fight it, but it was futile. The Saint Johns couldn't be overpowered, not in Savage Ridge, not like that.

But something had snapped in him, then. Something had changed.

And when Bethany died… that was it.

We'd been leaving the diner one night when he rolled by, told us to get in the cruiser.

We all squeezed into the back and he drove us up an old fire service road until we were on the hill above the Saint John

House. He got out, stood there in front of the truck and stared down at the place, the palace that it was.

He waited for us to get out, and then he made us watch as Sammy Saint John messed around in his heated pool, not a care in the world.

'She's dead,' he said, the words as cold and lifeless as we'd ever heard.

We didn't need to ask who. We all knew.

Emmy choked, spluttered, and then began to sob.

Pete's jaw shook as he took Emmy in his arms.

Pop's hand found my shoulder and squeezed, hard. 'I'm sorry,' he said.

It wasn't enough.

'I know,' he said.

'You don't.'

'I do. I know what you want. Because I want the same.'

I turned to look at him, saw in his eyes what I felt.

'What he did... what his father did... they got away with it, Nick. And now she's dead. Bethany is dead. She killed herself, Nick. Do you understand that?'

I felt the fire burning hot inside me.

'But we can do something.' His grip tightened on my shoulder so much that it hurt. 'Look at me, Nick. Look at me.' He jerked me, making me focus. 'Do you want to do something?'

I couldn't move. Couldn't do anything.

'Answer me, Nick. Do you want to do something? Do you want to make them pay?'

'I...'

'Listen to me,' he whispered, leaning forward so close that I could feel the warmth of his breath on my face. 'You can walk away, right now. And let her death mean nothing. Or you can do something. You can finally do something. You can finally *hurt* them like they hurt Bethany, like they hurt your family. Like they hurt everyone else. Do you want that?'

My heart was pounding. I nodded.

'Say it, Nick.'

'I want it.'

'What do you want?'

'I want to make them hurt.'

He searched my face for something, I still don't know what. And then he said it. 'Okay.'

'Okay?'

'Okay.' His grip loosened on my shoulder, a small, bitter-sweet smile playing across his lips. 'We're going to kill Sammy Saint John.'

I had no doubt that he'd been planning it since the moment he found out. He just needed help. And we were perfect for it.

There was no one else in the world who wanted him dead more than us. And Pop knew that. Exploited it.

God, I'd never been more scared in my life than when Pop picked me up after the pool party. After I'd threatened Sammy.

He'd shown up drunk, thrown up in the pool, then made an attempt to hit on Emmy. I tried to make him leave, begged him to, knowing that in a week he'd be dead anyway. That all this would be over.

But he wouldn't. He wouldn't do it. And when Emmy told him that he was a piece of shit, that he was a snivelling, pathetic creep that everyone hated, he tried to hit her. And I lost it.

Everything was a blur until I had Sammy out of the pool, face pressed against the concrete. He'd threatened to have my father fired. He'd threatened to take my house. And he bragged to my face about how Bethany had sucked his tiny, worthless cock, and how she would be again by the end of the week.

He didn't even know she was dead. He had no idea.

So, I told him. I leaned in, and I told him right to his measly fucking face.

I'm going to kill you.

He ran from there afterwards, and I knew. I knew I'd screwed up.

When Pop found out, I thought it was over.

He'd screamed at me, put his gun against my throat, told me that I'd ruined everything.

And I'd begged him.

Not for my life, not to let me live.

But to keep the plan in place. To please, please, let me kill Sammy Saint John.

I'd reminded him what he'd said on that hill above their house two weeks before, that Sammy Saint John deserves to die. And there's a way we could do it, and no one would ever know what we did. He'd beat on his chest with a closed fist then, said, 'But we'll know. And we'll know that he finally got what was coming to him. And that's the only justice we'll ever get.'

We'd looked at each other for a few seconds on that hilltop, stunned. And then without saying a word, we all just nodded.

And we did promise never to come back. But how could we have known? How could we have known what was waiting for us?

I looked down at Ellison Saint John's prostrate body, and I couldn't say I wasn't happy he was dead, but I didn't know... I just didn't know how I'd got there. How any of this had happened.

Something clanged to our right then and I looked up, saw that Pop had gone to the back of his truck and opened the trunk. That he'd taken out a pair of shovels and tossed them on the ground.

He pointed at them, looked right at us. 'Dig,' he said. 'Right here, next to his brother.'

'But—'

'Don't start with me, Pips,' he growled. 'That motherfucker just burned down your house. Paid dozens of investigators to persecute you, to peel apart your life, layer by layer. He threatened you, accused you, ran you out of your hometown. Don't you feel a single thing for him. For any of them. The

336

Saint Johns were a cancer, and you've got to cut a cancer out. If you don't, it'll just spread.' He cleared his throat, looked around. 'I'll deal with the PI's truck, and when I get back, I want to see this piece of shit in a hole.' He pointed down at Ellison. 'And then, you're gone. All three of you. For good this time. I never want to see your faces here again. You hear me?'

I swallowed, stared down at Ellison's vacant blue eyes, noticed how unlike Sammy's but sickeningly familiar they were, and thought I was going to vomit.

Though it was Emmy who spoke. Her words were distant and mumbled at first, and none of us caught them.

Pop stepped forward, leaned in a little. 'What did you say?'

She looked up then, tears still rolling. 'I said you're a fucking *animal*.'

Pop bunched his lips, then bent forward, reached out, and took Emmy by the face. He held her chin in his hand, fingers sinking into her cheeks. She pulled away but he gripped harder until she met his cold eyes. 'Sweetheart, this is Savage Ridge.' He let go and she slumped backwards. 'Down here, we're all animals.'

Chapter 49

Barry Poplar

When word came in that Thomas Saint John was finally dying, only then did Sheriff Barry Poplar make the drive up to the house.

Ellison Saint John had been missing for more than two months. After burning down Nicholas Pips' house, spurned by his father and locked out of his inheritance, he'd seemingly disappeared. State police had a BOLO on him, but Pop was confident that a man of Ellison Saint John's status and reach would have no problem evading them. He was wanted for arson and assault, but he wasn't a high priority for them by any stretch.

Pop pulled up at the gate and rolled down the window. He leaned out and pushed the buzzer, staring up through the black iron gates with the big, gold 'SJ' across them. A few seconds later, there was an answer. 'Saint John residence,' came the overly regal voice.

'Sheriff Poplar to see Mr Saint John,' he said, keeping his finger on the button. 'To pay my respects.'

'One moment.' The gate buzzed and then started to open and Pop took his truck sombrely up the driveway. He guessed that the procession of visitors had been irregular, if not Spartan. Business associates saving face, those who came to suckle at the money teat. Pop had been keeping an eye on things, biding his time, trying to ensure that the old man was really going to die before he made an appearance.

He parked and went up the steps, belt and boots creaking, and was welcomed into the entrance hall. A maid, and what

Pop guessed was probably a modern-day butler, stood at the foot of the stairs, hands clasped in front of them, heads bowed, faces expressionless. He wondered if they were glad the old man was finally withering away, or just dreading the coming unemployment. What would happen to the old place after he was gone? Pop figured it'd be sold off, maybe turned into a kitschy hotel, or possibly even flattened and turned into a suburb. No one would pay what the place was worth to live in Savage Ridge. And the fact that it made the place worthless brought Pop more than just a little pleasure.

'Please,' the man who answered the door said, 'this way.'

He led Pop through the halls towards Thomas Saint John's study, a wood-panelled room lined with old first edition leather-bound books, expensive crystal decanters filled with amber liquids, and soulless, expensive art that was nothing more than a tax write-off. The desk was stacked up with legal paper-work – all the things that would happen to his business and his money after he was gone. A legally ratified list of the pecking order of the vultures that would tear apart his carcass. And none of it would go to his sons. The Saint John dynasty ended right here. Right now.

Pop restrained a smile as he approached the bed by the window. The heart monitor beeped softly, the breathing machine hissing and sighing as it pumped air into the old man's lungs. A tube was lodged in his throat and up his nose, and his wrinkled hands laid next to his body looked pale and desiccated.

Two doctors stood at either side of the bed, making notes on charts and studying him. Trying to look busy, Pop thought, so they could earn their pay while they waited for his body to give out.

'Can I have a moment alone with him?' Pop asked, doing his best to sound solemn.

The doctors looked at each other, did everything except shrug, and then walked out, the doorman going with them.

Pop let the door latch, then waited a few more seconds, revelling in the old man's pain, and then pulled a chair across from in front of the bookcase, making sure the legs scraped the hardwood as roughly as possible.

The old man's hands twitched at the sound of money being wasted and his eyelids fluttered.

Pop sat, leaned in so he could whisper, and watched as consciousness took hold.

'There you are,' he said, laying a hand on the old man's stomach. Pop pressed a little and a small groan escaped his lips. Pop wanted him as lucid as possible for this, and there was nothing like a little pain to focus the mind.

Thomas Saint John opened his eyes, searched the ceiling, and then slowly lowered his gaze until he was looking at Pop.

'Seeing you like this,' Pop said slowly, 'brings me so much joy.'

The heart monitor quickened a little, the old man's brow creasing and furrowing.

'Almost as much joy,' Pop went on, taking his time, eyes never leaving Thomas Saint John's, 'as killing your son.'

The old man tried to rake in a breath, fighting the ventilator. It looked painful. If he could have made fists, he would have. Instead, his eyes widened and his body shook.

'Or should I say,' Pop continued, taking the old man's hand, feeling the meek, hateful squeeze, '*sons*. Both of them.' He sighed. 'Sammy first. Then Ellison. I won't bore you with the details, but know that they both were killed by their own arrogance. By their own entitlement. Both walked willingly to their deaths. And that made it even sweeter.'

Pop allowed himself to smile now, feeling a sense of uncontainable euphoria at the true revilement in Thomas Saint John's face. 'What Sammy did to Bethany Winlaw... he deserved worse. Something worse than death. And you know, the only thing I could think of that was worse than death, was making sure those who loved him – if there was any one—' Pop tsked '—had no idea what happened. The not knowing, I hear, is the worst. Was it? Was it torture? Losing a child... that's the

340

worst pain, isn't it? Bethany Winlaw's parents know. And now, you do, too.' He swallowed, looked out of the window for a few seconds, drinking in the silent beauty of the Savage Ridge visible through the glass. 'Sammy's buried out there, in an unmarked grave. Next to Ellison. And no one will ever know where, or will ever visit there, will ever mourn them, or think twice about them. And that's proof that their deaths are the only good thing the Saint Johns ever did. The only worthwhile thing. There'll be no funerals for them now. And though there'll be one for you, no one will come. Not your sons, not anyone.

'I see you're in pain. And I'm glad of it. And when you die, and the priest walks away, and they fill in the hole, I'm going to go out there, and I'm going to tear your stone down. I'm going to remove it, and wipe every trace of you from this earth. And then, I'm going to come back here, and I'm going to burn this place down. To cinders. I'm going to scrub the Saint Johns from the face of the earth like the stain they are.' He watched the old man's eyes, alight with hatred, and luxuriated in them. He listened to the heart rate monitor beep more vigorously, the blood pressure sensor whining with alarm as the numbers climbed. The old man shook, vibrated with anger. Pop hoped his heart would give out right then and there. That he could watch him die. But the old man held on. Stubbornly. It didn't matter, though. The longer he lived, the longer he'd live with the knowledge, with the pain. And that was almost as satisfying as his death would be. Perhaps even more so.

Pop stood, threw Thomas Saint John's liver spotted hand back at him, and straightened his belt. 'You know,' he said slowly, looking down on the old man, 'I haven't done much good in my life. But I can go to my death bed knowing I did at least one thing that made it all worth something. Bethany Winlaw's folks will never know, and they don't have to. Nothing could fix what they lost. Nothing could relieve their heartache, their guilt.' Their faces burned in his mind, the way they looked as they packed up the house, drove out of town, knowing they signed that paper, accepted that money, and put a price on what Sammy Saint John did to their daughter.

Pop thought about it every single day. Hated himself for letting it happen. It weighed on him, and it always would.

But this wouldn't.

Pop took one last look out the window, and then let out a long, slow breath. He allowed his eyes to fall on Thomas Saint John for the last time. 'Die slow,' he said, leaning down and pressing on his chest, hard enough that neither the old man nor the machine could fill his lungs. 'You fucking deserve it.'

Acknowledgements

When I think about all the people who impacted the writing of this book, the list begins small and then grows and grows. There are those closest to me who are my sounding boards and, well, victims – especially when I corner them and begin our conversations with the words, 'So, I've got this idea for a book...'

To those people – Sophie, Julie, Eddie, among others – thank you.

Then there are those who impacted the book without even realising. Set in a small town in the Pacific Northwest, it took moving to a place just like Savage Ridge to really understand the undercurrents that permeate through it. To understand the way the people think and feel, the almost gross divide between wealth and poverty at times; and the resentment that causes. And I wouldn't have been able to write this book without getting to know the people here, getting to hear them speak, and watch them live.

So, to all the people of Nelson, who'll likely never read this book or even know it exists, thank you.

Thank you, too, to those who took the time to put work into the book after it was written; my faithful advanced reading team, and especially the voracious Lesley for never mincing words or sugar coating it. It's always just what I need. You all take time out of your lives to read what is, frankly, usually a steaming mess – but you meet it with positivity and zeal and are always able to tease the good bits out, ignore the rest, and inspire me to get back to work and make it as good as it can be.

And finally, thank you to Viola, and to Kit. I pitched a lot of novels to a lot of agents, and every time I had a rejection, I thought it was a bad thing. But now I know, being where I am in life, and being the writer I am now, it was all leading up to the book I pitched you. I've been so very grateful for everything you've done, how hard you worked on this book, and how hard you worked to get it into the right hands. From our first meeting, I was sure I wanted to work with you, and I'm so glad that the road stretches out ahead. And to Kit, thank you for taking a chance on this book. When you came back to us, you were the only one that heard what we were trying to say, and from that first email, I knew you were the right champion to bring this to readers. And now, here we are.

So, to everyone that I know and that knows me as a writer, it really feels like you've done more than I have collectively to make what always felt like a pipe dream, a reality. Thank you for that. Thank you for everything.

Thank you for reading *Savage Ridge*

If you enjoyed it, and are eager for more from Morgan Greene, then you will love:

A PLACE CALLED HOPE

Coming September 2024

Read on for an exclusive extract…

Chapter 1

I guess it's pretty obvious you live in a nothing town in the middle of butt-fuck nowhere when the *Thanks for visiting!* sign as you head towards the horizon has the words 'Yep, that was it!' written across the bottom.

At least the scenery is pretty, if you like endless fields filled with dairy cows. Black and white, all quintessential looking. Dumb as fucking posts, the lot of them. Cows aren't my favourite animals, by any stretch, but they're about the most interesting thing about Hope. Which is saying a lot.

I thought that to myself for the thousandth time as we walked, Reuben and me, towards home. The highway split Hope right down the middle and a train track that brought freight through twice a day – once at 6 a.m. and once at 6 p.m. – split that highway in two, so the whole place was divided into four quarters. Each had its own personality – one was where the nice houses were built: they even had trees on the sidewalk. The one next to it was the 'affordable housing', where the farm hands and slaughterhouse workers lived.

Then there was Old Town, where the first buildings in Hope had been constructed back when it was a way-station on the old continental trail. Some of the houses were still used, but for the most part they weren't, kept as a living museum or something dumb. You could visit there, walk around what was once a western town. It used to be the centre of Hope until the new railroad was built and the highway got put in. Then the main street migrated about five hundred yards east to catch the few travellers that were unfortunate enough to drive through the place.

And squeezed in between rat-infested Old Town and the abattoir was the Wides. Trailer homes. Where we lived. Where we were headed right now on the way back from school. K through twelve. Less than two hundred kids total. Fucking shit-show.

As we approached the level crossing, Rueben gripped my hand. He was twelve now, but it'd been tradition since I could remember. He was getting big, almost too big to do this, his growth spurt barrelling down the line like the train did down these very tracks. I took a breath, gripped back, felt as his weight tugged on my shoulder, felt as he jumped.

I did my best to swing him, but it was 90 per cent his own doing these days.

His heels left the ground, landing clear of the tracks on the other side in a little plume of dust.

He slid, regaining his balance, his backpack jostling on his narrow shoulders. He turned then, grinning at me with shining braces, eyes icy blue through his round glasses, small on his face. He'd outgrown them a while back, but not like Mom could afford to replace them anytime soon.

'You're getting weak, Lucky,' he called.

I put my hands on my hips, staring at him. 'Maybe you're just getting fat.' He wasn't, though. He was all skin and bones.

He sneered at me, glanced around quickly to make sure no one was watching, then gave me the finger.

I lunged at him a step and he jumped, stumbling backwards and falling into the dirt next to the sidewalk. It was supposed to be a playful thing, a joke. But it looked like he fell hard. He grumbled, screwing up his face like he was going to cry.

'Ah fuck,' I muttered, stepping across the tracks and offering my hand. 'Come on, up you get. I didn't mean.'

'Fuck you,' he whispered, slapping my hand away. 'Not funny.'

No, it wasn't funny how weak Reubs was. Not like I was tough or anything. Five years older, sure, and bigger. But Hope didn't tend to breed them hard. Just stupid, I thought. Stupid enough to never leave the place.

But Reubs was gonna get stomped on for the rest of his life whether he left Hope or not. And it wasn't like Mom was gonna stick up for him. I was all he had. So, if he was stuck here, so was I.

Eventually he got himself out of the dirt and brushed himself off, his tatty thrift store flannel almost worn through in places.

'You hungry?' I asked, lowering my head a little to try and catch his eye.

'No,' he said, almost snivelling.

Jesus. I didn't even touch the kid. I had to swallow the urge to tell him he needed to man up. I'd done it before and it only made things worse.

'Yeah you are,' I said. 'There's fish sticks in the freezer.'

'And French fries?' he asked, trying to remain glum but brightening despite himself.

I sucked air between my teeth. 'Guess we'll have to see, won't we?' I said, knowing full well there was a box of the minute-microwave shit in there, too.

'Fine,' he said then, huffing. And then he lurched forward, made to shove me. His open palms rebounded off my chest and I let him move me back a step. 'Race you!'

And then he turned and began sprinting, skinny legs below his jean shorts whipping through the warm summer air.

I watched him go, glad he was happy, sad he was everything else.

I took another look around then, at Hope, at the deserted town that'd be my home forever, sighed, and took off after him.

He tore into the wides, spraying dirt everywhere as his hand gripped the metal pole that marked the end of the fence.

I let him stay ahead, knowing he'd be crushed if he lost. The kid didn't have much. It was the least I could do. And it wasn't like it cost me anything.

By the time we reached our double-wide, he was wheezing so bad it was almost painful to listen to. He didn't have asthma or anything, he was just sickly like that.

Our trailer was all beaten down and off-coloured, baked by the sun for forty years. The stairs creaked as Reubs climbed them, an ancient wooden set that'd been made long before I was even born. Though it wasn't the stairs that caught my eye, but Mom's old Camry in the driveway.

I paused for a second to look at it. She wasn't usually off work this early.

I realised I was being watched then. My eyes drifted up from the car to the trailer next to ours, to the porch opposite, to the curls of blue smoke drifting upwards from the cigarette between her thin fingers.

She was like a statue, leaning on her rail in her satin grown, her deep cleavage visible between the lapels, her skin tanned and leathery.

Mrs Newsham was heavily made up as always, but the face paint did little to hide her wrinkles, the purple lipstick stark against her skin. Her bleached hair hung in wide ringlets around her shoulders, her multitude of rings sparkling in the afternoon sunlight.

She didn't move, just watched me, her long legs lancing from the hem of her gown, shiny with the cocoa butter she used to keep them smooth.

I swallowed and looked away, hiding my grimace, and chased Reubs inside.

'Mom?' I asked, pushing into our living room.

She was striding back and forth, rummaging in her purse. She was sweating, looked frantic, her hair frizzy and the bags under her eyes deep. I knew that look. I hated that look.

Reubs was standing off to the side, watching her, hands at his sides, twitching. He didn't know what it was. But he knew something was wrong.

'Mom,' I said again, more forcefully. She stopped dead in her tracks and looked up at me, shocked, as though I'd materialised out of thin air.

'Lucas,' she said breathlessly. 'I— I— I'm late,' she stammered, her pupils so large I could barely see the pale blue ring of her irises. 'I need to find my keys.'

I kept quiet, not asking any of the questions that always came to my head when she was like this. *Did you go to work this morning? Did you sleep last night? Do you really think you should be driving right now?*

I couldn't blame her. She was doing her best. She was only thirty-one. Fourteen when she'd had me. Nineteen when she'd had Reubs. Different dads. But brothers all the same.

'My keys, Lucas. My keys!' she almost yelled then.

I just looked down, knowing they were on the ground in front of me. That's what she did when she came home after an all-nighter. Just dropped them on the ground in front of the door.

I stooped and picked them up, holding them out to her.

'Ah, you doll,' she sighed, darting forward at me with unnerving speed. She reached out and grabbed them and I could feel the shake of her hand even as her nails dragged them from my palm. She leaned in as though to kiss my cheek but I pulled out of reach. She froze, offended for a moment. But she and I both knew that it wasn't unwarranted. I didn't know where she'd been – she did – and we both knew she hadn't showered or brushed her teeth since.

She cleared her throat and stepped back, more like an older sister than a mother to me. Less than twice my age now.

'Where are you going?' I asked.

'I, uh… shift at the gas station. Someone called in sick, gotta cover.' She didn't meet my eyes, so I didn't know if it was bullshit or not.

'Did you work this morning?' I asked then, knowing she was supposed to be doing the six-four shift at the slaughterhouse, but knowing she hadn't. Not looking like that.

'It's Monday. You know I don't work Mondays,' she replied, almost incredulous. She shook her head, hair dancing.

'It's Wednesday,' I replied coolly.

She paused a moment, then shook her head again. 'Oh, yeah, no, Macy needed the hours. She asked me to switch days. So, yeah, it's all good. Don't even worry.'

I just swallowed. 'Okay. You want me to drive you to the gas station?' I knew the answer that was coming.

'No, no, I'm fine, I'm fine. I'm fine,' she repeated, telling herself.

I set my jaw. Knowing what was coming next. 'And what about Reubs? You know I'm doing clean-down at the pet store later. What time are you back?'

'It's a double,' she said, defensive now. 'Late. It's fine, though. Mrs Newsham's going to watch him.'

I clenched my teeth harder.

'Take Reubs over there, she said she'll fix him dinner.' Mom looked up, teary eyed for a moment. 'I don't know where we'd be without her.' She stared into space, then snapped back to reality. 'Alright. I'm off.' She put her hand against her mouth and blew a kiss to Reubs. 'Kisses. Alright? Be good, do what Mrs Newsham says.'

She rushed out then, slowing for just a second to put her hand on my shoulder and squeeze.

I didn't even look at her.

And then she was gone, the tappy, tired engine of the Camry sparking to life. She wheeled out of the drive quickly and then disappeared.

Reubs looked at me in the gloom of the living room. 'She okay?' he asked, his voice sad. He knew that I knew what was wrong with her. But I think he was scared to ask, scared that I might tell him the truth.

'Yeah,' I said, sighing a little. 'She's okay.' I steeled myself then. 'Come on, let's head over.' I extended my arm for him to walk into me and he did so gladly, squeezing tight.

Mom was supposed to be home this afternoon to watch him while I worked. Cleaning out the bird cages and rabbit hutches at the pet store wasn't glamorous, but it was enough to feed myself and Reubs when Mom didn't do the grocery shop, get him new pens and pencils for school, a shirt from the thrift store every now and then. A gift so he has *something* on his birthday.

We stayed there for a minute or so. I was the one who was reluctant to let go. At twelve, Reubs should have been able to take care of himself, but he couldn't. He couldn't make toast without risking burning the place down. He couldn't butter something without slicing his hand. It's one of the things Mom and I agreed on. Reubs needed watching. And Mrs Newsham did it for free – or so Mom thought.

'Come on then,' I said, my voice quiet.

We headed out the door and onto the porch.

Mrs Newsham was still standing there at the rail. She tapped the ash from the end of her cigarette and looked us over.

'Hey, Reubs,' she said, her voice raspy from the smoke.

'Hey, Mrs Newsham,' he replied.

She'd always been a Mrs, but there was no sign of a husband. And honestly, I didn't want to ask.

'Come inside,' she said, beckoning him. 'Dinner's in the oven.'

It wasn't gourmet, but she cooked better food than frozen value-store fish sticks. And Reuben needed all the decent food he could get.

'You too,' she added, looking at me then. 'Dinner'll be a few minutes.'

I suppressed a shudder, just nodding instead.

We went up the steps and she opened the door for us. I ushered Reubs in and he headed straight for the couch, the cartoons already playing.

I felt Mrs Newsham at my shoulder, could smell the mix of heavy perfume and Marlboro Golds.

She lingered there at the doorway as I headed forward, ruffled his hair from behind, and reached for the remote on the arm of the old brown couch. 'Dinner in ten,' I said, picking it up.

'Twenty,' Mrs Newsham corrected me.

'Watch close,' I told Reubs, turning the TV up loud. 'I'm gonna quiz you.'

''Kay,' he said, eyes glued to the screen. Spongebob.

I watched it for a moment, drinking in the innocence – until Mrs Newsham cleared her throat behind me.

I put the remote down, melting away from Reubs and towards Mrs Newsham's bedroom.

She followed me inside, closing the door behind her, untying her robe as she did.